In this volume

DEKKER: THE SHOEMAKERS' HOLIDAY
HEYWOOD: A WOMAN KILLED WITH KINDNESS
MARSTON: THE MALCONTENT
MIDDLETON AND ROWLEY: THE CHANGELING
MASSINGER: A NEW WAY TO PAY OLD DEBTS

Early Seventeenth Century Drama

EDITED WITH
AN INTRODUCTION BY
ROBERT G. LAWRENCE
*Associate Professor of English at the
University of Victoria, British Columbia*

DENT: LONDON
EVERYMAN'S LIBRARY
DUTTON: NEW YORK

© Introduction and editing,
J. M. Dent & Sons Ltd, 1963

All rights reserved
Made in Great Britain
at the
Aldine Press · Letchworth · Herts
for
J. M. DENT & SONS LTD
Aldine House · Bedford Street · London
This collection first published in Everyman's Library 1963
Last reprinted 1970

63-2574

NO. 390

ISBN: 0 460 00390 9

CONTENTS

Introduction by Robert G. Lawrence vii

THE SHOEMAKERS' HOLIDAY by Thomas Dekker 1

A WOMAN KILLED WITH KINDNESS by Thomas Heywood 75

THE MALCONTENT by John Marston 141

THE CHANGELING by Thomas Middleton and William
Rowley 223

A NEW WAY TO PAY OLD DEBTS by Philip Massinger .. 301

Glossary 389

v

INTRODUCTION

THIS volume of five plays is intended both to supplement other collections of plays in the Everyman series and to be useful in itself by providing a representative selection of the Elizabethan and Jacobean drama created by contemporaries of Shakespeare. Dekker's *Shoemakers' Holiday* (written in 1599) is a romantic comedy, Heywood's *A Woman Killed with Kindness* (1603) a domestic tragedy, Marston's *Malcontent* (1604) an Italianate intrigue melodrama, Middleton and Rowley's *Changeling* (1622) a Jacobean tragedy, and Massinger's *A New Way to Pay Old Debts* (1625) a comedy with overtones of social criticism. A comment on each play precedes the text.

Dekker, Heywood, and Marston were writing during the few years when the Elizabethan drama reached its highest point of achievement, the decade divided between the last years of the sixteenth century and the first years of the seventeenth. It was the period when Shakespeare and Jonson were most active, and these two dramatists inevitably overshadowed even the most distinguished of contemporary playwrights. Yet, had Shakespeare and Jonson pursued other careers, this and the era which followed would have been significant and interesting in the field of dramatic activity; both men influenced their contemporaries and successors, but neither created nor sustained single-handedly the Elizabethan and Jacobean drama.

England in 1599 was enjoying, in the form of relative peace, prosperity, and national pride, the aftermath of the defeat of the Spanish Armada eleven years earlier. Dekker, by his unsophisticated and unquizzical attitudes, reflects in *The Shoemakers' Holiday* the general tone of security and self-satisfaction. None the less there were critical rumblings in the background, and, even if Queen Elizabeth had lived beyond 1603, the relative simplicity of the drama would have changed with growing sophistication and criticism; indeed Dekker's contemporaries may have regarded his plays as old-fashioned when they were new.

Thomas Heywood, Dekker's immediate successor in this volume, shows a deeper penetration into the psychological motivations of his characters (as does Shakespeare in this period) and a questioning of traditional standards of morality; however, it is John Marston, writing *The Malcontent* probably at the very beginning of the reign of James I, who in his cynical disillusion displays most clearly the changing attitudes towards the court and aristocratic society.

Middleton's training ground during the first decade or so of the Jacobean era was in the *genre* of sophisticated city comedy. When he turned to tragedy he utilized some of this material, and added the pervasive influences of Marston and his great contemporary John Webster. Thus Middleton in *The Changeling* (1622) represented the climax of Jacobean 'psychological tragedy', when he (with the assistance of Rowley) explored with subtle irony the minds of two of the most memorable stage characters of the period, analysing unsentimentally their unconscious movements towards self-destruction.

Massinger's *A New Way to Pay Old Debts* appeared in the last year of the reign of King James. In this play the author looked back sentimentally on a more secure social order maintained by the gentry, the Lovells and Allworths, and at the same time he protested against the disintegration of established social values, a dissolution symbolized by the activities of opportunists like Overreach.

The dramatists represented here all show individual advances in technique, but their structural patterns and stage conventions had been largely settled before their day. It is in the areas of theatrical effectiveness and skill in imagery that these writers (especially the Jacobeans) are distinctive, although, naturally, not uniformly so. With the exception of *The Malcontent*, each of these plays has been produced several times in the modern theatre, evidence of their enduring vitality.

Space does not permit studies of the background influences on the Elizabethan and Jacobean drama, the dramatic and philosophical theories of the day, and the history of the theatres themselves. For these the reader is referred to the general studies of the drama listed in the bibliography (pages ix, x).

The earliest extant quarto editions of the plays have provided the sources for this anthology, with conservatively modernized spelling and punctuation. Square brackets (around act and scene divisions, settings, stage directions, a few textual additions, etc.) indicate material added by the editor. No editorial stage directions have been provided where the text of the play makes the accompanying action self-evident. Footnotes clarify puzzling points of action and unfamiliar words, but no footnotes appear for a variety of Elizabethan-Jacobean exclamatory words such as 'What!', 'How!' and so forth; the context usually makes clear that they are roughly equivalent to 'Indeed!'. The glossary at the end of the volume is provided in order to avoid the repeated footnoting of unfamiliar words used frequently. Both the footnotes and the glossary owe much to *O.E.D.* and to authoritative editors and scholars.

The quarto editions of only *A New Way to Pay Old Debts* and *The Malcontent* are completely divided by acts and scenes, although *The Changeling* quartos have act divisions. Conventional scene divisions have been added to the last, but the artificial French convention of *The Malcontent* has been modified (see the introduction to the play). The acts and scenes of *A Woman Killed with Kindness* largely conform to the customary arrangement, but the act and scene organization of *The Shoemakers' Holiday* follows that of Professor Fredson Bowers. The date at the beginning of each introduction and play is that of authorship.

The editor wishes to acknowledge the courtesy of the Library of the British Museum, the Folger Shakespeare Library, and the Huntington Library in making available copies and microfilms of the early quarto editions of the plays, and he is grateful to the authorities of Victoria College (Victoria, B.C.) who have provided financial and stenographic assistance.

ROBERT G. LAWRENCE

1963

SELECT BIBLIOGRAPHY

GENERAL. E. K. Chambers, *The Elizabethan Stage*, 4 vols., 1923; T. S. Eliot, *Elizabethan Essays*, 1934; G. E. Bentley, *The Jacobean and Caroline Stage*, 5 vols., 1941–56; B. I. Evans, *A Short History of English Drama*, 1948; M. C. Bradbrook, *The Growth and Structure of Elizabethan Comedy*, 1955; B. Ford, ed., *The Age of Shakespeare*, 1955; U. Ellis-Fermor, *The Jacobean Drama*, 1958; T. M. Parrott and R. H. Ball, *A Short View of Elizabethan Drama*, 1958.

DEKKER. W. K. Chandler, 'The Topography of Dekker's *The Shoemakers' Holiday*', *Studies in Philology*, XXVI (1929), 499–504; 'The Sources of the Characters in *The Shoemakers' Holiday*', *Modern Philology*, XXVII (1929–30), 175–82; T. Dekker, *Dramatic Works*, ed. F. Bowers, vol. i,

1953; P. Thomson, 'The Old Way and the New Way in Dekker and Massinger', *Modern Language Review*, LI (1956), 168–78; M. T. Jones-Davies, *Un Peintre de la Vie Londonienne: Thomas Dekker*, 2 vols., 1958; D. Novarr, 'Dekker's Gentle Craft and the Lord Mayor of London', *Modern Philology*, LVII (1960), 233–9; A. Brown, 'Citizen Comedy and Domestic Drama', *Jacobean Drama*, ed. J. R. Brown and B. Harris, 1960, pp. 63–84; H. E. Toliver, '*The Shoemakers' Holiday*: Theme and Image', *Boston University Studies in English*, V (1961), 208–18; G. R. Price, *Thomas Dekker*, 1969; J. H. Conover, *Thomas Dekker, an Analysis of Dramatic Structure*, 1969.

HEYWOOD. T. Heywood, *Best Plays* (Mermaid Series), ed. A. W. Verity, 1888; O. Cromwell, *Thomas Heywood*, 1928; A. M. Clark, *Thomas Heywood*, 1931; F. L. Townsend, 'The Artistry of Heywood's Double Plots', *Philological Quarterly*, XXV (1946), 97–119; F. S. Boas, *Thomas Heywood*, 1950; P. Ure, 'Marriage and Domestic Drama in Heywood and Ford', *English Studies*, XXXII (1951), 200–16; M. Grivelet, *Thomas Dekker et le Drame Domestique Élizabéthain*, 1957; P. M. Spacks, 'Honor and Perception in *A Woman Killed with Kindness*', *Modern Language Quarterly*, XX (1959), 321–32; W. F. McNeir, 'Heywood's Sources for the Main Plot of *A Woman Killed with Kindness*', *Studies in the English Renaissance Drama*, ed. J. W. Bennett *et al.*, 1959, pp. 189–211; D. Cook, '*A Woman Kill'd with Kindness*: an un-Shakespearian Tragedy', *English Studies*, XLV (1964), 353–72.

MARSTON. J. Marston, *Plays*, ed. H. H. Wood, 3 vols., 1934–9; C. Kiefer, 'Music and Marston's *The Malcontent*', *Studies in Philology*, LI (1954), 163–71; A. H. Axelrad, *Un Malcontent Élizabéthain: John Marston*, 1955; J. Peter, *Complaint and Satire in Early English Literature*, 1956; A. Caputi, *John Marston, Satirist*, 1961; P. J. Finkelpearl, *John Marston of the Middle Temple*, 1969.

MIDDLETON AND ROWLEY. T. Middleton, *Works*, ed. A. H. Bullen, 8 vols., 1885–6; S. Schoenbaum, *Middleton's Tragedies*, 1955; G. R. Hibbard, 'The Tragedies of Thomas Middleton and the Decadence of the Drama', *Renaissance and Modern Studies*, I (1957), 35–64; R. H. Barker, *Thomas Middleton*, 1958; T. Middleton and W. Rowley, *The Changeling*, ed. N. W. Bawcutt, 1958; C. Ricks, 'The Moral and Poetic Structure of *The Changeling*', *Essays in Criticism*, X (1960), 290–306; T. B. Tomlinson, 'Poetic Naturalism in *The Changeling*', *Journal of English and German Philology*, LXIII (1964), 648–59; D. M. Farr, 'The Changeling', *Modern Language Review*, LXII (1967), 586–97.

MASSINGER. P. Massinger, *Best Plays* (Mermaid Series), ed. A. Symons, 2 vols., 1887–9; A. H. Cruikshank, *Philip Massinger*, 1920; M. Chelli, *Le Drama de Massinger*, 1923; R. H. Ball, *The Amazing Career of Sir Giles Overreach*, 1939; T. A. Dunn, *Philip Massinger, the Man and Playwright*, 1957; P. Edwards, 'Massinger the Censor', *Essays on Shakespeare and Elizabethan Drama*, ed. R. Hosley, 1963, pp. 341–50; A. G. Cross, 'Social Change and Philip Massinger', *Studies in English Literature*, VII (1967), 329–42.

THOMAS DEKKER
(*c.* 1572–1632)

Born London; associated with producer Philip
Henslowe; wrote plays, including *Old Fortunatus*,
The Shoemakers' Holiday, *The Honest Whore* (two
parts); collaborated in *Satiromastix*, *The Roaring
Girl*, *The Witch of Edmonton*, etc.; pageants; prose
pamphlets, *The Wonderful Year*, *The Gull's Horn-
book*, etc.; involved in the War of the Theatres, 1599–
1601; imprisoned for debt, 1613–19.

The Shoemakers' Holiday (1599)

The romantic atmosphere and the unsophisticated charm of the three plots of this play show only a distant approach to the sharp social criticism evident in later plays of the period. *The Shoemakers' Holiday* reveals Dekker's gusto, his warm sympathies with ordinary people, and an intimate knowledge of contemporary London.

Simon Eyre, the extrovert shoemaker of Tower Street, provides the fundamental centre of interest in the play. The historical Eyre was a draper by trade, a sheriff of London in 1434, and Lord Mayor in 1445–6, when he made extensive additions to Leadenhall Market.

Dekker derived the outlines of the play principally from Thomas Deloney's collection of stories *The Gentle Craft* (1597), but the personalities of Eyre, Dame Margery, and the vigorously portrayed employees are chiefly Dekker's own. Firk, whose name means to be frisky, to beat, to cheat, or to trick, is the most memorable; he is outspoken, sometimes rude and vulgar, a lover of puns and *doubles entendres*.

The Jane-Rafe plot, while not entirely plausible in detail, must have been typical of an oft-repeated Elizabethan domestic crisis, with the odds inevitably against the safe return of the husband from foreign wars.

The third plot, the sentimental story of the love-affair between Rose Otley and Rowland Lacy, concerns social barriers, which were obviously higher in that day than this, although they were being breached. Dekker would certainly have known of Sir John Spencer, Lord Mayor of London in 1594–5; he, like Sir Roger Otley (the first Lord Mayor in the play), had a daughter whose marriage to a young nobleman he unsuccessfully opposed.

Rose Otley is self-assured and as emancipated as several of Shakespeare's heroines, and takes more of the initiative in the romance than her unsatisfying lover, Lacy. He is much more believable in his role as Hans, fraternizing with his fellow workmen and speaking eccentric stage-Dutch.

Hammon, the odd man out in the two romantic plots, is Dekker's least successful creation; a very mild-mannered

3

villain, he barely comes to life in his sentimental role, in striking contrast to the dynamic figures surrounding Simon Eyre.

The King, who appears in Act V, is not really identifiable with Henry VI, who reigned during Eyre's lifetime. This jolly, democratic king, alive with patriotism, owes much to the legendary personality of Henry V (1413–22), popularized in *The Famous Victories of Henry V* (*c.* 1588) and Shakespeare's *Henry V* (1599).

Few plays of the period present such a vital and varied social panorama as this one: glimpses of royalty and aristocracy, marital complications, social consciousness (Margery's new status goes to her head and her body), and a lively picture of Elizabethan shop life.

The Shoemakers' Holiday, written in 1599, was first performed on New Year's Day, 1600; it was published in the same year, and there were five successive editions, largely derivative, during the seventeenth century. The present edition is based essentially on the quarto of 1600, with a few borrowings from later quartos.

THE SHOEMAKERS' HOLIDAY
OR
THE GENTLE CRAFT
[by Thomas Dekker]
[1599]

[Dramatis Personae

KING OF ENGLAND
EARL OF LINCOLN
EARL OF CORNWALL
SIR ROGER OTLEY, Lord Mayor of London
SIMON EYRE, a shoemaker, and later Lord Mayor
ROWLAND LACY, nephew to Lincoln, later disguised as Hans Meulter
ASKEW, cousin to Lacy
HAMMON, a gentleman
WARNER, cousin to Hammon
MASTER SCOTT, friend to Otley
ROGER HODGE, foreman to Eyre
FIRK, journeyman to Eyre
RAFE DAMPORT, journeyman to Eyre
LOVELL, servant to the King
DODGER, parasite to Lincoln
DUTCH SKIPPER
BOY, apprentice to Eyre
BOY, servant to Otley
MARGERY, wife to Eyre
ROSE, daughter to Otley
JANE, wife to Rafe Damport
SYBIL, maid to Rose
NOBLEMEN, OFFICERS, SOLDIERS, HUNTSMEN, SHOEMAKERS, APPREN-
    TICES, SERVANTS]
[SCENE: London and Old Ford]

To all good fellows, professors of the gentle craft, of what degree soever :

Kind gentlemen, and honest boon companions, I present you here with a merry conceited comedy called *The Shoemakers' Holiday*, acted by my Lord Admiral's Players this present Christmas, before the Queen's Most Excellent Majesty, for the mirth and pleasant matter, by Her Highness graciously accepted, being indeed no way offensive. The argument of the play I will set down in this epistle: Sir Hugh Lacy, Earl of Lincoln, had a young gentleman of his own name, his near kinsman, that loved the lord mayor's daughter, of London; to prevent and cross which love, the Earl caused his kinsman to be sent colonel of a company into France; who resigned his place to another gentleman, his friend, and came, disguised like a Dutch shoemaker, to the house of Simon Eyre in Tower Street, who served the mayor and his household with shoes. The merriments that passed in Eyre's house, his coming to be mayor of London, Lacy's getting his love, and other accidents, with two merry three-men's songs—Take all in good worth that is well intended, for nothing is purposed but mirth—mirth lengtheneth long life—which, with all other blessings, I heartily wish you.

Farewell.

*The Prologue as it was pronounced before
the Queen's Majesty*

As wretches in a storm, expecting day,
With trembling hands and eyes cast up to heaven,
Make prayers the anchor of their conquer'd hopes,
So we, dear Goddess, wonder of all eyes,
Your meanest vassals, through mistrust and fear
To sink into the bottom of disgrace
By our imperfect pastimes, prostrate thus
On bended knees, our sails of hope do strike,
Dreading the bitter storms of your dislike.
Since then, unhappy men, our hap is such
That to ourselves ourselves no help can bring,
But needs must perish, if your saint-like ears,
Locking the temple where all mercy sits,
Refuse the tribute of our begging tongues.
Oh grant, bright mirror of true chastity,
From those life-breathing stars, your sun-like eyes,
One gracious smile; for your celestial breath
Must send us life, or sentence us to death.

10

[ACT I. SCENE 1]

[*A street in London*]

Enter LORD MAYOR (*Sir Roger Otley*) *and* EARL OF LINCOLN

LINC. My Lord Mayor, you have sundry times
    Feasted myself, and many courtiers more;
    Seldom or never can we be so kind
    To make requital of your courtesy.
    But, leaving this, I hear my cousin [1] Lacy
    Is much affected to your daughter Rose.
L. MAYOR. True, my good Lord, and she loves him so well
    That I mislike her boldness in the chase.
LINC. Why, my Lord Mayor, think you it then a shame
    To join a Lacy with an Otley's name?   10
L. MAYOR. Too mean is my poor girl for his high birth;
    Poor citizens must not with courtiers wed,
    Who will in silks and gay apparel spend
    More in one year than I am worth by far;
    Therefore your honour need not doubt [2] my girl.
LINC. Take heed, my Lord, advise you what you do;
    A verier [3] unthrift [4] lives not in the world
    Than is my cousin; for I'll tell you what,
    'Tis now almost a year since he requested
    To travel countries for experience;   20
    I furnish'd him with coin, bills of exchange,
    Letters of credit, men to wait on him,
    Solicited my friends in Italy
    Well to respect him; but to see the end:
    Scant had he journey'd through half Germany,
    But all his coin was spent, his men cast off,
    His bills [5] embezzl'd,[6] and my jolly coz,
    Asham'd to show his bankrupt presence here,
    Became a shoemaker in Wittenberg.

---

[1] Actually nephew. 'Cousin' was more casually used then to indicate relationship.
[2] Fear.   [3] Truer.   [4] Prodigal.
[5] Letters of credit.   [6] Squandered.

9

A goodly science for a gentleman   3 ●
Of such descent! Now judge the rest by this:
Suppose your daughter have a thousand pound,
He did consume me more in one half-year;
And make him heir to all the wealth you have,
One twelvemonth's rioting will waste it all.
Then seek, my Lord, some honest citizen
To wed your daughter to.
L. MAYOR.   I thank your lordship.
  [*Aside.*] Well, fox, I understand your subtlety.—
As for your nephew, let your lordship's eye
But watch his actions, and you need not fear,   4 ●
For I have sent my daughter far enough.
And yet your cousin Rowland might do well
Now he hath learn'd an occupation;
  [*Aside.*] And yet I scorn to call him son-in-law.
LINC. Ay, but I have a better trade for him;
I thank His Grace he hath appointed him
Chief colonel of all those companies
Muster'd in London and the shires about
To serve His Highness in those wars of France.
See where he comes.

Enter LOVELL, LACY, *and* ASKEW

                         Lovell, what news with you?   5 ●
LOVELL. My Lord of Lincoln, 'tis His Highness' will
That presently [1] your cousin ship for France
With all his powers; he would not for a million
But they should land at Dieppe within four days.
LINC. Go certify [2] His Grace it shall be done.   *Exit* LOVELL.
Now, cousin Lacy, in what forwardness
Are all your companies?
LACY.   All well prepar'd:
The men of Hertfordshire lie at Mile End,
Suffolk and Essex train in Tothill Fields;
The Londoners and those of Middlesex,   6 ●
All gallantly prepared in Finsbury,
With frolic spirits long for their parting hour.
L. MAYOR. They have their imprest,[3] coats, and furniture,[4]

----

[1] At once, soon.   [2] Inform.
[3] Enlistment pay.   [4] Equipment.

And if it please your cousin Lacy come
To the Guildhall, he shall receive his pay;
And twenty pounds besides my brethren [1]
Will freely give him to approve [2] our loves
We bear unto my lord your uncle here.

LACY. I thank your honour.

LINC.   Thanks, my good Lord Mayor.

L. MAYOR. At the Guildhall we will expect your coming. *Exit.*   70

LINC. To approve your loves to me? No, subtlety;
Nephew, that twenty pound he doth bestow
For joy to rid you from his daughter Rose.
But, cousins both, now here are none but friends,
I would not have you cast an amorous eye
Upon so mean a project as the love
Of a gay, wanton, painted citizen.
I know this churl, even in the height of scorn,
Doth hate the mixture of his blood with thine;
I pray thee do thou so. Remember, coz,   80
What honourable fortunes wait on thee;
Increase the king's love which so brightly shines
And gilds thy hopes. I have no heir but thee,
And yet not thee, if with a wayward spirit
Thou start from the true bias of my love.

LACY. My Lord, I will (for honour, not desire
Of land or livings, or to be your heir)
So guide my actions in pursuit of France
As shall add glory to the Lacys' name.

LINC. Coz, for those words here's thirty portuguese, [3]   90
And, nephew Askew, there's a few for you.
Fair Honour in her loftiest eminence
Stays in France for you till you fetch her thence.
Then, nephews, clap swift wings on your designs;
Be gone, be gone; make haste to the Guildhall;
There presently I'll meet you. Do not stay; [4]
Where honour beckons, shame attends delay.   *Exit.*

ASKEW. How gladly would your uncle have you gone!

LACY. True, coz, but I'll o'erreach his policies.
I have some serious business for three days   100
Which nothing but my presence can dispatch;
You, therefore, cousin, with the companies

---

[1] Aldermen.   [2] Acknowledge.
[3] Portagues: gold coins worth almost £5 each.   [4] Delay.

Shall haste to Dover; there I'll meet with you,
Or, if I stay past my prefixed time,
Away for France; we'll meet in Normandy.
The twenty pounds my lord mayor gives to me
You shall receive, and these ten portuguese,
Part of mine uncle's thirty. Gentle coz,
Have care to our great charge; I know your wisdom
Hath tried itself in higher consequence.   110

ASKEW. Coz, all myself am yours; yet have this care,
To lodge in London with all secrecy;
Our uncle Lincoln hath, besides his own,
Many a jealous eye, that in your face
Stares only to watch means for your disgrace.

LACY. Stay, cousin, who be these?

Enter SIMON EYRE, *his wife,* HODGE, FIRK, JANE, *and*
RAFE *with a piece [of work]*

EYRE. Leave whining, leave whining; away with this whimper-
ing, this puling, these blubbering tears and these wet eyes; I'll
get thy husband discharged, I warrant thee, sweet Jane. Go to.

HODGE. Master, here be the captains.   120

EYRE. Peace, Hodge; husht, ye knave, husht!

FIRK. Here be the cavaliers and the colonels, master.

EYRE. Peace, Firk; peace, my fine Firk; stand by with your
pishery-pashery; away! I am a man of the best presence; I'll
speak to them and [1] they were popes. Gentlemen, captains,
colonels, commanders, brave men, brave leaders, may it
please you to give me audience: I am Simon Eyre, the mad
shoemaker of Tower Street; this wench with the mealy
mouth that will never tire is my wife I can tell you; here's
Hodge, my man and my foreman; here's Firk, my fine   130
firking [2] journeyman, and this is blubbered Jane; all we come
to be suitors for this honest Rafe; keep him at home, and as I
am a true shoemaker and a gentleman of the gentle craft, buy
spurs yourself, and I'll find ye boots these seven years.

WIFE. Seven years, husband?

EYRE. Peace, midriff, peace; I know what I do; peace.

FIRK. Truly, master cormorant,[3] you shall do God good
service to let Rafe and his wife stay together; she's a young
new-married woman; if you take her husband away from her

---

[1] If.   [2] Frisking.   [3] A pun on 'colonel'.

a night, you undo her. She may beg in the day time, for he's   140
as good a workman at a prick and an awl as any is in our
trade.

JANE. Oh, let him stay, else I shall be undone!

FIRK. Ay, truly, she shall be laid at one side like a pair of old
shoes else, and be occupied for no use.

LACY. Truly, my friends, it lies not in my power;
The Londoners are press'd,[1] paid, and set forth
By the lord mayor; I cannot change a man.

HODGE. Why then, you were as good be a corporal as a colonel
if you cannot discharge one good fellow, and I tell you true, I   150
think you do more than you can answer, to press a man
within a year and a day of his marriage.

EYRE. Well said, melancholy Hodge; gramercy,[2] my fine
foreman.

WIFE. Truly, gentlemen, it were ill done for such as you to
stand so stiffly against a poor young wife, considering her
case; she is new married, but let that pass. I pray, deal not
roughly with her: her husband is a young man and but
newly entered, but let that pass.

EYRE. Away with your pishery-pashery, your polls and your   160
edipols;[3] peace, midriff; silence, Cicely Bumtrinket; let your
head speak.

FIRK. Yea, and the horns too, master.

EYRE. Too soon,[4] my fine Firk, too soon; peace, scoundrels.
See you this man, captains? You will not release him? Well,
let him go; he's a proper shot; let him vanish. Peace, Jane,
dry up thy tears, they'll make his powder dankish. Take him,
brave men; Hector of Troy was a hackney to him, Hercules
and Termagant scoundrels; Prince Arthur's Round-table, by
the Lord of Ludgate, ne'er fed such a tall,[5] such a dapper   170
swordman; by the life of Pharaoh, a brave, resolute swordman. Peace, Jane, I say; no more, mad knaves.

FIRK. See, see, Hodge, how my master raves in commendation
of Rafe.

HODGE. Rafe, th'art a gull by this hand, and thou goest not.

ASKEW. I am glad, good Master Eyre, it is my hap

---

[1] Conscripted.   [2] Thanks.
[3] Meaningless exclamations.
[4] Possibly a compositor's error for 'Taw soone', a Welsh phrase meaning
'keep quiet' (J. George, N. & Q., vol. 194).
[5] Brave, handsome.

To meet so resolute a soldier.
Trust me, for your report and love to him,
A common, slight regard shall not respect [1] him.

LACY. Is thy name Rafe?

RAFE.   Yes, sir.

LACY.   Give me thy hand;   18
Thou shalt not want, as I am a gentleman.
Woman, be patient. God, no doubt, will send
Thy husband safe again, but he must go;
His country's quarrel says it shall be so.

HODGE. Th'art a gull, by my stirrup,[2] if thou dost not go; I
will not have thee strike thy gimlet into these weak vessels;[3]
prick thine enemies, Rafe.

Enter DODGER

DODGER. My Lord, your uncle on the Tower Hill
Stays with the lord mayor and the aldermen,
And doth request you, with all speed you may,   1?
To hasten thither.

ASKEW.   Cousin, let us go.

LACY. Dodger, run you before; tell them we come.
                                        Exit DODGER.

This Dodger is mine uncle's parasite,
The arrant'st varlet that e'er breath'd on earth;
He sets more discord in a noble house
By one day's broaching of his pickthank [4] tales
Than can be salv'd again in twenty years,
And he, I fear, shall go with us to France
To pry into our actions.

ASKEW.   Therefore, coz,
It shall behove you to be circumspect.   2

LACY. Fear not, good cousin. Rafe, hie to your colours.
                    [*Exeunt* LACY *and* ASKEW.]

RAFE. I must, because there is no remedy;
But, gentle master and my loving dame,
As you have always been a friend to me,
So in mine absence think upon my wife.

JANE. Alas, my Rafe.

WIFE. She cannot speak for weeping.

---

[1] Refer to.   [2] A shoemaker's strap to hold the last on his knee.
[3] The shoes Rafe carries.   [4] Sycophantic.

EYRE. Peace, you cracked groats,[1] you mustard tokens,[2] disquiet not the brave soldier. Go thy ways, Rafe.

JANE. Ay, ay, you bid him go. What shall I do   210
    When he is gone?

FIRK. Why, be doing with me or my fellow Hodge; be not idle.

EYRE. Let me see thy hand, Jane. This fine hand, this white
    hand, these pretty fingers, must spin, must card, must work;
    work, you bombast[3] cotton-candle[4] quean,[5] work for your
    living with a pox to you. Hold thee, Rafe, here's five sixpences
    for thee. Fight for the honour of the gentle craft, for the
    gentlemen shoemakers, the courageous cordwainers,[6] the
    flower of Saint Martin's,[7] the mad knaves of Bedlam, Fleet
    Street, Tower Street, and Whitechapel; crack me the crowns   220
    of the French knaves. A pox on them! Crack them; fight, by
    the lord of Ludgate, fight, my fine boy.

FIRK. Here, Rafe, here's three twopences; two carry into
    France, the third shall wash our souls at parting, for sorrow is
    dry. For my sake, firk[8] the *Basa mon cues*.[9]

HODGE. Rafe, I am heavy at parting, but here's a shilling for
    thee; God send thee to cram thy slops[10] with French crowns
    and thy enemies' bellies with bullets.

RAFE. I thank you, master, and I thank you all.
    Now, gentle wife, my loving, lovely Jane,   230
    Rich men at parting give their wives rich gifts,
    Jewels and rings to grace their lily hands.
    Thou knowest our trade makes rings for women's heels;
    Here, take this pair of shoes, cut out by Hodge,
    Stitch'd by my fellow Firk, seam'd by myself,
    Made up and pink'd with letters for thy name.
    Wear them, my dear Jane, for thy husband's sake,
    And every morning when thou pull'st them on,
    Remember me and pray for my return;
    Make much of them, for I have made them so,   240
    That I can know them from a thousand mo.
        Sound drum; enter LORD MAYOR, LINCOLN, LACY,
        ASKEW, DODGER, *and soldiers. They pass over the stage;*
        RAFE *falls in amongst them;* FIRK *and the rest cry*
        'Farewell', *etc., and so exeunt*

[1] Coins worth fourpence.
[2] Shopkeepers' premiums, of very limited value.   [3] Cotton.
[4] A candle with a cotton wick.   [5] A jade.   [6] Shoemakers.
[7] i.e. good tipplers; by association with the patron saint of publicans.
[8] Beat.   [9] A vulgar expression of contempt.   [10] Loose-fitting breeches.

[ACT I. SCENE 2]

[*The garden of the* LORD MAYOR'S *house at Old Ford*]

Enter ROSE *alone, making a garland*

ROSE. Here sit thou down upon this flowery bank,
   And make a garland for thy Lacy's head.
   These pinks, these roses, and these violets,
   These blushing gillyflowers, these marigolds,
   The fair embroidery of his coronet,
   Carry not half such beauty in their cheeks
   As the sweet count'nance of my Lacy doth.
   O my most unkind father! O my stars!
   Why lower'd you so at my nativity,
   To make me love, yet live robb'd of my love?
   Here as a thief am I imprisoned,
   For my dear Lacy's sake, within those walls
   Which by my father's cost were builded up
   For better purposes; here must I languish
   For him that doth as much lament (I know)
   Mine absence, as for him I pine in woe.

Enter SYBIL

SYBIL. Good morrow, young mistress; I am sure you make
   that garland for me, against I shall be Lady of the Harvest.
ROSE. Sybil, what news at London?
SYBIL. None but good: my lord mayor, your father, and Master
   Philpot, your uncle, and Master Scott, your cousin, and
   Mistress Frigbottom by Doctors' Commons, do all, by my
   troth, send you most hearty commendations.
ROSE. Did Lacy send kind greetings to his love?
SYBIL. Oh yes, out of cry,[1] by my troth. I scant knew him;
   here 'a[2] wore a scarf, and here a scarf, here a bunch of
   feathers, and here precious stones and jewels, and a pair of
   garters; Oh, monstrous! Like one of our yellow silk curtains,
   at home here in Old Ford House, here in Master Belly-
   mount's chamber. I stood at our door in Cornhill, looked at
   him, he at me indeed, spake to him, but he not to me, not a

---

[1] Beyond expression.   [2] He.

word. Marry gup,[1] thought I, with a wanion.[2] He passed by
me as proud—marry foh! Are you grown humorous,[3]
thought I; and so shut the door and in I came.

ROSE. Oh, Sybil, how dost thou my Lacy wrong?
My Rowland is as gentle as a lamb,
No dove was ever half so mild as he.

SYBIL. Mild? Yea, as a bushel of stamped crabs;[4] he looked
upon me as sour as verjuice.[5] Go thy ways, thought I; thou
mayst be much in my gaskins, but nothing in my nether-   40
stocks.[6] This is your fault, mistress, to love him that loves not
you; he thinks scorn to do as he's done to, but if I were as you
I'd cry, 'Go by, Jeronimo, go by;[7]
I'd set mine old debts against my new driblets,[8]
And the hare's foot against the goose giblets;
For if ever I sigh when sleep I should take,
Pray God I may lose my maidenhead when I wake.'[9]

ROSE. Will my love leave me then and go to France?

SYBIL. I know not that, but I am sure I see him stalk before the
soldiers. By my troth, he is a proper[10] man, but he is proper   50
that proper doth; let him go snick-up,[11] young mistress.

ROSE. Get thee to London, and learn perfectly
Whether my Lacy go to France or no.
Do this, and I will give thee for thy pains
My cambric apron and my Romish[12] gloves,
My purple stockings and a stomacher.
Say, wilt thou do this, Sybil, for my sake?

SYBIL. Will I, quoth 'a?[13] At whose suit? By my troth, yes, I'll
go. A cambric apron, gloves, a pair of purple stockings, and a
stomacher! I'll sweat in purple, mistress, for you; I'll take   60
anything that comes a' God's name.[14] Oh rich, a cambric
apron! Faith then, have at up tails all;[15] I'll go jiggy-joggy to
London, and be here in a trice, young mistress.   *Exit.*

ROSE. Do so, good Sybil. Meantime, wretched I
Will sit and sigh for his lost company.   *Exit.*

---

[1] 'Go up': a conventional derisive expression.
[2] 'A plague upon you.'   [3] Capricious.
[4] Crushed crab-apples.   [5] The juice of sour or unripe fruit.
[6] 'My' is impersonal, equivalent to 'the'. A comment on self-importance:
you are less impressive in stockings than in trousers.
[7] A misquotation of Kyd's *Spanish Tragedy*, III. xii. 30.
[8] Small sums.
[9] A proverbial stanza implying 'Let the past take care of the past'.
[10] Handsome.   [11] Hang.   [12] Italian.
[13] She.   [14] Free.   [15] An old song and tune.

[ACT I. SCENE 3]
[Tower Street, London]

Enter ROWLAND LACY, *like a Dutch shoemaker*

LACY. How many shapes have gods and kings devis'd,
　　Thereby to compass their desired loves?
　　It is no shame for Rowland Lacy then
　　To clothe his cunning with the gentle craft,
　　That, thus disguis'd, I may unknown possess
　　The only happy presence of my Rose;
　　For her I have forsook my charge in France,
　　Incurr'd the king's displeasure, and stirr'd up
　　Rough hatred in mine uncle Lincoln's breast.
　　O love, how powerful art thou, that canst change
　　High birth to baseness, and a noble mind
　　To the mean semblance of a shoemaker!
　　But thus it must be; for her cruel father,
　　Hating the single union of our souls,
　　Hath secretly convey'd my Rose from London
　　To bar me of her presence, but I trust
　　Fortune and this disguise will further me
　　Once more to view her beauty, gain her sight.
　　Here in Tower Street, with Eyre the shoemaker,
　　Mean I a while to work; I know the trade,
　　I learnt it when I was in Wittenberg.
　　Then cheer thy hoping sprites, be not dismay'd,
　　Thou canst not want; do fortune what she can,
　　The gentle craft is living for a man.   *Exit.*

[ACT I. SCENE 4]
[*Before* EYRE'S *shop*]

Enter EYRE, *making himself ready*

EYRE. Where be these boys, these girls, these drabs, these
　　scoundrels? They wallow in the fat brewis [1] of my bounty,
　　and lick up the crumbs of my table, yet will not rise to see my

　　　　　　　　　　　　[1] Broth.

walks cleansed. Come out, you powder-beef[1] queans! What,
Nan! What, Madge Mumble-crust! Come out, you fat mid-
riff, swag-belly whores, and sweep me these kennels,[2] that the
noisome stench offend not the noses of my neighbours.
What, Firk, I say! What, Hodge! Open my shop windows.
What, Firk, I say!

Enter FIRK

FIRK. Oh, master, is 't you that speak bandog and bedlam[3] this   10
morning? I was in a dream and mused what madman was got
into the street so early. Have you drunk this morning that
your throat is so clear?

EYRE. Ah, well said, Firk, well said, Firk; to work, my fine
knave, to work; wash thy face, and thou 'lt be more blest.

FIRK. Let them wash my face that will eat it; good master, send
for a souse-wife,[4] if you 'll have my face cleaner.

Enter HODGE

EYRE. Away, sloven! Avaunt, scoundrel! Good morrow,
Hodge; good morrow, my fine foreman.

HODGE. Oh, master, good morrow; y 'are an early stirrer. Here 's   20
a fair morning. Good morrow, Firk; I could have slept this
hour. Here 's a brave day towards.

EYRE. Oh, haste to work, my fine foreman, haste to work.

FIRK. Master, I am dry as dust to hear my fellow Roger talk of
fair weather; let us pray for good leather, and let clowns and
ploughboys, and those that work in the fields, pray for brave
days. We work in a dry shop; what care I if it rain?

Enter EYRE'S wife

EYRE. How now, Dame Margery, can you see to rise? Trip and
go, call up the drabs, your maids.

WIFE. See to rise? I hope 'tis time enough; 'tis early enough for   30
any woman to be seen abroad. I marvel how many wives in
Tower Street are up so soon. Gods me, 'tis not noon! Here 's
a yawling.[5]

---

[1] Salted beef.   [2] Gutters.   [3] Like a chained dog and a madman.
[4] Woman who pickled pigs' feet, etc.   [5] A fuss, row.

EYRE. Peace, Margery, peace. Where's Cicely Bumtrinket, your
maid? She has a privy fault, she farts in her sleep. Call the
quean up; if my men want shoe-thread, I'll swinge her in a
stirrup.

FIRK. Yet that's but a dry beating; here's still a sign of drought.

Enter LACY [*as* HANS], *singing*

LACY. *Der was een bore van Gelderland,*
            Frolick si byen;
        He was als dronck he cold nyet stand,
            Upsolce si byen.
        Tap eens de canneken,
        Drincke, schone mannekin.[1]

FIRK. Master, for my life, yonder's a brother of the gentle
craft; if he bear not Saint Hugh's bones,[2] I'll forfeit my
bones. He's some uplandish[3] workman—hire him, good
master, that I may learn some gibble-gabble; 'twill make us
work the faster.

EYRE. Peace, Firk. A hard world; let him pass, let him vanish;
we have journeymen enow. Peace, my fine Firk.

WIFE. Nay, nay, y'are best follow your men's counsel; you
shall see what will come on't. We have not men enow, but we
must entertain[4] every butter-box;[5] but let that pass.

HODGE. Dame, 'fore God, if my master follow your counsel
he'll consume little beef;[6] he shall be glad of men, and he can
catch them.

FIRK. Ay, that he shall.

HODGE. 'Fore God, a proper man, and I warrant a fine workman. Master, farewell; dame, adieu; if such a man as he
cannot find work, Hodge is not for you.   *Offers to go.*

EYRE. Stay, my fine Hodge.

FIRK. Faith, and your foreman go, dame, you must take a

---

[1] 'There was a boor from Gelderland,—
        Jolly they be;
   He was so drunk he could not stand,—
        Drunken (?) they be:
   Clink on the cannikin,
   Drink, pretty little man!'
[2] Saint Hugh was the patron saint of the gentle craft; according to the
legend, the shoemakers made tools out of the saint's bones after his martyr-
dom.
[3] Rustic.   [4] Provide occupation for.
[5] Dutchman.   [6] Profit but little.

journey to seek a new journeyman; if Roger removes, Firk
follows. If Saint Hugh's bones shall not be set a-work, I may
prick mine awl in the walls and go play. Fare ye well, master;
goodbye, dame.

EYRE. Tarry, my fine Hodge, my brisk foreman; stay, Firk;
peace, pudding-broth. By the Lord of Ludgate, I love my
men as my life. Peace, you gallimaufry.[1] Hodge, if he want   70
work I'll hire him. One of you to him. Stay—he comes to us.

LACY. *Goeden dach, meester, ende u, vro, oak.*[2]

FIRK. Nails![3] If I should speak after him without drinking, I
should choke. And you, friend Oak, are you of the gentle
craft?

LACY. *Yaw, yaw, ik bin den skomawker.*

FIRK. 'Den skomaker', quoth 'a; and hark you, 'skomaker',
have you all your tools, a good rubbing-pin, a good stopper, a
good dresser, your four sorts of awls, and your two balls of
wax, your paring knife, your hand- and thumb-leathers, and   80
good Saint Hugh's bones to smooth up your work?

LACY. *Yaw, yaw, be niet vorveard.*[4] *Ik hab all de dingen voor
mack skoes groot and cleane.*[5]

FIRK. Ha, ha! Good master, hire him; he'll make me laugh, so
that I shall work more in mirth than I can in earnest.

EYRE. Hear ye, friend, have ye any skill in the mystery of
cordwainers?

LACY. *Ik weet* [6] *niet wat yow seg; ich verstaw you niet.*

FIRK. Why thus, man; 'Ich verste u niet,' quoth 'a.

LACY. *Yaw, yaw, yaw, ick can dat wel doen.*   90

FIRK. 'Yaw, yaw'; he speaks yawing like a jackdaw that gapes
to be fed with cheese-curds. Oh, he'll give a villainous pull at
a can of double-beer, but Hodge and I have the vantage: we
must drink first because we are the eldest journeymen.

EYRE. What is thy name?

LACY. Hans—Hans Meulter.

EYRE. Give me thy hand; th'art welcome. Hodge, entertain
him; Firk, bid him welcome; come, Hans. Run, wife, bid
your maids, your trullibubs,[7] make ready my fine men's breakfasts. To him, Hodge.   100

---

[1] Lit., a made dish; facetiously, a person of many parts.
[2] 'Good day, master, and you, madam, also.'
[3] 'By God's nails!'   [4] Afraid.
[5] i.e. *klein*, small.   [6] Know.
[7] A casual term of abuse; insignificant.

HODGE. Hans, th'art welcome; use thyself friendly, for we are
good fellows; if not, thou shalt be fought with, wert thou
bigger than a giant.

FIRK. Yea, and drunk with, wert thou Gargantua. My master
keeps no cowards, I tell thee. Ho, boy, bring him an heel-
block; here's a new journeyman.   *Enter boy.*

LACY. *Oh, ich wersto you; ich moet een halve dossen cans betaelen;
here, boy, nempt dis skilling, tap eens freelicke.*[1]   *Exit boy.*

EYRE. Quick, snipper-snapper, away; Firk, scour thy throat,
thou shalt wash it with Castilian liquor. Come, my last of the   11
fives,[2] (*Enter boy.*) give me a can. Have to thee, Hans; here,
Hodge; here, Firk. Drink, you mad Greeks, and work like
true Trojans, and pray for Simon Eyre the shoemaker. Here,
Hans, and th'art welcome.

FIRK. Lo, dame, you would have lost a good fellow that will
teach us to laugh; this beer came hopping in well.

WIFE. Simon, it is almost seven.

EYRE. Is't so, Dame Clapper-dudgeon?[3] Is't seven o'clock,
and my men's breakfast not ready? Trip and go, you soused
conger,[4] away! Come, you mad hyperboreans;[5] follow me,   12
Hodge; follow me, Hans; come after, my fine Firk; to work,
to work a while, and then to breakfast.   *Exit.*

FIRK. Soft! 'Yaw, yaw', good Hans; though my master have
no more wit but to call you afore me, I am not so foolish to go
behind you, I being the elder journeyman.   *Exeunt.*

[ACT II. SCENE 1]
[A field near Old Ford]

Hallooing within. Enter WARNER *and* HAMMON, *like hunters*

HAM. Cousin, beat every brake, the game's not far;
This way with winged feet he fled from death,
Whilst the pursuing hounds, scenting his steps,

[1] 'Oh, I understand you; I must pay for a half-dozen cans . . . take this
shilling, drink this once gayly'.
[2] A small-sized last.
[3] A casual term of reproach; a beggar (from the sound made with a beggar's
dish).
[4] A pickled eel.
[5] Mythological inhabitants of a northern land of perpetual happiness.

Find out his highway to destruction.
Besides, the miller's boy told me even now
He saw him take soil,[1] and he hallooed him,
Affirming him so emboss'd [2]
That long he could not hold.

WAR.   If it be so,
'Tis best we trace these meadows by Old Ford.

A noise of hunters within; enter a boy

HAM. How now, boy? Where's the deer? Speak—saw'st thou   10
him?

BOY. Oh, yea; I saw him leap through a hedge, and then over a
ditch, then at my lord mayor's pale; over he skipped me, and
in he went me, and 'Holla!' the hunters cried, and 'There,
boy, there, boy!' But there he is, a' mine honesty.

HAM. Boy, Godamercy.[3] Cousin, let's away;
I hope we shall find better sport today.   *Exeunt.*

[ACT II. SCENE 2]

[The garden of the LORD MAYOR'S *house at Old Ford]*

Hunting within. Enter ROSE *and* SYBIL

ROSE. Why, Sybil, wilt thou prove a forester?

SYBIL. Upon some,[4] no; forester, go by. No, faith, mistress, the
deer came running into the barn through the orchard and   20
over the pale; I wot well I looked as pale as a new cheese to
see him, but 'Whip!' says Goodman Pinclose, up with his
flail, and our Nick with a prong, and down he fell, and they
upon him, and I upon them. By my troth, we had such sport,
and in the end we ended him; his throat we cut, flayed him,
unhorned him, and my lord mayor shall eat of him anon when
he comes.   *Horns sound within.*

ROSE. Hark, hark, the hunters come; y'are best take heed;
They'll have a saying to you for this deed.

Enter HAMMON, WARNER, *huntsmen, and boy*

[1] To take to water for refuge.   [2] Exhausted.
[3] 'Thank you.'   [4] A mild assertion; 'indeed'.

HAM. God save you, fair ladies.

SYBIL.   Ladies! Oh, gross![1]

WAR. Came not a buck this way?

ROSE.   No, but two does.

HAM. And which way went they? Faith, we'll hunt at those.

SYBIL. At those? Upon some, no. When, can you tell?

WAR. Upon some, ay.

SYBIL.   Good Lord!

WAR.   Wounds! Then farewell.

HAM. Boy, which way went he?

BOY.   This way, sir, he ran.

HAM. This way he ran indeed, fair Mistress Rose;
  Our game was lately in your orchard seen.

WAR. Can you advise which way he took his flight?

SYBIL. Follow your nose; his horns will guide you right.

WAR. Th'art a mad wench.

SYBIL.   Oh, rich!

ROSE.   Trust me, not I.
  It is not like the wild forest deer
  Would come so near to places of resort.
  You are deceiv'd, he fled some other way.

WAR. Which way, my sugar-candy? Can you show?

SYBIL. Come up, good honeysops. Upon some, no.

ROSE. Why do you stay, and not pursue your game?

SYBIL. I'll hold my life their hunting-nags be lame.

HAM. A deer more dear is found within this place.

ROSE. But not the deer, sir, which you had in chase.

HAM. I chas'd the deer, but this dear chaseth me.

ROSE. The strangest hunting that ever I see;
  But where's your park?   *She offers to go away.*

HAM.   'Tis here—oh, stay.

ROSE. Impale [2] me, and then I will not stray.

WAR. They wrangle, wench; we are more kind than they.

SYBIL. What kind of hart [3] is that dear hart [3] you seek?

WAR. A hart, dear heart.

SYBIL.   Who ever saw the like?

ROSE. To lose your heart—is't possible you can?

HAM. My heart is lost.

ROSE.   Alack, good gentleman.

HAM. This poor lost heart would I wish you might find.

---

[1] Ignorant.   [2] Confine.
[3] So Q1; heart—later quartos and most modern editions.

ROSE. You by such luck might prove your hart a hind.   60
HAM. Why, Luck had horns, so have I heard some say.
ROSE. Now God, and't be his will, send Luck into your way.

Enter LORD MAYOR *and servants*

L. MAYOR. What, Master Hammon! Welcome to Old Ford.
SYBIL. [*To* WARNER.] God's pittikins! Hands off, sir; here's
    my lord.
L. MAYOR. I hear you had ill luck and lost your game.
HAM. 'Tis true, my lord.
L. MAYOR.   I am sorry for the same.
    What gentleman is this?
HAM.   My brother-in-law.
L. MAYOR. Y'are welcome both; sith Fortune offers you
    Into my hands, you shall not part from hence   70
    Until you have refresh'd your wearied limbs.
    Go, Sybil, cover the board. You shall be guest
    To no good cheer, but even a hunter's feast.
HAM. I thank your lordship. [*Aside, to* WARNER.] Cousin, on
    my life,
    For our lost venison, I shall find a wife.
                        Exeunt all, except LORD MAYOR.
L. MAYOR. In, gentlemen, I'll not be absent long.
    This Hammon is a proper gentleman,
    A citizen by birth, fairly allied;
    How fit a husband were he for my girl!   80
    Well, I will in, and do the best I can
    To match my daughter to this gentleman.   *Exit.*

[ACT II. SCENE 3]
[EYRE'S *workshop*]

Enter LACY [*as* HANS], *skipper,* HODGE, *and* FIRK

SKIP. *Ick sal yow wat seggen,*[1] *Hans; dis skip dat comen from
    Candy*[2] *is al wol,*[3] *by Got's sacrament, van sugar, civet, almonds,
    cambrick, end alle dingen, towsand towsand ding. Nempt*[4] *it,*

---

[1] 'I shall tell you what [it is].'   [2] Candia (Crete).
[3] Full.   [4] Take.

Hans, nempt it vor u meester; daer be de bils van laden. Your
meester Simon Eyre sal has good copen.[1] *Wat seggen yow, Hans?*

FIRK. 'Wat seggen de reggen de copen, slopen'—laugh,
Hodge, laugh.

LACY. *Mine liever* [2] *broder Firk, bringt meester Eyre tot den*
signe un Swannekin; daer sal yow finde dis skipper end me. Wat
seggen yow, broder Firk? Doot it, Hodge. Come, skipper.

Exeunt.

FIRK. Bring him, quoth you? Here's no knavery, to bring my
master to buy a ship worth the lading of two or three hundred
thousand pounds; alas, that's nothing, a trifle, a bauble,
Hodge.

HODGE. The truth is, Firk, that the merchant owner of the
ship dares not show his head, and therefore this skipper that
deals for him, for the love he bears to Hans, offers my master
Eyre a bargain in the commodities. He shall have a reasonable
day of payment; he may sell the wares by that time and be a
huge gainer himself.

FIRK. Yea, but can my fellow Hans lend my master twenty
porpentines [3] as an honest penny?

HODGE. Portagues, thou wouldst say; here they be, Firk;
hark, they jingle in my pocket like Saint Mary Overy's bells.

Enter EYRE *and his wife, with a boy*

FIRK. Mum; here comes my dame and my master. She'll scold,
on my life, for loitering this Monday, but all's one; let them
all say what they can, Monday's our holiday.

WIFE. You sing, Sir Sauce, but I beshrew your heart,
I fear for this your singing we shall smart.

FIRK. Smart for me, dame; why, dame, why?

HODGE. Master, I hope you'll not suffer my dame to take down
your journeymen.

FIRK. If she take me down, I'll take her up; yea, and take her
down too, a buttonhole lower.

EYRE. Peace, Firk; not I, Hodge; by the life of Pharaoh, by the
Lord of Ludgate, by this beard, every hair whereof I value at
a king's ransom, she shall not meddle with you. Peace, you
bombast cotton-candle quean; away, queen of clubs; quarrel

---

[1] Bargain.   [2] Dear.

[3] (Porcupines.) One of Firk's characteristic puns; see the next line.

not with me and my men, with me and my fine Firk; I'll firk
you if you do.   40

WIFE. Yea, yea, man, you may use me as you please, but let
that pass.

EYRE. Let it pass, let it vanish away. Peace, am I not Simon
Eyre? Are not these my brave men, brave shoemakers, all
gentlemen of the gentle craft? Prince am I none, yet am I
nobly born, as being the sole son of a shoemaker. Away,
rubbish, vanish; melt like kitchen-stuff.

WIFE. Yea, yea, 'tis well; I must be called rubbish, kitchen-
stuff, for a sort [1] of knaves.

FIRK. Nay, dame, you shall not weep and wail in woe for me.   50
Master, I'll stay no longer; here's a vennentory of my shop-
tools. Adieu, master; Hodge, farewell.

HODGE. Nay, stay, Firk, thou shalt not go alone.

WIFE. I pray, let them go; there be mo maids than Mawkin,
more men than Hodge, and more fools than Firk.

FIRK. Fools? Nails! If I tarry now, I would my guts might be
turned to shoe-thread.

HODGE. And if I stay, I pray God I may be turned to a Turk,
and set in Finsbury [2] for boys to shoot at. Come, Firk.

EYRE. Stay, my fine knaves, you arms of my trade, you pillars   60
of my profession. What, shall a tittle-tattle's words make you
forsake Simon Eyre? Avaunt, kitchen-stuff; rip, you brown-
bread Tannikin; [3] out of my sight; move me not! Have I not
ta'en you from selling tripes in Eastcheap, and set you in my
shop, and made you hail-fellow with Simon Eyre the shoemaker? And now do you deal thus with my journeymen?
Look, you powder-beef quean, on the face of Hodge—here's
a face for a lord.

FIRK. And here's a face for any lady in Christendom.

EYRE. Rip, you chitterling,[4] avaunt! Boy, bid the tapster of the   70
Boar's Head fill me a dozen cans of beer for my journeymen.

FIRK. A dozen cans? Oh, brave, Hodge; now I'll stay.

EYRE. [*Aside to boy.*] And the knave fills any more than two, he
pays for them.—[*Exit boy.*] A dozen cans of beer for my
journeymen! [*Enter boy with two cans and exit.*] Here, you
mad Mesopotamians, wash your livers with this liquor. Where

---

[1] Company.
[2] A well-known practice area for archery.
[3] Usually refers to a Dutch or German girl; a term of abuse.
[4] Sausage.

be the odd ten? No more, Madge, no more; well said.[1] Drink
and to work. What work dost thou, Hodge, what work? [2]

HODGE. I am making a pair of shoes for my lord mayor's
daughter, Mistress Rose.

FIRK. And I a pair of shoes for Sybil, my lord's maid; I deal
with her.

EYRE. Sybil? Fie, defile not thy fine workmanly fingers with
the feet of kitchen-stuff and basting-ladles. Ladies of the
court, fine ladies, my lads, commit their feet to our apparel-
ling; put gross work to Hans. Yerk [3] and seam, yerk and seam.

FIRK. For yerking and seaming let me alone, and I come to't.

HODGE. Well, master, all this is from the bias; [4] do you
remember the ship my fellow Hans told you of? The skipper
and he are both drinking at the Swan. Here be the portages
to give earnest; if you go through with it, you cannot choose
but be a lord at least.

FIRK. Nay, dame, if my master prove not a lord, and you a
lady, hang me.

WIFE. Yea, like enough, 'f you may loiter and tipple thus.

FIRK. Tipple, dame? No, we have been bargaining with
Skellum [5] Skanderbag [6]—'Can you Dutch sprecken?'—for
a ship of silk cypress,[7] laden with sugar-candy.

Enter the boy with a velvet coat and an alderman's gown;
EYRE *puts them on*

EYRE. Peace, Firk; silence, tittle-tattle. Hodge, I'll go through
with it. Here's a seal ring, and I have sent for a guarded [8]
gown, and a damask cassock. See where it comes. Look here,
Maggy; help me, Firk; apparel me, Hodge. Silk and satin,
you mad Philistines, silk and satin!

FIRK. Ha, ha; my master will be as proud as a dog in a doublet,
all in beaten [9] damask and velvet.

EYRE. Softly, Firk, for rearing of the nap, and wearing threadbare my garments. How dost thou like me, Firk? How do I
look, my fine Hodge?

---

[1] Well done.
[2] Dekker seems to have nodded here (*see above*, lines 25–7, the references to
Monday as the workmen's holiday).
[3] Stitch.   [4] Not to the point.   [5] Rascal.
[6] The Turkish name of John Kastriota, a fifteenth-century Albanian hero,
the subject of a contemporary play.
[7] Fine cloth, originally imported from or *via* Cyprus.
[8] Ornamented, trimmed with braid, etc.   [9] Embroidered.

HODGE. Why, now you look like yourself, master. I warrant you
there's few in the city but will give you the wall,[1] and come   110
upon you with the 'right worshipful'.

FIRK. Nails! My master looks like a threadbare cloak new
turned and dressed. Lord, Lord, to see what good raiment
doth! Dame, dame, are you not enamoured?

EYRE. How say'st thou, Maggy? Am I not brisk? Am I not fine?

WIFE. Fine? By my troth, sweetheart, very fine; by my troth, I
never liked thee so well in my life, sweetheart. But let that
pass. I warrant there be many women in the city have not such
handsome husbands, but only for their apparel, but let that
pass too.   120

Enter [LACY as] HANS [2] and skipper

LACY. *Godden day, mester. Dis be de skipper dat heb de skip van
marchandice; de commodity ben good; nempt it, master, nempt it.*

EYRE. Godamercy, Hans. Welcome, skipper; where lies this
ship of merchandise?

SKIP. *De skip ben in revere; dor be van sugar, civet, almonds,
cambrick, and a towsand towsand tings, gotz [3] sacrament;
nempt it, mester; yo sal heb good copen.*

FIRK. To him, master! O sweet master! O sweet wares!
Prunes, almonds, sugar-candy, carrot-roots, turnips! O brave
fatting meat! Let not a man buy a nutmeg but yourself.   130

EYRE. Peace, Firk. Come, skipper, I'll go aboard with you.
Hans, have you made him drink?

SKIP. *Yaw, yaw, ic veale gedrunck.*[4]

EYRE. Come, Hans, follow me. Skipper, thou shalt have my
countenance [5] in the city.   *Exeunt.*

FIRK. 'Yaw, heb veale gedrunck,' quoth 'a; they may well be
called butter-boxes, when they drink fat veal and thick beer
too. But come, dame, I hope you'll chide us no more.

WIFE. No, faith, Firk; no, perdy,[6] Hodge. I do feel honour
creep upon me, and, which is more, a certain rising in my   140
flesh, but let that pass.

FIRK. Rising in your flesh do you feel, say you? Ay, you may

---

[1] To step aside so that a higher ranking person might have the safer and
cleaner passage.
[2] In the quartos *Hans* is substituted for *Lacy* in all subsequent stage
directions and speech headings.
[3] God's.   [4] 'I have drunk much.'
[5] Patronage.   [6] Indeed; lit., by God (*par Dieu*).

be with child; but why should not my master feel a rising in
his flesh, having a gown and a gold ring on? But you are such
a shrew, you'll soon pull him down.

WIFE. Ha, ha! Prithee, peace! Thou mak'st my worship
laugh, but let that pass. Come, I'll go in; Hodge, prithee go
before me; Firk, follow me.

FIRK. Firk doth follow; Hodge, pass out in state.   *Exeunt.*

[ACT II. SCENE 4]

[*The* EARL OF LINCOLN'S *house, London*]

Enter LINCOLN *and* DODGER

LINC. How now, good Dodger, what's the news in France?
DODGER. My Lord, upon the eighteenth day of May
    The French and English were prepar'd to fight;
    Each side with eager fury gave the sign
    Of a most hot encounter. Five long hours
    Both armies fought together; at the length
    The lot of victory fell on our sides.
    Twelve thousand of the Frenchmen that day died,
    Four thousand English, and no man of name
    But Captain Hyam and young Ardington.   1(
LINC. Two gallant gentlemen; I knew them well.[1]
    But, Dodger, prithee tell me, in this fight
    How did my cousin Lacy bear himself?
DODGER. My Lord, your cousin Lacy was not there.
LINC. Not there?
DODGER.   No, my good Lord.
LINC.   Sure thou mistak'st;
    I saw him shipp'd, and a thousand eyes beside
    Were witnesses of the farewells which he gave,
    When I with weeping eyes bid him adieu.
    Dodger, take heed.
DODGER.   My Lord, I am advis'd [2]
    That what I spake is true: to prove it so,
    His cousin Askew, that supplied his place,   2(

[1] Quartos assign this line to Dodger. Emendation by Bowers.
[2] Assured.

Sent me for him from France, that secretly
He might convey himself hither.

LINC.   Is't even so?
Dares he so carelessly venture his life
Upon the indignation of a king?
Hath he despis'd my love and spurn'd those favours
Which I with prodigal hand pour'd on his head?
He shall repent his rashness with his soul.
Since of my love he makes no estimate,
I'll make him wish he had not known my hate.   30
Thou hast no other news?

DODGER.   None else, my Lord.

LINC. None worse I know thou hast. Procure the king
To crown his giddy brows with ample honours,
Send him chief colonel, and all my hope
Thus to be dash'd? But 'tis in vain to grieve;
One evil cannot a worse relieve.
Upon my life, I have found out his plot:
That old dog, Love, that fawn'd upon him so,
Love to that puling girl, his fair-cheek'd Rose,
The lord mayor's daughter, hath distracted him,   40
And in the fire of that love's lunacy
Hath he burnt up himself, consum'd his credit,
Lost the king's love, yea, and, I fear, his life,
Only to get a wanton to his wife.
Dodger, it is so.

DODGER.   I fear so, my good Lord.

LINC. It is so; nay, sure it cannot be.
I am at my wit's end. Dodger—

DODGER.   Yea, my Lord.

LINC. Thou art acquainted with my nephew's haunts;
Spend this gold for thy pains; go seek him out.
Watch at my lord mayor's; there if he live,   50
Dodger, thou shalt be sure to meet with him.
Prithee, be diligent. Lacy, thy name
Liv'd once in honour, now dead in shame.
Be circumspect.   *Exit.*

DODGER.   I warrant you, my Lord.   *Exit.*

[ACT III. SCENE 1]
[*The* LORD MAYOR'S *house, London*]

Enter LORD MAYOR *and* MASTER SCOTT

L. MAYOR. Good Master Scott, I have been bold with you,
To be a witness to a wedding knot [1]
Betwixt young Master Hammon and my daughter.
Oh, stand aside; see where the lovers come.

Enter HAMMON *and* ROSE

ROSE. Can it be possible you love me so?
No, no, within those eyeballs I espy
Apparent likelihoods of flattery.
Pray now, let go my hand.
HAM.   Sweet Mistress Rose,
Misconstrue not my words, nor misconceive
Of my affection, whose devoted soul
Swears that I love thee dearer than my heart.
ROSE. As dear as your own heart? I judge it right:
Men love their hearts best when th'are out of sight.
HAM. I love you, by this hand.
ROSE.   Yet hands off now!
If flesh be frail, how weak and frail's your vow?
HAM. Then by my life I swear.
ROSE.   Then do not brawl;
One quarrel loseth wife and life and all.
Is not your meaning thus?
HAM.   In faith, you jest.
ROSE. Love loves to sport; therefore, leave love, y'are best.
L. MAYOR. What? Square [2] they, Master Scott?
SCOTT.   Sir, never doubt,
Lovers are quickly in and quickly out.
HAM. Sweet Rose, be not so strange [3] in fancying me;
Nay, never turn aside, shun not my sight.
I am not grown so fond to fond [4] my love
On any that shall quit [5] it with disdain.
If you will love me, so; if not, farewell.

<hr>

[1] Betrothal.   [2] Quarrel.   [3] Reluctant.
[4] Establish; i.e. found.   [5] Requite.

L. MAYOR. Why, how now, lovers, are you both agreed?

HAM. Yes, faith, my Lord.

L. MAYOR.   'Tis well; give me your hand.
  Give me yours, daughter. How now, both pull back?
  What means this, girl?

ROSE.   I mean to live a maid.   30

HAM. (*Aside.*) But not to die one; pause ere that be said.

L. MAYOR. Will you still cross me, still be obstinate?

HAM. Nay, chide her not, my Lord, for doing well;
  If she can live a happy virgin's life,
  'Tis far more blessed than to be a wife.

ROSE. Say, sir, I cannot, I have made a vow;
  Whoever be my husband, 'tis not you.

L. MAYOR. Your tongue is quick; but, Master Hammon, know
  I bade you welcome to another end.

HAM. What, would you have me pule and pine and pray   40
  With 'Lovely lady', 'Mistress of my heart',
  'Pardon your servant', and the rhymer play,
  Railing on Cupid and his tyrant's dart?
  Or shall I undertake some martial spoil,
  Wearing your glove at tourney and at tilt,
  And tell how many gallants I unhors'd?
  Sweet, will this pleasure you?

ROSE.   Yea, when wilt begin?
  What, love rhymes, man? Fie on that deadly sin.

L. MAYOR. If you will have her, I'll make her agree.

HAM. Enforced love is worse than hate to me.   50
  [*Aside.*] There is a wench keeps shop in the Old Change,[1]
  To her will I; it is not wealth I seek,
  I have enough; and will prefer her love
  Before the world—My good Lord Mayor, adieu;
  Old love for me, I have no luck with new.   *Exit.*

L. MAYOR. Now, mammet,[2] you have well behav'd yourself,
  But you shall curse your coyness if I live.
  Who's within there? See you convey your mistress
  Straight to th'old Ford; I'll keep you straight enough.
  [*Aside.*] 'Fore God, I would have sworn the puling girl 60
  Would willingly accepted Hammon's love;
  But banish him, my thoughts.—Go, minion, in.   *Exit* ROSE.

[1] The Old Exchange, given over to drapers' shops and other businesses
after the new Royal Exchange was opened in 1566.
[2] A doll, puppet.

Now tell me, Master Scott, would you have thought
That Master Simon Eyre, the shoemaker,
Had been of wealth to buy such merchandise?
SCOTT. 'Twas well, my Lord, your honour and myself
Grew partners with him, for your bills of lading
Show that Eyre's gains in one commodity
Rise at the least to full three thousand pound,
Besides like gain in other merchandise. 7

L. MAYOR. Well, he shall spend some of his thousands now,
For I have sent for him to the Guildhall. *Enter* EYRE.
See where he comes. Good morrow, Master Eyre.

EYRE. Poor Simon Eyre, my Lord, your shoemaker.

L. MAYOR. Well, well, it likes yourself to term you so—
Enter DODGER.
Now, Master Dodger, what's the news with you?

DODGER. I'd gladly speak in private to your honour.

L. MAYOR. You shall, you shall. Master Eyre and Master
Scott,
I have some business with this gentleman;
I pray let me entreat you to walk before 8
To the Guildhall; I'll follow presently.
Master Eyre, I hope ere noon to call you sheriff.

EYRE. I would not care, my Lord, if you might call me King of
Spain. Come, Master Scott. [*Exeunt.*]

L. MAYOR. Now, Master Dodger, what's the news you bring?

DODGER. The Earl of Lincoln by me greets your lordship
And earnestly requests you, if you can,
Inform him where his nephew Lacy keeps.

L. MAYOR. Is not his nephew Lacy now in France? 9

DODGER. No, I assure your lordship, but disguis'd
Lurks here in London.

L. MAYOR. London? Is't even so?
It may be, but upon my faith and soul,
I know not where he lives, or whether he lives;
So tell my Lord of Lincoln. Lurch [1] in London?
Well, Master Dodger, you perhaps may start him;
Be but the means to rid him into France,
I'll give you a dozen angels [2] for your pains;
So much I love his honour, hate his nephew,
And prithee so inform thy lord from me. 100

---

[1] Lurk.
[2] Gold coins, worth 6s. 8d. each.

DODGER. I take my leave.

L. MAYOR.   Farewell, good Master Dodger.

Exit DODGER.

Lacy in London? I dare pawn my life
My daughter knows thereof, and for that cause
Denied young Master Hammon in his love.
Well, I am glad I sent her to Old Ford.
God's Lord, 'tis late! To Guildhall I must hie;
I know my brethren stay my company.   *Exit.*

[ACT III. SCENE 2]

[*Before* EYRE'S *shop*]

Enter FIRK, EYRE'S *wife*, [LACY *as*] HANS, *and* ROGER
[HODGE]

WIFE. Thou goest too fast for me, Roger. Oh, Firk.

FIRK. Ay, forsooth.

WIFE. I pray thee, run—do you hear?—Run to Guildhall and
learn if my husband, Master Eyre, will take that worshipful
vocation of Master Sheriff upon him; hie thee, good Firk.

FIRK. Take it? Well, I go; and he should not take it, Firk
swears to forswear him. Yes, forsooth, I go to Guildhall.

WIFE. Nay, when?[1] Thou art too compendious and tedious.

FIRK. Oh, rare! Your excellence is full of eloquence. [*Aside.*]
How like a new cart-wheel my dame speaks, and she looks   10
like an old musty ale-bottle going to scalding.

WIFE. Nay, when? Thou wilt make me melancholy.

FIRK. God forbid your worship should fall into that humour.
I run.   *Exit.*

WIFE. Let me see now, Roger and Hans.

HODGE. Ay, forsooth, dame—mistress, I should say, but the old
term so sticks to the roof of my mouth I can hardly lick it off.

WIFE. Even what thou wilt, good Roger; dame is a fair name
for any honest Christian, but let that pass. How dost thou,
Hans?   20

LACY. *Mee tanck you, vro.*

WIFE. Well, Hans and Roger, you see God hath blessed your
master, and, perdy, if ever he comes to be Master Sheriff of

---

[1] A vague expletive.

London (as we are all mortal), you shall see I will have some odd thing or other in a corner for you; I will not be your back-friend;[1] but let that pass. Hans, pray thee, tie my shoe.

LACY. *Yaw, ic sal, vro.*

WIFE. Roger, thou knowest the length of my foot; as it is none of the biggest, so I thank God, it is handsome enough; prithee, let me have a pair of shoes made—cork, good Roger, wooden heel too.

HODGE. You shall.

WIFE. Art thou acquainted with never a farthingale [2]-maker, nor a French hood-maker? I must enlarge my bum, ha, ha! How shall I look in a hood, I wonder? Perdy, oddly, I think.

HODGE. [*Aside.*] As a cat out of a pillory.—Very well, I warrant you, mistress.

WIFE. Indeed, all flesh is grass; and, Roger, canst thou tell where I may buy a good hair?

HODGE. Yes, forsooth, at the poulterer's in Gracious [3] Street.

WIFE. Thou art an ungracious wag; perdy, I mean a false hair for my periwig.

HODGE. Why, mistress, the next time I cut my beard you shall have the shavings of it, but they are all true hairs.

WIFE. It is very hot; I must get me a fan or else a mask.

HODGE. [*Aside.*] So had you need, to hide your wicked [4] face.

WIFE. Fie upon it, how costly this world's calling is! Perdy, but that it is one of the wonderful works of God, I would not deal with it. Is not Firk come yet? Hans, be not so sad; let it pass and vanish, as my husband's worship says.

LACY. *Ick bin vrolicke; lot see you soo.*[5]

HODGE. Mistress, will you drink a pipe of tobacco? [6]

WIFE. Oh, fie upon it, Roger! Perdy, these filthy tobacco pipes are the most idle slavering baubles that I ever felt. Out upon it! God bless us, men look not like men that use them.

Enter RAFE, *being lame*

HODGE. What, fellow Rafe? Mistress, look here, Jane's hus-band! Why, how now, lame? Hans, make much of him; he's a brother of our trade, a good workman, and a tall soldier.

---

[1] False friend.   [2] A petticoat extended with hoops.
[3] Later, Gracechurch.   [4] Unpleasant.
[5] 'I am happy; let us see you so.'
[6] An anachronism; tobacco was unknown in Eyre's day. Hodge is merely teasing the middle-class Dame Margery.

LACY. You be welcome, broder.

WIFE. Perdy, I knew him not. How dost thou, good Rafe? I am   60
glad to see thee well.

RAFE. I would God you saw me, dame, as well
As when I went from London into France.

WIFE. Trust me, I am sorry, Rafe, to see thee impotent.[1] Lord,
how the wars have made him sunburnt! The left leg is not
well; 'twas a fair gift of God the infirmity took not hold a little
higher, considering thou camest from France,[2] but let that
pass.

RAFE. I am glad to see you well and I rejoice
To hear that God hath bless'd my master so   70
Since my departure.

WIFE. Yea, truly, Rafe. I thank my Maker, but let that pass.

HODGE. And, sirrah Rafe, what news, what news in France?

RAFE. Tell me, good Roger, first, what news in England?
How does my Jane? When didst thou see my wife?
Where lives my poor heart? She'll be poor indeed,
Now I want limbs to get whereon to feed.

HODGE. Limbs? Hast thou not hands, man? Thou shalt never
see a shoemaker want bread, though he have but three fingers
on a hand.   80

RAFE. Yet all this while I hear not of my Jane.

WIFE. Oh, Rafe, your wife! Perdy, we know not what's become
of her; she was here a while, and, because she was married,
grew more stately than became her. I checked her, and so
forth away she flung, never returned, nor said bye nor bah;
and, Rafe, you know, 'Ka me, ka thee'.[3] And so, as I tell thee
—Roger, is not Firk come yet?

HODGE. No, forsooth.

WIFE. And so indeed we heard not of her, but I hear she lives
in London, but let that pass. If she wanted, she might have   90
opened her case to me or to my husband, or to any of my
men; I am sure there's not any of them, perdy, but would
have done her good to his power. Hans, look if Firk be come.

LACY. *Yaw, ic sal, vro.*   *Exit.*

WIFE. And so as I said; but, Rafe, why dost thou weep? Thou
knowest that naked we came out of our mother's womb, and
naked we must return, and therefore thank God for all things.

HODGE. No, faith, Jane is a stranger here; but, Rafe, pull up a

---

[1] Injured.   [2] An oblique allusion to a social disease.
[3] 'One good turn deserves another.'

good heart, I know thou hast one. Thy wife, man, is in
London; one told me he saw her a while ago very brave and 10
neat. We'll ferret her out, and London hold her.

WIFE. Alas, poor soul, he's overcome with sorrow; he does but
as I do, weep for the loss of any good thing. But, Rafe, get
thee in; call for some meat and drink; thou shalt find me
worshipful towards thee.

RAFE. I thank you, dame; since I want limbs and lands,
I'll trust to God, my good friends, and to my hands.   *Exit.*

Enter [LACY *as*] HANS *and* FIRK, *running*

FIRK. Run, good Hans. Oh, Hodge, oh, mistress! Hodge, heave
up thine ears; mistress, smug up [1] your looks, on with your
best apparel. My master is chosen, my master is called, nay, 110
condemned by the cry of the country to be sheriff of the city,
for this famous year now to come. And, time now being, a
great many men in black gowns were asked for their voices
and their hands, and my master had all their fists about his ears
presently, and they cried, 'Ay, ay, ay, ay!' and so I came
away;
Wherefore without all other grieve
I do salute you, Mistress Shrieve.[2]

LACY. *Yaw, my mester is de groot man, de shrieve.*

HODGE. Did not I tell you, mistress? Now I may boldly say, 120
'Good morrow to your worship'.

WIFE. Good morrow, good Roger. I thank you, my good
people all. Firk, hold up thy hand; here's a threepenny piece
for thy tidings.

FIRK. 'Tis but three halfpence, I think. Yes, 'tis threepence, I
smell [3] the rose.[4]

HODGE. But, mistress, be ruled by me, and do not speak so
pulingly.

FIRK. 'Tis her worship speaks so, and not she. No, faith,
mistress, speak to me in the old key: 'To it, Firk'; 'There, 130
good Firk'; 'Ply your business, Hodge'; 'Hodge, with a full
mouth'; 'I'll fill your bellies with good cheer till they cry
twang'.

Enter SIMON EYRE, *wearing a gold chain*

---

[1] Smarten.   [2] Sheriff.   [3] Discern.
[4] The rose design on the obverse of certain Elizabethan silver threepences.

LACY. *See, mine liever* [1] *broder, heer compt my meester.*

WIFE. Welcome home, Master Shrieve; I pray God continue
you in health and wealth.

EYRE. See here, my Maggy, a chain, a gold chain for Simon
Eyre. I shall make thee a lady; here's a French hood for thee;
on with it, on with it. Dress thy brows with this flap of a
shoulder of mutton,[2] to make thee look lovely. Where be my   140
fine men? Roger, I'll make over my shop and tools to thee;
Firk, thou shalt be the foreman; Hans, thou shalt have an
hundred for twenty. Be as mad knaves as your master Sim
Eyre hath been, and you shall live to be sheriffs of London.
How dost thou like me, Margery? Prince am I none, yet am I
princely born. Firk, Hodge, and Hans!

ALL THREE. Ay, forsooth, what says your worship, Master
Sheriff?

EYRE. Worship and honour, you Babylonian knaves, for the
gentle craft! But I forget myself; I am bidden by my lord   150
mayor to dinner to Old Ford; he's gone before, I must after.
Come, Madge, on with your trinkets. Now, my true Trojans,
my fine Firk, my dapper Hodge, my honest Hans, some
device, some odd crotchets,[3] some morris, or suchlike, for the
honour of the gentle shoemakers. Meet me at Old Ford; you
know my mind.

Come, Madge, away. Shut up the shop, knaves, and make
holiday.   *Exeunt.*

FIRK. Oh, rare, oh, brave! Come, Hodge; follow me, Hans;
We'll be with them for a morris-dance.   *Exeunt.*   160

[ACT III. SCENE 3]

[*The Lord Mayor's house at Old Ford*]

Enter LORD MAYOR, EYRE, *his wife, in a French hood*,
ROSE, SYBIL, *and other servants*

L. MAYOR. Trust me, you are as welcome to Old Ford
As I myself.

WIFE. Truly, I thank your lordship.

L. MAYOR. Would our bad cheer were worth the thanks you
give.

___

[1] Dear.   [2] A hood trimmed with wool.   [3] Fanciful devices.

EYRE. Good cheer, my Lord Mayor, fine cheer. A fine house, fine walls, all fine and neat.

L. MAYOR. Now, by my troth, I'll tell thee, Master Eyre,
It does me good and all my brethren
That such a madcap fellow as thyself
Is ent'red into our society.

WIFE. Ay, but, my Lord, he must learn now to put on gravity.

EYRE. Peace, Maggy; a fig for gravity! When I go to Guildhall in my scarlet gown, I'll look as demurely as a saint and speak as gravely as a justice of the peace; but now I am here at Old Ford, at my good lord mayor's house, let it go by. Vanish, Maggy; I'll be merry; away with flip-flap, these fooleries, these gulleries. What, honey? Prince am I none, yet am I princely born. What says my Lord Mayor?

L. MAYOR. Ha, ha, ha! I had rather than a thousand pound I had a heart but half so light as yours.

EYRE. Why, what should I do, my Lord? A pound of care pays not a dram of debt. Hum, let's be merry whiles we are young; old age, sack and sugar will steal upon us ere we be aware.

The First Three-men's Song [1]

Oh, the month of May, the merry month of May,
So frolic, so gay, and so green, so green, so green;
Oh, and then did I unto my true love say,
Sweet Peg, thou shalt be my summer's queen.

Now the nightingale, the pretty nightingale,
The sweetest singer in all the forest's choir,
Entreats thee, sweet Peggy, to hear my true love's tale;
Lo, yonder she sitteth, her breast against a briar.

But oh, I spy the cuckoo, the cuckoo, the cuckoo;
See where she sitteth; come away, my joy;
Come away, I prithee; I do not like the cuckoo
Should sing where my Peggy and I kiss and toy.

Oh, the month of May, the merry month of May,
So frolic, so gay, and so green, so green, so green;
And then did I unto my true love say,
Sweet Peg, thou shalt be my summer's queen.

[1] This song precedes the text of the play in the quartos. It is plausibly inserted here (without authority) by most modern editors.

L. MAYOR. It's well done. Mistress Eyre, pray give good
counsel to my daughter.

WIFE. I hope Mistress Rose will have the grace to take nothing
that's bad.

L. MAYOR. Pray God she do, for i' faith, Mistress Eyre,
I would bestow upon that peevish girl
A thousand marks more than I mean to give her
Upon condition she'd be rul'd by me.
The ape [1] still crosseth me. There came of late
A proper gentleman of fair revenues,   50
Whom gladly I would call [my] son-in-law,
But my fine cockney would have none of him.
You'll prove a coxcomb for it ere you die;
A courtier or no man must please your eye.

EYRE. Be ruled, sweet Rose; th'art ripe for a man. Marry not
with a boy that has no more hair on his face than thou hast on
thy cheeks. A courtier! Wash, go by, stand not upon pishery-
pashery; those silken fellows are but painted images—outsides, outsides, Rose; their inner linings are torn. No, my fine
mouse, marry me with a gentleman grocer like my lord mayor,   60
your father; a grocer is a sweet trade—plums, plums! Had I a
son or daughter should marry out of the generation and blood
of the shoemakers, he should pack. What, the gentle trade is a
living for a man through Europe, through the world.

A noise within of a tabor [2] and a pipe

L. MAYOR. What noise is this?

EYRE. Oh, my Lord Mayor, a crew of good fellows that for love
to your honour are come hither with a morris-dance. Come in,
my Mesopotamians, cheerily.

Enter HODGE, [LACY *as*] HANS, RAFE, FIRK, *and other shoemakers in a morris. After a little dancing, the* LORD
MAYOR *speaks*

L. MAYOR. Master Eyre, are all these shoemakers?

EYRE. All cordwainers, my good Lord Mayor.   70

ROSE. [*Aside.*] How like my Lacy looks yond shoemaker!

LACY. [*Aside.*] Oh, that I durst but speak unto my love.

---

[1] Fool.   [2] A small drum.

L. MAYOR. Sybil, go fetch some wine to make these drink.
  You are all welcome.
ALL. We thank your lordship.

ROSE *takes a cup of wine and goes to* HANS

ROSE. For his sake whose fair shape thou represent'st,
  Good friend, I drink to thee.
LACY. *Ic bedancke, good frister.*[1]
WIFE. I see, Mistress Rose, you do not want judgment; you
  have drunk to the properest man I keep.
FIRK. Here be some have done their parts to be as proper as he.
L. MAYOR. Well, urgent business calls me back to London.
  Good fellows, first go in and taste our cheer;
  And to make merry as you homeward go,
  Spend these two angels in beer at Stratford Bow.[2]
EYRE. To these two, my mad lads, Sim Eyre adds another.
  Then cheerily, Firk; tickle it, Hans, and all for the honour of
  shoemakers.   *The men go dancing out.*
L. MAYOR. Come, Master Eyre, let's have your company.
                                                    Exeunt.

ROSE. Sybil, what shall I do?
SYBIL. Why, what's the matter?
ROSE. That Hans the shoemaker is my love Lacy,
  Disguis'd in that attire to find me out.
  How should I find the means to speak with him?
SYBIL. What, mistress, never fear; I dare venture my maiden-
  head to nothing, and that's great odds, that Hans the Dutch-
  man, when we come to London, shall not only see and speak
  with you, but in spite of all your father's policies, steal you
  away and marry you. Will not this please you?
ROSE. Do this, and ever be assured of my love.
SYBIL. Away then, and follow your father to London, lest your
  absence cause him to suspect something.
  Tomorrow, if my counsel be obey'd,
  I'll bind you prentice to the gentle trade.   [*Exeunt.*]

---

[1] Sweetheart.   [2] An inn near Old Ford.

[ACT III. SCENE 4]
[*At the Old Change, London*]

Enter JANE *in a sempster's shop,*[1] *working, and* HAMMON,
muffled, at another door; he stands aloof

HAM. Yonder's the shop, and there my fair love sits;
   She's fair and lovely, but she is not mine.
   Oh, would she were. Thrice have I courted her,
   Thrice hath my hand been moist'ned with her hand,
   Whilst my poor famish'd eyes do feed on that
   Which made them famish. I am unfortunate;
   I still love one, yet nobody loves me.
   I muse in other men what women see
   That I so want.[2] Fine Mistress Rose was coy,
   And this too curious.[3] Oh, no, she is chaste,   10
   And for she thinks me wanton, she denies
   To cheer my cold heart with her sunny eyes.
   How prettily she works; O pretty hand!
   O happy work! It doth me good to stand
   Unseen to see her; thus I oft have stood
   In frosty evenings, a light burning by her,
   Enduring bitter cold, only to eye her.
   One only look hath seem'd as rich to me
   As a king's crown. Such is love's lunacy.
   Muffled I'll pass along, and by that try   20
   Whether she know me.
JANE.   Sir, what is't you buy?
   What is't you lack, sir? Calico, or lawn,
   Fine cambric shirts, or bands? [4] What will you buy?
HAM. [*Aside.*] That which thou wilt not sell; faith, yet I'll try.—
   How do you sell this handkercher?
JANE.   Good cheap.
HAM. And how these ruffs?
JANE.   Cheap too.
HAM.   And how this band?
JANE. Cheap too.
HAM.   All cheap. How sell you then this hand?

---

[1] The inner stage.   [2] Lack.
[3] Fastidious.   [4] Collars.

JANE. My hands are not to be sold.
HAM.   To be given then;
   Nay, faith, I come to buy.
JANE.   But none knows when.
HAM. Good sweet, leave work a little while; let's play.
JANE. I cannot live by keeping holiday.
HAM. I'll pay you for the time which shall be lost.
JANE. With me you shall not be at so much cost.
HAM. Look how you wound this cloth, so you wound me.
JANE. It may be so.
HAM.   'Tis so.
JANE.   What remedy?
HAM. Nay, faith, you are too coy.
JANE.   Let go my hand.
HAM. I will do any task at your command;
   I would let go this beauty, were I not
   In mind to disobey you by a power
   That controls kings: I love you.
JANE.   So, now part.
HAM. With hands I may, but never with my heart;
   In faith, I love you.
JANE.   I believe you do.
HAM. Shall a true love in me breed hate in you?
JANE. I hate you not.
HAM.   Then you must love.
JANE.   I do.
   What, are you better now? I love not you.
HAM. All this I hope is but a woman's fray [1]
   That means, 'Come to me', when she cried, 'Away!'
   In earnest, mistress, I do not jest;
   A true, chaste love has ent'red in my breast.
   I love you dearly as I love my life,
   I love you as a husband loves a wife;
   That, and no other love, my love requires.
   Thy wealth I know is little; my desires
   Thirst not for gold, sweet beauteous Jane; what's mine
   Shall, if thou make myself thine, all be thine.
   Say, judge, what is thy sentence, life or death?
   Mercy or cruelty lies in thy breath.
JANE. Good sir, I do believe you love me well;
   For 'tis a silly conquest, silly pride,

[1] Fear.

For one like you, I mean a gentleman,   60
To boast that by his love tricks he hath brought
Such and such women to his amorous lure.
I think you do not so, yet many do,
And make it even a very trade to woo.
I could be coy, as many women be,
Feed you with sunshine smiles and wanton looks,
But I detest witchcraft; say that I
Do constantly believe you constant, have—

HAM. Why dost thou not believe me?

JANE.   I believe you;
But yet, good sir, because I will not grieve you   70
With hopes to taste fruit which will never fall,
In simple truth this is the sum of all:
My husband lives, at least I hope he lives.
Press'd was he to these bitter wars in France;
Bitter they are to me by wanting him.
I have but one heart, and that heart's his due;
How can I then bestow the same on you?
Whilst he lives, his I live, be it ne'er so poor,
And rather be his wife than a king's whore.

HAM. Chaste and dear woman, I will not abuse thee,   80
Although it cost my life if thou refuse me.
Thy husband press'd for France? What was his name?

JANE. Rafe Damport.

HAM.   Damport? Here's a letter sent
From France to me, from a dear friend of mine,
A gentleman of place; here he doth write
Their names that hath been slain in every fight.

JANE. I hope death's scroll contains not my love's name.

HAM. Cannot you read?

JANE.   I can.

HAM.   Peruse the same;
To my remembrance such a name I read
Amongst the rest; see here.

JANE.   Aye me, he's dead,   90
He's dead! If this be true, my dear heart's slain!

HAM. Have patience, dear love.

JANE.   Hence, hence!

HAM.   Nay, sweet Jane,
Make not poor sorrow proud with these rich tears;
I mourn thy husband's death because thou mourn'st.

JANE. That bill is forg'd; 'tis sign'd by forgery.
HAM. I'll bring thee letters sent besides to many,
    Carrying the like report. Jane, 'tis too true;
    Come, weep not; mourning, though it rise from love,
    Helps not the mourned, yet hurts them that mourn.
JANE. For God's sake, leave me.
HAM.   Whither dost thou turn?
    Forget the dead, love them that are alive.
    His love is faded; try how mine will thrive.
JANE. 'Tis now no time for me to think on love.
HAM. 'Tis now best time for you to think on love,
    Because your love lives not.
JANE.   Though he be dead,
    My love to him shall not be buried.
    For God's sake, leave me to myself alone.
HAM. 'Twould kill my soul to leave thee drown'd in moan.
    Answer me to my suit, and I am gone;
    Say to me yea or no.
JANE.   No.
HAM.   Then farewell.
    One farewell will not serve, I come again;
    Come, dry these wet cheeks. Tell me, faith, sweet Jane,
    Yea or no once more.
JANE.   Once more I say no;
    Once more be gone, I pray, else will I go.
HAM. Nay, then I will grow rude; by this white hand,
    Until you change that cold 'No', here I'll stand
    Till by your hard heart—
JANE.   Nay, for God's love, peace.
    My sorrows by your presence more increase.
    Not that you thus are present, but all grief
    Desires to be alone; therefore, in brief
    Thus much I say, and saying, bid adieu,
    If ever I wed man it shall be you.
HAM. O blessed voice! Dear Jane, I'll urge no more;
    Thy breath hath made me rich.
JANE.   Death makes me poor.

                                Exeunt.

[ACT IV. SCENE 1]

[*The shoemaker's shop, formerly* EYRE'S]

Enter HODGE, *at his shop-board;* [1] RAFE, FIRK, [LACY *as*]
HANS, *and a boy, at work*

ALL. Hey, down a down, down derry.

HODGE. Well said, my hearts; ply your work today, we loitered
yesterday; to it pell-mell, that we may live to be lord mayors,
or aldermen at least.

FIRK. Hey, down a down, derry.

HODGE. Well said, i' faith; how sayst thou, Hans, doth not Firk
tickle it?

LACY. *Yaw, mester.*

FIRK. Not so neither; my organ-pipe squeaks this morning for
want of liquoring. Hey, down a down, derry.   10

LACY. *Forware,* [2] *Firk, tow best un jolly yongster. Hort,* [3] *ay,
mester, ic bid yo cut me un pair vampies* [4] *vor Mester Jeffre's
boots.*

HODGE. Thou shalt, Hans.

FIRK. Master.

HODGE. How now, boy?

FIRK. Pray, now you are in the cutting vein, cut me out a pair
of counterfeits, [5] or else my work will not pass current. Hey,
down a down.

HODGE. Tell me, sirs, are my cousin Mistress Priscilla's shoes   20
done?

FIRK. Your cousin? No, master, one of your aunts, [6] hang her;
let them alone.

RAFE. I am in hand with them; she gave charge that none but I
should do them for her.

FIRK. Thou do for her? Then 'twill be a lame thing, and that
she loves not. Rafe, thou might'st have sent her to me; in faith,
I would have yerked [7] and firked [8] your Priscilla. Hey, down a
down, derry. This gear will not hold.

HODGE. How say'st thou, Firk, were we not merry at Old Ford?   30

FIRK. How, merry? Why, our buttocks went jiggy-joggy like a

---

[1] Display counter or work table.   [2] Truly.
[3] Listen.   [4] Vamps, the upper part of a boot.
[5] Patterns.   [6] Prostitutes or bawds.
[7] Whipped or stitched up.   [8] Tricked or beaten.

quagmire. Well, Sir Roger Oatmeal, if I thought all meal of
that nature, I would eat nothing but bagpuddings.

RAFE. Of all good fortunes, my fellow Hans had the best.

FIRK. 'Tis true, because Mistress Rose drank to him.

HODGE. Well, well, work apace. They say seven of the aldermen be dead or very sick.

FIRK. I care not, I'll be none.

RAFE. No, nor I; but then my Master Eyre will come quickly to
be lord mayor.

Enter SYBIL

FIRK. Whoop, yonder comes Sybil.

HODGE. Sybil, welcome, i' faith, and how dost thou, mad
wench?

FIRK. Syb-whore, welcome to London.

SYBIL. Godamercy, sweet Firk. Good Lord, Hodge, what a
delicious shop you have got; you tickle it, i' faith.

RAFE. Godamercy, Sybil, for our good cheer at Old Ford.

SYBIL. That you shall have, Rafe.

FIRK. Nay, by the mass, we had tickling cheer, Sybil; and how
the plague dost thou and Mistress Rose, and my lord mayor?
I put the women in first.

SYBIL. Well, Godamercy; but God's me, I forget myself—
where's Hans the Fleming?

FIRK. Hark, butter box, now you must yelp out some 'spreken'.

LACY. *Vat begaie* [1] *you? Vat vod* [2] *you, frister?* [3]

SYBIL. Marry, you must come to my young mistress to pull on
her shoes you made last.

LACY. *Vare ben your egle fro?* [4] *Vare ben your mistress?*

SYBIL. Marry, here at our London house in Cornwall. [5]

FIRK. Will nobody serve her turn but Hans?

SYBIL. No, sir; come, Hans, I stand upon needles.

HODGE. Why then, Sybil, take heed of pricking.

SYBIL. For that let me alone; I have a trick in my budget. [6]
Come, Hans.

LACY. *Yaw, yaw, ic sall meet yo gane.* [7]

HODGE. Go, Hans, make haste again. Come, who lacks work?
                                    Exeunt HANS *and* SYBIL.

---

[1] Desire.   [2] Would.   [3] Sweetheart.
[4] Noble lady(?).   [5] An old, alternative name for Cornhill.
[6] Bag.   [7] 'I shall go with you.'

FIRK. I, master, for I lack my breakfast; 'tis munching-time
and past.

HODGE. Is't so? Why then, leave work, Rafe; to breakfast.
Boy, look to the tools. Come, Rafe; come, Firk.   *Exeunt.*   70

[ACT IV. SCENE 2]

[*Before* HODGE'S *shop*]

Enter a serving-man

SERV. Let me see now, the sign of the Last in Tower Street.
Mass, yonder's the house. What, haw! Who's within?

Enter RAFE

RAFE. Who calls there? What want you, sir?

SERV. Marry, I would have a pair of shoes made for a gentlewoman against tomorrow morning. What, can you do them?

RAFE. Yes, sir, you shall have them, but what length's her
foot?

SERV. Why, you must make them in all parts like this shoe; but,
at any hand, fail not to do them, for the gentlewoman is to be
married very early in the morning.   10

RAFE. How? By this shoe must it be made? By this? Are you
sure, sir, by this?

SERV. How? By this, am I sure, by this? Art thou in thy wits?
I tell thee, I must have a pair of shoes; dost thou mark me? A
pair of shoes, two shoes, made by this very shoe, this same
shoe, against tomorrow morning by four o'clock. Dost understand me? Canst thou do't?

RAFE. Yes, sir, yes; ay, ay, I can do't; by this shoe, you say. I
should know this shoe. Yes, sir, yes, by this shoe. I can do it;
four o'clock. Well, whither shall I bring them?   20

SERV. To the sign of the Golden Ball in Watling Street; inquire
for one Master Hammon, a gentleman, my master.

RAFE. Yea, sir; by this shoe, you say.

SERV. I say, Master Hammon at the Golden Ball; he's the
bridegroom, and those shoes are for his bride.

RAFE. They shall be done by this shoe. Well, well, Master
Hammon at the Golden Shoe; I would say, the Golden Ball.

Very well, very well; but I pray you, sir, where must Master
Hammon be married?

SERV. At Saint Faith's Church, under Paul's. But what's that
to thee? Prithee, dispatch those shoes, and so farewell.   *Exit.*

RAFE. By this shoe, said he. How am I amaz'd
At this strange accident! Upon my life,
This was the very shoe I gave my wife,
When I was press'd for France; since when, alas,
I never could hear of her. It is the same,
And Hammon's bride no other but my Jane.

Enter FIRK

FIRK. 'Snails, Rafe, thou has lost thy part of three pots a
countryman of mine gave me to breakfast.

RAFE. I care not; I have found a better thing.

FIRK. A thing? Away! Is it a man's thing or a woman's thing?

RAFE. Firk, dost thou know this shoe?

FIRK. No, by my troth; neither doth that know me. I have no
acquaintance with it; 'tis a mere stranger to me.

RAFE. Why then, I do; this shoe I durst be sworn
Once covered the instep of my Jane.
This is her size, her breadth; thus trod my love.
These true-love knots I prick'd; I hold my life,
By this old shoe I shall find out my wife.

FIRK. Ha, ha! Old shoe, that wert new. How a murrain [1] came
this ague-fit of foolishness upon thee?

RAFE. Thus, Firk: even now here came a serving-man;
By this shoe would he have a new pair made
Against tomorrow morning for his mistress,
That's to be married to a gentleman.
And why may not this be my sweet Jane?

FIRK. And why may'st not thou be my sweet ass? Ha, ha!

RAFE. Well, laugh and spare not; but the truth is this:
Against tomorrow morning I'll provide
A lusty crew of honest shoemakers,
To watch the going of the bride to church;
If she prove Jane, I'll take her in despite
From Hammon and the devil, were he by!
If it be not my Jane, what remedy? [2]

---

[1] Plague.   [2] 'What help for it?'

Hereof am I sure, I shall live till I die,
Although I never with a woman lie.   *Exit.*

FIRK. Thou lie with a woman to build nothing but Cripple-
gates.[1] Well, God send fools fortune, and it may be he may
light upon his matrimony by such a device, for wedding and
hanging goes by destiny.   *Exit.*   70

[ACT IV. SCENE 3]
[OTLEY'S *house, Cornhill*]

Enter [LACY *as*] HANS *and* ROSE, *arm in arm*

LACY. How happy am I embracing thee!
   Oh, I did fear such cross mishaps did reign
   That I should never see my Rose again.
ROSE. Sweet Lacy, since fair opportunity
   Offers herself to further our escape,
   Let not too over-fond esteem of me
   Hinder that happy hour. Invent the means,
   And Rose will follow thee through all the world.
LACY. Oh, how I surfeit with excess of joy,
   Made happy by the rich perfection;   10
   But since thou pay'st sweet interest to my hopes,
   Redoubling love on love, let me once more,
   Like a bold-fac'd debtor, crave of thee
   This night to steal abroad, and at Eyre's house,
   Who now, by death of certain aldermen,
   Is mayor of London,[2] and my master once,
   Meet thou thy Lacy, where, in spite of change,
   Your father's anger and mine uncle's hate,
   Our happy nuptials will we consummate.

Enter SYBIL

SYBIL. O God, what will you do, mistress? Shift for yourself—   20
   your father is at hand! He's coming, he's coming! Master

---

[1] An unkind allusion to Rafe's lameness: 'Your offspring will all be
cripples.'
[2] Eyre's civic advancement, here accomplished in two days, took twelve
years historically.

Lacy, hide yourself! In, my mistress! For God's sake, shift
for yourselves!

LACY. Your father come! Sweet Rose, what shall I do?
Where shall I hide me? How shall I escape?

ROSE. A man, and want wit in extremity?
Come, come, be Hans still; play the shoemaker.
Pull on my shoe.

Enter [SIR ROGER OTLEY, *formerly*] *lord mayor*

LACY. Mass, and that's well rememb'red.

SYBIL. Here comes your father.

LACY. *Forware,[1] mestresse, 'tis un good skow; it sal vel dute,[2] or
ye sal neit betallen.[3]*

ROSE. O God, it pincheth me; what will you do?

LACY. [*Aside.*] Your father's presence pincheth, not the shoe.

OTLEY. Well done; fit my daughter well, and she shall please
thee well.

LACY. *Yaw, yaw, ick weit [4] dat well; forware, 'tis un good skoo,
'tis gimait van neit's leider; se ever, mine here.[5]*

Enter a prentice

OTLEY. I do believe it.—What's the news with you?

PRENT. Please you, the Earl of Lincoln at the gate
Is newly lighted and would speak with you.

OTLEY. The Earl of Lincoln come to speak with me?
Well, well, I know his errand. Daughter Rose,
Send hence your shoemaker; dispatch, have done.
Syb, make things handsome. Sir boy, follow me.
                                    Exeunt OTLEY, SYBIL *and prentice.*

LACY. Mine uncle come! Oh, what may this portend?
Sweet Rose, this of our love threatens an end.

ROSE. Be not dismay'd at this; whate'er befall,
Rose is thine own. To witness I speak truth,
Where thou appoint'st the place, I'll meet with thee.
I will not fix a day to follow thee,
But presently [6] steal hence. Do not reply;
Love which gave strength to bear my father's hate
Shall now add wings to further our escape.   *Exeunt.*

---

[1] Truly.   [2] Fit(?).   [3] Pay.
[4] Know.   [5] 'Be assured(?), sir.'   [6] Immediately.

[ACT IV. SCENE 4]
[OTLEY'S *house, Cornhill*]

Enter OTLEY *and* LINCOLN

OTLEY. Believe me, on my credit,[1] I speak truth;
    Since first your nephew Lacy went to France,
    I have not seen him. It seem'd strange to me,
    When Dodger told me that he stay'd behind,
    Neglecting the high charge the king impos'd.
LINC. Trust me, Sir Roger Otley, I did think
    Your counsel had given head to this attempt,
    Drawn to it by the love he bears your child.
    Here I did hope to find him in your house,
    But now I see mine error, and confess   10
    My judgment wrong'd you by conceiving so.
OTLEY. Lodge in my house, say you? Trust me, my Lord,
    I love your nephew Lacy too too dearly,
    So much to wrong his honour; and [2] he hath done so,
    That first gave him advice to stay from France,
    To witness I speak truth, I let you know
    How careful I have been to keep my daughter
    Free from all conference or speech of him.
    Not that I scorn your nephew, but in love
    I bear your honour, lest your noble blood   20
    Should by my mean worth be dishonoured.
LINC. [*Aside.*] How far this churl's tongue wanders from his
    heart!—
    Well, well, Sir Roger Otley, I believe you,
    With more than many thanks for the kind love
    So much you seem to bear me. But, my Lord,
    Let me request your help to seek my nephew,
    Whom, if I find, I'll straight embark for France.
    So shall your Rose be free, my thoughts at rest,
    And much care die which now lies in my breast.   30

Enter SYBIL

SYBIL. O Lord! Help, for God's sake! My mistress; oh, my
    young mistress!
OTLEY. Where is thy mistress? What's become of her?

          [1] Reputation.   [2] If.

SYBIL. She's gone! She's fled!

OTLEY. Gone? Whither is she fled?

SYBIL. I know not, forsooth; she's fled out of doors with Hans the shoemaker; I saw them scud, scud, scud, apace, apace.[1]

OTLEY. Which way? What, John! Where be my men? Which way?

SYBIL. I know not, and it please your worship.

OTLEY. Fled with a shoemaker! Can this be true?

SYBIL. O Lord, sir, as true as God's in Heaven.

LINC. [*Aside.*] Her love turned shoemaker? I am glad of this.

OTLEY. A Fleming butter-box, a shoemaker!
Will she forget her birth, requite my care
With such ingratitude? Scorn'd she young Hammon
To love a honnikin,[2] a needy knave?
Well, let her fly, I'll not fly after her;
Let her starve if she will, she's none of mine.

LINC. Be not so cruel, sir.

Enter FIRK *with shoes*

SYBIL. [*Aside.*]   I am glad she's scap'd.

OTLEY. I'll not account of her as of my child.
Was there no better object for her eyes
But a foul, drunken lubber, swill-belly,
A shoemaker? That's brave!

FIRK. Yea, forsooth; 'tis a very brave shoe and as fit as a pudding.

OTLEY. How now, what knave is this? From whence comest thou?

FIRK. No knave, sir; I am Firk the shoemaker, lusty Roger's chief lusty journeyman, and I come hither to take up the pretty leg of sweet Mistress Rose, and thus hoping your worship is in as good health as I was at the making hereof, I bid you farewell. Yours, Firk.

OTLEY. Stay, stay, Sir Knave.

LINC. Come hither, shoemaker.

FIRK. 'Tis happy the knave is put before the shoemaker, or else I would not have vouchsafed to come back to you. I am moved, for I stir.

---

[1] Sybil apparently reveals the elopement (as soon as it is safely accomplished) in order to avoid possible later accusations of having been a party to it.
[2] Rascal.

OTLEY. My Lord, this villain calls us knaves by craft.

FIRK. Then 'tis by the gentle craft, and to call one knave gently   70
is no harm. Sit your worship merry. Syb, your young mistress— [*Aside.*] I'll so bob [1] them, now my master, Master
Eyre, is lord mayor of London.

OTLEY. Tell me, sirrah, whose man are you?

FIRK. I am glad to see your worship so merry; I have no maw [2]
to this gear, no stomach as yet to a red petticoat. *Points to*
SYBIL.

LINC. He means not, sir, to woo you to his maid,
But only doth demand whose man you are.

FIRK. I sing now to the tune of Rogero [3]; Roger, my fellow, is
now my master.   80

LINC. Sirrah, know'st thou one Hans, a shoemaker?

FIRK. Hans, shoemaker? Oh yes; stay; yes, I have him. I tell
you what—I speak it in secret: Mistress Rose and he are by
this time, no, not so, but shortly, are to come over one another
with, 'Can you dance "The Shaking of the Sheets"?' [4] It is
that Hans— [*Aside.*] I'll so gull these diggers.

OTLEY. Know'st thou then where he is?

FIRK. Yes, forsooth; yes, marry.

LINC. Canst thou, in sadness [5]—

FIRK. No, forsooth; no, marry.   90

OTLEY. Tell me, good honest fellow, where he is,
And thou shalt see what I'll bestow of [6] thee.

FIRK. 'Honest fellow?' No, sir, not so, sir; my profession is the
gentle craft. I care not for seeing, I love feeling; let me feel it
here; *aurium tenus*,[7] ten pieces of gold; *genuum tenus*,[7] ten
pieces of silver; and then Firk is your man— [*Aside.*] in a new
pair of stretchers.[8]

OTLEY. Here is an angel, part of thy reward,
Which I will give thee; tell me where he is.

FIRK. No point! [9] Shall I betray my brother? No. Shall I prove   100
Judas to Hans? No. Shall I cry treason to my corporation?
No. I shall be firked and yerked then; but give me your angel;
your angel shall tell you.

LINC. Do so, good fellow; 'tis no hurt to thee.

FIRK. Send simpering Syb away.

---

[1] Trick.   [2] Appetite.   [3] An Elizabethan tune and dance.
[4] A popular tune and ballad.   [5] Seriousness.   [6] Expend for.
[7] Lit., 'up to the ears'; 'up to the knees'. The phrases combine Firk's small
Latin and his love of a joke.
[8] Lit., a shoemaker's implement; here, 'lies'.   [9] Not at all.

OTLEY. Huswife, get you in.   *Exit* SYBIL.

FIRK. Pitchers have ears, and maids have wide mouths. But for
  Hans Prauns, upon my word, tomorrow morning he and
  young Mistress Rose go to this gear: they shall be married
  together, by this rush,[1] or else turn Firk to a firkin of butter to
  tan leather withal.

OTLEY. But art thou sure of this?

FIRK. Am I sure that Paul's steeple is a handful higher than
  London Stone?[2] Or that the Pissing Conduit[3] leaks nothing
  but pure Mother Bunch?[4] Am I sure I am lusty Firk? God's
  nails, do you think I am so base to gull you?

LINC. Where are they married? Dost thou know the church?

FIRK. I never go to church, but I know the name of it; it is a
  swearing church—stay awhile; 'tis—ay, by the mass, no, no;
  'tis—ay, by my troth, no, nor that ;'tis—ay, by my faith, that;
  that 'tis—ay, by my Faith's Church under Paul's Cross!
  There they shall be knit like a pair of stockings in matrimony;
  there they'll be inconie.[5]

LINC. Upon my life, my nephew Lacy walks
  In the disguise of this Dutch shoemaker.

FIRK. [*Aside.*] Yes, forsooth.

LINC. Doth he not, honest fellow?

FIRK. No, forsooth; I think Hans is nobody but Hans, no spirit.

OTLEY. My mind misgives me now; 'tis so indeed.

LINC. My cousin speaks the language, knows the trade.

OTLEY. Let me request your company, my Lord;
  Your honourable presence may, no doubt,
  Restrain their headstrong rashness, when myself,
  Going alone, perchance may be o'erborne.
  Shall I request this favour?

LINC.   This, or what else.

FIRK. Then you must rise betimes, for they mean to fall to their
  hey-pass and repass,[6] pindy-pandy, which hand will you
  have,[7] very early.

OTLEY. My care shall every way equal their haste.
  This night accept your lodging in my house,

---

[1] Floor-covering.
[2] The milestone from which all Roman roads out of London were
measured; in Cannon Street.
[3] Colloquial name for a drain near the Royal Exchange.
[4] An Elizabethan brewster; her name became a byword for ale of dubious
quality.
[5] Fine, rare.   [6] Jugglers' terms.   [7] A children's game.

The earlier shall we stir, and at Saint Faith's
Prevent this hare-brain'd nuptial.
This traffic of hot love shall yield cold gains;
They ban [1] our loves, and we'll forbid their banns.   *Exit.*

LINC. At Saint Faith's Church, thou say'st?

FIRK. Yes, by their troth.

LINC. Be secret, on thy life.   *Exit.*

FIRK. Yes, when I kiss your wife. Ha, ha, here's no craft in the
gentle craft; I came hither of purpose with shoes to Sir
Roger's worship, whilst Rose, his daughter, be cony-catched   150
by Hans. Soft now, these two gulls will be at Saint Faith's
Church tomorrow morning, to take Master Bridegroom and
Mistress Bride napping, and they, in the meantime, shall chop
up the matter at the Savoy.[2] But the best sport is, Sir Roger
Otley will find my fellow lame Rafe's wife going to marry a
gentleman, and then he'll stop her instead of his daughter.
Oh, brave! There will be fine tickling sport! Soft now, what
have I to do? Oh, I know now; a mess [3] of shoemakers meet
at the Woolsack in Ivy Lane, to cozen my gentleman of lame
Rafe's wife, that's true.   160
Alack, alack!
Girls, hold out tack; [4]
For now smocks for this jumbling
Shall go to wrack.   *Exit.*

[ACT V. SCENE 1]
[EYRE'S *house*]

Enter EYRE, *his wife,* [LACY *as*] HANS, *and* ROSE

EYRE. This is the morning then; say, my bully, my honest
Hans, is it not?

LACY. This is the morning that must make us two
Happy or miserable; therefore, if you—

EYRE. Away with these if's and and's, Hans, and these *et
ceteras*! By mine honour, Rowland Lacy, none but the king
shall wrong thee; come, fear nothing; am not I Sim Eyre? Is

---

[1] Denounce.   [2] The chapel of Savoy hospital.
[3] Company.   [4] Resist.

not Sim Eyre lord mayor of London? Fear nothing, Rose; let them all say what they can. Dainty, come thou to me; laughest thou?

WIFE. Good my Lord, stand her friend in what thing you may.

EYRE. Why, my sweet Lady Madgy, think you Simon Eyre can forget his fine Dutch journeyman? No, vah! Fie, I scorn it; it shall never be cast in my teeth that I was unthankful. Lady Madgy, thou had'st never covered thy Saracen's head with this French flap, nor loaden thy bum with this farthingale— 'tis trash, trumpery, vanity,—Simon Eyre had never walked in a red petticoat, nor wore a chain of gold, but for my fine journeyman's portagues; and shall I leave him? No! Prince am I none, yet bear a princely mind.

LACY. My Lord, 'tis time for us to part from hence.

EYRE. Lady Madgy, Lady Madgy, take two or three of my pie-crust eaters, my buff-jerkin varlets that do walk in black gowns at Simon Eyre's heels; take them, good Lady Madgy; trip and go, my brown queen of periwigs, with my delicate Rose and my jolly Rowland to the Savoy; see them linked, countenance the marriage; and when it is done, cling, cling together, you Hamborrow [1] turtle-doves. I'll bear you out; come to Simon Eyre; come dwell with me, Hans, thou shalt eat minced pies and marchpane.[2] Rose, away, cricket. Trip and go, my Lady Madgy, to the Savoy; Hans, wed and to bed, kiss and away; go, vanish.

WIFE. Farewell, my Lord.

ROSE. Make haste, sweet love.

WIFE. She'd fain the deed were done.

LACY. Come, my sweet Rose; faster than deer we'll run.

                    Exeunt LACY, ROSE, *and* MARGERY.

EYRE. Go, vanish, vanish! Avaunt, I say! By the Lord of Ludgate, it's a mad life to be a lord mayor; it's a stirring life, a fine life, a velvet life, a careful life! Well, Simon Eyre, yet set a good face on it, in the honour of Saint Hugh. Soft, the king this day comes to dine with me, to see my new buildings. His Majesty is welcome; he shall have good cheer, delicate cheer, princely cheer. This day my fellow prentices of London come to dine with me too; they shall have fine cheer, gentlemanlike cheer. I promised the mad Cappadocians, when we all served at the conduit together,[3] that if ever I came to be mayor of

---

[1] Hamburg.   [2] Marzipan.
[3] Carrying water, one of the duties of apprentices (*see* v. v. 174–84).

London, I would feast them all, and I 'll do 't! I 'll do 't, by the
life of Pharaoh; by this beard, Sim Eyre will be no flincher.
Besides, I have procured [1] that upon every Shrove Tuesday,
at the sound of the pancake bell, my fine dapper Assyrian lads   50
shall clap up their shop windows and away. This is the day,
and this day they shall do 't, they shall do 't.
Boys, that day are you free; let masters care,
And prentices shall pray for Simon Eyre.   *Exit.*

[ACT V. SCENE 2]

[A street near Saint Faith's Church]

Enter HODGE, FIRK, RAFE, *and five or six shoemakers, all
with cudgels or such weapons*

HODGE. Come, Rafe; stand to it, Firk. My masters, as we are
the brave bloods of the shoemakers, heirs apparent to Saint
Hugh, and perpetual benefactors to all good fellows, thou
shalt have no wrong; were Hammon a king of spades, he
should not delve in thy close [2] without thy sufferance. But tell
me, Rafe, art thou sure 'tis thy wife?

RAFE. Am I sure this is Firk? This morning when I stroked on [3]
her shoes, I looked upon her, and she upon me, and sighed,
asked me if ever I knew one Rafe. 'Yes,' said I. 'For his sake,'
said she, tears standing in her eyes, 'and for thou art somewhat   10
like him, spend this piece of gold.' I took it; my lame leg and
my travel beyond sea made me unknown. All is one for that;
I know she's mine.

FIRK. Did she give thee this gold? Oh, glorious, glittering
gold! She's thine own, 'tis thy wife, and she loves thee; for
I 'll stand to 't, there 's no woman will give gold to any man,
but she thinks better of him than she thinks of them she gives
silver to. And for Hammon, neither Hammon nor hangman
shall wrong thee in London. Is not our old master Eyre lord
mayor? Speak, my hearts.   20

ALL. Yes, and Hammon shall know it to his cost.

---

[1] Taken measures.   [2] Field.   [3] Fitted.

Enter HAMMON, *his man,* JANE, *and others*

HODGE. Peace, my bullies; yonder they come.

RAFE. Stand to't, my hearts; Firk, let me speak first.

HODGE. No, Rafe, let me. Hammon, whither away so early?

HAM. Unmannerly rude slave, what's that to thee?

FIRK. To him, sir? Yes, sir, and to me, and others. Good
morrow, Jane, how dost thou? Good Lord, how the world is
changed with you! God be thanked.

HAM. Villains, hands off! How dare you touch my love?

ALL. Villains? Down with them! Cry 'Clubs',[1] for prentices!   30

HODGE. Hold, my hearts. Touch her, Hammon? Yea, and more
than that, we'll carry her away with us. My masters and
gentlemen, never draw your bird-spits;[2] shoemakers are
steel to the back, men every inch of them, all spirit.

ALL OF HAMMON'S SIDE. Well, and what of all this?

HODGE. I'll show you. Jane, dost thou know this man? 'Tis
Rafe, I can tell thee; nay, 'tis he, in faith, though he be lamed
by the wars. Yet look not strange, but run to him, fold him
about the neck, and kiss him.

JANE. Lives then my husband? O God, let me go!   40
Let me embrace my Rafe.

HAM.   What means my Jane?

JANE. Nay, what meant you, to tell me he was slain?

HAM. Pardon me, dear love, for being misled;
[*To Rafe.*] 'Twas rumour'd here in London thou wert dead.

FIRK. Thou seest he lives. Lass, go pack home with him. Now
Master Hammon, where's your mistress, your wife?

SERV. 'Swounds, master, fight for her; will you thus lose her?

ALL. Down with that creature! Clubs! Down with him!

HODGE. Hold, hold.

HAM. Hold, fool. Sirs, he shall do no wrong.   50
Will my Jane leave me thus, and break her faith?

FIRK. Yea, sir; she must, sir; she shall, sir. What then? Mend it.

HODGE. Hark, fellow Rafe, follow my counsel; set the wench in
the midst, and let her choose her man, and let her be his
woman.

JANE. Whom should I choose? Whom should my thoughts
affect
But him whom Heaven hath made to be my love?

---

[1] A rallying call for apprentices.   [2] i.e. rapiers.

Thou art my husband, and these humble weeds
Make thee more beautiful than all his wealth.   60
Therefore, I will but put off his attire,
Returning it into the owner's hand,
And after ever be thy constant wife.

HODGE. Not a rag, Jane! The law's on our side; he that sows in
in another man's ground forfeits his harvest. Get thee home,
Rafe; follow him, Jane. He shall not have so much as a busk-
point [1] from thee.

FIRK. Stand to that, Rafe; the appurtenances are thine own.
Hammon, look not at her.

SERV. Oh, 'swounds, no!   70

FIRK. Blue coat,[2] be quiet, we'll give you a new livery else;
we'll make Shrove Tuesday Saint George's Day [3] for you.[4]
Look not, Hammon, leer not; I'll firk you. For [5] thy head
now, one glance, one sheep's eye, anything, at her; touch not a
rag, lest I and my brethren beat you to clouts.[6]

SERV. Come, Master Hammon, there's no striving here.

HAM. Good fellows, hear me speak; and, honest Rafe,
Whom I have injur'd most by loving Jane,
Mark what I offer thee: here in fair gold
Is twenty pound; I'll give it for thy Jane;   80
If this content thee not, thou shalt have more.

HODGE. Sell not thy wife, Rafe; make her not a whore.

HAM. Say, wilt thou freely cease thy claim in her,
And let her be my wife?

ALL. No, do not, Rafe.

RAFE. Sirrah Hammon, Hammon, dost thou think a shoemaker
is so base to be a bawd to his wife for commodity? Take thy
gold; choke with it! Were I not lame, I would make thee eat
thy words.

FIRK. A shoemaker sell his flesh and blood? Oh, indignity!   90

HODGE. Sirrah, take up your pelf,[7] and be packing.

HAM. I will not touch one penny, but in lieu
Of that great wrong I offered thy Jane,
To Jane and thee I give that twenty pound.
Since I have fail'd of her, during my life,

[1] Corset-lace.
[2] The usual garb of a liveried servant.
[3] 23rd April, a holiday for serving-men.
[4] Perhaps a reference to friction between servants and apprentices: 'We'll beat you black and blue as though this were your holiday.'
[5] For the sake of.   [6] Tatters.   [7] 'Filthy lucre.'

I vow, no woman else shall be my wife.
Farewell, good fellows of the gentle trade,
Your morning's mirth my mourning day hath made.   *Exit.*

FIRK. [*To* HAMMON'S *servant.*] Touch the gold, creature, if you
dare; y'are best be trudging. [*Exit servant.*] —Here, Jane, take   10(
thou it; now let's home, my hearts.

HODGE. Stay; who comes here? Jane, on again with thy mask.

Enter LINCOLN, OTLEY, *and servants*

LINC. Yonder's the lying varlet mock'd us so.

OTLEY. Come hither, sirrah!

FIRK. I, sir? I am sirrah? You mean me, do you not?

LINC. Where is my nephew married?

FIRK. Is he married? God give him joy, I am glad of it. They
have a fair day, and the sign is in a good planet; Mars in
Venus.[1]

OTLEY. Villain, thou toldst me that my daughter Rose   110
This morning should be married at Saint Faith's;
We have watch'd there these three hours at the least,
Yet see we no such thing.

FIRK. Truly, I am sorry for't; a bride's a pretty thing.

HODGE. Come to the purpose. Yonder's the bride and bridegroom you look for, I hope. Though you be lords, you are not
to bar, by your authority, men from women, are you?

OTLEY. See, see, my daughter's mask'd!

LINC.   True, and my nephew,
To hide his guilt, counterfeits him lame.

FIRK. Yea; truly, God help the poor couple, they are lame and   120
blind.

OTLEY. I'll ease her blindness.

LINC.   I'll his lameness cure.

FIRK. [*Aside to his colleagues.*] Lie down, sirs, and laugh; my
fellow Rafe is taken for Rowland Lacy, and Jane for Mistress
Damask Rose. This is all my knavery.

OTLEY. What, have I found you, minion?

LINC.   O base wretch!
Nay, hide thy face; the horror of thy guilt
Can hardly be wash'd off. Where are thy powers?
What battles have you made? Oh yes, I see

---

[1] Astrological nonsense.

Thou fought'st with Shame, and Shame hath conquered thee.   130
This lameness will not serve.
OTLEY.   Unmask yourself.
LINC. Lead home your daughter.
OTLEY.   Take your nephew hence.
RAFE. Hence! 'Swounds, what mean you? Are you mad? I hope
you cannot enforce my wife from me. Where's Hammon?
OTLEY. Your wife?
LINC. What, Hammon?
RAFE. Yea, my wife; and therefore the proudest of you that lays
hands on her first, I'll lay my crutch 'cross his pate.
FIRK. To him, lame Rafe! Here's brave sport!
RAFE. Rose call you her? Why, her name is Jane. Look here else   140
[*Unmasks* JANE.]; do you know her now?
LINC. Is this your daughter?
OTLEY.   No, nor this your nephew.
My Lord of Lincoln, we are both abus'd
By this base, crafty varlet.
FIRK. Yea, forsooth, no varlet; forsooth, no base; forsooth, I
am but mean; [1] no crafty neither, but of the gentle craft.
OTLEY. Where is my daughter Rose? Where is my child?
LINC. Where is my nephew Lacy married?
FIRK. Why, here is good lac'd-mutton,[2] as I promised you.
LINC. Villain, I'll have thee punish'd for this wrong.   150
FIRK. Punish the journeyman villain, but not the journeyman
shoemaker.

Enter DODGER

DODGER. My Lord, I come to bring unwelcome news:
Your nephew Lacy and your daughter Rose
Early this morning wedded at the Savoy,
None being present but the lady mayoress.
Besides, I learnt among the officers
The lord mayor vows to stand in their defence
'Gainst any that shall seek to cross the match.
LINC. Dares Eyre the shoemaker uphold the deed?   160
FIRK. Yes, sir, shoemakers dare stand in a woman's quarrel, I
warrant you, as deep as another, and deeper too.

----

[1] Tenor; punning on 'bass'.
[2] Strumpet; Firk uses the word for the sake of the pun on 'Lacy'.

DODGER. Besides, His Grace today dines with the mayor,
    Who on his knees humbly intends to fall,
    And beg a pardon for your nephew's fault.
LINC. But I'll prevent him. Come, Sir Roger Otley;
    The king will do us justice in this cause.
    Howe'er their hands have made them man and wife,
    I will disjoin the match, or lose my life.

                    Exeunt OTLEY, LINCOLN, *and* DODGER.

FIRK. Adieu, Monsieur Dodger; farewell, fools; ha, ha!   170
    Oh, if they had stayed I would have lammed them with flouts!
    O heart, my codpiece-point is ready to fly in pieces every time
    I think upon Mistress Rose; but let that pass, as my lady
    mayoress says.
HODGE. This matter is answered. Come, Rafe, home with thy
    wife; come, my fine shoemakers, let's to our master's, the new
    lord mayor, and there swagger this Shrove Tuesday. I'll
    promise you wine enough, for Madge keeps the cellar.
ALL. Oh, rare! Madge is a good wench.
FIRK. And I'll promise you meat enough, for simpering Susan   180
    keeps the larder; I'll lead you to victuals, my brave soldiers.
    Follow your captain. Oh, brave! Hark, hark!   *Bell rings.*
ALL. The pancake-bell rings, the pancake bell! Trilill, my
    hearts!
FIRK. Oh, brave! O sweet bell! O delicate pancakes! Open the
    doors, my hearts, and shut up the windows; keep in the house,
    let out the pancakes! Oh, rare, my hearts! Let's march
    together for the honour of Saint Hugh to the great new hall [1]
    in Gracious Street corner, which our master the new lord
    mayor hath built.   190
RAFE. Oh, the crew of good fellows that will dine at my lord
    mayor's cost today!
HODGE. By the Lord, my lord mayor is a most brave man.
    How shall prentices be bound to pray for him and the
    honour of gentlemen shoemakers! Let's feed and be fat with
    my lord's bounty.
FIRK. O musical bell, still! O Hodge, O my brethren! There's
    cheer for the heavens: venison-pasties walk up and down
    piping hot, like sergeants; beef and brewis [2] comes marching
    in dry-fats; [3] fritters and pancakes comes trowling [4] in in   200
    wheelbarrows; hens and oranges hopping in porters' baskets;

----

[1] Leadenhall, actually rebuilt by Eyre.   [2] Broth.
[3] Vats.   [4] Trundling.

collops [1] and eggs in scuttles; and tarts and custards comes
quavering in in malt-shovels.

Enter more prentices

ALL. Whoop, look here, look here!

HODGE. How now, mad lads, whither away so fast?

1 PRENT. Whither? Why, to the great new hall; know you not
    why? The lord mayor hath bidden all the prentices of London
    to breakfast this morning.

ALL. O brave shoemaker! O brave lord of incomprehensible
    good-fellowship! Whoo! Hark you, the pancake-bell rings.   210
                                            Cast up their caps.

FIRK. Nay, more, my hearts: every Shrove Tuesday is our year
    of jubilee; and when the pancake-bell rings, we are as free as
    my lord mayor; we may shut up our shops, and make holiday.
    I'll have it called Saint Hugh's Holiday.

ALL. Agreed, agreed! Saint Hugh's Holiday!

HODGE. And this shall continue for ever.

ALL. Oh, brave! Come, come, my hearts, away, away.

FIRK. Oh, eternal credit to us of the gentle craft. March fair,
    my hearts. Oh, rare!   *Exeunt.*

[ACT V. SCENE 3]

[*A street near Leadenhall*]

Enter KING and his train over the stage

KING. Is our lord mayor of London such a gallant?

NOBLEMAN. One of the merriest madcaps in your land.
    Your Grace will think, when you behold the man,
    He's rather a wild ruffian than a mayor;
    Yet thus much I'll ensure Your Majesty,
    In all his actions that concern his state,
    He is as serious, provident, and wise,
    As full of gravity amongst the grave,
    As any mayor hath been these many years.

KING. I am with child [2] till I behold this huff-cap; [3]   10

---

[1] Slices of meat.   [2] In suspense.   [3] Swashbuckler.

But all my doubt is, when we come in presence,
His madness will be dash'd clean out of countenance.
NOBLEMAN. It may be so, my Liege.
KING.   Which to prevent,
Let someone give him notice, 'tis our pleasure
That he put on his wonted merriment.
Set forward.
ALL. On afore!   *Exeunt.*

[ACT V. SCENE 4]
[*Near Leadenhall*]

Enter EYRE, HODGE, FIRK, RAFE, *and other shoemakers,*
all with napkins on their shoulders [1]

EYRE. Come, my fine Hodge, my jolly gentlemen shoemakers.
Soft, where be these cannibals, these varlets, my officers? Let
them all walk and wait upon my brethren; for my meaning is,
that none but shoemakers, none but the livery of my company
shall in their satin hoods wait upon the trencher of my
sovereign.
FIRK. Oh, my Lord, it will be rare.
EYRE. No more, Firk; come lively! Let your fellow prentices
want no cheer; let wine be plentiful as beer, and beer as water.
Hang these penny-pinching fathers, that cram wealth in   10
innocent lamb-skins. [2] Rip, knaves, avaunt! Look to my
guests.
HODGE. My Lord, we are at our wit's end for room; those
hundred tables will not feast the fourth part of them.
EYRE. Then cover me those hundred tables again and again,
till all my jolly prentices be feasted. Avoid, [3] Hodge! Run,
Rafe! Frisk about, my nimble Firk! Carouse me fathom-
healths to the honour of the shoemakers! Do they drink lively,
Hodge? Do they tickle it, Firk?
FIRK. Tickle it? Some of them have taken their liquor standing   20
so long that they can stand no longer; but for meat, they would
eat it, and they had it.

[1] Symbolic of their privilege of serving the king (*see* lines 4–6 above).
[2] Purses(?).   [3] Withdraw.

EYRE. Want they meat? Where's this swag-belly, this greasy kitchen-stuff cook? Call the varlet to me. Want meat! Firk, Hodge, lame Rafe; run, my tall men, beleaguer the shambles,[1] beggar all Eastcheap, serve me whole oxen in chargers, and let sheep whine [2] upon the tables like pigs, for want of good fellows to eat them. Want meat! Vanish, Firk! Avaunt, Hodge!

HODGE. Your lordship mistakes my man Firk: he means their 30 bellies want meat, not the boards; for they have drunk so much they can eat nothing.

Enter [LACY as] HANS, ROSE, and MISTRESS EYRE

WIFE. Where is my lord?

HODGE. How now, Lady Madgy?

WIFE. The King's Most Excellent Majesty is new come; he sends me for thy honour. One of his most worshipful peers bade me tell thou must be merry, and so forth; but let that pass.

EYRE. Is my sovereign come? Vanish, my tall shoemakers, my nimble brethren; look to my guests, the prentices. Yet stay a 40 little; how now, Hans? How looks my little Rose?

LACY. Let me request you to remember me.
I know your honour easily may obtain
Free pardon of the king for me and Rose,
And reconcile me to my uncle's grace.

EYRE. Have done, my good Hans, my honest journeyman; look cheerily. I'll fall upon both my knees till they be as hard as horn, but I'll get thy pardon.

WIFE. Good my Lord, have a care what you speak to His Grace. 50

EYRE. Away, you Islington whitepot;[3] hence, you hopper-arse,[4] you barleypudding full of maggots, you broiled carbonado! [5] Avaunt, avaunt, avoid, Mephistophilis! Shall Sim Eyre learn to speak of you, Lady Madgy? Vanish, Mother Miniver-cap; [6] vanish, go, trip and go! Meddle with your partlets [7] and your pishery-pashery, your flewes [8] and your whirligigs; go, rub,[9] out of mine alley! Sim Eyre knows how

---

[1] Meat markets.   [2] Cry.   [3] Baked pudding.
[4] Large-of-hip.   [5] Meat scored for cooking over coals.
[6] Fur-cap.   [7] Collars or ruffs.
[8] The sides or flaps of her hood.
[9] 'Don't impede me'—a term from bowling.

to speak to a pope, to Sultan Soliman, to Tamburlaine, and he were here; and shall I melt, shall I droop before my sovereign? No! Come, my Lady Madgy; follow me, Hans; about your business, my frolic free-booters. Firk, frisk about, and about, and about, and about, for the honour of mad Simon Eyre, lord mayor of London.

FIRK. Hey, for the honour of the shoemakers!   *Exeunt.*

[ACT V. SCENE 5]

[*Before Leadenhall*]

A long flourish or two; enter KING, *nobles*, EYRE, *his wife*, LACY, *and* ROSE. LACY *and* ROSE kneel

KING. Well, Lacy, though the fact was very foul
Of your revolting from our kingly love
And your own duty, yet we pardon you.
Rise both, and, Mistress Lacy, thank my lord mayor
For your young bridegroom here.

EYRE. So, my dear Liege, Sim Eyre and my brethren, the gentlemen shoemakers, shall set your sweet Majesty's image cheek by jowl by Saint Hugh, for this honour you have done poor Simon Eyre. I beseech Your Grace pardon my rude behaviour; I am a handicraftsman, yet my heart is without craft. I would be sorry at my soul that my boldness should offend my king.

KING. Nay, I pray thee, good Lord Mayor, be even as merry
As if thou wert among thy shoemakers.
It does me good to see thee in this humour.

EYRE. Say'st thou me so, my sweet Diocletian?[1] Then, hump! Prince am I none, yet am I princely born. By the Lord of Ludgate, my Liege, I'll be as merry as a pie.[2]

KING. Tell me, in faith, mad Eyre, how old thou art.

EYRE. My Liege, a very boy, a stripling, a younker; you see not a white hair on my head, not a grey in this beard. Every hair, I assure Thy Majesty, that sticks in this beard Sim Eyre

---

[1] Another of Eyre's meaningless epithets; rather inappropriate here because Emperor Diocletian (A.D. 284–305) persecuted Christians, among them Saint Hugh.

[2] Magpie.

values at the King of Babylon's ransom. Tamar Cham's [1]
beard was a rubbing brush to't; yet I'll shave it off and stuff
tennis balls with it, to please my bully [2] king.

KING. But all this while I do not know your age.

EYRE. My Liege, I am six-and-fifty year old, yet I can cry
'Hump' with a sound heart for the honour of Saint Hugh.
Mark this old wench, my King; I danced the shaking of the
sheets with her six-and-thirty years ago, and yet I hope to get   30
two or three young lord mayors ere I die. I am lusty still, Sim
Eyre still. Care and cold lodging brings white hairs. My
sweet Majesty, let care vanish; cast it upon thy nobles. It will
make thee look always young like Apollo, and cry 'Hump!'
Prince am I none, yet am I princely born.

KING. Ha, ha!
    Say, Cornwall, didst thou ever see his like?

NOBLEMAN. Not I, my Lord.

Enter LINCOLN *and* OTLEY

KING.   Lincoln, what's news with you?

LINC. My gracious Lord, have care unto yourself,
    For there are traitors here.

ALL.   Traitors? Where? Who?   40

EYRE. Traitors in my house? God forbid! Where be my
    officers? I'll spend my soul ere my king feel harm.

KING. Where is the traitor, Lincoln?

LINC.   Here he stands.
                                        [*Points to Lacy.*]

KING. Cornwall, lay hold on Lacy. Lincoln, speak;
    What canst thou lay unto thy nephew's charge?

LINC. This, my dear Liege: Your Grace, to do me honour,
    Heap'd on the head of this degenerous [3] boy
    Desertless favours; you made choice of him
    To be commander over powers in France,
    But he—

KING.   Good Lincoln, prithee, pause awhile.   50
    Even in thine eyes I read what thou wouldst speak;
    I know how Lacy did neglect our love,
    Ran himself deeply, in the highest degree,
    Into vile treason.

----

¹ Tamburlaine's.   ² Fine.   ³ Degenerate.

LINC.   Is he not a traitor?

KING. Lincoln, he was. Now have we pardon'd him;
  'Twas not a base want of true valour's fire
  That held him out of France, but love's desire.

LINC. I will not bear his shame upon my back.

KING. Nor shalt thou, Lincoln; I forgive you both.

LINC. Then, good my Liege, forbid the boy to wed
  One whose mean birth will much disgrace his bed.

KING. Are they not married?

LINC.   No, my Liege.

BOTH.   We are.

KING. Shall I divorce them then? Oh, be it far
  That any hand on earth should dare untie
  The sacred knot knit by God's Majesty!
  I would not for my crown disjoin their hands,
  That are conjoin'd in holy nuptial bands.
  How say'st thou, Lacy? Wouldst thou lose thy Rose?

LACY. Not for all India's wealth, my sovereign.

KING. But Rose, I am sure, her Lacy would forgo.

ROSE. If Rose were asked that question, she'd say no.

KING. You hear them, Lincoln.

LINC.   Yea, my Liege, I do.

KING. Yet canst thou find i' th' heart to part these two?
  Who seeks, besides you, to divorce these lovers?

OTLEY. I do, my gracious Lord; I am her father.

KING. Sir Roger Otley, our last mayor, I think?

NOBLEMAN. The same, my Liege.

KING.   Would you offend love's laws?
  Well, you shall have your wills. You sue to me
  To prohibit the match. Soft, let me see—
  You both are married, Lacy, art thou not?

LACY. I am, dread sovereign.

KING.   Then upon thy life,
  I charge thee not to call this woman wife.

OTLEY. I thank Your Grace.

ROSE.   O my most gracious Lord!

                               Kneels.

KING. Nay, Rose, never woo me; I tell you true,
  Although as yet I am a bachelor,[1]
  Yet I believe I shall not marry you.

    [1] Henry VI married in 1444, before Eyre became lord mayor.

ROSE. Can you divide the body from the soul,
  Yet make the body live?
KING.   Yea, so profound?
  I cannot, Rose; but you I must divide.
  Fair maid, this bridegroom cannot be your bride.[1]   90
  Are you pleas'd, Lincoln? Otley, are you pleas'd?
BOTH. Yes, my Lord.
KING.   Then must my heart be eas'd;
  For, credit me, my conscience lives in pain,
  Till these whom I divorc'd be join'd again.
  Lacy, give me thy hand; Rose, lend me thine;
  Be what you would be. Kiss now; so—that's fine.
  At night, lovers, to bed. Now let me see,
  Which of you all mislikes this harmony?
OTLEY. Will you then take from me my child perforce?
KING. Why, tell me, Otley, shines not Lacy's name   100
  As bright in the world's eye as the gay beams
  Of any citizen?
LINC.   Yea, but, my gracious Lord,
  I do mislike the match far more than he;
  Her blood is too too base.
KING.   Lincoln, no more.
  Dost thou not know that love respects no blood,
  Cares not for difference of birth or state?
  The maid is young, well born, fair, virtuous,
  A worthy bride for any gentleman.
  Besides, your nephew for her sake did stoop
  To bare necessity, and, as I hear,   110
  Forgetting honours and all courtly pleasures,
  To gain her love, became a shoemaker.
  As for the honour which he lost in France,
  Thus I redeem it: Lacy, kneel thee down;
  Arise, Sir Rowland Lacy. Tell me now,
  Tell me in earnest, Otley, canst thou chide,
  Seeing thy Rose a lady and a bride?
OTLEY. I am content with what Your Grace hath done.
LINC. And I, my Liege, since there's no remedy.
KING. Come on then, all shake hands; I'll have you friends.   120
  Where there is much love all discord ends.
  What says my mad Lord Mayor to all this love?

----

[1] Spouse.

EYRE. O my Liege, this honour you have done to my fine journeyman here, Rowland Lacy, and all these favours which you have shown to me this day in my poor house will make Simon Eyre live longer by one dozen of warm summers more than he should.

KING. Nay, my mad Lord Mayor—that shall be thy name—
If any grace of mine can length thy life,
One honour more I'll do thee: that new building,   1:
Which at thy cost in Cornhill is erected,
Shall take a name from us; we'll have it call'd
The Leadenhall, because in digging it
You found the lead that covereth the same.

EYRE. I thank Your Majesty.

WIFE.   God bless Your Grace.

KING. Lincoln, a word with you.

Enter HODGE, FIRK, RAFE, *and more shoemakers*

EYRE. How now, my mad knaves? Peace, speak softly; yonder is the king.

KING. With the old troop, which here we keep in pay,
We will incorporate a new supply.   1·
Before one summer more pass o'er my head,
France shall repent England was injured.
What are all those?

LACY.   All shoemakers, my Liege,
Sometime my fellows; in their companies
I liv'd as merry as an emperor.

KING. My mad Lord Mayor, are all these shoemakers?

EYRE. All shoemakers, my Liege, all gentlemen of the gentle craft, true Trojans, courageous cordwainers; they all kneel to the shrine of holy Saint Hugh.

ALL. God save Your Majesty!   1:

KING. Mad Simon, would they anything with us?

EYRE. Mum, mad knaves; not a word; I'll do't, I warrant you. They are all beggars, my Liege; all for themselves, and I for them all, on both my knees, do entreat that for the honour of poor Simon Eyre and the good of his brethren, these mad knaves, Your Grace would vouchsafe some privilege to my

new Leadenhall, that it may be lawful for us to buy and sell
leather there two days a week.

KING. Mad Sim, I grant your suit; you shall have patent
    To hold two market-days in Leadenhall.[1]   160
Mondays and Fridays, those shall be the times.
    Will this content you?

ALL.   Jesus bless Your Grace!

EYRE. In the name of these my poor brethren shoemakers, I
    most humbly thank Your Grace. But before I rise, seeing you
    are in the giving vein, and we in the begging, grant Sim Eyre
    one boon more.

KING. What is it, my Lord Mayor?

EYRE. Vouchsafe to taste of a poor banquet that stands sweetly
    waiting for your sweet presence.

KING. I shall undo thee, Eyre, only with feasts.   170
Already I have been too troublesome;
    Say, have I not?

EYRE.[2] O my dear King, Sim Eyre was taken unawares upon a
    day of shroving [3] which I promised long ago to the prentices
    of London.
For, and 't please Your Highness, in time past
I bare the water tankard, and my coat
Sits not a whit the worse upon my back.
And then upon a morning some mad boys—
    It was Shrove Tuesday even as 'tis now—   180
gave me my breakfast, and I swore then by the stopple of my
    tankard, if ever I came to be lord mayor of London, I would
    feast all the prentices. This day, my Liege, I did, and the
    slaves had an hundred tables five times covered; they are gone
    home and vanished.
Yet add more honour to the gentle trade;
Taste of Eyre's banquet, Simon's happy made.

KING. Eyre, I will taste of thy banquet, and will say
I have not met more pleasure on a day.
Friends of the gentle craft, thanks to you all,   190
Thanks, my kind lady mayoress, for our cheer.
Come, Lords, awhile let's revel it at home;
When all our sports and banqueting are done,
Wars must right wrongs which Frenchmen have begun.

[1] Not effected until Elizabeth's reign.
[2] The mixture of verse and prose in this speech is evidently the result of
some confusion in Dekker's manuscript.
[3] Rejoicing.

The Second Three-men's Song [1]

Cold's the wind and wet's the rain,
    Saint Hugh be our good speed;
Ill is the weather that bringeth no gain,
    Nor helps good hearts in need.

Troll [2] the bowl, the jolly nut-brown bowl,
    And here, kind mate, to thee:
Let's sing a dirge for Saint Hugh's soul,
    And down it merrily.

Down a down, hey, down a down,
    (*Close with the tenor boy.*)
Hey, derry derry, down a down.
Ho, well done, to me let come;
    Ring, compass gentle joy. [3]

Troll the bowl, the nut-brown bowl,
    And here, kind, *etc., as often as there be men to drink.*

At last when all have drunk, this verse

Cold's the wind and wet's the rain,
    Saint Hugh be our good speed;
Ill is the weather that bringeth no gain,
    Nor helps good hearts in need.

                                      Exeunt.

---

[1] Like the first part-song (III. iii. 24), this precedes the text of the play in the quartos. The ambiguous quarto stage direction, '*This is to be sung at the latter end*', justifies the present location of the song, but it may have been sung at v. iv (so several modern editors).

[2] Pass round.

[3] 'The circle of fellowship or comrades should surround gentle joy(?).'

THOMAS HEYWOOD
(*c.* 1573–1641)

Born Lincolnshire; attended Cambridge 1591–3; poet, translator, journalist, actor (*Apology for Actors*, 1612), dramatist; wrote pageants (was City Poet, 1631–41), masques and plays, including *The Four Prentices of London, Edward IV* (two parts), *A Woman Killed with Kindness, The Wise Woman of Hogsden*, and *The Fair Maid of the West* (two parts).

A Woman Killed with Kindness (1603)

Heywood's remarkable distinction of having had a hand in over two hundred plays (only about twenty survive) suggests a facility of composition and implicitly a casualness in matters of detail. This play is a complex study in confusion of moral values, but it fails to clarify certain plot situations and to develop fully the relationships between the two plots.

The more interesting and important plot appears at first to be a conventional melodrama centring on the disruption of the Frankfords' marriage through the seduction of the wife by her husband's protégé. It is primarily in the punishment of the erring woman that Heywood rose memorably above the average for this type of play and showed a sensitivity bordering on the modern in his insight into psychology. (It is of interest to contrast the situation in *Othello*, c. 1604.)

The Charles-Susan-Acton plot is unremarkable in both action and characterization. Heywood's intention, imperfectly developed, was to show a contrasting relationship between the two plots, both dealing with seduction and the redemption of honour. Anne Frankford, the possessor of many graces and virtues, yields precipitously to her seducer, whereas Susan Mountford agrees to submit to Acton only to satisfy the Mountford honour, somewhat tarnished by Susan's treacherous intentions and Charles's acquiescence in them. (In *The Changeling* Middleton and Rowley developed a similarly contrasting pair of female characters, Beatrice and Isabella.) The enemies of virtue in the two plots, Wendoll and Acton, are also contrasting figures; likewise, the proponents of virtue, Frankford and Mountford, differ in their reactions to problems of social morality.

Heywood's casualness of writing is illustrated in his handling of the passage of time in this play. It begins with the marriage of John and Anne Frankford; the rapid pace of the action gives the impression that only a few days have passed before the appearance of their two children in Act IV, Scene 4. Frankford (although he banishes Anne for infidelity) accepts the children

77

as his own, and thus Heywood has left ambiguous the relationship of events in Wendoll's seduction of Anne.

The slender evidence suggests that about two years pass between Wendoll's arrival and his declaration of passion; had Heywood been a more painstaking dramatist he might have intensified the characterization in the play by establishing clearly the lengthy development of Wendoll's passion and Anne's capitulation.

The greatest strengths of the play lie in Frankford's tolerance and in the intensity of Anne's chagrin and her self-realization; her self-punishment, starvation, demonstrates her concentration on requalifying herself for admission to heaven.

The Puritan themes of conscience, retribution and justice are reinforced by the large number of *sententiae* in the form of rhyming couplets. *A Woman Killed with Kindness*, based on three stories in Painter's *Palace of Pleasure* (1566–7), survives in its quarto form in editions of 1607 and 1617. The edition in this volume is based on the latter, with a few variants drawn from the first edition.

A WOMAN KILLED WITH KINDNESS
by Thomas Heywood
[1603]

[Dramatis Personae

SIR FRANCIS ACTON, brother to Mistress Anne Frankford
SIR CHARLES MOUNTFORD
MASTER JOHN FRANKFORD, newly married to Mistress Anne
MASTER MALBY, friend to Acton
MASTER WENDOLL ⎫
⎬ friends to Frankford
MASTER CRANWELL ⎭
MASTER SHAFTON, false friend to Mountford
OLD MOUNTFORD, uncle to Mountford
MASTER SANDY
MASTER RODER
MASTER TIDY
NICHOLAS ⎫
JENKIN ⎪
SPIGOT, the butler ⎬ servants to Frankford
ROGER BRICKBAT ⎪
JACK SLIME ⎭
SHERIFF
SERGEANT
KEEPER OF THE PRISON
MISTRESS ANNE FRANKFORD
SUSAN MOUNTFORD, sister to Sir Charles
CICELY, maid to Mistress Anne
FALCONERS, HUNTSMEN, OFFICERS, SERVANTS, MUSICIANS
SCENE: Rural Yorkshire]

The Prologue

I come but as a harbinger, being sent
To tell you what these preparations mean.
Look for no glorious state; our Muse is bent
Upon a barren subject, a bare scene.
We could afford [1] this twig a timber tree,
Whose strength might boldly on your favours build;
Our russet,[2] tissue;[3] drone, a honey-bee;
Our barren plot, a large and spacious field;
Our coarse fare, banquets; our thin water, wine;
Our brook, a sea; our bat's eyes, eagle's sight;
Our poet's full and earthly Muse, divine;
Our ravens, doves; our crow's black feathers, white;
    But gentle thoughts, when they may give the foil,[4]
    Save them that yield, and spare where they may spoil.

---

[1] 'We would have.'   [2] Coarse woollen cloth.
[3] A rich kind of fabric.   [4] A throw, as in wrestling.

[ACT I. SCENE 1]

[FRANKFORD'S *house*]

Enter MASTER JOHN FRANKFORD, MISTRESS ANNE, SIR
FRANCIS ACTON, SIR CHARLES MOUNTFORD, MASTER
MALBY, MASTER WENDOLL, *and* MASTER CRANWELL

FRANCIS. Some music there! None lead the bride a dance?
CHAR. Yes, would she dance 'The Shaking of the Sheets',[1]
  But that's a dance her husband means to lead her.
WEND. That's not the dance that every man must dance,
  According to the ballad.
FRAN.   Music, ho!
  By your leave, sister; by your husband's leave,
  I should have said. The hand that but this day
  Was given you in church I'll borrow. Sound!
  This marriage music hoists me from the ground.
FRANK. Ay, you may caper, you are light and free;   10
  Marriage hath yok'd my heels; pray, pardon me.
FRAN. I'll have you dance too, brother.
CHAR.   Master Frankford,
  Y'are a happy man, sir, and much joy
  Succeed your marriage mirth. You have a wife
  So qualified, and with such ornaments
  Both of mind and body; first, her birth
  Is noble, and her education such
  As might become the daughter of a prince;
  Her own tongue speaks all tongues, and her own hand
  Can reach all strings to speak in their best grace,   20
  From the shrill'st treble to the hoarsest bass.
  To end her many praises in one word,
  She's Beauty and Perfection's eldest daughter,
  Only found by yours, though many a heart hath sought her.
FRANK. But that I know your virtues and chaste thoughts,
  I should be jealous of your praise, Sir Charles.
CRAN. He speaks no more than you approve.
MAL. Nor flatters he that gives to her her due.
ANNE. I would your praise could find a fitter theme

---

[1] An Elizabethan tune and ballad.

Than my imperfect beauties to speak on;
Such as they be, if they my husband please,
They suffice me now I am married.
His sweet content is like a flatt'ring glass,
To make my face seem fairer to mine eye;
But the least wrinkle from his stormy brow
Will blast the roses in my cheeks that grow.

FRAN. A perfect wife already, meek and patient.
How strangely the word husband fits your mouth,
Not married three hours since. Sister, 'tis good;
You that begin betimes thus must needs prove
Pliant and duteous in your husband's love.
Gramercies,[1] brother! Wrought her to't already?—
'Sweet husband,' and a curtsy the first day!
Mark this, mark this, you that are bachelors,
And never took the grace of honest man,[2]
Mark this, against you marry, this one phrase:
In good time that man both wins and woos
That takes his wife down [3] in her wedding shoes.

FRANK. Your sister takes not after you, Sir Francis;
All his wild blood your father spent on you;
He got her in his age, when he grew civil.
All his mad tricks were to his land entail'd,
And you are heir to all; your sister, she
Hath to her dower her mother's modesty.

CHAR. Lord, sir, in what a happy state live you!
This morning, which to many seems a burden,
Too heavy to bear, is unto you a pleasure.
This lady is no clog, as many are;
She doth become you like a well-made suit,
In which the tailor hath us'd all his art;
Not like a thick coat of unseason'd frieze,[4]
Forc'd on your back in summer. She's no chain
To tie your neck and curb ye to the yoke;
But she's a chain of gold to adorn your neck;
You both adorn each other, and your hands,
Methinks, are matches. There's equality
In this fair combination; y'are both scholars,
Both young, both being descended nobly.
There's music in this sympathy; it carries

---

[1] 'Mercy on us.'   [2] Acquired the dignity of husband.
[3] Compels her submission.   [4] Coarse woollen cloth.

Consort and expectation of much joy,   70
Which God bestow on you from this first day
Until your dissolution—that's for aye.

FRAN. We keep you here too long, good brother Frankford.
Into the hall; away! Go cheer your guests.
What, bride and bridegroom both withdrawn at once?
If you be miss'd, the guests will doubt their welcome,
And charge you with unkindness.

FRANK.   To prevent it,
I'll leave you here, to see the dance within.

ANNE. And so will I.   *Exeunt* ANNE *and* FRANKFORD.

FRAN.   To part you it were sin.
Now, gallants, while the town musicians   80
Finger their frets within, and the mad lads
And country lasses, every mother's child,
With nosegays and bride-laces [1] in their hats,
Dance all their country measures, rounds, and jigs,
What shall we do? Hark, they're all on the hoigh; [2]
They toil like mill-horses, and turn as round;
Marry, not on the toe. Ay, and they caper,
Not [3] without cutting.[4] You shall see tomorrow
The hall floor peck'd and dinted like a millstone,
Made by their high shoes; though their skill be small,   90
Yet they tread heavy where their hobnails fall.

CHAR. Well, leave them to their sports. Sir Francis Acton,
I'll make a match with you: Meet tomorrow
At Chevy Chase; [5] I'll fly my hawk with yours.

FRAN. For what? For what?

CHAR.   Why, for a hundred pound.

FRAN. Pawn me some gold [6] of that.

CHAR.   Here are ten angels;
I'll make them good a hundred pound tomorrow
Upon my hawk's wing.

FRAN.   'Tis a match, 'tis done;
Another hundred pound upon your dogs—
Dare ye, Sir Charles?

---

[1] Wedding favours.   [2] Excited.
[3] But—quartos.   [4] Scarring [the floor].
[5] Named erroneously, or perhaps used generically = a hunting park. The Chevy Chase of the ballads, near the Scottish border (the site of the battle of Otterburn, 1388), is a considerable distance from York, the general locale of the rest of the play (*see* IV. ii. 47–68).
[6] Put up some security.

CHAR.   I dare; were I sure to lose,   1
 I durst do more than that. Here's my hand:
 The first course for a hundred pound.
FRAN.   A match.
WEND. Ten angels on Sir Francis Acton's hawk;
 As much upon his dogs!
CRAN. I am for Sir Charles Mountford; I have seen
 His hawk and dog both tried. What, clap [1] ye hands,
 Or is't no bargain?
WEND.   Yes, and stake them down. [2]
 Were they five hundred, they were all my own.
FRAN. Be stirring early with the lark tomorrow;
 I'll rise into my saddle ere the sun   1
 Rise from his bed.
CHAR.   If there you miss me, say
 I am no gentleman. I'll hold my day. [3]
FRAN. It holds on all sides. Come, tonight let's dance;
 Early tomorrow let's prepare to ride.
 We had need be three hours up before the bride.   *Exeunt.*

[ACT I. SCENE 2]

[*The yard at* FRANKFORD'S *house*]

Enter NICK, JENKIN, JACK SLIME, ROGER BRICKBAT,
CICELY, *other country wenches, and two or three musicians*

JENK. Come, Nick, take you Joan Miniver to trace [4] withal;
 Jack Slime, traverse [4] you with Cicely Milkpail; I will take
 Jane Trubkin, and Roger Brickbat shall have Isbell Motley;
 and now that they are busy in the parlour, come, strike up,
 we'll have a crash [5] here in the yard.
NICH. My humour is not compendious; [6] dancing I possess not,
 though I can foot it; yet, since I am fallen into the hands of
 Cicely Milkpail, I consent.
JACK. Truly, Nick, though we were never brought up like
 serving courtiers, yet we have been brought up with serving
 creatures; ay, and God's creatures too; for we have been

    [1] Shake.   [2] 'Deposit a sum as a wager.'
    [3] 'Adhere to my commitment.'   [4] Dance.
    [5] Frolic.   [6] Comprehensive.

brought up to serve sheep, oxen, horses, hogs, and suchlike; and, though we be but country fellows, it may be in the way of dancing we can do the horse-trick [1] as well as the serving-men.

ROGER. Ay, and the cross-point [1] too.

JENK. Oh, Slime, oh, Brickbat, do you not know that comparisons are odious? Now we are odious ourselves too; therefore there are no comparisons to be made betwixt us.

NICH. I am sudden, and not superfluous;
I am quarrelsome, and not seditious;   20
I am peaceable, and not contentious;
I am brief, and not compendious.

JACK. Foot it quickly. If the music overcome not my melancholy, I shall quarrel; and if they suddenly do not strike up, I shall presently strike thee down.

JENK. No quarrelling, for God's sake; truly, if you do, I shall set a knave between ye.

JACK. I come to dance, not to quarrel. Come, what shall it be? 'Rogero'? [2]

JENK. 'Rogero'? No; we will dance 'The Beginning of the   30
World'.

CICELY. I love no dance so well as 'John, Come Kiss Me Now'.

NICH. I, that have ere now deserved a cushion, call for the Cushion dance.

ROGER. For my part, I like nothing so well as 'Tom Tyler'.

JENK. No; we'll have 'The Hunting of the Fox'.

JACK. 'The Hay'! 'The Hay'! There's nothing like 'The Hay'!

NICH. I have said, do say, and will say again—

JENK. Every man agree to have it as Nick says.   40

ALL. Content.

NICH. It hath been, it now is, and it shall be—

CICELY. What, Master Nicholas, what?

NICH. 'Put on your Smock o' Monday'.

JENK. So, the dance will come cleanly off! Come, for God's sake, agree of something. If you like not that, put it to the musicians. Or let me speak for all, and we'll have 'Sellenger's Round'.

ALL. That, that, that!

NICH. No, I am resolved; thus it shall be.   50
First take hands, then take ye to your heels.

JENK. Why, would ye have us run away?

---

[1] A dance step.   [2] A dance tune, and so the names that follow.

NICH. No; but I would have you shake your heels.
 Music! Strike up!
  They dance; NICK, *dancing, speaks stately and scurvily,*[1] *the*
  rest after the country fashion
JENK. Hey! Lively, my lasses, here's a turn for thee! *Exeunt.*

[ACT I. SCENE 3]

[*Chevy Chase*]

 Wind horns. Enter SIR CHARLES, SIR FRANCIS, MALBY,
 CRANWELL, WENDOLL, *falconers, and huntsmen*

CHAR. So, well cast off. Aloft, aloft! Well flown.
 Oh, now she takes her at the souse,[2] and strikes her
 Down to the earth like a swift thunder-clap.
WEND. She hath struck ten angels out of my way.
FRAN. A hundred pound from me.
CHAR. What, falconer!
FALC. At hand, sir.
CHAR. Now she hath seiz'd the fowl and 'gins to plume [3] her,
 Rebuke [4] her not; rather stand still and cherk [5] her.
 So, seize her gets,[6] her jesses,[6] and her bells.
 Away!
FRAN. My hawk kill'd too.
CHAR.   Ay, but 'twas at the querre,[7]
 Not at the mount, like mine.
FRAN.   Judgment, my masters.
CRAN. Yours miss'd her at the ferre.[8]
WEND. Ay, but our merlin first had plum'd the fowl,
 And twice renew'd [9] her from the river too.
 Her bells, Sir Francis, had not both one weight,
 Nor was one semi-tune above the other.
 Methinks these Milan bells do sound too full,
 And spoil the mounting of your hawk.

---

[1] Rudely.   [2] The rise of the prey.
[3] Pluck.   [4] Startle.
[5] Chirp, whistle (to calm the falcon). This line emended by K. L. Bates.
'Rebeck her . . . check her'—quartos. Miss Bates's edition (Boston, 1917)
deals with falconry in detail.
[6] Leg straps.   [7] Seizing the prey on the ground.
[8] Highest point.   [9] Recovered.

CHAR.   'Tis lost.[1]
FRAN. I grant it not. Mine likewise seiz'd a fowl
    Within her talons, and you saw her paws
    Full of the feathers; both her petty singles [2]
    And her long singles grip'd her more than other.
    The terrials [3] of her legs [4] were stain'd with blood,
    Not of the fowl only; she did discomfit
    Some of her feathers, but she brake away.
    Come, come, your hawk is but a rifler.[5]
CHAR.   How!
FRAN. Ay, and your dogs are trindle-tails [6] and curs.
CHAR. You stir my blood!
    You keep not one good hound in all your kennel,
    Nor one good hawk upon your perch.
FRAN.   How, knight!
CHAR. So, knight; you will not swagger, sir?
FRAN. Why, say I did?
CHAR.   Why, sir,
    I say you would gain as much by swagg'ring
    As you have got by wagers on your dogs.
    You will come short in all things.
FRAN.   Not in this.
    Now I'll strike home.   [*Strikes* SIR CHARLES.]
CHAR.   Thou shalt to thy long home,
    Or I will want my will.
FRAN. All they that love Sir Francis follow me!
CHAR. All that affect Sir Charles draw on my part!
CRAN. On this side heaves my hand.
WEND.   Here goes my heart.
    They divide themselves. SIR CHARLES, CRANWELL, *his
    falconer and huntsman fight against* SIR FRANCIS,
    WENDOLL, *his falconer and huntsman;* SIR CHARLES
    hath the better and beats them away, killing both of SIR
    FRANCIS'S *men.*
CHAR. My God, what have I done? What have I done?
    My rage hath plung'd into a sea of blood,
    In which my soul lies drown'd. Poor innocents,
    For whom we are to answer. Well, 'tis done,

[1] i.e. Sir Francis's wager.   [2] Outer claws.
[3] An obscure word, possibly 'terriets' (Bates); rings on the harness of the
hawk.   [4] The legs of Mountford's hawk.
[5] A spoiler.   [6] Low-bred.

And I remain the victor. A great conquest,
When I would give this right hand—nay, this head—
To breathe in them new life whom I have slain.
Forgive me, God; 'twas in the heat of blood,
And anger quite removes me from myself.
It was not I, but rage, did this vile murder;
Yet I, and not my rage, must answer it.
Sir Francis Acton, he is fled the field;
With him all those that did partake his quarrel,
And I am left alone, with sorrow dumb,
And in my height of conquest overcome.

Enter SUSAN

SUSAN. O God! My brother wounded 'mong the dead!
    Unhappy jest, that in such earnest ends.
    The rumour of this fear stretch'd to my ears,
    And I am come to know if you be wounded.
CHAR. Oh, sister, sister, wounded at the heart.
SUSAN. My God forbid!
CHAR. In doing that thing which he forbad,
    I am wounded, sister.
SUSAN.   I hope not at the heart.
CHAR. Yes, at the heart.
SUSAN.   O God! A surgeon there!
CHAR. Call me a surgeon, sister, for my soul;
    The sin of murder, it hath pierced my heart
    And made a wide wound there. But for these scratches,
    They are nothing, nothing.
SUSAN.   Charles, what have you done?
    Sir Francis hath great friends, and will pursue you
    Unto the utmost danger [1] of the law.
CHAR. My conscience is become mine enemy,
    And will pursue me more than Acton can.
SUSAN. Oh, fly, sweet brother!
CHAR.   Shall I fly from thee?
    Why, Sue, art weary of my company?
SUSAN. Fly from your foe.
CHAR.   You, sister, are my friend,
    And flying you, I shall pursue my end.

[1] Liability.

SUSAN. Your company is as my eye-ball dear;
   Being far from you, no comfort can be near;   80
   Yet fly to save your life. What would I care
   To spend my future age in black despair,
   So you were safe? And yet to live one week
   Without my brother Charles, though every cheek
   My streaming tears would downwards run so rank,
   Till they could set on either side a bank,
   And in the midst a channel; so my face
   For two salt-water brooks shall still find place.
CHAR. Thou shalt not weep so much, for I will stay,
   In spite of danger's teeth. I'll live with thee,   90
   Or I'll not live at all. I will not sell
   My country and my father's patrimony,
   Nor thy sweet sight, for a vain hope of life.

Enter SHERIFF, *with officers*

SHER. Sir Charles, I am made the unwilling instrument
   Of your attach [1] and apprehension.
   I'm sorry that the blood of innocent men
   Should be of you exacted. It was told me
   That you were guarded with a troop of friends,
   And therefore [I] came thus arm'd.
CHAR.   Oh, Master Sheriff,
   I came into the field with many friends,   100
   But see, they all have left me; only one
   Clings to my sad misfortune, my dear sister.
   I know you for an honest gentleman;
   I yield my weapons and submit to you.
   Convey me where you please.
SHER.   To prison then,
   To answer for the lives of these dead men.
SUSAN. O God! O God!
CHAR.   Sweet sister, every strain
   Of sorrow from your heart augments my pain;
   Your grief abounds [2] and hits against my breast.
SHER. Sir, will you go?
CHAR.   Even where it likes you best.   110
                         [Exeunt.]

---

[1] Arrest.   [2] Pours forth.

[ACT II. SCENE 1]

[FRANKFORD'S *house*]

Enter MASTER FRANKFORD *in a study* [1]

FRANK. How happy am I amongst other men,
　　That in my mean [2] estate embrace content.
　　I am a gentleman, and by my birth
　　Companion with a king; a king's no more.
　　I am possess'd of many fair revenues,
　　Sufficient to maintain a gentleman.
　　Touching my mind, I am studied in all arts,
　　The riches of my thoughts; and of my time
　　Have been a good proficient; [3] but the chief
　　Of all the sweet felicities on earth,
　　I have a fair, a chaste, and loving wife;
　　Perfection all, all truth, all ornament.
　　If man on earth may truly happy be,
　　Of these at once possess'd, sure I am he.

Enter NICHOLAS

NICH. Sir, there's a gentleman attends without
　　To speak with you.
FRANK.　　　　　　On horseback?
NICH.　　　　　　　　　　　Yes, on horseback.
FRANK. Entreat him to alight, and I'll attend him.
　　Know'st thou him, Nick?
NICH. Know him? Yes; his name's Wendoll.
　　It seems he comes in haste: his horse is booted [4]
　　Up to the flank in mire, himself all spotted
　　And stain'd with plashing. Sure, he rid in fear,
　　Or for a wager. Horse and man both sweat;
　　I ne'er saw two in such a smoking heat.
FRANK. Entreat him in; about it instantly.　[*Exit* NICHOLAS.]
　　This Wendoll I have noted, and his carriage
　　Hath pleas'd me much; by observation
　　I have noted many good deserts in him.

---

[1] Reverie.　　　[2] Inferior.
[3] 'I have used my time to good advantage.'　　　　　Covered.

He's affable, and seen [1] in many things,
Discourses well, a good companion;   30
And though of small means, yet a gentleman
Of a good house, somewhat press'd by want.
I have preferr'd him to a second place
In my opinion and my best regard.

Enter WENDOLL, MISTRESS FRANKFORD, *and* NICK

ANNE. Oh, Master Frankford, Master Wendoll here
  Brings you the strangest news that e'er you heard.
FRANK. What news, sweet wife? What news, good Master
  Wendoll?
WEND. You know the match made 'twixt Sir Francis Acton
  And Sir Charles Mountford?
FRANK.   True; with their hounds and hawks.   40
WEND. The matches were both play'd.
FRANK.   Ha! And which won?
WEND. Sir Francis, your wife's brother, had the worst,
  And lost the wager.
FRANK.   Why, the worse his chance.
  Perhaps the fortune of some other day
  Will change his luck.
WEND.[2]   Oh, but you hear not all.
  Sir Francis lost, and yet was loath to yield;
  At length the two knights grew to difference,
  From words to blows, and so to banding [3] sides;
  Where valorous Sir Charles slew, in his spleen,
  Two of your brother's [4] men: his falconer,   50
  And his good huntsman, whom he lov'd so well.
  More men were wounded, no more slain outright.
FRAN. Now, trust me, I am sorry for the knight;
  But is my brother safe?
WEND.   All whole and sound,
  His body not being blemish'd with one wound.
  But poor Sir Charles is to the prison led,
  To answer at th'assize for them that's dead.
FRANK. I thank your pains, sir; had your news been better,
  Your will was to have brought it, Master Wendoll.

[1] Versed.   [2] *Anne*—quartos.
[3] Taking.   [4] i.e. brother-in-law's.

Sir Charles will find hard friends; his case is heinous,
And will be most severely censur'd on;
I'm sorry for him. Sir, a word with you:
I know you, sir, to be a gentleman
In all things; your possibility [1] but mean.
Please you to use my table and my purse;
They are yours.

WEND.　　　　　O Lord, sir, I shall never deserve it!

FRANK. Oh, sir, disparage not your worth too much;
　　You are full of quality and fair desert.
　　Choose of my men which shall attend you, sir,
　　And he is yours. I will allow you, sir,
　　Your man, your gelding, and your table, all
　　At mine own charge; be my companion.

WEND. Master Frankford, I have oft been bound to you
　　By many favours; this exceeds them all,
　　That I shall never merit your least favour.
　　But when your last remembrance I forget,
　　Heaven at my soul exact that weighty debt.

FRANK. There needs no protestation, for I know you
　　Virtuous, and therefore grateful. Prithee, Nan,
　　Use him with all thy loving'st courtesy.

ANNE. As far as modesty may well extend,
　　It is my duty to receive your friend.

FRANK. To dinner. Come, sir, from this present day
　　Welcome to me for ever. Come, away!
　　　　　　　Exeunt ANNE, FRANKFORD, *and* WENDOLL.

NICH. I do not like this fellow by no means;
　　I never see him but my heart still earns.[2]
　　Zounds! I could fight with him, yet know not why;
　　The devil and he are all one in mine eye.

Enter JENKIN

JENK. Oh, Nick, what gentleman is that that comes to lie at our
　　house? My master allows him one to wait on him, and I
　　believe it will fall to thy lot.

NICH. I love my master; by these hilts, I do;
　　But rather than I'll ever come to serve him,[3]
　　I'll turn away my master.

　　　　　[1] Prospects.　　　　　[2] Grieves.　　　　　[3] Wendoll.

Enter CICELY

CICELY. Nich'las, where are you, Nich'las? You must come in,
   Nich'las, and help the young gentleman off with his boots.
NICH. If I pluck off his boots, I'll eat the spurs,
   And they shall stick fast in my throat like burrs.
CICELY. Then, Jenkin, come you.
JENK. Nay, 'tis no boot [1] for me to deny it. My master hath   100
   given me a coat here, but he takes pains himself to brush it
   once or twice a day with a holly-wand.
CICELY. Come, come; make haste, that you may wash your
   hands again and help to serve in dinner.
JENK.[2] You may see, my masters, though it be afternoon with
   you, 'tis but early days with us, for we have not dined yet.
   Stay a little, I'll but go in and help to bear up the first course,
   and come to you again presently.   *Exeunt.*

[ACT II. SCENE 2]
[*The prison*]

Enter MALBY *and* CRANWELL

MAL. This is the sessions day; pray, can you tell me
   How young Sir Charles hath sped? Is he acquit,
   Or must he try the law's strict penalty?
CRAN. He's clear'd of all, spite of his enemies,
   Whose earnest labour was to take his life;
   But in this suit of pardon he hath spent [3]
   All the revenues that his father left him,
   And he is now turn'd a plain countryman,
   Reform'd in all things. See, sir, here he comes.

Enter SIR CHARLES *and his keeper*

KEEP. Discharge your fees, and you are then at freedom.   10
CHAR. Here, Master Keeper, take the poor remainder
   Of all the wealth I have; my heavy foes

----

[1] Use.   [2] He speaks to the audience.
[3] In gifts and bribes.

Have made my purse light. But, alas, to me
'Tis wealth enough that you have set me free.
MAL. God give you joy of your delivery!
I am glad to see you abroad, Sir Charles.
CHAR. The poorest knight in England, Master Malby.
My life hath cost me all my patrimony
My father left his son. Well, God forgive them
That are the authors of my penury.

Enter SHAFTON

SHAF. Sir Charles, a hand, a hand! At liberty?
Now, by the faith I owe, I am glad to see it.
What want you? Wherein may I pleasure you?
CHAR. O me, O most unhappy gentleman!
I am not worthy to have friends stirr'd up,
Whose hands may help me in this plunge of want.
I would I were in Heaven, to inherit there
Th'immortal birthright which my Saviour keeps,
And by no unthrift [1] can be bought and sold;
For here on earth what pleasures should we trust?
SHAF. To rid you from these contemplations,
Three hundred pounds you shall receive of me;
Nay, five [2] for fail.[3] Come, sir, the sight of gold
Is the most sweet receipt [4] for melancholy,
And will revive your spirits. You shall hold law
With your proud adversaries. Tush! Let Frank Acton
Wage, [with] his knighthood, like expense with me,
And 'a will sink, he will. Nay, good Sir Charles,
Applaud your fortune and your fair escape
From all these perils.
CHAR.   Oh, sir, they have undone me.
Two thousand and five hundred pound a year
My father at his death possess'd me of;
All which the envious Acton made me spend;
And, notwithstanding all this large expense,
I had much ado to gain my liberty.
And I have only now a house of pleasure,[5]

[1] Extravagance.
[2] He seems actually to have given Charles only £300 (*see* III. i. 29).
[3] 'To prevent your failure.'
[4] Remedy.   [5] A country retreat.

With some five hundred pounds reserv'd,
Both to maintain me and my loving sister.
SHAF. [*Aside.*] That must I have; it lies convenient for me.
If I can fasten but one finger on him,   50
With my full hand I'll gripe him to the heart.
'Tis not for love I proffer'd him this coin,
But for my gain and pleasure.—Come, Sir Charles,
I know you have need of money; take my offer.
CHAR. Sir, I accept it, and remain indebted
Even to the best of my unable [1] power.
Come, gentlemen, and see it tend'red down.[2]   [*Exeunt.*]

[ACT II. SCENE 3]
[FRANKFORD's *house*]

Enter WENDOLL, *melancholy*

WEND. I am a villain if I apprehend [3]
But such a thought! Then, to attempt the deed,
Slave, thou art damn'd without redemption.
I'll drive away this passion with a song.
A song! Ha, ha! A song! As if, fond [4] man,
Thy eyes could swim in laughter, when thy soul
Lies drench'd and drowned in red tears of blood.
I'll pray, and see if God within my heart
Plant better thoughts. Why, prayers are meditations;
And when I meditate—O God, forgive me!—   10
It is on her divine perfections.
I will forget her; I will arm myself
Not t'entertain a thought of love to her,
And, when I come by chance into her presence,
I'll hale [5] these balls until my eye-strings crack,
From being pull'd and drawn to look that way.

Enter, over the stage, FRANKFORD, *his wife, and* NICK [6]

O God, O God! With what a violence
I'm hurried to mine own destruction!

    [1] Weak.   [2] Paid.   [3] Consider.
    [4] Foolish.   [5] Pull.   [6] They pass across upstage.

There goest thou, the most perfect'st man
That ever England bred a gentleman;
And shall I wrong his bed? Thou God of thunder,
Stay, in Thy thoughts of vengeance and of wrath,
Thy great, almighty, and all-judging hand
From speedy execution on a villain;
A villain and a traitor to his friend!

Enter JENKIN [1]

JENK. Did your worship call?
WEND. He doth maintain me; he allows me largely [2]
    Money to spend,—
JENK. [*Aside.*] By my faith, so do not you me; I cannot get a
    cross [3] of you.
WEND. —My gelding, and my man;—
JENK. [*Aside.*] That's Sorrel and I.
WEND. —This kindness grows of no alliance [4] 'twixt us.—
JENK. [*Aside.*] Nor is my service of any great acquaintance.[5]
WEND. —I never bound him to me by desert.
    Of a mere stranger, a poor gentleman,
    A man by whom in no kind could he gain;
    And he hath plac'd me in his highest thoughts,
    Made me companion with the best and chiefest
    In Yorkshire. He cannot eat without me,
    Nor laugh without me. I am to his body
    As necessary as his digestion,
    And equally do make him whole or sick.
    And shall I wrong this man? Base man! Ingrate!
    Hast thou the power, straight with thy gory hands,
    To rip thy image from his bleeding heart?
    To scratch thy name from out the holy book
    Of his remembrance, and to wound his name
    That holds thy name so dear? Or rend his heart
    To whom thy heart was knit and join'd together?
    And yet I must. Then, Wendoll, be content.
    Thus villains, when they would, cannot repent.
JENK. [*Aside.*] What a strange humour is my new master in!
    Pray God he be not mad; if he should be so, I should never

---

[1] Unnoticed by Wendoll until line 57.   [2] Generously.
[3] A piece of money; the obverse of several coins was marked with a cross.
[4] Kinship.   [5] Intimacy.

have any mind to serve him in Bedlam. It may be he's mad
for missing of me.

WEND. What, Jenkin! Where's your mistress?

JENK. Is your worship married?

WEND. Why dost thou ask?

JENK. Because you are my master, and if I have a mistress, I   60
would be glad, like a good servant, to do my duty to her.

WEND. I mean Mistress Frankford.

JENK. Marry, sir, her husband is riding out of town, and she
went very lovingly to bring him on his way to horse. Do you
see, sir? Here she comes, and here I go.

WEND. Vanish!   [*Exit* JENKIN.]

Enter MISTRESS FRANKFORD

ANNE. Y'are well met, sir. Now, in troth, my husband,
Before he took horse, had a great desire
To speak with you; we sought about the house,
Halloo'd into the fields, sent every way,   70
But could not meet you; therefore he enjoin'd me
To do unto you his most kind commends.
Nay, more; he wills you, as you prize his love,
Or hold in estimation his kind friendship,
To make bold in his absence, and command
Even as himself were present in the house.
For you must keep his table, use his servants,
And be a present Frankford in his absence.

WEND. I thank him for his love.
[*Aside.*] Give me a name, you whose infectious tongues   80
Are tipp'd with gall and poison. As you would
Think on a man that had your father slain,
Murd'red your children, made your wives base strumpets,
So call me, call me so; print in my face
The most stigmatic title of a villain,
For hatching treason to so true a friend.

ANNE. Sir, you are much beholding to my husband;
You are a man most dear in his regard.

WEND. I am bound unto your husband, and you too.
[*Aside.*] I will not speak to wrong a gentleman   90
Of that good estimation, my kind friend;
I will not; zounds, I will not! I may choose,
And I will choose. Shall I be so misled,

Or shall I purchase to my father's crest
The motto of a villain? If I say
I will not do it, what thing can enforce me?
What can compel me? What sad destiny
Hath such command upon my yielding thoughts?
I will not. Ha! Some fury pricks me on;
The swift Fates drag me at their chariot wheel,
And hurry me to mischief. Speak I must;
Injure myself, wrong her, deceive his trust.

ANNE. Are you not well, sir, that ye seem thus troubled?
There is sedition [1] in your countenance.

WEND. And in my heart, fair angel, chaste and wise.
I love you. Start not, speak not, answer not.
I love you. Nay, let me speak the rest.
Bid me to swear, and I will call to record
The host of Heaven.

ANNE.   The host of Heaven forbid
Wendoll should hatch such a disloyal thought.

WEND. Such is my fate. To this suit I was born,
To wear rich pleasure's crown, or fortune's scorn.

ANNE. My husband loves you.

WEND.   I know it.

ANNE.   He esteems you,
Even as his brain, his eye-ball, or his heart.

WEND. I have tried it. [2]

ANNE. His purse is your exchequer, and his table
Doth freely serve you.

WEND.   So I have found it.

ANNE. Oh, with what face of brass, what brow of steel,
Can you, unblushing, speak this to the face
Of the espous'd wife of so dear a friend?
It is my husband that maintains your state;
Will you dishonour him? I am his wife,
That in your power hath left his whole affairs;
It is to me you speak.

WEND.   Oh, speak no more;
For more than this I know, and have recorded
Within the red-leav'd table [3] of my heart.
Fair, and of all belov'd, I was not fearful
Bluntly to give my life into your hand,

---

[1] Tumult.   [2] Tested his esteem.
[3] Memorandum book; cf. *Hamlet*, I. v. 98.

And at one hazard all my earthly means.
Go, tell your husband; he will turn me off,   130
And I am then undone. I care not, I;
'Twas for your sake. Perchance, in rage he'll kill me;
I care not; 'twas for you. Say I incur
The general name of villain through the world,
Of traitor to my friend; I care not, I.
Beggary, shame, death, scandal, and reproach,—
For you I'll hazard all; why, what care I?
For you I'll live,[1] and in your love I'll die.
ANNE. You move me, sir, to passion [2] and to pity.
The love I bear my husband is as precious   140
As my soul's health.
WEND.   I love your husband too,
And for his love I will engage my life.
Mistake me not; the augmentation
Of my sincere affection borne to you
Doth no whit lessen my regard of him.
I will be secret, lady, close as night;
And not the light of one small glorious star
Shall shine here in my forehead to bewray [3]
That act of night.
ANNE.   What shall I say?
My soul is wand'ring and hath lost her way.   150
Oh, Master Wendoll, oh!
WEND.   Sigh not, sweet saint;
For every sigh you breathe draws from my heart
A drop of blood.
ANNE.   I ne'er offended yet;
My fault, I fear, will in my brow be writ.
Women that fall, not quite bereft of grace,
Have their offences noted in their face.
I blush and am asham'd. Oh, Master Wendoll,
Pray God I be not born to curse your tongue,
That hath enchanted me. This maze I am in   160
I fear will prove the labyrinth of sin.

Enter NICK [*unseen*]

WEND. The path of pleasure and the gate to bliss,
Which on your lips I knock at with a kiss.
           [1] Love—quartos.   [2] Suffering.   [3] Divulge.

NICH. [*Aside.*] I'll kill the rogue.
WEND. Your husband is from home, your bed's no blab;
  Nay, look not down and blush.
                         Exeunt WENDOLL *and* ANNE.
NICH.   Zounds, I'll stab!
  Ay, Nick, was it thy chance to come just in the nick?
  I love my master, and I hate that slave;
  I love my mistress, but these tricks I like not.
  My master shall not pocket up this wrong,
  I'll eat my fingers first. What say'st thou, metal? 17
  Does not that rascal Wendoll go on legs
  That thou must cut off? Hath he not hamstrings
  That thou must hough? [1] Nay, metal, thou shalt stand
  To all I say. I'll henceforth turn a spy,
  And watch them in their close conveyances. [2]
  I never look'd for better of that rascal,
  Since he came miching [3] first into our house.
  It is that Satan hath corrupted her,
  For she was fair and chaste. I'll have an eye
  In all their gestures. Thus I think of them, 18
  If they proceed as they have done before:
  Wendoll's a knave, my mistress is a ——.   *Exit.*

[ACT III. SCENE 1]
[MOUNTFORD'S *house in the country*]

Enter CHARLES *and* SUSAN

CHAR. Sister, you see we are driven to hard shift,
  To keep this poor house we have left unsold.
  I am now enforc'd to follow husbandry,
  And you to milk. And do we not live well?
  Well, I thank God.
SUSAN.   Oh, brother, here's a change,
  Since old Sir Charles died in our father's house.
CHAR. All things on earth thus change, some up, some down;
  Content's a kingdom, and I wear that crown.

      [1] Cut.   [2] Private conduct.   [3] Skulking.

Enter SHAFTON, *with a sergeant*

SHAF. Good morrow, morrow, Sir Charles. What, with your
  sister,   10
  Plying your husbandry?—Sergeant, stand off.—
  You have a pretty house here, and a garden,
  And goodly ground about it. Since it lies
  So near a lordship [1] that I lately bought,
  I would fain buy it of you. I will give you—
CHAR. Oh, pardon me; this house successively
  Hath long'd to me and my progenitors
  Three hundred years. My great-great-grandfather,
  He in whom first our gentle style [2] began,
  Dwelt here, and in this ground increas'd this mole-hill   20
  Unto that mountain which my father left me.
  Where he the first of all our house began,
  I now the last will end, and keep this house,
  This virgin title, never yet deflower'd
  By any unthrift of the Mountfords' line.
  In brief, I will not sell it for more gold
  Than you could hide or pave the ground withal.
SHAF. Ha, ha! A proud mind and a beggar's purse.
  Where's my three hundred pounds, besides the use? [3]
  I have brought it to an execution [4]   30
  By course of law. What, is my monies ready?
CHAR. An execution, sir, and never tell me
  You put my bond in suit? You deal extremely. [5]
SHAF. Sell me the land, and I'll acquit you straight.
CHAR. Alas, alas, 'tis all trouble hath left me
  To cherish me and my poor sister's life.
  If this were sold, our names [6] should then be quite
  Raz'd from the bead-roll [7] of gentility.
  You see what hard shift we have made to keep it
  Allied still to our own name; this palm you see,   40
  Labour hath glow'd within; her silver brow,
  That never tasted a rough winter's blast
  Without a mask or fan, doth with a grace
  Defy cold winter, and his storms outface.
SUSAN. Sir, we feed sparingly, and we labour hard;

---

[1] An estate.   [2] Title, rank.   [3] Interest.
[4] Action.   [5] With great severity. [6] Means—quartos.
[7] Pedigree.

We lie uneasy, to reserve to us
And our succession this small plot of ground.

CHAR. I have so bent my thoughts to husbandry,
  That I protest I scarcely can remember
  What a new fashion is, how silk or satin
  Feels in my hand. Why, pride is grown to us
  A mere, mere stranger. I have quite forgot
  The names of all that ever waited on me.
  I cannot name ye any of my hounds,
  Once from whose echoing mouths I heard all music
  That e'er my heart desir'd. What should I say?
  To keep this place, I have chang'd myself away.

SHAF. Arrest him at my suit. Actions and actions
  Shall keep thee in continual bondage fast;
  Nay, more, I'll sue thee by a late appeal,
  And call thy former life in question.
  The keeper is my friend; thou shalt have irons,
  And usage such as I'll deny to dogs.
  Away with him!

CHAR.   Ye are too timorous; [1]
  But trouble is my master,
  And I will serve him truly. My kind sister,
  Thy tears are of no force to mollify
  This flinty man. Go to my father's brother,
  My kinsmen, and allies; entreat them for me,
  To ransom me from this injurious man
  That seeks my ruin.

SHAF.   Come, irons, irons! Come, away;
  I'll see thee lodg'd far from the sight of day.

              [*Exeunt* SHAFTON, CHARLES, *and sergeant.*]

SUSAN. My heart's so hard'ned with the frost of grief,
  Death cannot pierce it through. Tyrant too fell!
  So lead the fiends condemned souls to hell!   [*Stands aside.*]

Enter SIR FRANCIS ACTON *and* MALBY

FRAN. Again to prison! Malby, hast thou seen
  A poor slave better tortur'd? Shall we hear
  The music of his voice cry from the grate,[2]
  'Meat, for the Lord's sake'? No, no; yet I am not

----

    [1] Terrible.   [2] The prison.

Throughly reveng'd. They say he hath a pretty wench 80
To his sister; shall I, in my mercy-sake
To him and to his kindred, bribe the fool
To shame herself by lewd, dishonest lust?
I'll proffer largely; but, the deed being done,
I'll smile to see her base confusion.

MAL. Methinks, Sir Francis, you are full reveng'd
For greater wrongs than he can proffer you.
See where the poor sad gentlewoman stands.

FRAN. Ha, ha! Now will I flout her poverty,
Deride her fortunes, scoff her base estate; 90
My very soul the name of Mountford hates.
But stay, my heart; oh, what a look did fly
To strike my soul through with thy piercing eye!
I am enchanted; all my spirits are fled,
And with one glance my envious spleen struck dead.

SUSAN. Acton that seeks our blood!   *Runs away.*

FRAN.   O chaste and fair!

MAL. Sir Francis! Why, Sir Francis! In a trance?
Sir Francis! What cheer, man? Come, come, how is't?

FRAN. Was she not fair? Or else this judging eye
Cannot distinguish beauty.

MAL.   She was fair. 100

FRAN. She was an angel in a mortal's shape,
And ne'er descended from old Mountford's line.
But soft, soft; let me call my wits together.
A poor, poor wench, to my great adversary
Sister, whose very souls denounce stern war
Each against other. How now, Frank? Turn'd fool
Or madman, whether? [1] But no; master of
My perfect senses and directest wits.
Then why should I be in this violent humour
Of passion and of love? And with a person 110
So different every way, and so opposed
In all contractions [2] and still-warring actions?
Fie, fie! How I dispute against my soul!
Come, come; I'll gain her, or in her fair quest
Purchase my soul free and immortal rest.   [*Exeunt.*]

Which.   [2] Lawsuits.

[ACT III. SCENE 2]

[FRANKFORD'S *house*]

Enter three or four serving-men, one with a voider [1] *and a wooden knife, to take away;* [2] *another the salt and bread; another the tablecloth and napkins; another the carpet;* [3] JENKIN *with two lights after them*

JENK. So; march in order, and retire in battle array. My master and the guests have supped already; all's taken away. Here, now spread for the serving-men in the hall. Butler, it belongs to your office.

SPIGOT. I know it, Jenkin. What d'ye call the gentleman that supped there tonight?

JENK. Who, my master?

SPIGOT. No, no; Master Wendoll, he's a daily guest. I mean the gentleman that came but this afternoon.

JENK. His name's Master Cranwell. God's light! Hark, within there! My master calls to lay more billets upon the fire. Come, come! Lord, how we that are in office here in the house are troubled! One spread the carpet in the parlour, and stand ready to snuff the lights; the rest be ready to prepare their stomachs. More lights in the hall there. Come, Nich'las.

Exeunt, except NICHOLAS.

NICH. I cannot eat; but, had I Wendoll's heart,
I would eat that; the rogue grows impudent.
Oh, I have seen such vile, notorious tricks,
Ready to make my eyes dart from my head.
I'll tell my master; by this air, I will;
Fall what may fall, I'll tell him. Here he comes.

Enter MASTER FRANKFORD, *as it were brushing the crumbs from his clothes with a napkin, as newly risen from supper*

FRANK. Nich'las, what make you here? Why are not you
At supper in the hall among your fellows?

NICH. Master, I stay'd your rising from the board,
To speak with you.

---

[1] A tray or basket for removing remnants of a meal.
[2] To clear off the table.
[3] A heavy undercovering for a table.

FRANK.   Be brief then, gentle Nich'las;
  My wife and guests attend me in the parlour.
  Why dost thou pause? Now, Nich'las, you want money,
  And, unthrift-like, would eat into your wages
  Ere you have earn'd it; here, sir, 's half a crown;
  Play the good husband,[1] and away to supper.   30

NICH. [*Aside.*] By this hand, an honourable gentleman; I will
  not see him wronged.—
  Sir, I have serv'd you long; you entertain'd [2] me
  Seven years before your beard. You knew me, sir,
  Before you knew my mistress.

FRANK. What of this, good Nich'las?

NICH. I never was a makebate [3] or a knave;
  I have no fault but one: I'm given to quarrel,
  But not with women. I will tell you, master,
  That which will make your heart leap from your breast,   40
  Your hair to startle from your head, your ears to tingle.

FRANK. What preparation's this to dismal news?

NICH. 'Sblood, sir, I love you better than your wife;
  I'll make it good.

FRANK. Y'are a knave, and I have much ado
  With wonted patience to contain my rage,
  And not to break thy pate. Th'art a knave;
  I'll turn you, with your base comparisons,
  Out of my doors.

NICH.   Do, do.
  There is not room for Wendoll and me too,   50
  Both in one house. Oh, master, master,
  That Wendoll is a villain!

FRANK. [*Strikes him.*]   Ay, saucy?

NICH. Strike, strike, do; strike! Yet hear me. I am no fool;
  I know a villain, when I see him act
  Deeds of a villain. Master, master, that base slave
  Enjoys my mistress, and dishonours you!

FRANK. Thou hast kill'd me with a weapon whose sharp point
  Hath prick'd quite through and through my shiv'ring heart.
  Drops of cold sweat sit dangling on my hairs,
  Like morning's dew upon the golden flowers,   60
  And I am plung'd into strange agonies.
  What did'st thou say? If any word that touch'd

---

[1] Be thrifty.   [2] Provided occupation for.
[3] Mischief-maker.

His credit or her reputation,
It is as hard to enter my belief
As Dives into Heaven.

NICH.   I can gain nothing;
They are two that never wrong'd me. I knew before
'Twas but a thankless office, and perhaps
As much as is my service, or my life
Is worth; all this I know. But this, and more,
More by a thousand dangers, could not hire me
To smother such a heinous wrong from you;
I saw, and I have said.

FRANK. [*Aside.*] 'Tis probable;[1] though blunt, yet he is honest.
Though I durst pawn my life, and on their faith
Hazard the dear salvation of my soul,
Yet in my trust I may be too secure.
May this be true? Oh, may it? Can it be?
Is it by any wonder possible?
Man, woman, what thing mortal can we trust,
When friends and bosom wives prove so unjust?—
What instance[2] hast thou of this strange report?

NICH. Eyes, master, eyes.

FRANK. Thy eyes may be deceiv'd, I tell thee;
For should an angel from the heavens drop down,
And preach this to me that thyself hast told,
He should have much ado to win belief,
In both their loves I am so confident.

NICH. Shall I discourse the same by circumstance?[3]

FRANK. No more. To supper, and command your fellows
To attend us and the strangers. Not a word,
I charge thee, on thy life. Be secret then,
For I know nothing.

NICH. I am dumb; and now that I have eas'd my stomach,[4]
I will go fill my stomach.   *Exit.*

FRANK.   Away, begone.
She is well born, descended nobly;
Virtuous her education; her repute
Is in the general voice of all the country
Honest and fair; her carriage, her demeanour,
In all her actions that concern the love
To me her husband, modest, chaste, and godly.
Is all this seeming gold plain copper?

---

[1] Plausible.   [2] Proof.   [3] In detail.   [4] Anger.

But he, that Judas that hath borne my purse
And sold me for a sin! O God, O God!
Shall I put up [1] these wrongs? No! Shall I trust
The bare report of this suspicious groom
Before the double-gilt,[2] the well-hatch'd [3] ore,
Of their two hearts? No! I will lose these thoughts;
Distraction I will banish from my brow,
And from my looks exile sad discontent.
Their wonted favours in my tongue shall flow;   110
Till I know all, I'll nothing seem to know.
Lights and a table there! Wife, Master Wendoll,
And gentle Master Cranwell!

Enter MISTRESS FRANKFORD, MASTER WENDOLL,
MASTER CRANWELL, NICK *and* JENKIN, *with cards,
carpets, stools and other necessaries*

FRANK. Oh, Master Cranwell, you are a stranger here,
And often balk [4] my house; faith, y'are a churl.[5]
Now we have supp'd, a table, and to cards!
JENK. A pair [6] of cards, Nich'las, and a carpet to cover the
table. Where's Cicely, with her counters and her box? Candles
and candlesticks there! Fie, we have such a household of
serving creatures! Unless it be Nick and I, there's not one   120
amongst them all can say boo to a goose. Well said,[7] Nick.
They spread a carpet, set down lights and cards
ANNE. Come, Master Frankford, who shall take my part? [8]
FRANK. Marry, that will I, sweet wife.
WEND. No, by my faith; when you are together I sit out. It
must be Mistress Frankford and I, or else it is no match.
FRANK. I do not like that match.
NICH. [*Aside.*] You have no reason, marry, knowing all.
FRANK. 'Tis no great matter neither. Come, Master Cranwell,
shall you and I take them up?
CRAN. At your pleasure, sir.   130
FRANK. I must look to you, Master Wendoll, for you'll be
playing false; nay, so will my wife too.
NICH. [*Aside.*] I will be sworn she will.
ANNE. Let them that are taken false, forfeit the set.

[1] Endure.	[2] Heavy gold or silve- plating.	[3] Richly inlaid.
[4] Pass by.	[5] Base fellow.	[6] Pack.
[7] Well done.	[8] 'Be my partner.'	

FRANK. Content; it shall go hard, but I'll take [1] you.

CRAN. Gentlemen, what shall our game be?

WEND. Master Frankford, you play best at noddy.[2]

FRANK. You shall not find it so; indeed you shall not.

ANNE. I can play at nothing so well as double ruff.

FRANK. If Master Wendoll and my wife be together, there's no
    playing against them at double-hand.

NICH. I can tell you, sir, the game that Master Wendoll is best
    at.

WEND. What game is that, Nick?

NICH. Marry, sir, knave out of doors.

WEND. She and I will take you at loadum.

ANNE. Husband, shall we play at saint?

FRANK. [*Aside.*] My saint's turn'd devil—No, we'll none of
    saint.
    You are best at new-cut, wife; you'll play at that.

WEND. If you play at new-cut, I'm soonest hitter [3] of any here,
    for a wager.

FRANK. [*Aside.*] 'Tis me they play on.—Well, you may draw
    out; [4]
    For all your cunning, 'twill be to your shame;
    I'll teach you, at your new-cut, a new game.
    Come, come!

CRAN. If you cannot agree upon the game,
    To post and pair.

WEND. We shall be soonest pairs, and my good host,
    When he comes late home, he must kiss the post.[5]

FRANK. Whoever wins, it shall be to thy cost.

CRAN. Faith, let it be vide-ruff, and let's make honours.[6]

FRANK. If you make honours, one thing let me crave:
    Honour the king and queen, except [7] the knave.

WEND. Well, as you please for that. Lift [8] who shall deal.

ANNE. The least in sight. What are you, Master Wendoll?

WEND. I am a knave.

NICH. [*Aside.*]   I'll swear it.

ANNE.   I am queen.

---

[1] Defeat.
  [2] A game like cribbage; also, a simpleton. One of a series of *doubles entendres* involving Elizabethan card games. See K. L. Bates's edition of the
play (Boston, 1917), and C. Cotton, *The Compleat Gamester* (London, 1674).
  [3] Winner.   [4] Begin play.   [5] Be shut out.
  [6] To count the highest ranking honour cards in scoring.
  [7] Exclude.   [8] Cut.

FRANK. [*Aside*.] A quean, thou should'st say.—Well, the cards
    are mine;   170
    They are the grossest pair that e'er I felt.

ANNE. Shuffle; I'll cut. Would I had never dealt.

FRANK. [*Misdeals*.] I have lost my dealing.

WEND.   Sir, the fault's in me;
    This queen I have more than mine own, you see.
    Give me the stock.[1]

FRANK.   My mind's not on my game.
    Many a deal I have lost, the more's your shame.
    You have serv'd me a bad trick, Master Wendoll.

WEND. Sir, you must take your lot. To end this strife,
    I know I have dealt better to your wife.

FRANK. Thou hast dealt falsely then.   180

ANNE. What's trumps?

WEND. Hearts. Partner, I rub.[2]

FRANK. [*Aside*.] Thou robb'st me of my soul, of her chaste love;
    In thy false dealing thou hast robb'd my heart.—
    Booty you play;[3] I like a loser stand.
    Having no heart, or[4] here or in my hand.
    I will give o'er the set, I am not well.
    Come, who will hold my cards?

ANNE. Not well, sweet Master Frankford?
    Alas, what ails you? 'Tis some sudden qualm.   190

WEND. How long have you been so, Master Frankford?

FRANK. Sir, I was lusty, and I had my health,
    But I grew ill when you began to deal.
    Take hence this table. Gentle Master Cranwell,
    Y'are welcome; see your chamber at your pleasure.
    I am sorry that this megrim[5] takes me so,
    I cannot sit and bear you company.
    Jenkin, some lights, and show him to his chamber!

                 [*Exeunt* CRANWELL *and* JENKIN.]

ANNE. A night-gown[6] for my husband; quickly there!
    It is some rheum or cold.

WEND.   Now, in good faith,   200
    This illness you have got by sitting late
    Without your gown.

---

[1] The remaining, undealt cards.   [2] To take all the cards of one suit.
[3] To play, or lose, by confederacy in order to trick another player.
[4] Either.
[5] Headache; with the implication of the cuckold's horns?
[6] Dressing-gown.

FRANK.   I know it, Master Wendoll.
  Go, go to bed, lest you complain like me.
  Wife, prithee, wife, into my bed-chamber;
  The night is raw and cold, and rheumatic.
  Leave me my gown and light; I'll walk away my fit.
WEND. Sweet sir, good night.
FRANK.   Myself, good night.
                                        [*Exit* WENDOLL.]
ANNE. Shall I attend you, husband?
FRANK. No, gentle wife, thou'lt catch cold in thy head;
  Prithee, begone, sweet; I'll make haste to bed.
ANNE. No sleep will fasten on mine eyes, you know,
  Until you come.
FRANK.   Sweet Nan, I prithee, go.   *Exit* ANNE.
  I have bethought me; get me by degrees
  The keys of all my doors, which I will mould
  In wax, and take their fair impression,
  To have by them new keys. This being compass'd,
  At a set hour a letter shall be brought me,
  And when they think they may securely play,
  They nearest are to danger. Nick, I must rely
  Upon thy trust and faithful secrecy.
NICH. Build on my faith.
FRANK.   To bed then, not to rest;
  Care lodges in my brain, grief in my breast.   [*Exeunt.*]

[ACT III. SCENE 3]
[OLD MOUNTFORD'S *house*]

Enter SIR CHARLES'S *sister*, OLD MOUNTFORD, SANDY,
    RODER, *and* TIDY

MOUNT. You say my nephew is in great distress.
  Who brought it to him but his own lewd life?
  I cannot spare a cross. I must confess
  He was my brother's son; why, niece, what then?
  This is no world in which to pity men.
SUSAN. I was not born a beggar, though his extremes [1]

----

[1] Straits.

Enforce this language from me; I protest
No fortune of mine own could lead my tongue
To this base key. I do beseech you, uncle,
For the name's sake, for Christianity,—   10
Nay, for God's sake, to pity his distress.
He is deni'd the freedom of the prison,
And in the hole [1] is laid with men condemn'd;
Plenty he hath of nothing but of irons,
And it remains in you to free him thence.

MOUNT. Money I cannot spare. Men should take heed;
 He lost my kindred [2] when he fell to need.   *[Exit.]*

SUSAN. Gold is but earth; thou earth enough shalt have,
 When thou hast once took measure of thy grave.
 You know me, Master Sandy, and my suit.   20

SANDY. I knew you, lady, when the old man liv'd;
 I knew you ere your brother sold his land.
 Then you were Mistress Sue, trick'd up in jewels;
 Then you sung well, play'd sweetly on the lute;
 But now I neither know you nor your suit.   *[Exit.]*

SUSAN. You, Master Roder, was my brother's tenant;
 Rent-free he plac'd you in that wealthy farm,
 Of which you are possess'd.

RODER.   True, he did;
 And have I not there dwelt still for his sake?
 I have some business now; but, without doubt,   30
 They that have hurl'd him in will help him out.   *Exit.*

SUSAN. Cold comfort still. What say you, cousin Tidy?

TIDY. I say this comes of roisting,[3] swagg'ring;
 Call me not cousin. Each man for himself.
 Some men are born to mirth, and some to sorrow;
 I am no cousin unto them that borrow.   *Exit.*

SUSAN. O Charity, why art thou fled to Heaven,
 And left all things on this earth uneven?
 Their scoffing answers I will ne'er return;
 But to myself his grief in silence mourn.   40

Enter SIR FRANCIS *and* MALBY

FRAN. She is poor; I'll therefore tempt her with this gold.
 Go, Malby, in my name deliver it,

   ¹ Dungeon. ² Kinship. ³ Rioting.

And I will stay thy answer.

MAL. Fair mistress, as I understand your grief
   Doth grow from want, so I have here in store
   A means to furnish you, a bag of gold,
   Which to your hands I freely tender you.

SUSAN. I thank you, Heavens; I thank you, gentle sir.
   God make me able to requite this favour!

MAL. This gold Sir Francis Acton sends by me,
   And prays you—

SUSAN. Acton! O God! That name I'm born to curse.
   Hence, bawd; hence, broker! See, I spurn his gold;
   My honour never shall for gain be sold.

FRAN. Stay, lady, stay!

SUSAN.   From you I'll posting hie,
   Even as the doves from feather'd eagles fly.   *Exit.*

FRAN. She hates my name, my face; how should I woo?
   I am disgrac'd in everything I do.
   The more she hates me and disdains my love,
   The more I am rapt in admiration
   Of her divine and chaste perfections.
   Woo her with gifts I cannot, for all gifts
   Sent in my name she spurns; with looks I cannot,
   For she abhors my sight; nor yet with letters,
   For none she will receive. How then? How then?
   Well, I will fasten such a kindness on her,
   As shall o'ercome her hate and conquer it.
   Sir Charles, her brother, lies in execution [1]
   For a great sum of money; and besides,
   The appeal is sued still for my huntsmen's death,
   Which only I have power to reverse.
   In her I'll bury all my hate of him.
   Go seek the keeper, Malby; bring him to me.
   To save his body, I his debts will pay;
   To save his life, I his appeal will stay.   *[Exeunt.]*

---

[1] Legal action.

[Act IV. Scene I]

[*The prison in York Castle*]

Enter Sir Charles *with irons, his feet bare, his garments all
ragged and torn*

Char. Of all on the earth's face most miserable,
Breathe in this hellish dungeon thy laments.
Thus like a slave ragg'd, like a felon gyv'd,—
That hurls thee headlong to this base estate.
O unkind uncle! O my friends ingrate!
Unthankful kinsmen! Mountford's all too base,
To let thy name be fetter'd in disgrace.
A thousand deaths here in this grave I die;
Fear, hunger, sorrow, cold, all threat my death,
And join together to deprive my breath.   10
But that which most torments me, my dear sister
Hath left [1] to visit me, and from my friends
Hath brought no hopeful answer; therefore, I
Divine they will not help my misery.
If it be so, shame, scandal, and contempt
Attend their covetous thoughts; need make their graves!
Usurers they live, and may they die like slaves!

Enter keeper

Keep. Knight, be of comfort, for I bring thee freedom
From all thy troubles.
Char.   Then I am doomed to die;
Death is the end of all calamity.   20
Keep. Live. Your appeal is stay'd, the execution
Of your debts discharg'd, your creditors,
Even to the utmost penny, satisfied.
In sign whereof, your shackles I knock off.
You are not left so much indebted to us
As for your fees; all is discharg'd, all paid.
Go freely to your house, or where you please;
After long miseries, embrace your ease.
Char. Thou grumblest out the sweetest music to me

---

[1] Ceased.

That ever organ play'd. Is this a dream,
Or do my waking senses apprehend
The pleasing taste of these applausive [1] news?
Slave that I was, to wrong such honest friends,
My loving kinsmen, and my near allies!
Tongue, I will bite thee for the scandal breath'd
Against such faithful kinsmen; they are all
Compos'd of pity and compassion,
Of melting charity, and of moving ruth.[2]
That which I spake before was in my rage;
They are my friends, the mirrors of this age,
Bounteous and free. The noble Mountfords' race
Ne'er bred a covetous thought or humour base.

Enter SUSAN

SUSAN. [*Aside.*] I can no longer stay from visiting
    My woeful brother; while I could, I kept
    My hapless tidings from his hopeful ear.
CHAR. Sister, how much am I indebted to thee
    And to thy travail!
SUSAN.   What, at liberty?
CHAR. Thou seest I am, thanks to thy industry.
    Oh, unto which of all my courteous friends
    Am I thus bound? My uncle Mountford, he
    Even of an infant lov'd me; was it he?
    So did my cousin Tidy: was it he?
    So Master Roder, Master Sandy too;
    Which of all these did this high kindness do?
SUSAN. Charles, can you mock me in your poverty,
    Knowing your friends deride your misery?
    Now I protest I stand so much amaz'd,
    To see your bonds free, and your irons knock'd off,
    That I am rapt into a maze of wonder;
    The rather for I know not by what means
    This happiness hath chanc'd.
CHAR.   Why, by my uncle,
    My cousins, and my friends; who else, I pray,
    Would take upon them all my debts to pay?
SUSAN. Oh, brother, they are men [made] all of flint,

---

[1] Agreeable.   [2] Sorrow.

Pictures of marble, and as void of pity
As chased bears. I begg'd, I sued, I kneel'd,
Laid open all your griefs and miseries,
Which they derided; more than that, deni'd us
A part in their alliance; but, in pride,
Said that our kindred with our plenty died.   70

CHAR. Drudges too much! What, did they? Oh, known evil!
Rich fly the poor as good men shun the devil.
Whence should my freedom come? Of whom alive,
Saving of those, have I deserv'd so well?
Guess, sister, call to mind, remember [1] me.
These I have rais'd,[2] they follow the world's guise,
Whom rich they [3] honour, they in woe despise.

SUSAN. My wits have lost themselves; let's ask the keeper.

CHAR. Jailer!

KEEP. At hand, sir.   80

CHAR. Of courtesy, resolve me one demand.
What was he took the burden of my debts
From off my back, stay'd my appeal to death,
Discharg'd my fees, and brought me liberty?

KEEP. A courteous knight, and call'd Sir Francis Acton.

CHAR. Ha! Acton! O me, more distress'd in this
Than all my troubles! Hale me back,
Double my irons, and my sparing meals
Put into halves, and lodge me in a dungeon
More deep, more dark, more cold, more comfortless.   90
By Acton freed! Not all thy manacles
Could fetter so my heels, as this one word
Hath thrall'd [4] my heart; and it must now lie bound
In more strict prison than thy stony jail.
I am not free; I go but under bail.

KEEP. My charge is done, sir, now I have my fees;
As we get little, we will nothing leese.[5]

CHAR. By Acton freed, my dangerous opposite!
Why, to what end? Or what occasion? Ha!
Let me forget the name of enemy,   100
And with indifference balance [6] this high favour. Ha!

SUSAN. [Aside.] His love to me; upon my soul, 'tis so!
That is the root from whence these strange things grow.

CHAR. Had this proceeded from my father, he

---

[1] Remind.   [2] Produced.   [3] In—quartos.
[4] Enslaved.   [5] Abate.   [6] Impartially weigh.

That by the law of nature is most bound
In offices of love, it had deserv'd
My best employment to requite that grace.
Had it proceeded from my friends, or him,[1]
From them this action had deserv'd my life,
And from a stranger more, because from such
There is less execution of good deeds.
But he, nor father, nor ally, nor friend,
More than a stranger, both remote in blood,
And in his heart oppos'd my enemy,
That this high bounty should proceed from him—
Oh, there I lose myself. What should I say,
What think, what do, his bounty to repay?

SUSAN. You wonder, I am sure, whence this strange kindness
Proceeds in Acton; I will tell you, brother:
He dotes on me, and oft hath sent me gifts,
Letters, and tokens. I refus'd them all.

CHAR. I have enough, though poor; my heart is set,
In one rich gift to pay back all my debt.   *Exeunt.*

[ACT IV. SCENE 2]

[FRANKFORD'S *house*]

Enter FRANKFORD, *with a letter in his hand, and* NICK, *with keys*

FRANK. This is the night that I must play my part,
To try two seeming angels. Where's my keys?

NICH. They are made according to your mould in wax.
I bade the smith be secret, gave him money,
And here they are. The letter, sir.

FRANK. True; take it, there it is;
And when thou seest me in my pleasant'st vein,
Ready to sit to supper, bring it me.

NICH. I'll do't; make no more question but I'll do't.   *Exit.*

Enter MISTRESS FRANKFORD, CRANWELL, WENDOLL,
and JENKIN

[1] 'My father.'

ANNE. Sirrah, 'tis six o'clock already struck;   10
  Go bid them spread the cloth and serve in supper.
JENK. It shall be done, forsooth, Mistress. Where's Spigot, the
  butler, to give us our salt and trenchers? [1]
WEND. We that have been a-hunting all the day
  Come with prepared stomachs. Master Frankford,
  We wish'd you at our sport.
FRANK. My heart was with you, and my mind was on you.
  Fie, Master Cranwell, you are still thus sad;
  A stool, a stool! Where's Jenkin, and where's Nick?
  'Tis supper time at least an hour ago.   20
  What's the best news abroad?
WEND.   I know none good.
FRANK. [Aside.] But I know too much bad.

Enter SPIGOT *and* JENKIN *with a tablecloth, bread, trenchers,*
   and salt [and exeunt shortly]

CRAN. Methinks, sir, you might have that interest
  In [2] your wife's brother, to be more remiss [3]
  In his hard dealing against poor Sir Charles,
  Who, as I hear, lies in York Castle,
  Needy, and in great want.
FRANK. Did not more weighty business of mine own
  Hold me away, I would have labour'd peace
  Betwixt them with all care; indeed I would, sir.   30
ANNE. I'll write unto my brother earnestly
  In that behalf.
WEND.   A charitable deed,
  And will beget the good opinion
  Of all your friends that love you, Mistress Frankford.
FRANK. That's you for one. I know you love Sir Charles.—
  [Aside.] And my wife too well.
WEND.   He deserves the love
  Of all true gentlemen; be yourselves judge.
FRANK. But supper, ho! Now as thou lov'st me, Wendoll,
  Which I am sure thou dost, be merry, pleasant,
  And frolic it tonight. Sweet Master Cranwell,   40
  Do you the like. Wife, I protest my heart

---

[1] Serving-dishes or plates, usually of wood.
[2] Influence with.   [3] Lenient.

Was ne'er more bent on sweet alacrity.[1]
Where be those lazy knaves to serve in supper?

Enter NICK

NICH. Here's a letter, sir.
FRANK. Whence comes it, and who brought it?
NICH. A stripling that below attends your answer,
    And, as he tells me, it is sent from York.
FRANK. Have him into the cellar; let him taste
    A cup of our March beer. Go, make him drink.
                                    [*Reads the letter.*]
NICH. I'll make him drunk, if he be a Trojan.[2]
FRANK. My boots and spurs! Where's Jenkin? God forgive me,
    How I neglect my business! Wife, look here;
    I have a matter to be tri'd tomorrow
    By eight o'clock, and my attorney writes me
    I must be there betimes with evidence,
    Or it will go against me. Where's my boots?

Enter JENKIN, *with boots and spurs*

ANNE. I hope your business craves no such dispatch
    That you must ride tonight.
WEND. [*Aside.*]   I hope it doth.
FRANK. God's me, no such dispatch?
    Jenkin, my boots. Where's Nick? Saddle my roan,
    And the grey dapple for himself. Content ye,
    It much concerns me. Gentle Master Cranwell,
    And Master Wendoll, in my absence use
    The very ripest pleasures of my house.
WEND. Lord, Master Frankford, will you ride tonight?
    The ways are dangerous.
FRANK.   Therefore will I ride
    Appointed [3] well, and so shall Nick, my man.
ANNE. I'll call you up by five o'clock tomorrow.
FRANK. No, by my faith, wife, I'll not trust to that;
    'Tis not such easy rising in a morning
    From one I love so dearly. No, by my faith,
    I shall not leave so sweet a bedfellow

        [1] Sprightliness.   [2] Good fellow.   [3] Armed.

But with much pain; you have made me a sluggard
Since I first knew you.
ANNE.   Then, if you needs will go
  This dangerous evening, Master Wendoll,
  Let me entreat you bear him company.
WEND. With all my heart, sweet mistress. My boots there!
FRANK. Fie, fie, that for my private business
  I should disease [1] my friend, and be a trouble
  To the whole house. Nick?
NICH.   Anon, sir.   80
FRANK. Bring forth my gelding.—As you love me, sir,
                                        [*Exit* NICHOLAS.]
  Use no more words. A hand, good Master Cranwell.
CRAN. Sir, God be your good speed.
FRANK. Good night, sweet Nan; nay, nay, a kiss, and part.—
  [*Aside.*] Dissembling lips, you suit not with my heart.   *Exit.*
WEND. [*Aside.*] How business, time, and hours, all gracious
    prove,
  And are the furtherers to my new-born love!
  I am husband now in Master Frankford's place,
  And must command the house. [*To* ANNE.] My pleasure is   90
  We will not sup abroad so publicly,
  But in your private chamber, Mistress Frankford.
ANNE. [*Aside to Wendoll.*] Oh, sir, you are too public in your
    love,
  And Master Frankford's wife—
CRAN.   Might I crave favour,
  I would entreat you I might see my chamber;
  I am on the sudden grown exceeding ill,
  And would be spar'd from supper.
WEND.   Light there, ho!
  See you want nothing, sir; for if you do,
  You injure that good man, and wrong me too.   100
CRAN. I will make bold. Good night.   *Exit.*
WEND.   How all conspire
  To make our bosom [2] sweet, and full entire!
  Come, Nan, I prithee, let us sup within.
ANNE. Oh, what a clog unto the soul is sin!
  We pale offenders are still full of fear;
  Every suspicious eye brings danger near.
  When [3] they whose clear heart from offence is free

          [1] Inconvenience.   [2] Intimacy.   [3] While.

    Despise report, base scandals do outface,
    And stand at mere [1] defiance with disgrace.
WEND. Fie, fie! You talk too like a Puritan!
ANNE. You have tempted me to mischief, Master Wendoll;
    I have done I know not what. Well, you plead custom;
    That which for want of wit I granted erst,[2]
    I now must yield through fear. Come, come, let's in.
    Once o'er shoes, we are straight o'er head in sin.
WEND. My jocund soul is joyful above measure;
    I'll be profuse [3] in Frankford's richest treasure.   *Exeunt.*

[ACT IV. SCENE 3]
[*Another room in* FRANKFORD'S *house*]

Enter CICELY, JENKIN, *and* SPIGOT

JENK. My mistress and Master Wendoll, my master, sup in her
    chamber tonight. Cicely, you are preferred [4] from being the
    cook to be chambermaid. Of all the loves betwixt thee and me,
    tell me what thou think'st of this.
CICELY. Mum; there's an old proverb: when the cat's away,
    the mouse may play.
JENK. Now you talk of a cat, Cicely, I smell a rat.
CICELY. Good words, Jenkin, lest you be called to answer
    them.
JENK. Why, God make my mistress an honest woman! Are not
    these good words? Pray God my new master play not the
    knave with my old master! Is there any hurt in this? God send
    no villainy intended; and if they do sup together, pray God
    they do not lie together! God make my mistress chaste, and
    make us all His servants! What harm is there in all this? Nay,
    more; here is my hand; thou shalt never have my heart unless
    thou say Amen.
CICELY. Amen, I pray God, I say.

Enter serving-man

SERV. My mistress sends that you should make less noise, to
    lock up the doors, and see the household all got to bed. You,

---

[1] Absolute.   [2] Earlier, formerly.   [3] Lavish.   [4] Advanced.

Jenkin, for this night are made the porter, to see the gates shut in.

JENK. Thus by little and little I creep into office. Come, to kennel, my masters, to kennel; 'tis eleven o'clock already.

SERV. When you have locked the gates in, you must send up the keys to my mistress.

CICELY. Quickly, for God's sake, Jenkin, for I must carry them! I am neither pillow nor bolster, but I know more than both.

JENK. To bed, good Spigot; to bed, good honest serving-creatures; and let us sleep as snug as pigs in pease-straw.   30

Exeunt.

[ACT IV. SCENE 4]

[*Outside* FRANKFORD's *house*]

Enter FRANKFORD *and* NICK

FRANK. Soft, soft; we have tied our geldings to a tree
Two flight-shot [1] off, lest by their thundering hoofs
They blab our coming. Hear'st thou no noise?

NICH. I hear nothing but the owl and you.

FRANK. So; now my watch's hand points upon twelve,
And it is just midnight. Where are my keys?

NICH. Here, sir.

FRANK. This is the key that opes my outward gate;
This, the hall door; this, the withdrawing-chamber;
But this, that door that's bawd unto my shame,   10
Fountain and spring of all my bleeding thoughts,
Where the most hallowed order and true knot
Of nuptial sanctity hath been profan'd;
It leads to my polluted bed-chamber,
Once my terrestrial Heaven, now my earth's hell,
The place where sins in all their ripeness dwell.
But I forget myself; now to my gate.

NICH. It must ope with far less noise than Cripplegate, or your plot's dashed.

FRANK. So; reach me my dark lantern to the rest; [2]   20
Tread softly, softly.   [*They pass through the outer gate.*]

---

[1] A bow-shot.   [2] In addition to the keys.

NICH. I will walk on eggs this pace.

FRANK. A general silence hath surpris'd [1] the house,
And this is the last door.[2] Astonishment,
Fear, and amazement beat upon my heart,
Even as a madman beats upon a drum.
Oh, keep my eyes, you Heavens, before I enter,
From any sight that may transfix my soul;
Or if there be so black a spectacle,
Oh, strike mine eyes stark blind; or if not so,
Lend me such patience to digest my grief,
That I may keep this white and virgin hand
From any violent outrage, or red murder;
And with that prayer I enter.   [*Enter the bedroom.*]

NICH.[3] Here's a circumstance [4] indeed! A man may be made a
cuckold in the time he's about it. And the case were mine, as
'tis my master's,—'Sblood! (That makes me swear!)—
I would have plac'd his action,[5] enter'd there,
I would, I would.

                    [*Enter* FRANKFORD]

FRANK.   Oh, oh!

NICH. Master! 'Sblood! Master, master!

FRANK. O me unhappy! I have found them lying
Close in each other's arms, and fast asleep.
But that I would not damn two precious souls
Bought with my Saviour's blood, and send them, laden
With all their scarlet sins upon their backs,
Unto a fearful judgment, their two lives
Had met upon my rapier.

NICH. Master! What, have you left them sleeping still?
Let me go wake 'em!

FRANK.   Stay, let me pause awhile.
O God, O God, that it were possible
To undo things done; to call back yesterday!
That Time could turn up his swift sandy glass,
To untell the days, and to redeem these hours;

---

[1] Overtaken.
[2] Between lines 17 and 24 they move across the stage towards the entrance
to the inner stage.
[3] Many modern editors print this speech in whole or part as poetry.
[4] An ado.   [5] Established his situation.

Or that the sun
Could, rising from the west, draw his coach backward,
Take from th'account of time so many minutes,
Till he had all these seasons call'd again,
Those minutes, and those actions done in them,
Even from her first offence; that I might take her
As spotless as an angel in my arms!   60
But, oh, I talk of things impossible,
And cast beyond the moon.[1] God give me patience,
For I will in and wake them.   *Exit.*
NICH.   Here's patience perforce;
He needs must trot afoot that tires his horse.

Enter WENDOLL, *running over the stage in a nightgown,*
FRANKFORD *after him with his sword drawn; a maid in her*
smock [2] *stays his hand and clasps hold on him. He pauses for*
a while

FRANK. I thank thee, maid; thou, like an angel's hand,
Hast stay'd me from a bloody sacrifice.[3]—
Go, villain, and my wrongs sit on thy soul
As heavy as this grief doth upon mine.
When thou record'st my many courtesies,
And shalt compare them with thy treacherous heart,   70
Lay them together, weigh them equally,
'Twill be revenge enough. Go, to thy friend
A Judas. Pray, pray, lest I live to see
Thee, Judas-like, hang'd on an elder-tree.

Enter MISTRESS FRANKFORD *in her smock, nightgown, and*
night attire

ANNE. Oh, by what word, what title, or what name,
Shall I entreat your pardon? Pardon! Oh,
I am as far from hoping such sweet grace
As Lucifer from Heaven. To call you husband—
O me, most wretched!—I have lost that name;
I am no more your wife.
NICH.   'Sblood, sir, she sounds![4]   80

---

[1] Aim unrealistically.   [2] Chemise.
[3] Genesis xxii. 10–11.   [4] Swoons.

FRANK. [*To* ANNE.] Spare thou thy tears, for I will weep for
      thee;
   And keep thy count'nance, for I'll blush for thee.
   Now, I protest, I think 'tis I am tainted,
   For I am most asham'd; and 'tis more hard
   For me to look upon thy guilty face
   Than on the sun's clear brow. What, would'st thou speak?
ANNE. I would I had no tongue, no ears, no eyes,
   No apprehension, no capacity.
   When do you spurn me like a dog? When tread me
   Under feet? When drag me by the hair?
   Though I deserve a thousand thousand fold
   More than you can inflict; yet, once my husband,
   For womanhood, to which I am a shame,[1]
   Though once an ornament; even for His sake
   That hath redeem'd our souls, mark not my face,
   Nor hack me with your sword; but let me go
   Perfect and undeformed to my tomb.
   I am not worthy that I should prevail
   In the least suit; no, not to speak to you,
   Nor look on you, nor to be in your presence.
   Yet, as an abject, this one suit I crave,
   This granted, I am ready for my grave.
FRANK. My God, with patience arm me! Rise, nay, rise,
   And I'll debate with thee. Was it for want
   Thou play'dst the strumpet? Wast thou not supplied
   With every pleasure, fashion, and new toy,
   Nay, even beyond my calling?[2]
ANNE.   I was.
FRANK. Was it then disability in me?
   Or in thine eye seem'd he a properer[3] man?
ANNE.   Oh no.
FRANK. Did I not lodge thee in my bosom,
   Wear thee in my heart?
ANNE.   You did.
FRANK. I did, indeed; witness my tears, I did.
   Go, bring my infants hither.
                    [*Exit maid, returning with two children.*]
                        O Nan, O Nan,
   If neither fear of shame, regard of honour,

---

[1] Asham'd—quartos.   [2] Estate.
[3] More handsome.

The blemish of my house, nor my dear love
Could have withheld thee from so lewd a fact,[1]
Yet for these infants, these young, harmless souls,
On whose white brows thy shame is character'd,
And grows in greatness as they wax in years—   120
Look but on them, and melt away in tears.
Away with them; lest, as her spotted body
Hath stain'd their names with stripe of bastardy,
So her adulterous breath may blast their spirits
With her infectious thoughts. Away with them!
                              [*Exeunt maid and children.*]

ANNE. [*Kneeling.*] In this one life I die ten thousand deaths.
FRANK. Stand up, stand up. I will do nothing rashly;
    I will retire awhile into my study,
    And thou shalt hear thy sentence presently.   *Exit.*

ANNE. 'Tis welcome, be it death. O me, base strumpet,   130
    That having such a husband, such sweet children,
    Must enjoy neither! Oh, to redeem mine honour,
    I would have this hand cut off, these my breasts sear'd,
    Be rack'd, strappado'd,[2] put to any torment;
    Nay, to whip but this scandal out, I would hazard
    The rich and dear redemption of my soul!
    He cannot be so base as to forgive me,
    Nor I so shameless to accept his pardon.
    O women, women, you that yet have kept
    Your holy matrimonial vow unstain'd,   140
    Make me your instance; when you tread awry,
    Your sins, like mine, will on your conscience lie.

Enter CICELY, JENKIN, SPIGOT, *and all the serving-men,
    as newly come out of bed*

ALL. O mistress, mistress! What have you done, mistress?
NICH. What a caterwauling keep you here!
JENK. O Lord, mistress, how comes this to pass? My master is
    run away in his shirt, and never so much as called me to bring
    his clothes after him.
ANNE. [*Aside.*] See what guilt is; here stand I in this place,
    Asham'd to look my servants in the face.

---

[1] Evil deed.   [2] Tortured.

Enter MASTER FRANKFORD *and* CRANWELL; *whom seeing,
she falls on her knees*

FRANK. My words are register'd in Heaven already;   15
  With patience hear me. I'll not martyr thee,
  Nor mark thee for a strumpet; but with usage
  Of more humility torment thy soul,
  And kill thee even with kindness.
CRAN.   Master Frankford,—
FRANK. Good Master Cranwell.—Woman, hear thy judgment.
  Go make thee ready in thy best attire;
  Take with thee all thy gowns, all thy apparel;
  Leave nothing that did ever call thee mistress,
  Or by whose sight, being left here in the house,
  I may remember such a woman by.   16
  Choose thee a bed and hanging for thy chamber;
  Take with thee everything which hath thy mark,
  And get thee to my manor seven mile off,
  Where live.—'Tis thine; I freely give it thee.
  My tenants by [1] shall furnish thee with wains
  To carry all thy stuff within two hours;
  No longer will I limit [2] thee my sight.
  Choose which of all my servants thou lik'st best,
  And they are thine to attend thee.
ANNE.   A mild sentence.
FRANK. But, as thou hop'st for Heaven, as thou believ'st   17
  Thy name's recorded in the book of life,
  I charge thee never after this sad day
  To see me, or to meet me, or to send,
  By word, or writing, gift, or otherwise,
  To move me, by thyself, or by thy friends;
  Nor challenge [3] any part in my two children.
  So farewell, Nan; for we will henceforth be
  As we had never seen, ne'er more shall see.
ANNE. How full my heart is, in mine eyes appears;
  What wants in words, I will supply in tears.   18
FRANK. Come, take your coach, your stuff; all must along.
  Servants and all make ready; all begone.
  It was thy hand cut two hearts out of one.   [*Exeunt.*]

      [1] Near by.   [2] Allot.   [3] Claim.

[ACT V. SCENE 1]
[*Near* SIR FRANCIS ACTON'S *house*]

Enter SIR CHARLES, *gentlemanlike, and his sister, gentle-*
   womanlike

SUSAN. Brother, why have you trick'd [1] me like a bride,
   Bought me this gay attire, these ornaments?
   Forget you our estate, our poverty?
CHAR. Call me not brother, but imagine me
   Some barbarous outlaw, or uncivil kern; [2]
   For if thou shutt'st thy eye, and only hear'st
   The words that I shall utter, thou shalt judge me
   Some staring ruffian, not thy brother Charles.
   Oh, sister—
SUSAN. Oh, brother, what doth this strange language mean?   10
CHAR. Dost love me, sister? Wouldst thou see me live
   A bankrupt beggar in the world's disgrace,
   And die indebted to mine enemies?
   Wouldst thou behold me stand like a huge beam
   In the world's eye, a byword and a scorn?
   It lies in thee of these to acquit me free,
   And all my debt I may outstrip by thee.
SUSAN. By me? Why, I have nothing, nothing left;
   I owe even for the clothes upon my back.
   I am not worth—
CHAR.   Oh, sister, say not so;   20
   It lies in you my downcast state to raise,
   To make me stand on even points with the world.
   Come, sister, you are rich; indeed you are,
   And in your power you have, without delay,
   Acton's five hundred pound back to repay.
SUSAN. Till now I had thought y'had lov'd me. By my honour,
   Which I have kept as spotless as the moon,
   I ne'er was mistress of that single doit [3]
   Which I reserv'd not to supply your wants;
   And do ye think that I would hoard from you?   30
   Now, by my hopes in Heaven, knew I the means
   To buy you from the slavery of your debts

---

[1] Dressed.   [2] Boor.   [3] Half a farthing.

(Especially from Acton, whom I hate),
I would redeem it with my life or blood.

CHAR. I challenge [1] it, and, kindred set apart,
Thus, ruffian-like, I lay siege to thy heart.
What do I owe to Acton?

SUSAN. Why, some five hundred pounds; towards which, I
swear,
In all the world I have not one denier.[2]   4

CHAR. It will not prove so. Sister, now resolve [3] me:
What do you think (and speak your conscience)
Would Acton give, might he enjoy your bed?

SUSAN. He would not shrink to spend a thousand pound,
To give the Mountfords' name so deep a wound.

CHAR. A thousand pound! I but five hundred owe;
Grant him your bed, he's paid with interest so.

SUSAN. Oh, brother!

CHAR.   Oh, sister, only this one way,
With that rich jewel you my debts may pay.
In speaking so my cold heart shakes with shame;   5
Nor do I woo you in a brother's name,
But in a stranger's. Shall I die in debt
To Acton, my grand foe, and you still wear
The precious jewel that he holds so dear?

SUSAN. My honour I esteem as dear and precious
As my redemption.

CHAR.   I esteem you, sister,
As dear, for so dear prizing it.

SUSAN.   Will Charles
Have me cut off my hands and send them Acton,
Rip up my breast, and with my bleeding heart
Present him as a token?

CHAR.   Neither, sister;   6
But hear me in my strange assertion.
Thy honour and my soul are equal in my regard;
Nor will thy brother Charles survive thy shame.
His [4] kindness, like a burden, hath surcharg'd [5] me,
And under his good deeds I stooping go,
Not with an upright soul. Had I remain'd
In prison still, there doubtless I had died.
Then, unto him that freed me from that prison

---

[1] Claim.   [2] Penny.   [3] Answer.
[4] Acton's.   [5] Overwhelmed.

Still do I owe this life. What mov'd my foe
To enfranchise me? 'Twas, sister, for your love.   70
With full five hundred pounds he bought your love,
And shall he not enjoy it? Shall the weight
Of all this heavy burden lean on me,
And will you not bear part? You did partake
The joy of my release; will you not stand
In joint-bond bound to satisfy the debt?
Shall I be only charg'd?

SUSAN.   But that I know
These arguments come from an honour'd mind,
As in your most extremity of need
Scorning to stand in debt to one you hate—   80
Nay, rather would engage your unstain'd honour
Than to be held ingrate—I should condemn you.
I see your resolution, and assent;
So Charles will have me, and I am content.

CHAR. For this I trick'd you up.

SUSAN.   But here's a knife,
To save my honour, shall slice out my life.

CHAR. I know thou pleasest me a thousand times
More in thy resolution than thy grant.—
[*Aside.*] Observe her love; to sooth it to my suit,
Her honour she will hazard, though not lose.   90
To bring me out of debt, her rigorous hand
Will pierce her heart. Oh wonder, that will choose,
Rather than stain her blood, her life to lose!—
Come, you sad sister to a woeful brother,
This is the gate. I'll bear him such a present,
Such an acquittance for the knight to seal,[1]
As will amaze his senses, and surprise
With admiration [2] all his fantasies.[3]

Enter SIR FRANCIS ACTON *and* MALBY [*at a distance*]

SUSAN. Before his unchaste thoughts shall seize on me,
'Tis here [4] shall my imprison'd soul set free.   100

FRAN. How! Mountford with his sister, hand in hand!
What miracle's afoot?

---

[1] Ratify.   [2] Wonder.   [3] Faculties of perception.
[4] An allusion to her knife (lines 85-6).

MAL.   It is a sight
  Begets in me much admiration.
CHAR. Stand not amaz'd to see me thus attended.
  Acton, I owe thee money, and being unable
  To bring thee the full sum in ready coin,
  Lo, for thy more assurance here's a pawn,
  My sister, my dear sister, whose chaste honour
  I prize above a million. Here; nay, take her;
  She's worth your money, man; do not forsake her.   1?
FRAN. [*Aside.*] I would he were in earnest.
SUSAN. Impute it not to my immodesty;
  My brother, being rich in nothing else
  But in his interest that he hath in me,
  According to his poverty hath brought you
  Me, all his store; whom, howsoe'er you prize
  As forfeit to your hand, he values highly,
  And would not sell, but to acquit your debt,
  For any emperor's ransom.
FRAN. [*Aside.*]   Stern heart, relent,
  Thy former cruelty at length repent.   1?
  Was ever known, in any former age,
  Such honourable, wrested [1] courtesy?
  Lands, honours, life, and all the world forgo,
  Rather than stand engag'd to such a foe.
CHAR. Acton, she is too poor to be thy bride,
  And I too much oppos'd to be thy brother.
  There, take her to thee; if thou hast the heart
  To seize her as a rape or lustful prey,
  To blur our house, that never yet was stain'd,
  To murder her that never meant thee harm,   1?
  To kill me now, whom once thou sav'dst from death;—
  Do them at once; on her all these rely,
  And perish with her spotted chastity. [2]
FRAN. You overcome me in your love, Sir Charles.
  I cannot be so cruel to a lady
  I love so dearly. Since you have not spar'd
  To engage [3] your reputation to the world,
  Your sister's honour, which you prize so dear,
  Nay, all the comfort which you hold on earth,
  To grow out of my debt, being your foe,   14

----

    [1] Distorted.   [2] When her purity is stained.
    [3] Pledge.

Your honour'd thoughts, lo, thus I recompense.
Your metamorphos'd foe receives your gift
In satisfaction of all former wrongs.
This jewel I will wear here in my heart,
And where before I thought her, for her wants,
Too base to be my bride, to end all strife,
I seal [1] you my dear brother, her my wife.
SUSAN. You still exceed us. I will yield to fate,
    And learn to love, where I till now did hate.
CHAR. With that enchantment you have charm'd my soul,   150
    And made me rich even in those very words.
    I pay no debt, but I am indebted more;
    Rich in your love, I never can be poor.
FRAN. All's mine is yours; we are alike in state;
    Let's knit in love what was oppos'd in hate.
    Come; for our nuptials we will straight provide,
    Bless'd only in our brother and fair bride.   [*Exeunt.*]

[ACT V. SCENE 2]

[FRANKFORD'S *house*]

Enter CRANWELL, FRANKFORD, *and* NICHOLAS

CRAN. Why do you search each room about your house,
    Now that you have dispatch'd your wife away?
FRANK. Oh, sir, to see that nothing may be left
    That ever was my wife's. I lov'd her dearly,
    And when I do but think of her unkindness,
    My thoughts are all in hell; to avoid which torment,
    I would not have a bodkin [2] or a cuff,
    A braclet, necklace, or rebato wire,[3]
    Nor anything that ever was call'd hers
    Left me, by which I might remember her.   10
    Seek round about.
NICH. 'Sblood, master; here's her lute flung in a corner!
FRANK. Her lute! O God! Upon this instrument
    Her fingers have ran quick division,[4]

_____

[1] Designate.   [2] A pin or ornament for the hair.
[3] A wire used to support a rebato (a ruff or collar).
[4] Accompaniment.

Sweeter than that which now divides our hearts.
These frets have made me pleasant,[1] that have now
Frets of my heart-strings made. Oh, Master Cranwell,
Oft hath she made this melancholy wood,
Now mute and dumb for her disastrous chance,[2]
Speak sweetly many a note, sound many a strain
To her own ravishing voice; which being well strung,
What pleasant strange airs have they jointly rung.
Post with it after her. Now nothing's left;
Of her and hers I am at once bereft.

NICH. I'll ride and overtake her, do my message,
    And come back again.   [*Exit.*]

CRAN.   Meantime, sir, if you please,
    I'll to Sir Francis Acton, and inform him
    Of what hath pass'd betwixt you and his sister.

FRANK. Do as you please. How ill I am bested,
    To be a widower ere my wife be dead!   [*Exeunt.*]

[ACT V. SCENE 3]
[*The road near* FRANKFORD'S *manor-house*]

Enter MISTRESS FRANKFORD, *with* JENKIN, *her maid*
CICELY, *her coachman, and three carters*

ANNE. Bid my coach stay; why should I ride in state,
    Being hurl'd so low down by the hand of fate?
    A seat like to my fortunes let me have,
    Earth for my chair, and for my bed a grave.

JENK. Comfort, good mistress; you have watered your coach
with tears already. You have but two mile now to go to your
manor. A man cannot say by my old master Frankford as he
may say by me, that he wants manors; for he has three or four,
of which this is one that we are going to now.

CICELY. Good mistress, be of good cheer; sorrow, you see,
hurts you, but helps you not. We all mourn to see you so sad.

CARTER. Mistress, I see some of my landlord's men
    Come riding post; 'tis like he brings some news.

ANNE. Comes he from Master Frankford, he is welcome;
    So is his news, because they come from him.

        [1] Gay.   [2] Because of her misfortune.

Enter NICHOLAS

NICH. [*Handing her the lute.*] There!

ANNE. I know the lute. Oft have I sung to thee;
We are both out of tune, being out of time.

NICH. Would that had been the worst instrument that e'er you
played on. My master commends him unto ye; there's all he   20
can find that was ever yours. He hath nothing left that ever
you could lay claim to but his own heart, and he could afford [1]
you that. All that I have to deliver you is this: he prays you to
forget him, and so he bids you farewell.

ANNE. I thank him; he is kind, and ever was.
All you that have true feeling for my grief,
That know my loss, and have relenting hearts,
Gird me about, and help me with your tears
To wash my spotted sins. My lute shall groan;
It cannot weep, but shall lament my moan.   30
                          [*She plays and sings.*]

Enter WENDOLL [*at a distance*]

WEND. Pursu'd with horror of a guilty soul,
And with the sharp scourge of repentance lash'd,
I fly from mine own shadow. O my stars!
What have my parents in their lives deserv'd,
That you should lay this penance on their [2] son?
When I but think of Master Frankford's love,
And lay it to [3] my treason, or compare
My murdering him for his relieving me,
It strikes a terror like a lightning's flash
To scorch my blood up. Thus I, like the owl,   40
Asham'd of day, live in these shadowy woods,
Afraid of every leaf or murmuring blast,
Yet longing to receive some perfect knowledge
How he hath dealt with her. [*Sees* MISTRESS FRANKFORD.]
                          O my sad fate!
Here, and so far from home, and thus attended!
O God, I have divorc'd the truest turtles [4]
That ever liv'd together, and, being divided,
In several places make their several moan;
She in the fields laments, and he at home.
So poets write that Orpheus made the trees   50

[1] Yield.   [2] Your—quartos.   [3] Blame.   [4] Turtle-doves.

And stones to dance to his melodious harp,
Meaning the rustic and the barbarous hinds,
That had no understanding part in them;
So she from these rude carters tears extracts,
Making their flinty hearts with grief to rise,
And draw down rivers from their rocky eyes.

ANNE. [*To Nicholas.*] If you return unto my master, say
(Though not from me, for I am all unworthy
To blast his name so with a strumpet's tongue)
That you have seen me weep, wish myself dead.
Nay, you may say too, for my vow is pass'd,[1]
Last night you saw me eat and drink my last.
This to your master you may say and swear,
For it is writ in Heaven, and decreed here.

NICH. I'll say you wept; I'll swear you made me sad.
Why, how now, eyes? What now? What's here to do?
I'm gone, or I shall straight turn baby too.

WEND. [*Aside.*] I cannot weep, my heart is all on fire;
Curs'd be the fruits of my unchaste desire!

ANNE. Go, break this lute upon my coach's wheel,
As the last music that I e'er shall make:
Not as my husband's gift, but my farewell
To all earth's joys; and so your master tell.

NICH. If I can for crying.

WEND. [*Aside.*]   Grief, have done,
Or, like a madman, I shall frantic run.

ANNE. You have beheld the woefull'st wretch on earth,
A woman made of tears. Would you had words
To express but what you see! My inward grief
No tongue can utter; yet unto your power
You may describe my sorrow, and disclose
To thy sad master my abundant woes.

NICH. I'll do your commendations.[2]

ANNE.   Oh no!
I dare not so presume; nor to my children.
I am disclaim'd in both; alas, I am.
Oh, never teach them, when they come to speak,
To name the name of mother. Chide their tongue,
If they by chance light on that hated word;
Tell them 'tis naught; for when that word they name,
Poor, pretty souls, they harp on their own shame.

---

[1] Pledged.   [2] Charges.

WEND. [*Aside.*] To recompense her wrongs, what canst thou do?   90
    Thou hast made her husbandless, and childless too.

ANNE. I have no more to say. Speak not for me;
    Yet you may tell your master what you see.

NICH. I'll do't.   *Exit.*

WEND. [*Aside.*] I'll speak to her, and comfort her in grief.
    Oh, but her wound cannot be cur'd with words!
    No matter, though; I'll do my best good will
    To work a cure on her whom I did kill.

ANNE. So, now unto my coach, then to my home,
    So to my death-bed; for from this sad hour,   100
    I never will nor [1] eat, nor drink, nor taste
    Of any cates [2] that may preserve my life.
    I never will nor smile, nor sleep, nor rest;
    But when my tears have wash'd my black soul white,
    Sweet Saviour, to Thy hands I yield my sprite.

WEND. [*Approaching.*] Oh, Mistress Frankford!

ANNE.   Oh, for God's sake, fly!
    The devil doth come to tempt me ere I die.
    My coach! This sin that with an angel's face
    Conjur'd [3] mine honour, till he sought my wrack,
    In my repentant eye seems ugly black.   110

    Exeunt all, except WENDOLL *and* JENKIN, *the carters
    whistling*

JENK. What, my young master, that fled in his shirt! How come
you by your clothes again? You have made our house in a
sweet pickle, ha' ye not, think you? What, shall I serve you
still, or cleave to the old house?

WEND. Hence, slave! Away with thy unseason'd [4] mirth!
    Unless thou canst shed tears, and sigh, and howl,
    Curse thy sad fortunes, and exclaim on fate,
    Thou art not for my turn.

JENK. Marry, and you will not, another will. Farewell, and be
hanged! Would you had never come to have kept this coil [5]   120
within our doors! We shall ha' you run away like a sprite
again.   [*Exit.*]

WEND. She's gone to death; I live to want and woe,
    Her life, her sins, and all upon my head.
    And I must now go wander, like a Cain,
    In foreign countries and remoted climes,

---

[1] Neither.   [2] Viands.   [3] Bewitched.
[4] Unseasonable.   [5] Disturbance.

Where the report of my ingratitude
Cannot be heard. I'll over first to France,
And so to Germany and Italy;
Where, when I have recover'd, and by travel
Gotten those perfect tongues,[1] and that [2] these rumours
May in their height abate, I will return;
And I divine, however now dejected,
My worth and parts being by some great man prais'd,
At my return I may in court be rais'd.   *Exit.*

[ACT V. SCENE 4]
[*Before* FRANKFORD'S *manor-house*]

Enter SIR FRANCIS, SIR CHARLES, CRANWELL, MALBY, *and* SUSAN

FRAN. Brother, and now my wife, I think these troubles
   Fall on my head by justice of the Heavens,
   For being so strict to you in your extremities;
   But we are now aton'd.[3] I would my sister
   Could with like happiness o'ercome her griefs
   As we have ours.
SUSAN. You tell us, Master Cranwell, wondrous things
   Touching the patience of that gentleman,
   With what strange virtue he demeans [4] his grief.
CRAN. I told you what I was witness of;
   It was my fortune to lodge there that night.
FRAN. Oh, that same villain, Wendoll! 'Twas his tongue
   That did corrupt her; she was of herself
   Chaste and devoted well.[5] Is this the house?
CRAN. Yes, sir; I take it here your sister lies.
FRAN. My brother Frankford show'd too mild a spirit
   In the revenge of such a loathed crime.
   Less than he did, no man of spirit could do.
   I am so far from blaming his revenge,
   That I commend it. Had it been my case,
   Their souls at once had from their breasts been freed;
   Death to such deeds of shame is the due meed.

---

[1] 'Learned those languages perfectly.'   [2] 'In the hope that.'
[3] Reconciled.   [4] Expresses.   [5] Faithful.

Enter JENKIN *and* CECILY

JENK. Oh, my mistress, mistress, my poor mistress!

CICELY. Alas, that ever I was born! What shall I do for my poor
  mistress?

CHAR. Why, what of her?

JENK. O Lord, sir, she no sooner heard that her brother and her
  friends were come to see how she did, but she, for very shame
  of her guilty conscience, fell into such a swoon that we had
  much ado to get life in her.   30

SUSAN. Alas, that she should bear so hard a fate!
  Pity it is repentance comes too late.

FRAN. Is she so weak in body?

JENK. Oh, sir, I can assure you there's no hope of life in her,
  for she will take no sustenance; she hath plainly starved herself, and now she's as lean as a lath. She ever looks for the
  good hour. Many gentlemen and gentlewomen of the country
  are come to comfort her.

[ACT V. SCENE 5]

[MISTRESS FRANKFORD'S *bedroom*]

Enter MISTRESS FRANKFORD *in her bed*[1]

MAL. How fare you, Mistress Frankford?

ANNE. Sick, sick, oh, sick! Give me some air, I pray you.
  Tell me, oh, tell me, where's Master Frankford?
  Will not he deign to see me ere I die?

MAL. Yes, Mistress Frankford; divers gentlemen,
  Your loving neighbours, with that just request
  Have mov'd, and told him of your weak estate;
  Who, though with much ado to get belief,
  Examining of the general circumstance,
  Seeing your sorrow and your penitence,   10
  And hearing therewithal the great desire
  You have to see him ere you left the world,

---

[1] An impressionistic scene change; the characters remain on stage, the
setting being changed by the revelation of the bed, from behind a curtain,
perhaps that of the inner stage. Anne's bed may have been moved downstage, as the original direction implies.

He gave to us his faith [1] to follow us,
And sure he will be here immediately.

ANNE. You have half reviv'd me with the pleasing news;
Raise me a little higher in my bed.
Blush I not, brother Acton? Blush I not, Sir Charles?
Can you not read my fault writ in my cheek?
Is not my crime there? Tell me, gentlemen.

CHAR. Alas, good mistress, sickness hath not left you
Blood in your face enough to make you blush.

ANNE. Then sickness, like a friend, my fault would hide.
Is my husband come? My soul but tarries
His arrive; then I am fit for Heaven.

FRAN. I came to chide you, but my words of hate
Are turn'd to pity and compassionate grief.
I came to rate you, but my brawls,[2] you see,
Melt into tears, and I must weep by thee.
Here's Master Frankford now.

Enter FRANKFORD

FRANK. Good morrow, brother; morrow, gentlemen.
God, that hath laid this cross upon our heads,
Might, had He pleas'd, have made our cause of meeting
On a more fair and more contented ground;
But He that made us made us to this woe.

ANNE. And is he come? Methinks that voice I know.

FRANK. How do you, woman?

ANNE. Well, Master Frankford, well; but shall be better,
I hope, within this hour. Will you vouchsafe,
Out of your grace and your humanity,
To take a spotted strumpet by the hand?

FRANK. This hand once held my heart in faster bonds
Than now 'tis gripp'd by me. God pardon them
That made us first break hold.

ANNE.   Amen, amen.
Out of zeal to Heaven, whither I'm now bound,
I was so impudent to wish you here,
And once more beg your pardon. O good man,
And father to my children, pardon me!
Pardon, oh, pardon me! My fault so heinous is,
That if you in this world forgive it not,

----

[1] Pledge.   [2] Reproaches.

Heaven will not clear it in the world to come.   50
Faintness hath so usurp'd [1] upon my knees
That kneel I cannot; but on my heart's knees
My prostrate soul lies thrown down at your feet,
To beg your gracious pardon. Pardon, oh, pardon me!

FRANK. As freely, from the low depth of my soul,
As my Redeemer hath forgiven His death,
I pardon thee. I will shed tears for thee,
Pray with thee; and, in mere pity of thy weak estate,
I'll wish to die with thee.

ALL.   So do we all.

NICH. [*Aside.*] So will not I;   60
I'll sigh and sob, but, by my faith, not die.

FRAN. O Master Frankford, all the near alliance
I lose by her shall be suppli'd in thee.
You are my brother by the nearest way;
Her kindred hath fall'n off, but yours doth stay.[2]

FRANK. [*To* ANNE.] Even as I hope for pardon at that day
When the great Judge of Heaven in scarlet sits,
So be thou pardon'd. Though thy rash offence
Divorc'd our bodies, thy repentant tears
Unite our souls.

CHAR.   Then comfort, Mistress Frankford;   70
You see your husband hath forgiven your fall.
Then rouse your spirits and cheer your fainting soul.

SUSAN. How is it with you?

FRAN.   How d'ye feel yourself?

ANNE. Not of this world.

FRANK. I see you are not, and I weep to see it.
My wife, the mother to my pretty babes—
Both those lost names I do restore thee back,
And with this kiss I wed thee once again.
Though thou art wounded in thy honour'd name,
And with that grief upon thy death-bed liest,   80
Honest in heart, upon my soul, thou diest.

ANNE. Pardon'd on earth, soul, thou in Heaven art free;
Once more thy wife—dies thus embracing thee.

FRANK. New married, and new widow'd. Oh, she's dead;
And a cold grave must be her nuptial bed.

---

[1] Seized.
[2] 'My relationship with her diminishes [as she dies], but it remains constant with you.'

CHAR. Sir, be of good comfort; and your heavy sorrow
  Part equally amongst us. Storms divided
  Abate their force, and with less rage are guided.
CRAN. Do, Master Frankford; he that hath least part
  Will find enough to drown one troubled heart.
FRAN. Peace with thee, Nan. Brothers and gentlemen,
  All we that can plead interest in her grief,
  Bestow upon her body funeral tears.
  Brother, had you with threats and usage bad
  Punish'd her sin, the grief of her offence
  Had not with such true sorrow touch'd her heart.
FRANK. I see it had not; therefore, on her grave
  Will I bestow this funeral epitaph,
  Which on her marble tomb shall be engrav'd.
  In golden letters shall these words be fill'd: [1]
  Here lies she whom her husband's kindness kill'd.

FINIS

The Epilogue

An honest crew, disposed to be merry,
Came to a tavern by,[2] and call'd for wine.
The drawer brought it, smiling like a cherry,
And told them it was pleasant, neat,[3] and fine.
  'Taste it,' quoth one. He did so; 'Fie,' quoth he,
  'This wine was good; now 't runs too near the lee.' [4]

Another sipp'd, to give the wine his due,
And said unto the rest it drunk too flat;
The third said it was old; the fourth, too new;
'Nay,' quoth the fifth, 'the sharpness likes me not.'
  Thus, gentlemen, you see how in one hour
  The wine was new, old, flat, sharp, sweet, and sour.

Unto this wine we do allude [5] our play,
Which some will judge too trivial, some too grave.
You as our guests we entertain this day,
And bid you welcome to the best we have.
  Excuse us then; good wine may be disgrac'd
  When every several mouth hath sundry taste.

[1] 'The incised letters will be filled in with gold.'   [2] Near by.
[3] Pure, undiluted.   [4] Dregs.   [5] Compare.

JOHN MARSTON
(c. 1575–1634)

Born Oxfordshire; graduated from Oxford (1591);
studied at Middle Temple. After brief career as
dramatist (1598–c. 1609) entered the Church. Collaborated with Dekker and others in *Satiromastix*
and *Eastward Ho!* Best known independent plays
Antonio and Mellida, *Antonio's Revenge*, *The Dutch
Courtesan*, and *The Malcontent*.

THE MALCONTENT (1604)

'HONESTY is but an art to seem so'; this line from the play brings its cynical and satirical tone clearly into focus and conveys the Italianate or Machiavellian atmosphere of the plot and setting. Marston's sordid but untragic Genoa is in sharp contrast to the sunny optimism of Dekker's London, but *The Malcontent* represents a *genre* which had great popularity, revealing changing tastes and social values. Its commentary on social decadence may well reflect the author's personal disillusion with life, as he concentrated on Malvole's railing at the deficiencies of his fellow men from behind a fictional façade.

The plot of the play advances through a series of interwoven intrigues (with a few minor side excursions), uniting Malvole's efforts to reinstate himself in his lost position and Mendoza's villainous attempts to strengthen his illegitimate position. The final outcome of the tragicomedy, with its abrupt and casual dismissal of Mendoza, seems disproportionate to the elaborate preparation for it (compare Kyd's *Spanish Tragedy*). The implication behind the events is that, in spite of a purging in Genoa, the world beyond remains still receptive to the practice of Mendoza's treacherous arts.

Marston's uneven, surging poetry which drifts easily into prose mirrors the unrest and violence of the play; there is much sharp-edged imagery, especially of lust, deception, and filth. Old Bilioso is brilliantly described as 'a pigeon-house . . . smooth, round, and white without, and full of holes and stink within'. One of the author's milder sarcastic allusions to feminine vanity concerns 'an old lady gracious by torchlight'.

Marston had a considerable dramatic ability; it is occasionally heavy-handed, but he did convey memorably the bitterness of his commentary on the state of the word he saw, a world of corruption, decadence, and intrigue still recognizable to the pessimist today.

In the seventeenth-century quarto editions of the play the five acts are conventionally divided, but within each act Marston followed the elaborate and artificial French convention of scene division; it is distinguished by beginning a new scene with the entrance of a new major character or group of characters, although Marston was inconsistent and arbitrary in his practice. This edition retains the five-act structure of the quartos, but the scenes are set off to conform to more familiar later conventions of scene division. (A footnote locates Marston's divisions.)

The three early editions of the play all date from 1604; the content of the three quartos is similar, with the exception of the induction (by John Webster) and additions to the text which supplement the third quarto. The order and arrangement of information on the Q_3 title-page and in the heading of the induction suggest ambiguously and erroneously that Webster wrote both the additions and the induction.

Since Q_3 obviously represented Marston's final intention in the play, that text is the foundation of the present edition, with a few minor readings from Q_1 and Q_2. A footnote indicates the presence of important Q_3 additions.

The Malcontent
by John Marston
1604

Benjamino Jonsonio, poetae elegantissimo, gravissimo, amico
suo, candido et cordato, Johannes Marston, Musarum alumnus,
asperam hanc suam thaliam d[ono] d[edit].[1]

[1] To Benjamin Jonson, the most elegant and weighty poet, his sincere and
judicious friend, John Marston, disciple of the Muses, gives and dedicates
this his rough comedy. [Marston and Jonson quarrelled frequently before and
after this occasion.]

To the Reader

I am an ill orator; and, in truth, use to indite more honestly than eloquently, for it is my custom to speak as I think, and write as I speak.

In plainness, therefore, understand that in some things I have willingly erred, as in supposing a Duke of Genoa, and in taking names different from that city's families; for which some may wittily [1] accuse me, but my defence shall be as honest as many reproofs unto me have been most malicious; since, I heartily protest, it was my care to write so far from reasonable offence that even strangers, in whose state I laid my scene, should not from thence draw any disgrace to any, dead or living. Yet, in despite of my endeavours, I understand some have been most unadvisedly over-cunning in misinterpreting me, and with subtlety as deep as hell have maliciously spread ill rumours, which, springing from themselves, might to themselves have heavily returned. Surely I desire to satisfy every firm spirit, who, in all his actions, proposeth to himself no more ends than God and virtue do, whose intentions are always simple. To such I protest that, with my free understanding, I have not glanced at disgrace of any, but of those whose unquiet studies labour innovation, [2] contempt of holy policy, reverend, comely superiority, and established unity. For the rest of my supposed tartness, I fear not, but unto every worthy mind it will be approved so general and honest as may modestly pass with the freedom of a satire. I would fain leave the paper; only one thing afflicts me: to think that scenes invented merely to be spoken should be enforcively published to be read, and that the least hurt I can receive is to do myself the wrong. But, since others otherwise would do me more, the least inconvenience is to be accepted. I have myself, therefore, set forth this comedy; but so, [3] that my enforced absence must much rely upon the printer's discretion; but I shall entreat slight errors in orthography may be as slightly [4] overpassed, and that the unhandsome shape, which this trifle in reading presents, may be pardoned for the pleasure it once afforded you, when it was presented with the soul of lively action.

Sine aliqua dementia nullus Phoebus. [5]

J. M.

---

[1] Shrewdly. [2] Work towards revolution.
[3] In such circumstances. [4] Readily.
[5] No poetic genius without some madness. Some copies of Q₁ have *Me mea sequentur fata* ('My fates will follow me').

[*Dramatis Personae* of the Induction (members of the Company of
  His Majesty's Servants, at the Globe Theatre)

WILLIAM SLY
JOHN SINKLO
RICHARD BURBAGE
HENRY CONDELL
JOHN LOWIN
TIRE-MAN [1]]

Dramatis Personae

GIOVANNI ALTOFRONTO, disguised Malvole, sometime Duke of Genoa
PIETRO JACOMO, Duke of Genoa
MENDOZA, a minion [2] to the duchess of Pietro Jacomo
CELSO, a friend to Altofronto
BILIOSO, an old choleric marshal
PREPASSO, a gentleman usher
FERNEZE, a young courtier, enamoured on the duchess
FERRARDO, a minion to Duke Pietro Jacomo
EQUATO } two courtiers
GUERRINO }
PASSARELLO, fool to Bilioso [3]
[CAPTAIN OF THE CITADEL]
[MERCURY]
AURELIA, duchess to Duke Pietro Jacomo
MARIA, duchess to Duke Altofronto
EMILIA } two ladies attending Duchess Aurelia
BIANCA }
MAQUERELLE, an old panderess
[COURTIERS, PAGES, GUARDS]
[SCENE: Genoa.]

[1] The stage-manager, also in charge of properties and costumes.
[2] Favourite.
[3] This character was added in Q₃.

The Induction to *The Malcontent*.[1]

Written by John Webster.

[The stage of the Globe Theatre]

Enter WILLIAM SLY, *a tire-man following him with a stool*

TIRE. Sir, the gentlemen will be angry if you sit here.

SLY. Why? We may sit upon the stage at the private house.[2]
Thou dost not take me for a country gentleman, dost? Dost
think I fear hissing? I'll hold my life thou took'st me for one
of the players.

TIRE. No, sir.

SLY. By God's lid, if you had, I would have given you but sixpence for your stool. Let them that have stale suits sit in the
galleries. Hiss at me! He that will be laughed out of a tavern or
an ordinary shall seldom feed well or be drunk in good com-   10
pany. Where's Harry Condell, Dick Burbage, and Will Sly?
Let me speak with some of them.

TIRE. An 't please you to go in, sir, you may.

SLY. I tell you, no. I am one that hath seen this play often, and
can give them intelligence for the action. I have most of the
jests here in my table-book.

Enter SINKLO

SINK. Save you, coz.

SLY. Oh, cousin, come; you shall sit between my legs here.

SINK. No, indeed, cousin; the audience then will take me for a
viol da gamba,[3] and think that you play upon me.   20

SLY. Nay, rather that I work upon you, coz.

SINK. We stayed for you at supper last night at my cousin
Honeymoon's, the woollen-draper. After supper we drew cuts
for a score of apricots, the longest cut still to draw an apricot.
By this light, 'twas Mistress Frank Honeymoon's fortune still
to have the longest cut; I did measure for the women. What be
these, coz?

[1] Q₃ has as well, 'And the additions acted by the King's Majesty's
Servants.' The additions were actually written by Marston.
[2] Blackfriars Theatre, where the Children of the Queen's Revels originally
performed *The Malcontent*.   [3] Bass viol.

Enter DICK BURBAGE, HENRY CONDELL, *and* JOHN
LOWIN

SLY. The players.—God save you.

BUR. You are very welcome.

SLY. I pray you, know this gentleman, my cousin; 'tis Master
Doomsday's son, the usurer.

COND. I beseech you, sir, be covered.

SLY. No, in good faith—for mine ease. Look you, my hat's the
handle to this fan.[1] God's so,[2] what a beast was I, I did not
leave my feather at home. Well, but I'll take an order with
you. *Puts his feather in his pocket.*

BUR. Why do you conceal your feather, sir?

SLY. Why, do you think I'll have jests broken upon me in the
play, to be laughed at? This play hath beaten all your gallants
out of the feathers. Blackfriars hath almost spoiled Blackfriars
for feathers.[3]

SINK. God's so, I thought 'twas for somewhat our gentlewomen at home counselled me to wear my feather to the play;
yet I am loath to spoil it.

SLY. Why, coz?

SINK. Because I got it in the tilt-yard.[4] There was a herald
broke my pate for taking it up; but I have worn it up and
down the Strand, and met him forty times since, and yet he
dares not challenge it.

SLY. Do you hear, sir? This play is a bitter play.

COND. Why, sir, 'tis neither satire nor moral, but the mean
passage of a history. Yet there are a sort of discontented
creatures that bear a stingless envy to great ones, and these
will wrest the doings of any man to their base, malicious
applyment. But should their interpretation come to the test,
like your marmoset,[5] they presently turn their teeth to their
tail and eat it.

SLY. I will not go so far with you; but I say any man that hath
wit may censure, if he sit in the twelve-penny room;[6] and I
say again, the play is bitter.

BUR. Sir, you are like a patron that, presenting a poor scholar to
a benefice, enjoins him not to rail against anything that stands

[1] His feather.
[2] A variation of 'Catso', an Italian exclamation.
[3] This play, first presented at Blackfriars Theatre, ridiculed affectation, to
the discomfiture of the wearers and vendors of feathers.
[4] Tournament ground.   [5] Monkey.   [6] Box.

within compass of his patron's folly. Why should not we
enjoy the ancient freedom of poesy? Shall we protest to the
ladies that their painting makes them angels, or to my young
gallant that his expense in the brothel shall gain him reputation? No, sir, such vices as stand not accountable to law should
be cured as men heal tetters,[1] by casting ink upon them.
Would you be satisfied in anything else, sir?

SLY. Ay, marry, would I. I would know how you came by this   70
    play.

COND. Faith, sir, the book was lost, and because 'twas pity so
    good a play should be lost, we found it and play it.

SLY. I wonder you would play it, another company having an
    interest in it.

COND. Why not Malvole in folio with us, as Jeronimo in
    decimo-sexto with them? They taught us a name for our
    play: we call it *One for Another*.[2]

SLY. What are your additions?

BUR. Sooth, not greatly needful; only as your sallet[3] to your   80
    great feast, to entertain a little more time, and to abridge the
    not-received custom of music in our theatre. I must leave
    you, sir.   *Exit* BURBAGE.

SINK. Doth he play the malcontent?

COND. Yes, sir.

SINK. I durst lay[4] four of mine ears the play is not so well acted
    as it hath been.

COND. Oh no, sir, nothing *ad Parmenonis suem*.[5]

LOW. Have you lost your ears, sir, that you are so prodigal of
    laying them?   90

SINK. Why did you ask that, friend?

LOW. Marry, sir, because I have heard of a fellow would offer to
    lay a hundred-pound wager, that was not worth five baubees;[6]
    and in this kind you might venture four of your elbows. Yet
    God defend[7] your coat should have so many.

SINK. Nay, truly, I am no great censurer; and yet I might have

---

[1] Skin eruptions.
[2] The King's Men (i.e. 'folio' actors) had evidently appropriated *The
Malcontent* from the Children of the Queen's Revels ('16mo' actors) in
retaliation for their having pirated *The First Part of Jeronimo* (an anonymous
comedy), the property of the King's Men.
[3] Salad.   [4] Wager.
[5] 'Nothing to Parmeno's pig'; the implication is, 'Don't make disparaging
comparisons rashly.' Roman critics were tricked into claiming that the actor
Parmeno's imitation of the grunting of a pig was superior to the real thing.
[6] Scotch halfpennies.   [7] Forbid.

been one of the college of critics once. My cousin here hath an
excellent memory indeed, sir.

SLY. Who, I? I'll tell you a strange thing of myself; and I can
tell you, for one that never studied the art of memory, 'tis
very strange too.

COND. What's that, sir?

SLY. Why, I'll lay a hundred pound, I'll walk but once down
by the Goldsmiths' Row in Cheap, take notice of the signs,
and tell you them with a breath instantly.

LOW. 'Tis very strange.

SLY. They begin as the world did, with Adam and Eve.
There's in all just five-and-fifty.[1] I do use to meditate much
when I come to plays too. What do you think might come
into a man's head now, seeing all this company?

COND. I know not, sir.

SLY. I have an excellent thought: if some fifty of the Grecians
that were crammed in the horse-belly had eaten garlic, do you
not think the Trojans might have smelt out their knavery?

COND. Very likely.

SLY. By God, I would they had, for I love Hector horribly.

SINK. Oh, but, coz, coz,—
    'Great Alexander, when he came to the tomb of Achilles,
    Spake with a big loud voice, "O thou thrice blessed and
        happy."'[2]

SLY. Alexander was an ass to speak so well of a filthy cullion.[3]

LOW. Good sir, will you leave the stage? I'll help you to a
private room.

SLY. Come, coz, let's take some tobacco. Have you never a
prologue?

LOW. Not any, sir.

SLY. Let me see; I will make one extempore. Come to them,
and fencing of a congee [4] with arms and legs, be round [5] with
them. 'Gentlemen, I could wish for the women's sakes you
had all soft cushions; and, gentlewomen, I could wish that for
the men's sakes you had all more easy standings.' What would
they wish more but the play now? And that they shall have
instantly.   [*Exeunt.*]

---

[1] An exaggerated figure; the number was probably closer to a dozen.
[2] Petrarch, Sonnet 153, trans. John Harvey.
[3] Rascal.   [4] Ceremonious bow.   [5] Severe.

THE MALCONTENT

ACT I. SCENE 1 [1]
[The palace of PIETRO, *Duke of Genoa]*

The vilest out-of-tune music being heard, enter BILIOSO *and*
PREPASSO

BIL. Why, how now? are ye mad, or drunk, or both, or what?
PREP. Are ye building Babylon there?
BIL. Here's a noise in court! You think you are in a tavern, do
you not?
PREP. You think you are in a brothel-house, do you not?
This room is ill-scented.

Enter one with a perfume

So, perfume, perfume; some upon me, I pray thee.
The duke is upon instant entrance; so, make place there!

Enter DUKE PIETRO, FERRARDO, COUNT EQUATO,
COUNT CELSO, *and* GUERRINO [2]

PIET. Where breathes that music?
BIL. The discord rather than the music is heard from the mal-   10
content Malvole's chamber.
FERR. Malvole!
MAL. (*Out of his chamber.*[3]) Yaugh, God o' man, what dost
thou there? Duke's Ganymede,[4] Juno's jealous of thy long
stockings. Shadow of a woman, what wouldst, weasel? Thou
lamb o' court, what dost thou bleat for? Ah, you smooth-
chinned catamite.[4]
PIET. Come down, thou ragged cur, and snarl here. I give thy
dogged sullenness free liberty; trot about and bespurtle whom
thou pleasest.   20

[1] In the right margin of the quartos: '*Vexat censura columbas.*' ('Censor-
ship troubles the doves.'—Juvenal, *Satires*, ii. 63.)
[2] Act I, Scene 2—quartos.
[3] The upper stage.   [4] Male prostitute.

153

MAL. I'll come among you, you goatish-blooded toderers,[1] as
gum into taffeta, to fret, to fret. I'll fall like a sponge into
water to suck up, to suck up. Howl again. I'll go to church and
come to you.   [*Exit.*]

PIET. This Malvole is one of the most prodigious affections [2]
that ever conversed with nature; a man, or rather, a monster,
more discontent than Lucifer when he was thrust out of the
presence. His appetite is insatiable as the grave, as far from
any content as from Heaven. His highest delight is to procure
others' vexation, and therein he thinks he truly serves
Heaven; for 'tis his position,[3] whosoever in this earth can be
contented is a slave and damned; therefore does he afflict all
in that to which they are most affected.[4] Th' elements struggle
within him; his own soul is at variance within herself; his
speech is halter-worthy at all hours. I like him, faith; he gives
good intelligence to my spirit, makes me understand those
weaknesses which others' flattery palliates. Hark, they sing.

[*A Song*]

Enter MALVOLE, *after the song* [5]

See, he comes. Now shall you hear the extremity of a malcontent. He is as free as air; he blows over every man.—And,
sir, whence come you now?

MAL. From the public place of much dissimulation, the
church.[6]

PIET. What didst there?

MAL. Talk with a usurer; take up at interest.

PIET. I wonder what religion thou art of.

MAL. Of a soldier's religion.

PIET. And what dost think makes most infidels now?

MAL. Sects, sects. I have seen seeming Piety change her robe so
oft that sure none but some arch-devil can shape her a new
petticoat.

PIET. Oh, a religious policy.

MAL. But damnation on a politic religion! I am weary; would I
were one of the duke's hounds now.

---

[1] Libertines.   [2] Dispositions.   [3] Thesis.
[4] Partial.   [5] I. 3—quartos.
[6] 'The church' is censored from some copies of the quartos.

PIET. But what's the common news abroad, Malvole? Thou dogg'st rumour still.

MAL. Common news? Why, common words are, 'God save ye', 'Fare ye well'; common actions, flattery and cozenage; common things, women and cuckolds. And how does my little Ferrard? Ah, ye lecherous animal, my little ferret; he goes sucking up and down the palace into every hen's nest, like a weasel; and to what dost thou addict thy time to now, more than to those antique painted drabs that are still affected of [1] young courtiers: Flattery, Pride, and Venery? 60

FERR. I study languages. Who dost think to be the best linguist of our age?

MAL. Phew! The devil! Let him possess thee; he'll teach thee to speak all languages most readily and strangely—and great reason, marry, he's travelled greatly in the world and is everywhere.

FERR. Save i' th' court. 70

MAL. Ay, save i' th' court. (To BILIOSO.) And how does my old muckhill, overspread with fresh snow? Thou half a man, half a goat, all a beast. How does thy young wife, old huddle? [2]

BIL. Out, you improvident rascal!

MAL. Do; kick, thou hugely-horned old duke's ox, good Master Make-place.

PIET. How dost thou live nowadays, Malvole?

MAL. Why, like the knight, Sir Patrick Penlolians, [3] with killing o' spiders for my lady's monkey.

PIET. How dost spend the night? I hear thou never sleep'st. 80

MAL. Oh no, but dream the most fantastical. O Heaven! O fubbery, [4] fubbery!

PIET. Dream? What dream'st?

MAL. Why, methinks I see that signior pawn his foot-cloth, [5] that metreza [6] her plate; this madam take physic that t'other monsieur may minister to her; here is a pander jeweled; there is a fellow in shift of satin this day that could not shift a shirt t'other night; here a Paris supports that Helen; there's a Lady Guinever bears up that Sir Lancelot. Dreams, dreams, visions, fantasies, chimeras, imaginations, tricks, conceits! (To 90 PREPASSO.) Sir Tristram Trimtram, come aloft, Jackanapes, [7]

---

[1] Cherished by.   [2] Miserly old man.
[3] Not identified.   [4] Deception.
[5] An ornamented cloth for the back of a horse.
[6] Mistress (Ital.).   [7] A trainer's call to his monkey or ape.

with a whim-wham; here's a knight of the land of Catito [1]
shall play at trap [2] with any page in Europe; do the sword-
dance with any morris-dancer in Christendom; ride at the
ring [3] till the fin [4] of his eyes look as blue as the welkin; and
run the wild-goose chase even with Pompey the Huge.

PIET. You run—

MAL. To the devil. Now, Signior Guerrino, that thou from a
most pitied prisoner shouldst grow a most loathed flatterer!—
Alas, poor Celso, thy star's oppressed; thou art an honest
lord, 'tis pity.

EQUATO. Is't pity?

MAL. Ay, marry is't, philosophical Equato, and 'tis pity that
thou, being so excellent a scholar by art, shouldst be so
ridiculous a fool by nature. I have a thing to tell you, Duke;
bid 'um avaunt, bid 'um avaunt.

PIET. Leave us, leave us.
                              Exeunt all saving PIETRO *and* MALVOLE.
Now, sir, what is't?

MAL. Duke, thou art a becco,[5] a cornuto.[5]

PIET. How!

MAL. Thou art a cuckold.

PIET. Speak! Unshale [6] him quick.

MAL. With most tumbler-like nimbleness.

PIET. Who? By whom? I burst with desire.

MAL. Mendoza is the man makes thee a horned beast. Duke,
'tis Mendoza cornutes thee.

PIET. What conformance? [7] Relate—short, short.

MAL. As a lawyer's beard.
    [*Sings.*] 'There is an old crone in the court, her name is
        Maquerelle;
    She is my mistress, sooth to say, and she doth ever tell me.'
    Blirt [8] o' rhyme! Maquerelle is a cunning bawd, I am an
    honest villain, thy wife is a close drab,[9] and thou art a
    notorious cuckold. Farewell, Duke.

PIET. Stay, stay.

MAL. Dull, dull Duke, can lazy patience make lame revenge?
O God, for a woman to make a man that which God never
created, never made!

---

[1] i.e. the land of children's games, such as cat.   [2] A ball game.
[3] To tilt at a ring suspended on a post.   [4] Lid.
[5] Cuckold (Ital.).   [6] Unshell, reveal.   [7] Confirmation.
[8] Outburst.   [9] A secret strumpet.

PIET. What did God never make?

MAL. A cuckold; to be made a thing that's hoodwinked with   130
kindness, whilst every rascal fillips his brows; to have a coxcomb [1] with egregious horns pinned to a lord's back, every
page sporting himself with delightful laughter, whilst he must
be the last must know it. Pistols and poniards, pistols and
poniards!

PIET. Death and damnation!

MAL. Lightning and thunder!

PIET. Vengeance and torture!

MAL. Catso!

PIET. Oh, revenge!   140

MAL. Nay, to select among ten thousand fairs [2]
A lady far inferior to the most,
In fair proportion both of limb and soul;
To take her from austerer check of parents,
To make her his by most devoutful rites,
Make her commandress of a better essence
Than is the gorgeous world, even, of a man,
To hug her with as rais'd an appetite
As usurers do their delv'd-up treasury,
Thinking none tells [3] it but his private self;   150
To meet her spirit in a nimble kiss,
Distilling panting ardour to her heart;
True to her sheets, nay, diets strong his blood,[4]
To give her height of hymeneal sweets—

PIET. O God!

MAL. Whilst she lisps and gives him some court *quelquechose*,[5]
Made only to provoke, not satiate;
And yet, even then, the thaw of her delight
Flows from the lewd heat of apprehension,[6]
Only from strange imagination's rankness,   160
That forms the adulterer's presence in her soul,
And makes her think she clips [7] the foul knave's loins.

PIET. Affliction to my blood's root!

MAL. Nay, think, but think what may proceed of this; adultery
is often the mother of incest.

PIET. Incest?

MAL. Yes, incest. Mark: Mendoza of his wife begets perchance

---

[1] Fool's cap.   [2] Lines 141–82 added in Q₃.
[3] Counts.   [4] Regulates his passion severely.
[5] Kickshaw, delicacy.   [6] Anticipation.   [7] Embraces.

a daughter; Mendoza dies; his son marries this daughter; say
you? Nay, 'tis frequent; not only probable, but no question
often acted, whilst ignorance, fearless ignorance, clasps his
own seed.

PIET. Hideous imagination!

MAL. Adultery? Why, next to the sin of simony, 'tis the most
horrid transgression under the cope of salvation.[1]

PIET. Next to simony?

MAL. Ay, next to simony, in which our men in next age shall
not sin.

PIET. Not sin? Why?

MAL. Because, thanks to some churchmen, our age will leave
them nothing to sin with. But adultery—O dullness!—
should show exemplary punishment, that intemperate bloods
may freeze but to think it. I would damn him and all his
generation; my own hands should do it. Ha! I would not trust
Heaven with my vengeance, anything.

PIET. Anything, anything, Malvole! Thou shalt see instantly
what temper my spirit holds. Farewell; remember I forget
thee not; farewell.   *Exit.*

MAL. Farewell.[2]
    Lean thoughtfulness, a shallow meditation
    Suck thy veins dry! Distemperance rob thy sleep!
    The heart's disquiet is revenge most deep.
    He that gets blood, the life of flesh but spills,
    But he that breaks heart's peace, the dear soul kills.
    Well, this disguise doth yet afford me that
    Which kings do seldom hear, or great men use,
    Free speech; and though my state's usurp'd,
    Yet this affected strain gives me a tongue
    As fetterless as is an emperor's.
    I may speak foolishly, ay, knavishly,
    Always carelessly; yet no one thinks it fashion
    To poise [3] my breath; for he that laughs and strikes
    Is lightly felt, or seldom struck again.[4]
    Duke, I'll torment thee; now my just revenge
    From thee than crown a richer gem shall part.
    Beneath God, naught's so dear as a calm heart.

---

[1] The cloak of salvation; i.e. Heaven.
[2] Lines 188–205 added in Q3.
[3] Weigh, value.   [4] In return.

Enter CELSO [1]

CEL. My honour'd Lord,—
MAL. Peace, speak low, peace. O Celso, constant lord,
   Thou to whose faith I only rest discover'd,[2]
   Thou, one of full ten millions of men,
   That lovest virtue only for itself,   210
   Thou in whose hands old Ops [3] may put her soul,
   Behold for ever-banish'd Altofront,
   This Genoa's last year's duke. Oh, truly noble!
   I wanted [4] those old instruments of state,
   Dissemblance and suspect; I could not time it,[5] Celso;
   My throne stood like a point in midst of a circle,
   To all of equal nearness; bore with [6] none;
   Reign'd all alike; so slept in fearless virtue,
   Suspectless, too suspectless; till the crowd,
   Still lickerous [7] of untried novelties,   220
   Impatient with severer government,
   Made strong with Florence, banish'd Altofront.
CEL. Strong with Florence! Ay, thence your mischief rose;
   For when the daughter of the Florentine
   Was match'd once with this Pietro, now duke,
   No stratagem of state untri'd was left,
   Till you of all—
MAL.   Of all was quite bereft.
   Alas, Maria too, close prisoned,
   My true-faith'd duchess, i' th' citadel!
CEL. I'll still adhere; let's mutiny and die.   230
MAL. Oh no; climb not a falling tower, Celso;
   'Tis well held desperation, no zeal,
   Hopeless to strive with fate. Peace; temporize.
   Hope, hope, that never forsak'st the wretched'st man,
   Yet bidd'st me live, and lurk in this disguise.
   What, play I well the free-breath'd discontent?
   Why, man, we are all philosophical monarchs
   Or natural fools. Celso, the court's afire;
   The duchess' sheets will smoke for't ere it be long.
   Impure Mendoza, that sharp-nos'd lord, that made   240

---

[1] I. 4—quartos.   [2] 'I stand revealed only to your trust.'
[3] The goddess of plenty.   [4] Lacked.
[5] 'I could not adapt myself to these conditions.'
[6] Favoured.   [7] Greedy.

The cursed match link'd Genoa with Florence,
Now broad-horns the duke, which he now knows.
Discord to malcontents is very manna;
When the ranks are burst, then scuffle, Altofront.
CEL. Ay, but durst—
MAL. 'Tis gone; 'tis swallow'd like a mineral.[1]
  Some way 'twill work—Pheut! I'll not shrink;
  He's resolute who can no lower sink.

BILIOSO *entering,* MALVOLE *shifteth his speech* [2]

Oh, the father of Maypoles! Did you never see a fellow whose
strength consisted in his breath, respect in his office, religion
in his lord, and love in himself? Why, then, behold.
BIL. Signior,—
MAL. My right worshipful Lord, your court night-cap makes
  you have a passing high forehead.
BIL. I can tell you strange news, but I am sure you know them
  already: the duke speaks much good of you.
MAL. Go to,[3] then; and shall you and I now enter into a strict
  friendship?
BIL. Second one another?
MAL. Yes.
BIL. Do one another good offices?
MAL. Just. What though I called thee old ox, egregious wittol,[4]
  broken-bellied coward, rotten mummy? Yet, since I am in
  favour—
BIL. Words of course, terms of disport. His grace presents you
  by me a chain, as his grateful remembrance for—I am
  ignorant for what. Marry, ye may impart. Yet howsoever—
  come—dear friend. Dost know my son?
MAL. Your son?
BIL. He shall eat woodcocks, dance jigs, make possets,[5] and
  play at shuttlecock with any young lord about the court. He
  has as sweet a lady too; dost know her little bitch?
MAL. 'Tis a dog, man.
BIL. Believe me, a she-bitch. Oh, 'tis a good creature. Thou
  shalt be her servant.[6] I'll make thee acquainted with my

---

[1] Medicine.   [2] The stage direction and lines 249–93 added in Q₃.
[3] An expression of impatience.
[4] Complacent cuckold.
[5] Hot mixed drinks, often medicinal.   [6] Paramour.

young wife too. What, I keep her not at court for nothing.
'Tis grown to supper time; come to my table; that, anything
I have, stands open to thee.

MAL. (*Aside to* CELSO.) How smooth to him that is in state of   280
grace,
How servile is the rugged'st courtier's face!
What profit, nay, what nature would keep down,
Are heav'd to them are minions to a crown.
Envious ambition never sates his thirst,
Till, sucking all, he swells and swells, and bursts.

BIL. I shall now leave you with my always-best wishes; only
let's hold betwixt us a firm correspondence,[1] a mutual
friendly-reciprocal kind of steady-unanimous-heartily-
leagued—

MAL. Did your signiorship ne'er see a pigeon-house that was   290
smooth, round, and white without, and full of holes and stink
within? Ha' ye not, old courtier?

BIL. Oh yes; 'tis the form, the fashion of them all.

MAL. Adieu, my true court-friend; farewell, my dear Castilio.[2]
                                        Exit BILIOSO.

CEL. (*Descrying* MENDOZA.) Yonder's Mendoza.

MAL.   True, the privy key.

CEL. I take my leave, sweet Lord.

MAL.   'Tis fit; away!
                                        Exit CELSO.

Enter MENDOZA *with three or four suitors* [3]

MEND. Leave your suits with me; I can and will. Attend my
secretary; leave me.   [*Exeunt suitors.*]

MAL. Mendoza, hark ye, hark ye. You are a treacherous
villain. God b' wi' ye.   300

MEND. Out, you base-born rascal!

MAL. We are all the sons of Heaven, though a tripe-wife [4] were
our mother. Ah, you whoreson, hot-rein'd [5] he-marmoset!
Aegisthus [6]—didst ever hear of one Aegisthus?

MEND. 'Gisthus?

---

[1] Agreement.
[2] A sarcastic allusion to the name which Castiglione gave himself in *The Courtier*.
[3] I. 5—quartos.   [4] A seller of tripe.
[5] Lecherous.   [6] Clytemnestra's paramour.

MAL. Ay, Aegisthus; he was a filthy, incontinent flesh-monger, such a one as thou art.

MEND. Out, grumbling rogue!

MAL. Orestes,[1] beware Orestes!

MEND. Out, beggar!

MAL. I once shall rise.

MEND. Thou rise?

MAL. Ay, at the resurrection.

No vulgar seed but once may rise and shall;
No king so huge but 'fore he die may fall.   *Exit.*

MEND. Now, good Elysium! What a delicious Heaven is it for a man to be in a prince's favour! O sweet God! O pleasure! O fortune! O all thou best of life! What should I think, what say, what do? To be a favourite, a minion! To have a general timorous respect observe [2] a man, a stateful silence in his presence, solitariness in his absence, a confused hum and busy murmur of obsequious suitors training [3] him; the cloth held up, the way proclaimed before him; petitionary vassals licking the pavement with their slavish knees, whilst some odd palace-lamprels [4] that engender with snakes, and are full of eyes on both sides, with a kind of insinuated humbleness, fix all their delights upon his brow. O blessed state! What a ravishing prospect doth the Olympus of favour yield! Death, I cornute the duke! Sweet women, most sweet ladies; nay, angels! By Heaven, he is more accursed than a devil that hates you, or is hated by you, and happier than a god that loves you, or is beloved by you! You preservers of mankind, life-blood of society, who would live, nay, who can live without you? O paradise, how majestical is your austerer presence, how imperiously chaste is your more modest face! But, oh, how full of ravishing attraction is your pretty, petulant, languishing, lasciviously-composed countenance! These amorous smiles, those soul-warming, sparkling glances, ardent as those flames that singed the world by heedless Phaeton! In body how delicate, in soul how witty, in discourse how pregnant, in life how wary, in favours how judicious, in day how sociable, and in night how—O pleasure unutterable! Indeed, it is most certain, one man cannot deserve only to enjoy a beauteous woman; but a duchess! In despite of Phoebus, I'll write a sonnet instantly in praise of her.   *Exit.*

[1] The son of Agamemnon who avenged the death of his father.
[2] Defer to.   [3] Following.   [4] Young lampreys.

[ACT I. SCENE 2] [1]

[*Another room in the palace*]

Enter FERNEZE *ushering* AURELIA; EMILIA *and*
MAQUERELLE *bearing up her train*, BIANCA *attending.*
All go out but AURELIA, MAQUERELLE, *and* FERNEZE

AUR. And is't possible? Mendoza slight me? Possible?

FERN. Possible!
What can be strange in him that's drunk with favour,
Grows insolent with grace? Speak, Maquerelle, speak.

MAQ. To speak feelingly, more, more richly in solid sense than
worthless words, give me those jewels of your ears to receive
my enforced duty. (FERNEZE *privately feeds* MAQUERELLE'S
hands with jewels during this speech.) As for my part, 'tis well
known I can put up [2] anything, can bear patiently with any
man; but when I heard he wronged your precious sweetness,   10
I was enforced to take deep offence. 'Tis most certain he loves
Emilia with high appetite, and, as she told me—as you know,
we women impart our secrets one to another—when she
repulsed his suit, in that he was possessed with your endeared
grace, Mendoza most ingratefully renounced all faith to you.

FERN. Nay, called you—speak, Maquerelle, speak.

MAQ. By Heaven, 'witch', 'dried biscuit'; and contested
blushlessly he loved you but for a spurt [3] or so.

FERN. For maintenance.

MAQ. Advancement and regard.   20

AUR. O villain! O impudent Mendoza!

MAQ. Nay, he is the rustiest jade,[4] the foulest-mouthed knave
in railing against our sex. He will rail against women—

AUR. How? How?

MAQ. I am ashamed to speak't, I.

AUR. I love to hate him; speak.

MAQ. Why, when Emilia scorned his base unsteadiness, the
black-throated rascal scolded and said—

AUR. What?

MAQ. Troth, 'tis too shameless.   30

AUR. What said he?

---

[1] I. 6—quartos.   [2] Endure.
[3] Brief period.   [4] Roughest old horse.

MAQ. Why, that at four, women were fools; at fourteen, drabs; at forty, bawds; at fourscore, witches; and [at] a hundred, cats.

AUR. Oh, unlimitable impudency!

FERN. But as for poor Ferneze's fixed heart,
Was never shadeless meadow drier parch'd
Under the scorching heat of heaven's dog [1]
Than is my heart with your enforcing [2] eyes.

MAQ. A hot simile.

FERN. Your smiles have been my Heaven, your frowns my hell;
Oh, pity then; grace should with beauty dwell.

MAQ. Reasonable perfect, by'r lady.

AUR. I will love thee, be it but in despite
Of that Mendoza. 'Witch!' Ferneze,—'Witch!'—
Ferneze, thou art the duchess' favourite;
Be faithful, private; but 'tis dangerous.

FERN. His love is lifeless that for love fears breath;
The worst that's due to sin, oh, would 'twere death.

AUR. Enjoy my favour. I will be sick instantly and take physic; therefore in depth of night visit—

MAQ. Visit her chamber, but conditionally: you shall not offend her bed. By this diamond.

FERN. By this diamond.   *Gives it to* MAQUERELLE.

MAQ. Nor tarry longer than you please. By this ruby.

FERN. By this ruby.   *Gives again.*

MAQ. And that the door shall not creak.

FERN. And that the door shall not creak.

MAQ. Nay, but swear.

FERN. By this purse.   *Gives her his purse.*

MAQ. Go to; I'll keep your oaths for you. Remember, visit.

Enter MENDOZA, *reading a sonnet; [he remains apart]*

AUR. 'Dried biscuit!' Look where the base wretch comes.

MEND. 'Beauty's life, Heaven's model, love's queen . . .'

MAQ. That's his Emilia.

MEND. 'Nature's triumph, best on earth . . .'

MAQ. Meaning Emilia.

MEND. 'Thou only wonder that the world hath seen . . .'

[1] Sirius, the dog star, which at certain times rises with the sun.
[2] Compelling.

MAQ. That's Emilia.

AUR. Must I then hear her praised? Mendoza!   70

MEND. [*Coming forward.*] Madam, your excellency is graciously
encount'red; I have been writing passionate flashes in honour
of—

Exit FERNEZE.

AUR. Out, villain, villain!
O judgment, where have been my eyes? What
Bewitch'd election made me dote on thee?
What sorcery made me love thee? But begone;
Bury thy head. Oh, that I could do more
Than loathe thee! Hence, worst of ill!
No reason ask; our reason is our will.   80

Exit, with attendants.

MEND. Women? Nay, Furies! Nay, worse; for they torment
only the bad; but women, good and bad. Damnation of mankind! Breath, hast thou praised them for this? And is't you,
Ferneze, are wriggled into smock-grace? Sit sure. Oh, that I
could rail against these monsters in nature, models of hell,
curse of the earth, women that dare attempt anything, and
what they attempt, they care not how they accomplish; without all premeditation or prevention, rash in asking, desperate
in working, impatient in suffering, extreme in desiring, slaves
unto appetite, mistresses in dissembling, only constant in   90
unconstancy, only perfect in counterfeiting; their words are
feigned, their eyes forged,[1] their sighs dissembled, their looks
counterfeit, their hair false, their given [2] hopes deceitful, their
very breath artificial; their blood [3] is their only god; bad
clothes and old age are only the devils they tremble at. That
I could rail now!

Enter PIETRO, *his sword drawn* [4]

PIET. A mischief fill thy throat, thou foul-jaw'd slave!
Say thy prayers.

MEND.   I ha' forgot 'um.

PIET.   Thou shalt die.

MEND. So shalt thou. I am heart-mad.

PIET.   I am horn-mad.[5]

---

[1] 'Made up.'   [2] Stated.
[3] Passion.   [4] I. 7—quartos.
[5] Stark mad (with implications of cuckoldry).

MEND. Extreme mad?

PIET.   Monstrous mad.

MEND.   Why?

PIET. Why? Thou, thou hast dishonoured my bed.

MEND. I? Come, come, sit. Here's my bare heart to thee,
As steady as is the centre to the glorious world.
And yet, hark: thou art a cornuto; but, by me?

PIET. Yes, slave, by thee.

MEND. Do not, do not, with tart and spleenful breath,
Loose him that can loose thee. I offend my duke?
Bear record, O ye dumb and raw-air'd nights,
How vigilant my sleepless eyes hath been
To watch the traitor! Record, thou spirit of truth,
With what debasement I ha' thrown myself
To under offices, only to learn
The truth, the party, time, the means, the place,
By whom, and when, and where thou wert disgrac'd!
And am I paid with 'slave'? Hath my intrusion
To places private and prohibited,
Only to observe the closer passages,[1]—
Heaven knows with vows of revelation,—
Made me suspected, made me deem'd a villain?
What rogue hath wrong'd us?

PIET.   Mendoza, I may err.

MEND. Err? 'Tis too mild a name. But err and err,
Run giddy with suspect, for through me thou know
That which most creatures, save thyself, do know.
Nay, since my service hath so loath'd reject,[2]
'Fore I'll reveal, shalt find them clipp'd together.

PIET. Mendoza, thou know'st I am a most plain-breasted man.

MEND. The fitter to make a cuckold. Would your brows were
most plain too!

PIET. Tell me; indeed, I heard thee rail—

MEND. At women, true. Why, what cold phlegm[3] could
choose,
Knowing a lord so honest, virtuous,
So boundless loving, bounteous, fair-shap'd, sweet,
To be condemn'd, abus'd, defam'd, made cuckold?
Heart! I hate all women for't: sweet sheets, wax lights,
antique bedposts, cambric smocks, villainous curtains, arras

---

[1] More secret proceedings.   [2] Rejection.
[3] Apathy, dullness.

pictures, oiled hinges, and all the tongue-tied lascivious witnesses of great creatures' wantonness. What salvation can you
expect?

PIET. Wilt thou tell me?   140

MEND. Why, you may find it yourself: observe, observe.

PIET. I ha' not the patience. Wilt thou deserve me? [1] Tell, give
it.

MEND. Take't. Why, Ferneze is the man, Ferneze. I'll prove
it; this night you shall take him in your sheets. Will't serve?

PIET. It will; my bosom's in some peace. Till night—

MEND. What?

PIET. Farewell.

MEND. God! How weak a lord are you!
Why, do you think there is no more but so?   150

PIET. Why?

MEND. Nay, then will I presume to counsel you.
It should be thus: you, with some guard, upon the sudden
Break into the princess' chamber; I stay behind,
Without the door through which he needs must pass;
Ferneze flies—let him; to me he comes; he's kill'd
By me—observe, by me. You follow; I rail,
And seem to save the body. Duchess comes,
On whom, respecting her advanced birth
And your fair nature, I know, nay, I do know,   160
No violence must be us'd. She comes; I storm,
I praise, excuse Ferneze, and still maintain
The duchess' honour; she for this loves me.
I honour you, shall know her soul, you mine;
Then naught shall she contrive in vengeance
(As women are most thoughtful in revenge)
Of her Ferneze, but you shall sooner know't
Than she can think't. Thus shall his death come sure,
Your duchess brain-caught; [2] so your life secure.

PIET. It is too well, my bosom and my heart.   170
When nothing helps, cut off the rotten part.   *Exit.*

MEND. Who cannot feign friendship can ne'er produce the
effects of hatred. Honest fool Duke, subtle, lascivious Duchess,
silly novice Ferneze—I do laugh at ye! My brain is in labour
till it produce mischief, and I feel sudden throes, proofs
sensible [3] the issue is at hand.

---

[1] 'Be deserving of my favour or rewards.'
[2] Deceived.   [3] Evident.

As bears shape young, so I'll form my device,
Which grown, proves horrid; vengeance makes men wise.

Exit.

[ACT I. SCENE 3][1]

[*Another room in the palace*]

Enter MALVOLE *and* PASSARELLO

MAL. Fool, most happily encount'red; canst sing, fool?

PASS. Yes, I can sing, fool, if you'll bear the burden; and I can
play upon instruments, scurvily, as gentlemen do. Oh, that I
had been gelded! I should then have been a fat fool for a
chamber, a squeaking fool for a tavern, and a private fool for
all the ladies.

MAL. You are in good case[2] since you came to court, fool.
What? Guarded,[3] guarded?

PASS. Yes, faith, even as footmen and bawds wear velvet, not for
an ornament of honour, but for a badge of drudgery; for now
the duke is discontented I am fain to fool him asleep every
night.

MAL. What are his griefs?

PASS. He hath sore eyes.

MAL. I never observed so much.

PASS. Horrible sore eyes; and so hath every cuckold; for the
roots of the horns spring in the eyeballs, and that's the reason
the horn of a cuckold is as tender as his eye, or as that growing
in the woman's forehead twelve years since, that could not
endure to be touched.[4] The duke hangs down his head like a
columbine.

MAL. Passarello, why do great men beg fools?[5]

PASS. As the Welshman stole rushes when there was nothing
else to filch: only to keep begging in fashion.

MAL. Pooh! Thou givest no good reason; thou speakest like a
fool.

---

[1] This scene added in Q3.   [2] Well off.
[3] Wearing a coat with facing or embroidery.
[4] Such a peculiarity was reported in an English pamphlet in 1588.
[5] To apply to the king for the guardianship of idiots in order to profit from
their estates.

PASS. Faith, I utter small fragments, as your knight courts your
city widow with jingling of his gilt spurs, advancing his bush-
coloured beard, and taking tobacco. This is all the mirror of
their knightly complements.[1] Nay, I shall talk when my   30
tongue is a-going once; 'tis like a citizen on horseback, evermore in a false gallop.

MAL. And how doth Maquerelle fare nowadays?

PASS. Faith, I was wont to salute her as our English women are
at their first landing in Flushing: [2] I would call her whore; but
now that antiquity leaves her as an old piece of plastic [3] t' work
by, I only ask her how her rotten teeth fare every morning,
and so leave her. She was the first that ever invented perfumed smocks for the gentlewomen and wooden shoes, for
fear of creaking, for the visitant. She were an excellent lady,   40
but that her face peeleth like Muscovy glass.[4]

MAL. And how doth thy old lord [5] that hath wit enough to be a
flatterer and conscience enough to be a knave?

PASS. Oh, excellent; he keeps, beside me, fifteen jesters, to
instruct him in the art of fooling, and utters their jests in
private to the duke and duchess. He'll lie like to your Switzer
or lawyer; he'll be of any side for most money.

MAL. I am in haste; be brief.

PASS. As your fiddler when he is paid. He'll thrive, I warrant
you, while your young courtier stands like Good Friday in   50
Lent; men long to see it, because more fatting days come after
it; else he's the leanest and pitiful'st actor in the whole
pageant. Adieu, Malvole.

MAL. O world most vile, when thy loose vanities,
Taught by this fool, do make the fool seem wise!

PASS. You'll know me again, Malvole.

MAL. Oh, ay, by that velvet.

PASS. Ay, as a pettifogger [6] by his buckram bag. I am as
common in the court as a hostess's lips in the country.
Knights and clowns and knaves and all share me; the court   60
cannot possibly be without me. Adieu, Malvole.   *Exeunt.*

---

[1] Qualities.
[2] A Dutch city in English hands for several years after 1585 as security for
a loan.
[3] A model for sculpture.
[4] Mica or talc, which tends to flake.
  Bilioso.   [6] Rascally lawyer.

ACT II. SCENE 1

[The hallway outside the duchess's apartments]

Enter MENDOZA, *with a sconce,*[1] *to observe* FERNEZE'S *entrance, who, whilst the act is playing,*[2] *enters unbraced,*[3] *two pages before him with lights; is met by* MAQUERELLE *and conveyed in. The pages are sent away*

MEND. He's caught! The woodcock's head is i' th' noose.
Now treads Ferneze in dangerous path of lust,
Swearing his sense is merely [4] deified.
The fool grasps clouds, and shall beget centaurs;
And now, in strength of panting faint delight,
The goat bids Heaven envy him. Good goose,
I can afford thee nothing
But the poor comfort of calamity, pity;
Lust's like the plummets hanging on clock-lines,
Will ne'er ha' done till all is quite undone.
Such is the course salt,[5] sallow lust doth run,
Which thou shalt try. I'll be reveng'd. Duke, thy suspect;
Duchess, thy disgrace; Ferneze, thy rivalship—
Shall have swift vengeance. Nothing so holy,
No band of nature so strong,
No law of friendship so sacred,
But I'll profane, burst, violate, 'fore I'll
Endure disgrace, contempt, and poverty.
Shall I, whose very 'Hum' struck all heads bare,
Whose face made silence, creaking of whose shoe
Forc'd the most private passages fly ope,
Scrape like a servile dog at some latch'd door?
Learn now to make a leg,[6] and cry, 'Beseech ye,
Pray ye, is such a lord within?'—be aw'd
At some odd usher's scoff'd formality?
First sear my brains! *Unde cadis, non quo, refert.*[7]
My heart cries, 'Perish all!' How! How! What fate
Can once avoid revenge that's desperate?
I'll to the duke; if all should ope—if? Tush!
Fortune still dotes on those who cannot blush.   *Exit.*

[1] Lantern.   [2] *Entr'acte* music.   [3] *Déshabillé.*
[4] Absolutely.   [5] Salacious.   [6] To bow.
[7] 'Whence you fall, not whither, matters' (Seneca, *Thyestes,* 1. 926).

Act II. Scene 2

[*The hallway outside the duchess's apartments*]

Enter MALVOLE *at one door*, BIANCA, EMILIA, *and*
MAQUERELLE *at the other*

MAL. Bless ye, cast [1] o' ladies. Ha, Dipsas; [2] how dost thou, old
coal?

MAQ. Old coal?

MAL. Ay, old coal. Methinks thou liest like a brand under these
billets of green wood. He that will enflame a young wench's
heart, let him lay close to her an old coal that hath first been
fired, a panderess, my half-burnt lint,[3] who, though thou
canst not flame thyself, yet art able to set a thousand virgins'
tapers afire. [*To* BIANCA.] And how dost January thy husband,
my little periwinkle? Is he troubled with the cough of the   10
lungs still? Does he hawk o' nights still? He will not bite.

BIAN. No, by my troth, I took him with his mouth empty of old
teeth.

MAL. And he took thee with thy belly full of young bones.
Marry, he took his maim by the stroke of his enemy.

BIAN. And I mine by the stroke of my friend.

MAL. The close stock! [4] O mortal wench! Lady, ha' ye no
restoratives for your decayed Jasons? Look ye, crab's guts
baked, distilled ox-pith, the pulverized hairs of a lion's upper
lip, jelly of cock-sparrows, he-monkey's marrow, or powder of   20
fox-stones.[5] And whither are all you ambling now?

BIAN. Why, to bed, to bed.

MAL. Do your husbands lie with ye?

BIAN. That were country fashion, i' faith.

MAL. Ha' ye no foregoers [6] about you? Come, whither in good
deed, la now?

MAQ. In good indeed, la now, to eat the most miraculously,
admirably, astonishable-composed posset with three curds,
without any drink. Will ye help me to a he-fox?—Here's the
duke.   *Exeunt ladies.*   30

MAL. (*To* BIANCA.) Fri'd frogs are very good, and French-like
too.

---

[1] Couple (a hawking term).   [2] i.e. bawd (Ovid, *Amores*, I. 8. 2).
[3] Tinder.   [4] Stoccado, thrust (fencing).
[5] A series of aphrodisiacs.   [6] Forerunners.

Enter DUKE PIETRO, COUNT CELSO, COUNT EQUATO,
BILIOSO, FERRARDO, *and* MENDOZA[1]

PIET. The night grows deep and foul; what hour is 't?

CEL. Upon the stroke of twelve.

MAL. Save ye, Duke.

PIET. From thee.—Begone; I do not love thee. Let me see thee
no more; we are displeased.

MAL. Why, God b' wi' thee. Heaven hear my curse:
May thy wife and thee live long together!

PIET. Begone, sirrah.

MAL. 'When Arthur first in court began'[2]—Agamemnon,
Menelaus[3]—was ever any duke a cornuto?

PIET. Begone; hence!

MAL. What religion wilt thou be of next?

MEND. Out with him.

MAL. With most servile patience. Time will come
When wonder of thy error will strike dumb
Thy bezzl'd[4] sense.
Slaves! Ay, favour! Ay, marry, shall he rise!
Good God! How subtle hell doth flatter vice,
Mounts him aloft and makes him seem to fly;
As fowl the tortoise mock'd, who to the sky
Th'ambitious shellfish rais'd. Th'end of all
Is only that from height he might dead fall.

BIL. Why, when? Out, ye rogue! Begone, ye rascal![5]

MAL. I shall now leave ye with all my best wishes.

BIL. Out, ye cur!

MAL. Only let's hold together a firm correspondence.

BIL. Out!

MAL. A mutual, friendly-reciprocal, perpetual kind of steady-
unanimous-heartily-leagued—

BIL. Hence, ye gross-jaw'd, peasantly—out, go!

MAL. Adieu, pigeon-house, thou burr that only stickest to
nappy fortunes. The serpigo,[6] the strangury,[7] an eternal,
uneffectual priapism[8] seize thee!

BIL. Out, rogue!

MAL. May'st thou be a notorious wittoly pander to thine own

---

[1] II. 3—quartos.
[2] The first line of an old ballad; two lines are sung in *2 Henry IV*, ii. 4.
[3] These three men are referred to here because they had unfaithful wives.
[4] Muddled.   [5] Lines 55–69 added in Q₃.
[6] Ringworm.   [7] A disease of the bladder.   [8] A sexual disability.

wife, and yet get no office, but live to be the utmost misery of
mankind, a beggarly cuckold. *Exit.*

PIET. It shall be so.   70

MEND. It must be so, for where great states revenge
'Tis requisite the parts which piety
And lost respect forbears be closely dogg'd.
Lay one into his breast shall sleep with him,
Feed in the same dish, run in self-faction,
Who may discover any shape of danger;
For once disgrac'd, discover'd in offence,
It makes man blushless, and man is, all confess,
More prone to vengeance than to gratefulness.
Favours are writ in dust, but stripes we feel   80
Deprav'd nature stamps in lasting steel.

PIET. You shall be leagu'd with the duchess.

EQUATO. The plot is very good.

MEND. You shall both kill, and seem the corse to save.

FERR. A most fine brain-trick.

CEL. (*Aside.*) Of a most cunning knave.

PIET. My lords, the heavy action we intend
Is death and shame, two of the ugliest shapes
That can confound a soul. Think, think of it.
I strike, but yet, like him that 'gainst stone walls   90
Directs, his shafts rebound in his own face.
My lady's shame is mine; O God, 'tis mine!
Therefore I do conjure [1] all secrecy.
Let it be as very little as may be,
Pray ye, as may be;
Make frightless entrance, salute her with soft eyes,
Stain naught with blood. Only Ferneze dies,
But not before her brows. O gentlemen,
God knows I love her! Nothing else, but this:
I am not well; if grief, that sucks veins dry,   100
Rivels [2] the skin, casts ashes in men's faces,
Bedulls the eye, unstrengthens all the blood,
Chance to remove me to another world,
As sure I once must die, let him succeed.
I have no child; all that my youth begot
Hath been your loves, which shall inherit me;
Which as it ever shall, I do conjure it,

---

[1] Implore.   [2] Wrinkles.

Mendoza may succeed; he's nobly born,
With me of much desert.

CEL. (*Aside.*) Much.

PIET. Your silence answers 'Ay';
I thank you. Come on now. Oh, that I might die
Before her shame's display'd! Would I were forc'd
To burn my father's tomb, unhele [1] his bones,
And dash them in the dirt, rather than this.
This both the living and the dead offends:
Sharp surgery where naught but death amends.   *Exeunt.*

[ACT II. SCENE 3] [2]

[MAQUERELLE'S *apartment*]

Enter MAQUERELLE, EMILIA, *and* BIANCA, *with a posset*

MAQ. Even here it is: three curds in three regions individually distinct, most methodical, according to art composed, without any drink.

BIAN. Without any drink?

MAQ. Upon my honour; will you sit and eat?

EMIL. Good. The composure, [3] the receipt, how is't?

MAQ. 'Tis a pretty pearl; [4] by this pearl—how does't with me? [5]—thus it is: seven-and-thirty yolks of Barbary hens' eggs, eighteen spoonfuls and a half of the juice of cock-sparrow bones, one ounce, three drams, four scruples and one quarter of the syrup of Ethiopian dates; sweetened with three-quarters of a pound of pure candied Indian eryngoes; [6] strewed over with the powder of pearl of America, amber of Cataia, [7] and lamb-stones of Muscovia.

BIAN. Trust me, the ingredients are very cordial, [8] and, no question, good, and most powerful in restoration.

MAQ. I know not what you mean by restoration, but this it doth; it purifieth the blood, smootheth the skin, enliveneth the eye,

---

[1] Uncover.   [2] II. 4—quartos.   [3] Composition.
[4] Anything precious or fine.   [5] 'How does it look?'
[6] Roots of sea-holly; aphrodisiac in reputation, like the other ingredients.
[7] Cathay (China).   [8] Restorative.

strengtheneth the veins, mundifieth [1] the teeth, comforteth the
stomach, fortifieth the back, and quickeneth the wit; that's all.   20

EMIL. By my troth, I have eaten but two spoonfuls, and methinks I could discourse most swiftly and wittily already.

MAQ. Have you the art to seem honest? [2]

BIAN. Ay, thank advice and practice.

MAQ. Why, then, eat me of this posset, quicken your blood, and
preserve your beauty. Do you know Doctor Plaster-face? By
this curd, he is the most exquisite in forging of veins, [3]
spritening of eyes, dyeing of hair, sleeking of skins, blushing
of cheeks, surfling [4] of breasts, blanching and bleaching of
teeth, that ever made an old lady gracious by torchlight; by   30
this curd, la.

BIAN. Well, we are resolved; what God has given us we'll
cherish.

MAQ. Cherish anything saving your husband; keep him not too
high, lest he leap the pale. But for your beauty, let it be your
saint; bequeath two hours to it every morning in your closet.
I ha' been young, and yet, in my conscience, I am not above
five-and-twenty; but, believe me, preserve and use your
beauty; for youth and beauty once gone, we are like beehives
without honey, out o' fashion, apparel that no man will wear;   40
therefore, use me your beauty. [5]

EMIL. Ay, but men say—

MAQ. Men say? Let men say what they will. Life o' woman!
They are ignorant of our wants. The more in years, the more in
perfection they grow; if they lose youth and beauty, they gain
wisdom and discretion; but when our beauty fades, good
night with us. There cannot be an uglier thing to see than an
old woman; from which, O pruning, pinching, and painting,
deliver all sweet beauties.

BIAN. Hark! Music!   50

MAQ. Peace; 'tis in the duchess' bed-chamber. Good rest, most
prosperously-graced ladies.

EMIL. Good night, sentinel.

BIAN. 'Night, dear Maquerelle. *Exeunt all but* MAQUERELLE.

MAQ. May my posset's operation send you my wit and honesty,
And me your youth and beauty; the pleasing'st rest.   *Exit.*

[1] Cleanseth.   [2] Chaste.
[3] The elimination of unsightly facial veins (?).
[4] Painting with cosmetics.
[5] 'Employ your beauty at my behest.'

[ACT II. SCENE 4][1]
[*The hallway outside* AURELIA'S *apartment*]
A song [*within*]

Whilst the song is singing, enter MENDOZA *with his sword drawn, standing ready to murder* FERNEZE *as he flies from the duchess's chamber*

ALL. [*Within.*] Strike, strike!
AUR. [*Within.*] Save my Ferneze! Oh, save my Ferneze!

Enter FERNEZE *in his shirt, and is received upon* MENDOZA'S *sword*

ALL. [*Within.*] Follow! Pursue!
AUR. Oh, save Ferneze!
MEND. Pierce, pierce! Thou shallow fool, drop there!
He that attempts a princess' lawless love
Must have broad hands, close heart, with Argus' eyes,
And back of Hercules, or else he dies.
                    Thrusts his rapier in FERNEZE.

Enter AURELIA, DUKE PIETRO, FERRARDO, BILIOSO, CELSO, *and* EQUATO

ALL. Follow, follow!
MEND. Stand off, forbear, ye most uncivil lords!
PIET. Strike!
MEND. Do not. Tempt not a man resolv'd;
                    [*Seems to protect the body of* FERNEZE.]
Would you, inhuman murderers, more than death?
AUR. O poor Ferneze!
MEND. Alas, now all defence too late.
AUR. He's dead.
PIET. I am sorry for our shame. Go to bed;
Weep not too much, but leave some tears to shed
When I am dead.
AUR. What, weep for thee? My soul no tears shall find.
PIET. Alas, alas, that women's souls are blind.

[1] II. 5—quartos.

MEND. Betray such beauty, murder such youth, contemn
    civility!
  He loves him not that rails not at him.
PIET. Thou canst not move us; we have blood enough.
  And please you, lady, we have quite forgot
  All your defects; if not, why then—
AUR. Not.
PIET. Not. The best of rest, good night.

                Exit PIETRO, *with the other courtiers.*

AUR. Despite go with thee!   30
MEND. Madam, you ha' done me foul disgrace;
  You have wrong'd him much loves you too much.
  Go to; your soul knows you have.
AUR. I think I have.
MEND. Do you but think so?
AUR. Nay, sure I have; my eyes have witnessed thy love.
  Thou hast stood too firm for me.
MEND. Why, tell me, fair-cheek'd lady, who even in tears
  Art powerfully beauteous, what unadvised passion
  Struck ye into such a violent heat against me?   40
  Speak; what mischief wrong'd us? What devil injur'd us?
  Speak.
AUR. That thing ne'er worthy of the name of man, Ferneze;
  Ferneze swore thou lov'st Emilia;
  Which to advance, with most reproachful breath
  Thou both didst blemish and denounce my love.
MEND. Ignoble villain, did I for this bestride
  Thy wounded limbs? For this, rank [1] opposite
  Even to my sovereign? For this, O God, for this,
  Sunk all my hopes, and with my hopes, my life?   50
  Ripp'd bare my throat unto the hangman's axe?
  Thou most dishonour'd trunk! Emilia!
  By life, I know her not! Emilia!
  Did you believe him?
AUR.   Pardon me, I did.
MEND. Did you? And thereupon you grac'd him?
AUR. I did.
MEND. Took him to favour, nay, even clasp'd with him?
AUR. Alas, I did.
MEND.   This night?
AUR.   This night.

               'Place myself.'

MEND. And in your lustful twines the duke took you?

AUR. A most sad truth.

MEND. O God! O God! How we dull honest souls,
Heavy-brain'd men, are swallow'd in the bogs
Of a deceitful ground, whilst nimble bloods,
Light-jointed spirits, speed, cut good men's throats,
And scape! Alas, I am too honest for this age,
Too full of phlegm and heavy steadiness;
Stood still whilst this slave case a noose about me;
Nay, then to stand in honour of him and her
Who had even slic'd my heart.

AUR. Come; I did err, and am most sorry I did err.

MEND. Why, we are both but dead: the duke hates us;
And those whom princes do once groundly [1] hate,
Let them provide to die, as sure as fate.
Prevention [2] is the heart of policy.

AUR. Shall we murder him?

MEND. Instantly?

AUR. Instantly; before he casts a plot,
Or further blaze my honour's much-known blot,
Let's murder him.

MEND. I would do much for you; will ye marry me?

AUR. I'll make thee duke. We are of Medicis,
Florence our friend; in court my faction
Not meanly strengthful; the duke then dead,
We well prepar'd for change; the multitude
Irresolutely reeling, we in force;
Our party seconded, the kingdom maz'd; [3]
No doubt of [4] swift success all shall be grac'd.

MEND. You do confirm me; we are resolute.
Tomorrow look for change; rest confident.
'Tis now about the immodest waist of night;
The mother of moist dew with pallid light
Spreads gloomy shades about the numbed earth.
Sleep, sleep, whilst we contrive our mischief's birth.
This man I'll get inhum'd. Farewell; to bed.
I kiss the pillow; dream the duke is dead.   *Exit* AURELIA.
So, so, good night. How fortune dotes on impudence!
I am in private the adopted son
Of yon good prince;

---

[1] Profoundly.   [2] Anticipation.
[3] Bewildered.   [4] By.

I must be duke; why, if I must, I must.
Most silly lord, name me? O heaven! I see   100
God made honest fools to maintain crafty knaves.
The duchess is wholly mine too; must kill her husband
To quit her shame; much; then marry her, ay—
Oh, I grow proud in prosperous treachery!
As wrestlers clip, so I'll embrace you all,
Not to support, but to procure your fall.

Enter MALVOLE

MAL. God arrest thee.
MEND. At whose suit?
MAL. At the devil's. Ah, you treacherous, damnable monster,
How dost? How dost, thou treacherous rogue?   110
Ah, ye rascal. I am banish'd the court, sirrah.
MEND. Prithee, let's be acquainted; I do love thee, faith.
MAL. At your service, by the Lord, la. Shall's go to supper?
Let's be once drunk together, and so unite a most virtuously
strengthened friendship; shall's, Huguenot,[1] shall's?
MEND. Wilt fall upon my chamber tomorrow morn?
MAL. As a raven to a dunghill. They say there's one dead here,
pricked for the pride of the flesh.
MEND. Ferneze. There he is; prithee, bury him.
MAL. Oh, most willingly; I mean to turn pure Rochelle church-   120
man,[2] I.
MEND. Thou churchman? Why? Why?
MAL. Because I'll live lazily, rail upon authority, deny kings'
supremacy in things indifferent, and be a pope in my own
parish.
MEND. Wherefore dost thou think churches were made?
MAL. To scour ploughshares; I have seen oxen plough up
altars; *et nunc seges ubi Sion fuit.*[3]
MEND. Strange.
MAL. Nay, monstrous. I ha' seen a sumptuous steeple turned to   130
a stinking privy; more beastly, the sacredest place made a
dog's kennel; nay, most inhuman, the stoned coffins of long-
dead Christians burst up and made hogs' troughs—*Hic finis*

[1] Used ironically in the original sense of oath-comrade.
[2] i.e. Huguenot. Many Huguenots settled in La Rochelle, France.
[3] 'And now there is a cornfield where Zion was.' (A paraphrase of Ovid, *Heroides*, I. 53.)

Priami.[1] Shall I ha' some sack and cheese at thy chamber?
Good night, good mischievous incarnate devil; good night,
Mendoza; ah, you inhuman villain, good night; 'night, fub.[2]

MEND. Good night; tomorrow morn?   *Exit* MENDOZA.

MAL. Ay, I will come, friendly damnation, I will come.
I do descry cross-points;[3] honesty and courtship straddle as
far asunder as a true Frenchman's legs.

FERN. Oh!

MAL. Proclamations, more proclamations!

FERN. Oh, a surgeon!

MAL. Hark! Lust cries for a surgeon; what news from Limbo?
How dost the grand cuckold, Lucifer?

FERN. Oh, help, help! Conceal and save me.

   FERNEZE *stirs, and* MALVOLE *helps him up and conveys him
   away*

MAL. Thy shame more than thy wounds do grieve me far;
   Thy wounds but leave upon thy flesh some scar;
   But fame ne'er heals, still rankles worse and worse;
   Such is of uncontrolled lust the curse.
   Think what it is in lawless sheets to lie;
   But, O Ferneze, what in lust to die!
   Then thou that shame respects, oh, fly converse
   With women's eyes and lisping wantonness.
   Stick candles 'gainst a virgin wall's white back;
   If they not burn, yet at the least they'll black.
   Come, I'll convey thee to a private port,[4]
   Where thou shalt live, O happy man, from court.
   The beauty of the day begins to rise,
   From whose bright form night's heavy shadow flies.
   Now 'gins close plots to work, the scene grows full,
   And craves his eyes who hath a solid skull.   *Exeunt.*

---

[1] 'Here [was] the end of Priam.' (A misquotation of Virgil, *Aeneid*, II. 554.)
[2] Imposter.   [3] Trickery.   [4] Refuge.

ACT III. Scene 1

[A room in the palace]

Enter Duke Pietro, Mendoza, Count Equato, *and*
Bilioso

Piet. 'Tis grown to youth of day; how shall we waste this light?
My heart's more heavy than a tyrant's crown.
Shall we go hunt? Prepare for field.   *Exit* Equato.
Mend. Would ye could be merry.
Piet. Would God I could. Mendoza, bid 'um haste.
                                                    Exit Mendoza.
  I would fain shift place. Oh, vain relief!
  Sad souls may well change place, but not change grief;
  As deer, being struck, fly through many soils,[1]
  Yet still the shaft sticks fast, so—
Bil. A good simile, my honest Lord.   10
Piet. I am not much unlike to some sick man
  That long desired hurtful drink; at last
  Swills in and drinks his last, ending at once
  Both life and thirst. Oh, would I ne'er had known
  My own dishonour! Good God, that men should
  Desire to search out that, which being found, ills all
  Their joy in life! To taste the tree of knowledge,
  And then be driven from out Paradise!
  Canst give me some comfort?
Bil. My Lord, I have some books which have been dedicated   20
  to my honour, and I ne'er read 'um, and yet they had very fine
  names: *Physic for Fortune*; *Lozenges of Sanctified Sincerity*;
  very pretty works of curates, scriveners, and schoolmasters.
  Marry, I remember one Seneca, Lucius Annaeus Seneca.
Piet. Out upon him! He writ of temperance and fortitude, yet
  lived like a voluptuous epicure, and died like an effeminate
  coward.
  Haste thee to Florence.
  Here, take our letters; see 'um seal'd; away.
  Report in private to the honour'd duke   30
  His daughter's forc'd disgrace; tell him at length

---

[1] Stretches of water (to lose their scent).

We know too much; due compliments advance.
There's naught that's safe and sweet but ignorance.   *Exit.*

Enter BIANCA [1]

BIL. Madam, I am going ambassador for Florence; 'twill be great charges [2] to me.

BIAN. No matter, my Lord, you have the lease of two manors come out [3] next Christmas; you may lay your tenants on the greater rack for it; and when you come home again, I'll teach you how you shall get two hundred pounds a year by your teeth.

BIL. How, madam?

BIAN. Cut off so much from housekeeping; that which is saved by the teeth, you know, is got by the teeth.

BIL. 'Fore God, and so I may; I am in wondrous credit,[4] lady.

BIAN. See the use of flattery. I did ever counsel you to flatter greatness, and you have profited well; any man that will do so shall be sure to be like your Scotch barnacle: [5] now a block, instantly a worm, and presently a great goose. This it is to rot and putrefy in the bosom of greatness.

BIL. Thou art ever my politician. Oh, how happy is that old lord that hath a politician to his young lady! I'll have fifty gentlemen shall attend upon me; marry, the most of them shall be farmers' sons because they shall bear their own charges; and they shall go apparelled thus: in sea-water green suits, ash-colour cloaks, watchet [6] stockings, and popinjay-green feathers. Will not these colours do excellent?

BIAN. Out upon't! They'll look like citizens riding to their friends at Whitsuntide, their apparel just so many several parishes.[7]

BIL. I'll have it so; and Passarello, my fool, shall go along with me; marry, he shall be in velvet.

BIAN. A fool in velvet?

BIL. Ay, 'tis common for your fool to wear satin; I'll have mine in velvet.

BIAN. What will you wear then, my Lord?

---

[1] The remainder of the scene is added in Q₃.   [2] Expense.
[3] Expire (subject to renewal).   [4] Reputation.
[5] The wild goose, said in folk-lore to be engendered from rotting timbers (blocks), etc., in the sea.
[6] Light blue.   [7] i.e. variegated.

BIL. Velvet too; marry, it shall be embroidered, because I'll differ from the fool somewhat. I am horribly troubled with the gout; nothing grieves me but that my doctor hath forbidden me wine, and you know your ambassador must drink. Didst thou ask thy doctor what was good for the gout?   70

BIAN. Yes; he said ease, wine and women were good for it.

BIL. Nay, thou has such a wit. What was good to cure it, said he?

BIAN. Why, the rack; all your empirics [1] could never do the like cure upon the gout the rack did in England, or your Scotch boot.[2] The French harlequin [3] will instruct you.

BIL. Surely, I do wonder how thou, having for the most part of thy lifetime been a country body, shouldst have so good a wit.

BIAN. Who, I? Why, I have been a courtier thrice two months.

BIL. So have I these twenty year, and yet there was a gentle-   80
man-usher called me coxcomb t'other day, and to my face too. Was't not a backbiting rascal? I would I were better travelled, that I might have been better acquainted with the fashions of several countrymen,[4] but my secretary, I think, he hath sufficiently instructed me.

BIAN. How, my Lord?

BIL. 'Marry, my good Lord,' quoth he, 'your lordship shall ever find amongst a hundred Frenchmen forty hot-shots; [5] amongst a hundred Spaniards, three-score braggards; amongst a hundred Dutchmen, four-score drunkards;   90
amongst a hundred Englishmen, four-score and ten madmen; and amongst a hundred Welshmen,—'

BIAN. What, my Lord?

BIL. 'Four-score and nineteen gentlemen.' [6]

BIAN. But since you go about a sad embassy, I would have you go in black, my Lord.

BIL. Why, dost think I cannot mourn unless I wear my hat in cypress,[7] like an alderman's heir? That's vile, very old, in faith.

BIAN. I'll learn of you shortly. Oh, we should have a fine   100
gallant of you should not I instruct you. How will you bear yourself when you come into the Duke of Florence' court?

BIL. Proud enough, and 'twill do well enough. As I walk up and

---

[1] Physicians who relied on experiment and experience.
[2] Like the rack, an instrument of torture.   [3] Buffoon, clown.
[4] Men of several countries.   [5] Hotheads.
[6] A hit at Welsh pride in gentility.   [7] Mourning.

down the chamber, I'll spit frowns about me, have a strong perfume in my jerkin, let my beard grow to make me look terrible, salute no man below the fourth button,[1] and 'twill do excellent.

BIAN. But there is a very beautiful lady there; how will you entertain her?

BIL I'll tell you that when the lady hath entertained me; but to satisfy thee, here comes the fool.

Enter PASSARELLO

Fool, thou shalt stand for the fair lady.

PASS. Your fool will stand for your lady most willingly and most uprightly.

BIL. I'll salute her in Latin.

PASS. Oh, your fool can understand no Latin.

BIL. Ay, but your lady can.

PASS. Why, then, if your lady take down your fool, your fool will stand no longer for your lady.

BIL. A pestilent fool! 'Fore God, I think the world be turned upside-down too.

PASS. Oh no, sir; for then your lady and all the ladies in the palace should go with their heels upward, and that were a strange sight, you know.

BIL. There be many will repine at my preferment.

PASS. Oh ay, like the envy of an elder sister that hath her younger made a lady before her.

BIL. The duke is wondrous discontented.

PASS. Ay, and more melancholic than a usurer having all his money out at the death of a prince.

BIL. Didst thou see Madam Floria today?

PASS. Yes, I found her repairing her face today; the red upon the white showed as if her cheeks should have been served in for two dishes of barberries [2] in stewed broth, and the flesh to them a woodcock.

BIL. A bitter fool! [3] Come, madam, this night thou shalt enjoy me freely, and tomorrow for Florence.

[*Exeunt* BILIOSO *and* BIANCA.]

PASS. What a natural fool is he that would be a pair of bodies [4]

---

[1] Refuse to make a low bow.   [2] Barbary hens.
[3] Fowle—quartos; perhaps intended as a pun.
[4] Bodice, a corset-like outer garment.

to a woman's petticoat, to be trussed and pointed [1] to them.
Well, I'll dog my lord; and the word is proper, for when I   140
fawn upon him he feeds me; when I snap him by the fingers,
he spits in my mouth. If a dog's death were not strangling, I
had rather be one than a serving-man; for the corruption of
coin is either the generation of a usurer, or a lousy beggar.

                                                            [*Exit.*]

ACT III. SCENE 2

[*Another room in the palace*]

Enter MALVOLE *in a frieze gown, and* BILIOSO, *reading his
     patent* [2]

MAL. [*Aside.*] I cannot sleep; my eyes' ill-neighbouring lids
     Will hold no fellowship. O thou pale, sober night,
     Thou that in sluggish fumes all sense doth steep,
     Thou that gives all the world full leave to play,
     Unbend'st the feebled veins of sweaty labour!
     The galley-slave that all the toilsome day
     Tugs at his oar against the stubborn wave,
     Straining his rugged veins, snores fast;
     The stooping scythe-man that doth barb [3] the field
     Thou mak'st wink sure. In night all creatures sleep;   10
     Only the malcontent, that 'gainst his fate
     Repines and quarrels,—alas, he's goodman tell-clock.
     His sallow jawbones sink with wasting moan;
     Whilst others' beds are down, his pillow's stone.
BIL. Malvole.
MAL. Elder of Israel, thou honest defect of wicked nature and
     obstinate ignorance, when did thy wife let thee lie with her?
BIL. I am going ambassador to Florence.
MAL. Ambassador! Now, for thy country's honour, prithee, do
     not put up mutton and porridge in thy cloak-bag. Thy young   20
     lady wife goes to Florence with thee too, does she not?
BIL. No, I leave her at the palace.
MAL. At the palace? Now discretion shield, man. For God's
     love, let's ha' no more cuckolds. Hymen begins to put off his

---

[1] Tied and laced.   [2] Letters patent, commission.
[3] Cut, mow.

saffron robe. Keep thy wife i' a state of grace. Heart o' truth, I
would sooner leave my lady singled [1] in a bordello than in the
Genoa palace;
Sin there [2] appearing in her sluttish shape
Would soon grow loathsome, even to blushes' sense;
Surfeit would choke intemperate appetite,
Make the soul scent the rotten breath of lust.
When in an Italian lascivious palace,
A lady guardianless,
Left to the push of all allurement,
The strongest incitements to immodesty,
To have her bound, incens'd with wanton sweets,
Her veins fill'd with heating delicacies,
Soft rest, sweet music, amorous masquerers,
Lascivious banquets, sin itself gilt o'er,
Strong fantasy tricking up strange delights,
Presenting it dress'd pleasingly to sense,
Sense leading it unto the soul, confirm'd
With potent example, impudent custom,
Entic'd by that great bawd, Opportunity;
Thus being prepar'd, clap to her easy ear
Youth in good clothes, well-shap'd, rich,
Fair-spoken, promising-noble, ardent, blood-full,
Witty, flattering,—Ulysses absent,
O Ithaca, can chastest Penelope hold out?
BIL. Mass, I 'll think on't; farewell.   *Exit* BILIOSO.
MAL. Farewell; take thy wife with thee; farewell.
To Florence? Um. It may prove good, it may;
And we may once unmask our brows.

Enter COUNT CELSO [3]

CEL. My honour'd Lord,—
MAL. Celso, peace; how is 't? Speak low; pale fears
Suspect that hedges, walls, and trees have ears.
Speak, how runs all?
CEL. I' faith, my Lord, that beast with many heads,
The staggering multitude, recoils apace;
Though through great men's envy, most men's malice,
Their much intemperate heat hath banish'd you,

---

[1] Alone.   [2] In a bordello.   [3] III. 3—quartos.

Yet now they find envy and malice ne'er
Produce faint reformation.
The duke, the too soft duke, lies as a block,
For which two tugging factions seem to saw;
But still the iron through the ribs they draw.

MAL. I tell thee, Celso, I have ever found
Thy breast most far from shifting cowardice
And fearful baseness; therefore I'll tell thee, Celso,
I find the wind begins to come about;   70
I'll shift my suit of fortune.
I know the Florentine, whose only force,[1]
By marrying his proud daughter to this prince,
Both banish'd me and made this weak lord duke,
Will now forsake them all; be sure he will.
I'll lie in ambush for conveniency,
Upon their severance to confirm myself.

CEL. Is Ferneze interr'd?

MAL. Of that at leisure; he lives.

CEL. But how stands Mendoza? How is't with him?   80

MAL. Faith, like a pair of snuffers: snibs [2] filth in other men
and retains it in himself.

CEL. He does fly from public notice, methinks, as a hare does
from hounds; the feet whereon he flies betrays him.

MAL. I can track him, Celso.
Oh, my disguise fools him most powerfully;
For that I seem a desperate malcontent,
He fain would clasp with me; he's the true slave
That will put on the most affected grace
For some vile second cause.

Enter MENDOZA

CEL.   He's here.
MAL.   Give place.   90
                                   Exit CELSO.
Illo, ho, ho, ho! Art there, old truepenny? [3] Where hast thou
spent thyself this morning? I see flattery in thine eyes and
damnation in thy soul. Ha, thou huge rascal!

MEND. Thou art very merry.

---

[1] Whose power alone.   [2] Reproves.
[3] Phrases from *Hamlet*, I. 5.

MAL. As a scholar, *futuens gratis*.[1] How dost the devil go with thee now?

MEND. Malvole, thou art an arrant knave.

MAL. Who, I? I have been a sergeant, man.

MEND. Thou art very poor.

MAL. As Job, an alchemist, or a poet.

MEND. The dukes hates thee.

MAL. As Irishmen do bum-cracks.[2]

MEND. Thou hast lost his amity.

MAL. As pleasing as maids lose their virginity.

MEND. Would thou wert of a lusty spirit! Would thou wert noble!

MAL. Why, sure my blood gives [3] me I am noble; sure I am of noble kind, for I find myself possessed with all their qualities: love dogs, dice, and drabs, scorn wit in stuff-clothes,[4] have beat my shoemaker, knocked [5] my seamstress, cuckolded my pothecary, and undone my tailor. Noble? Why not? Since the Stoic said, *Neminem servum non ex regibus, neminem regem non ex servis esse oriundum*,[6] only busy Fortune touses,[7] and the provident Chances blends them together. I'll give you a simile: did you ever see a well with two buckets; whilst one comes up full to be emptied, another goes down empty to be filled? Such is the state of all humanity. Why, look you, I may be the son of some duke; for, believe me, intemperate lascivious bastardy makes nobility doubtful. I have a lusty, daring heart, Mendoza.

MEND. Let's grasp; [8] I do like thee infinitely. Wilt enact one thing for me?

MAL. Shall I get by it? (MENDOZA *gives him his purse.*) Command me; I am thy slave beyond death and hell.

MEND. Murder the duke.

MAL. My heart's wish, my soul's desire, my fantasy's dream, my blood's longing, the only height of my hopes! How, O God, how? Oh, how my united spirits throng together, to strengthen my resolve!

MEND. The duke is now a-hunting.

MAL. Excellent, admirable, as the devil would have it! Lend me, lend me rapier, pistol, cross-bow; so, so, I'll do it.

MEND. Then we agree.

---

[1] Making love gratuitously. [2] Breaking of wind.
[3] Shows. [4] Garments of coarse cloth. [5] Struck.
[6] 'There is no slave not born of kings, no king not born of slaves' (Seneca, *Epistles*, xliv). [7] Disorders. [8] Embrace.

MAL. As Lent and fishmongers. Come, a-cap-a-pie,[1] how?
Inform.

MEND. Know that this weak-brain'd duke, who only stands
On Florence' stilts, hath out of witless zeal
Made me his heir, and secretly confirm'd
The wreath to me after his life's full point.

MAL. Upon what merit?   140

MEND. Merit? By Heaven, I horn him!
Only Ferneze's death gave me state's life.
Tut, we are politic; he must not live now.

MAL. No reason, marry; but how must he die now?

MEND. My utmost project is to murder the duke, that I might
have his state, because he makes me his heir; to banish the
duchess, that I might be rid of a cunning Lacedaemonian,[2]
because I know Florence will forsake her; and then to marry
Maria, the banished Duke Altofront's wife, that her friends
might strengthen me and my faction. This is all, la.   150

MAL. Do you love Maria?

MEND. Faith, no great affection, but as wise men do love great
women, to ennoble their blood and augment their revenue.
To accomplish this now, thus now: the duke is in the forest
next the sea; single him, kill him, hurl him in the main, and
proclaim thou sawest wolves eat him.

MAL. Um. Not so good; methinks when he is slain,
To get some hypocrite, some dangerous wretch
That's muffled o'er with feigned holiness,
To swear he heard the duke on some steep cliff   160
Lament his wife's dishonour, and in an agony
Of his heart's torture, hurl'd his groaning sides
Into the swollen sea. This circumstance
Well made sounds probable, and hereupon
The duchess—

MEND.   May well be banish'd.
O unpeerable invention! Rare!
Thou god of policy, it honeys me.

MAL. Then fear not for the wife of Altofront;
I'll close to [3] her.

MEND. Thou shalt, thou shalt! Our excellency is pleas'd.   170
Why wert not thou an emperor? When we
Are duke, I'll make thee some great man, sure.

---

[1] 'From head to foot', i.e. comprehensively.
[2] Strumpet.   [3] 'Come to terms with.'

MAL. Nay, make me some rich knave, and I'll make myself
    Some great man.
MEND.   In thee be all my spirit;
    Retain ten souls, unite thy virtual [1] powers;
    Resolve; ha, remember greatness. Heart, farewell;
    The fate of all my hopes in thee doth dwell.   *[Exit.]*

Enter CELSO

MAL. Celso, didst hear? O Heaven, didst hear
    Such devilish mischief? Sufferest thou the world
    Carouse damnation even with greedy swallow,   1?
    And still dost wink, still does thy vengeance slumber?
    If now thy brows are clear, when will they thunder?
                              Exeunt.

[ACT III. SCENE 3] [2]
[*A forest*]

Enter PIETRO, FERRARDO, PREPASSO, *and three pages*

FERR. The dogs are at a fault.   *Cornets like horns.*
PIET. Would God nothing but the dogs were at it! Let the deer
    pursue safety, the dogs follow the game, and do you follow
    the dogs. As for me, 'tis unfit one beast should hunt another;
    I ha' one chaseth me. And 't please you, I would be rid of you
    a little.
FERR. Would your grief would as soon leave you as we to
    quietness.   *Exeunt* FERRARDO *and* PREPASSO.
PIET. I thank you. Boy, what dost thou dream of now?
PAGE. Of a dry summer, my Lord, for here's a hot world
    towards; but, my Lord, I had a strange dream last night.
PIET. What strange dream?
PAGE. Why, methought I pleased you with singing, and then I
    dreamt you gave me that short sword.
PIET. Prettily begged. Hold thee, I'll prove thy dream true;
    tak't.
PAGE. My duty; but still I dreamt on, my Lord, and methought,

              [1]Effective.   [2] III. 4—quartos.

and't please your excellency, you would needs out of your
royal bounty give me that jewel in your hat.

PIET. Oh, thou didst but dream, boy; do not believe it; dreams   20
prove not always true. They may hold in a short sword, but not
in a jewel. But now, sir, you dreamt you had pleased me with
singing; make that true, as I have made the other.

PAGE. Faith, my Lord, I did but dream, and dreams, you say,
prove not always true; they may hold in a good sword, but not
in a good song. The truth is, I ha' lost my voice.

PIET. Lost thy voice? How?

PAGE. With dreaming, faith; but here's a couple of sirenical
rascals shall enchant ye. What shall they sing, my good Lord?

PIET. Sing of the nature of women, and then the song shall be   30
surely full of variety, old crotchets [1] and most sweet closes; [2]
it shall be humorous, grave, fantastic, amorous, melancholy,
sprightly, all in all, and all in one.

PAGE. All in one?

PIET. By 'r lady, too many. Sing; my speech grows culpable of
unthrifty idleness; sing.

Song [3]

Enter MALVOLE, *with cross-bow and pistol* [4]

PIET. Ah, so, so; sing. I am heavy; walk off; I shall talk in my
sleep; walk off.   *Exeunt pages.*

MAL. [*Aside.*] Brief,[5] brief; who? The duke? Good Heaven,
that fools   40
Should stumble upon greatness!—Do not sleep, Duke;
Give ye good morrow. I must be brief, Duke;
I am fee'd to murder thee.—Start not. Mendoza,
Mendoza hir'd me; here's his gold, his pistol,
Cross-bow and sword; 'tis all as firm as earth.
O fool, fool, chok'd with the common maze
Of easy idiots, credulity!
Make him thine heir? What, thy sworn murderer?

PIET. Oh, can it be?

MAL. Can?   50

[1] Musical notes and fanciful devices.   [2] Conclusions.
[3] Not included in the quartos.   [4] III. 5—quartos.
[5] In short.

PIET. Discover'd he not Ferneze?
MAL. Yes; but why? But why? For love to thee?
  Much, much! To be reveng'd upon his rival,
  Who had thrust his jaws awry;
  Who, being slain, suppos'd by thine own hands,
  Defended by his sword, made thee the most loathsome,
  Him most gracious with thy loose princess;
  Thou, closely [1] yielding egress and regress to her,
  Madest him heir, whose hot, unquiet lust
  Straight tous'd thy sheets, and now would seize thy state.   6
  Politician! Wise man! Death, to be
  Led to the stake like a bull by the horns,
  To make even kindness cut a gentle throat!
  Life, why art thou numb'd? Thou foggy dullness, speak.
  Lives not more faith in a home-thrusting tongue
  Than in these fencing, tip-tap [2] courtiers?

Enter CELSO, *with a hermit's gown and beard*

PIET. Lord Malvole, if this be true—
MAL. If? Come, shade thee with this disguise. If? Thou shalt
  handle it; he shall thank thee for killing thyself. Come, follow
  my directions, and thou shalt see strange sleights.   7
PIET. World, whither wilt thou?
MAL. Why, to the devil. Come, the morn grows late;
  A steady quickness is the soul of state.   *Exeunt.*

ACT IV. SCENE 1

[*The hallway near* BIANCA *and* EMILIA'S *apartment*]

Enter MAQUERELLE, *knocking at the ladies' door*

MAQ. Medam, medam, are you stirring, medam? If you be
  stirring, medam—if I thought I should disturb ye—
                                  [*Enter page.*]
PAGE. My lady is up, forsooth.
MAQ. A pretty boy, faith; how old art thou?
PAGE. I think fourteen.

            [1] Secretly.   [2] Frivolous.

MAQ. Nay, and ye be in the teens—are ye a gentleman born?
Do you know me? My name is Medam Maquerelle; I lie in
the old Cunnycourt.[1]

Enter BIANCA *and* EMILIA

[PAGE.] See, here the ladies.

BIAN. A fair day to ye, Maquerelle.   10

EMIL. Is the duchess up yet, sentinel?

MAQ. Oh, ladies, the most abominable mischance! Oh, dear
ladies, the most piteous disaster! Ferneze was taken last night
in the duchess' chamber. Alas, the duke catched him and
killed him.

BIAN. Was he found in bed?

MAQ. Oh no, but the villainous certainty is, the door was not
bolted. The tongue-tied hatch held his peace;[2] so the naked
troth is, he was found in his shirt, whilst I, like an arrant
beast, lay in the outward chamber, heard nothing; and yet   20
they came by me in the dark, and yet I felt them not, like a
senseless creature as I was. Oh, beauties, look to your busk-
points[3]—if not chastely, yet charily; be sure the door is
bolted. Is your lord gone to Florence?

BIAN. Yes, Maquerelle.

MAQ. I hope you'll find the discretion to purchase a fresh
gown for his return. Now, by my troth, beauties, I would ha' ye
once wise: He loves ye; pish! He is witty; bubble! Fair pro-
portioned; mew! Nobly born; wind! Let this be still your
fixed position: esteem me every man according to his good   30
gifts, and so ye shall ever remain most dear, and most worthy
to be most dear ladies.

EMIL. Is the duke returned from hunting yet?

MAQ. They say not yet.

BIAN. 'Tis now in midst of day.

EMIL. How bears the duchess with this blemish now?

MAQ. Faith, boldly; strongly defies defame, as one that has a
duke to her father. And there's a note to you: be sure of a
stout friend in a corner, that you may always awe your
husband. Mark the haviour of the duchess now: She dares   40

[1] Probably an informal name for the area; 'cony' or 'cunny' often
described a woman of doubtful character.
[2] 'The divided door opened silently(?).'
[3] Corset-laces.

defame, cries, 'Duke, do what thou canst, I'll quit[1] mine honour'; nay, as one confirmed in her own virtue against ten thousand mouths that mutter her disgrace, she's presently for dances.

Enter FERRARDO [*apart*]

BIAN. For dances?

MAQ. Most true.

BIAN. Most strange. See, here's my servant,[2] young Ferrard. How many servants thinkest thou I have, Maquerelle?

MAQ. The more, the merrier. 'Twas well said, use your servants as you do your smocks: have many, use one, and change often; for that's most sweet and court-like.

FERR. Save ye, fair ladies. Is the duke returned?

BIAN. Sweet sir, no voice of him as yet in court.

FERR. 'Tis very strange.

BIAN. [*Aside.*] And how do you like my servant, Maquerelle?

MAQ. [*Aside.*] I think he could hardly draw Ulysses' bow, but, by my fidelity, were his nose narrower, his eyes broader, his hands thinner, his lips thicker, his legs bigger, his feet lesser, his hair blacker, his teeth whiter, he were a tolerable sweet youth, i' faith. And he will come to my chamber, I will read him the fortune of his beard.

Cornets sound.

FERR. Not yet returned; I fear—but the duchess approacheth.

ACT IV. SCENE 2

[*The hall of the palace*][3]

Enter MENDOZA, *supporting the duchess;* GUERRINO. *The ladies that are on the stage rise.* FERRARDO *ushers in the duchess, and then takes a lady to tread a measure*

AUR. We will dance. Music! We will dance.

GUERR. '*Les quanto*,' lady, '*Pensez bien*', '*Passa regis*', or '*Bianca's brawl*'?[4]

---

[1] Redeem.   [2] Paramour.

[3] None of the actors leaves the stage, the change of scene probably being indicated by a general movement downstage.

[4] Names of dances.

AUR. We have forgot the brawl.

FERR. So soon? 'Tis wonder.

GUERR. Why, 'tis but two singles on the left, two on the right,
three doubles forward, a traverse of six round; do this twice;
three singles side, galliard trick of twenty, coronto-pace; a
figure of eight, three singles broken down; come up, meet
two doubles, fall back, and then honour.[1]

AUR. O Dedalus, thy maze! I have quite forgot it.

MAQ. [*Aside.*] Trust me, so have I, saving the falling back, and
then honour.

Enter PREPASSO

AUR. Music, music!

PREP. Who saw the duke? The duke?

Enter EQUATO

AUR. Music, music!

EQUATO. The duke? Is the duke returned?

AUR. Music!

Enter CELSO

CEL. The duke is either quite invisible, or else is not.

AUR. We are not pleased with your intrusion upon our private
retirement. We are not pleased; you have forgot yourselves.

Enter a page

CEL. Boy, thy master? Where's the duke?

PAGE. Alas, I left him burying the earth with his spread joyless
limbs. He told me he was heavy, would sleep; bid me walk off,
for that the strength of fantasy oft made him talk in his dreams.
I straight obeyed, nor ever saw him since; but whereso'er he is,
he's sad.

AUR. Music, sound high, as is our heart! Sound high!

Enter MALVOLE, *and* PIETRO, *disguised like a hermit* [2]

---

[1] Bow or curtsy.   [2] IV. 3—quartos.

MAL. The duke—peace!—the duke is dead.

AUR. Music!

MAL. Is't music?

MEND. Give proof.

FERR. How?

CEL. Where?

PREP. When?

MAL. Rest in peace, as the duke does; quietly sit. For my own
part, I beheld him but dead, that's all. Marry, here's one can
give you a more particular account of him.

MEND. Speak, holy father, nor let any brow
Within this presence fright thee from the truth;
Speak confidently and freely.

AUR.   We attend.

PIET. Now had the mounting sun's all-ripening wings
Swept the cold sweat of night from the earth's dank breast,
When I, whom men call Hermit of the Rock,
Forsook my cell and clamber'd up a cliff,
Against whose base the heady Neptune dash'd
His high-curl'd brows; there 'twas I eas'd my limbs,
When, lo! my entrails melted with the moan
Someone, who far 'bove me was climb'd, did make—
I shall offend.

MEND. Not.

AUR. On.

PIET. Methinks I hear him yet: 'O female faith!
Go sow the ingrateful sand, and love a woman.
And do I live to be the scoff of men?
To be the wittol-cuckold, even to hug
My poison? Thou knowest, O truth!
Sooner hard steel will melt with southern wind,
A seaman's whistle calm the ocean,
A town on fire be extinct with tears,
Than women, vow'd to blushless impudence,
With sweet behaviour and soft minioning,
Will turn from that where appetite is fix'd.
O powerful blood! How thou dost slave their soul!
I wash'd an Ethiop, who, for recompense,
Sullied my name. And must I then be forc'd
To walk, to live thus black? Must? Must? Fie!
He that can bear with "must", he cannot die.'
With that he sigh'd so passionately deep

That the dull air even groan'd. At last he cries,   70
'Sink shame in seas, sink deep enough!' So dies.
For then I view'd his body fall and souse [1]
Into the foamy main. Oh, then I saw
That which methinks I see: it was the duke,
Whom straight the nicer-stomach'd sea belch'd up;
But then—
MAL. Then came I in, but, 'las, all was too late,
For even straight he sunk.
PIET.   Such was the duke's sad fate.
CEL. A better fortune to our Duke Mendoza!
OMNES. Mendoza!   *Cornets flourish.*   80
MEND. A guard, a guard!   *Enter a guard.*
                         We, full of hearty tears
For our good father's loss,
For so we well may call him,
Who did beseech your loves for our succession,
Cannot so lightly over-jump his death
As leave his woes revengeless. (*To* AURELIA.) Woman of
     shame,
We banish thee for ever to the place
From whence this good man comes; nor permit,
On death, unto thy body any ornament;   90
But, base as was thy life, depart away.
AUR. Ungrateful!
MEND. Away!
AUR. Villain, hear me.
     PREPASSO *and* GUERRINO *lead away the duchess*
MEND. Be gone! My lords,
Address to [2] public council; 'tis most fit;
The train of Fortune is borne up by wit.
Away! Our presence shall be sudden. Haste.
     All depart saving MENDOZA, MALVOLE, *and* PIETRO
     [*disguised*]
MAL. Now, you egregious devil; ha, ye murdering politician!
How dost, Duke? How dost look now? Brave Duke, i' faith!   100
MEND. How did you kill him?
MAL. Slatted [3] his brains out, then soused him in the briny
   sea.
MEND. Brained him and drowned him too?

----

     [1] Plunge.   [2] Prepare for.   [3] Knocked.

MAL. Oh, 'twas best—sure work. For he that strikes a great
    man, let him strike home, or else 'ware, he'll prove no man.
    Shoulder not a huge fellow, unless you may be sure to lay him
    in the kennel.[1]

MEND. A most sound brain-pan! I'll make you both emperors.

MAL. Make us Christians, make us Christians.

MEND. I'll hoist ye; ye shall mount.

MAL. To the gallows, say ye? Come; *praemium incertum petit,*
    certum scelus.[2] How stands the progress?

MEND. Here, take my ring unto the citadel;
    Have entrance to Maria, the grave duchess
    Of banish'd Altofront. Tell her we love her;
    Omit no circumstance to grace our person. Do't.

MAL. I'll make an excellent pander. Duke, farewell; 'dieu,
    adieu, Duke.

MEND. Take Maquerelle with thee; for 'tis found
    None cuts a diamond but a diamond. (*Exit* MALVOLE.)—
      Hermit,
    Thou art a man for me, my confessor.
    O thou selected spirit, born for my good,
    Sure thou wouldst make
    An excellent elder in a deform'd church.
    Come, we must be inward,[3] thou and I all one.

PIET. I am glad I was ordained for ye.

MEND. Go to, then; thou must know that Malvole is a strange
    villain; dangerous, very dangerous; you see how broad 'a
    speaks, a gross-jawed rogue. I would have thee poison him;
    he's like a corn upon my great toe: I cannot go for him; he
    must be cored out, he must. Wilt do't, ha?

PIET. Anything, anything.

MEND. Heart of my life! Thus then to the citadel:
    Thou shalt consort with this Malvole;
    There being at supper, poison him. It shall be laid
    Upon Maria, who yields love or dies.
    Scud quick.

PIET. Like lightning. Good deeds crawl, but mischief flies.
                                  Exit PIETRO.

Enter MALVOLE

[1] Gutter.
[2] 'Uncertain the reward he seeks, certain the guilt.' (Adapted from Seneca,
Phoenissae, l. 632.)
[3] Intimate.

MAL. Your devilship's ring [1] has no virtue; the buff-captain,[2] the sallow Westphalian gammon-faced zaza [3] cries, 'Stand out!' Must have a stiffer warrant, or no pass into the castle of comfort.

MEND. Command our sudden letter. Not enter, sha't' [4]? What place is there in Genoa but thou shalt? Into my heart, into my very body. Come, let's love; we must love, we two, soul and body.

MAL. How didst like the hermit? A strange hermit, sirrah.

MEND. A dangerous fellow, very perilous; he must die.   150

MAL. Ay, he must die.

MEND. Thou'st [5] kill him. We are wise; we must be wise.

MAL. And provident.

MEND. Yea, provident; beware an hypocrite.
  A churchman once corrupted; oh, avoid!
  A fellow that makes religion his stalking-horse, [6]
  He breeds a plague. Thou shalt poison him.

MAL. Ho, 'tis wondrous necessary. How?

MEND. You both go jointly to the citadel;
  There sup; there poison him; and Maria,   160
  Because she is our opposite,[7] shall bear
  The sad suspect, on which she dies or loves us.

MAL. I run.   *Exit* MALVOLE.

MEND. We that are great, our sole self-good still moves us.
  They shall die both, for their deserts craves more
  Than we can recompense; their presence still
  Imbraids [8] our fortunes with beholdingness,
  Which we abhor; like deed, like doer; then conclude,
  They live not to cry out ingratitude.
  One stick burns t'other; steel cuts steel alone.   170
  'Tis good trust few, but, oh, 'tis best trust none.   *Exit.*

---

[1] See 1. 114.
[2] The leather-jerkined guardian of the citadel.
[3] The ruffian(?) with a ham-like face.
[4] Shalt thou.   [5] Thou must.
[6] 'Shoots under his belly' appears in margin of quartos. Conjectured to be a stage direction (H. H. Wood, ed., *Plays of John Marston*, London, 1934), but more likely intended by Marston to cancel 'He breeds a plague', to convey the image of trickery.
[7] Opponent.   [8] Upbraids.

[ACT IV. SCENE 3] [1]

[*Another room in the palace*]

Enter MALVOLE *and* PIETRO, *still disguised, at several doors*

MAL. How do you? How dost, Duke?

PIET. Oh, let
The last day fall; drop, drop on our curs'd heads!
Let Heaven unclasp itself, vomit forth flames.

MAL. Oh, do not rave, do not turn player; there's more of them than can well live one by another already. What, art an infidel still?

PIET. I am amazed, struck in a swoon with wonder. I am commanded to poison thee!

MAL. I am commanded to poison thee at supper.

PIET. At supper?

MAL. In the citadel.

PIET. In the citadel?

MAL. Cross-capers! Tricks! Truth o' Heaven, he would discharge us as boys do eldern guns: [2] one pellet to strike out another. Of what faith art now?

PIET. All is damnation, wickedness extreme;
There is no faith in man.

MAL. In none but usurers and brokers; they deceive no man. Men take 'um for blood-suckers, and so they are. Now God deliver me from my friends!

PIET. Thy friends?

MAL. Yes, from my friends; for from mine enemies I'll deliver myself. Oh, cut-throat friendship is the rankest villainy! Mark this Mendoza; mark him for a villain; but Heaven will send a plague upon him for a rogue.

PIET. O world!

MAL. World! 'Tis the only region of death, the greatest shop of the devil, the cruelest prison of men, out of which none pass without paying their dearest breath for a fee; there's nothing perfect in it, but extreme, extreme calamity, such as comes yonder.

----

[1] IV. 4—quartos.
[2] Popguns made of elder wood.

Enter AURELIA, *two halberds* [1] *before and two after, supported*
by CELSO *and* FERRARDO; AURELIA *in base mourning*
attire [2]

AUR. To banishment! Lead [3] on to banishment!
PIET. Lady, the blessedness of repentance to you.
AUR. Why? Why? I can desire nothing but death,
Nor deserve anything but hell.
If Heaven should give me sufficiency of grace
To clear my soul, it would make Heaven graceless;
My sins would make the stock of mercy poor;
Oh, they would tire Heaven's goodness to reclaim them.   40
Judgment is just, yet [4] from that vast villain!
But sure he shall not miss sad punishment
'Fore he shall rule. On to my cell of shame!
PIET. My cell 'tis, lady; where, instead of masques,
Music, tilts, tourneys, and such court-like shows,
The hollow murmur of the checkless winds
Shall groan again, whilst the unquiet sea
Shakes the whole rock with foamy battery.
There, usherless, the air comes in and out,
The rheumy vault will force your eyes to weep,   50
Whilst you behold true desolation.
A rocky barrenness shall pierce your eyes,
Where all at once one reaches where he stands,
With brows the roof, both walls with both his hands.
AUR. It is too good. Bless'd spirit of my lord,
Oh, in what orb soe'er thy soul is thron'd,
Behold me worthily most miserable!
Oh, let the anguish of my contrite spirit
Entreat some reconciliation!
If not, oh, joy,[5] triumph in my just grief.   60
Death is the end of woes and tears' relief.
PIET. Belike your lord not lov'd you, was unkind.
AUR. O Heaven!
As the soul loves the body, so lov'd he;
'Twas death to him to part my presence,
Heaven to see me pleas'd.
Yet I, like a wretch given o'er to hell,

---

[1] Soldiers bearing battle-axes.
[2] IV. 5—quartos.   [3] Led—quartos.
[4] Even.   [5] A verb.

Brake all the sacred rites of marriage,
To clip a base, ungentle, faithless villain;
O God, a very pagan reprobate—
What should I say?—ungrateful, throws me out,
For whom I lost soul, body, fame, and honour;
But 'tis most fit. Why should a better fate
Attend on any who forsake chaste sheets,
Fly the embrace of a devoted heart,
Join'd by a solemn vow 'fore God and man,
To taste the brackish blood [1] of beastly lust
In an adulterous touch? O ravenous immodesty,
Insatiate impudence of appetite!
Look, here's your end; for mark what sap in dust,
What good in sin, even so much love in lust.
Joy to thy ghost, sweet Lord; pardon to me.

CEL. 'Tis the duke's pleasure this night you rest in court.

AUR. Soul, lurk in shades; run, shame, from frightsome skies;
In night the blind man misseth not his eyes.

Exeunt all except MALVOLE *and* PIETRO.

MAL. Do not weep, kind cuckold; take comfort, man; thy
betters have been beccos: [2] Agamemnon, emperor of all the
merry Greeks, that tickled all the true Trojans, was a cornuto;
Prince Arthur, that cut off twelve kings' beards, was a cornuto; Hercules, whose back bore up heaven, and got forty
wenches with child in one night—

PIET. Nay, it was fifty.

MAL. Faith, forty's enow, a' conscience; yet was a cornuto.
Patience; mischief grows proud; be wise.

PIET. Thou pinchest too deep, art too keen upon me.

MAL. Tut, a pitiful surgeon makes a dangerous sore; I'll tent [3]
thee to the ground. Thinkest I'll sustain myself by flattering
thee, because thou art a prince? I had rather follow a
drunkard, and live by licking up his vomit than by servile
flattery.

PIET. Yet great men ha' done 't.

MAL. Great slaves fear better than love, born naturally for a
coal-basket; [4] though the common usher of princes' presence,
Fortune, hath blindly given them better place. I am vowed to
be thy affliction.

---

[1] Licentious passion.   [2] Cuckolds.
[3] Probe.   [4] i.e. servile employment.

PIET. Prithee, be;
   I love much misery, and be thou son to me.
MAL. Because you are an usurping duke—

Enter BILIOSO

(*To* BILIOSO.) Your lordship's well return'd from Florence.
BIL. Well returned, I praise my horse.   110
MAL. What news from the Florentines?
BIL. I will conceal the great duke's pleasure; only this was his
   charge: His pleasure is, that his daughter die; Duke Pietro
   be banished, for banishing [1] his blood's dishonour; and that
   Duke Altofront be reaccepted. This is all; but I hear Duke
   Pietro is dead.
MAL. Ay, and Mendoza is duke. What will you do?
BIL. Is Mendoza strongest?
MAL. Yet he is.
BIL. Then yet I'll hold to him.   120
MAL. But if that Altofront should turn straight again? [2]
BIL. Why, then I would turn straight again.
   'Tis good run still with him that has most might;
   I had rather stand with wrong than fall with right.
MAL. What religion will you be of now?
BIL. Of the duke's religion, when I know what it is.
MAL. O Hercules!
BIL. Hercules? Hercules was the son of Jupiter and Alcmena.
MAL. Your lordship is a very wit-all.
BIL. Wittol?   130
MAL. Ay, all-wit.
BIL. Amphitryon [3] was a cuckold.
MAL. Your lordship sweats; your young lady will get you a
   cloth for your old worship's brows. (*Exit* BILIOSO.) Here's a
   fellow to be damned; this is his inviolable maxim: flatter the
   greatest, and oppress the least. A whoreson flesh-fly, that still
   gnaws upon the lean, galled backs.
PIET. Why dost then salute him?
MAL. I' faith, as bawds go to church, for fashion sake. Come, be
   not confounded; thou art but in danger to lose a dukedom.   140
   Think this: This earth is the only grave and Golgotha wherein
   all things that live must rot; 'tis but the draught [4] wherein the

---

[1] 'In order to banish.'   [2] 'Return immediately.'
[3] The husband of Alcmena.   [4] Privy.

heavenly bodies discharge their corruption, the very muckhill
on which the sublunary orbs cast their excrements; man is the
slime of this dung-pit, and princes are the governors of these
men; for, for our souls, they are as free as emperors, all of one
piece; there goes but a pair of shears [1] betwixt an emperor and
the son of a bagpiper; only the dyeing, dressing, pressing,
glossing makes the difference.
Now, what art thou like to lose?
A jailer's office to keep men in bonds,
Whilst toil and treason all life's good confounds.

PIET. I here renounce for ever regency.
O Altofront, I wrong thee to supplant thy right,
To trip thy heels up with a devilish sleight!
For which I now from throne am thrown; world tricks abjure;
For vengeance, though 't comes slow, yet it comes sure.
Oh, I am chang'd; for here, 'fore the dread power,
In true contrition I do dedicate
My breath to solitary holiness,
My lips to prayer; and my breast's care shall be
Restoring Altofront to regency.

MAL. Thy vows are heard, and we accept thy faith.
                                    Undisguiseth himself.

Enter FERNEZE *and* CELSO

Banish amazement; come, we four must stand
Full shock of fortune; be not so wonder-stricken.

PIET. Doth Ferneze live?

FERN. For your pardon.

PIET. Pardon and love. Give leave to recollect
My thoughts dispers'd in wild astonishment.
My vows stand fix'd in Heaven, and from hence
I crave all love and pardon.

MAL. Who doubts of providence,
That sees this change? A hearty faith to all!
He needs must rise who can no lower fall.
For still impetuous vicissitude
Touseth the world, then let no maze [2] intrude
Upon your spirits. Wonder not I rise;
For who can sink that close can temporize?

---

[1] The different cutting of cloth.   Bewilderment.

The time grows ripe for action; I'll detect [1]
My privat'st plot, lest ignorance fear suspect.   180
Let's close [2] to counsel, leave the rest to fate;
Mature discretion is the life of state.   *Exeunt.*

ACT V. SCENE 1 [3]

[*A room in the palace*]

Enter BILIOSO *and* PASSARELLO

BIL. Fool, how dost like my calf in a long stocking?

PASS. An excellent calf, my Lord.

BIL. This calf hath been a reveller this twenty year. When
  Monsieur Gundi lay here ambassador, I could have carried a
  lady up and down at arms' end in a platter; and I can tell you,
  there were those at that time who, to try the strength of a
  man's back and his arm would be coistered.[4] I have measured
  calves with most of the palace, and they come nothing near
  me; besides, I think there be not many armours in the arsenal
  will fit me, especially for the headpiece. I'll tell thee—   10

PASS. What, my Lord?

BIL. I can eat stewed broth as it comes seething off the fire, or a
  custard as it comes reeking out of the oven; and I think there
  are not many lords can do it. [*Displays his pomander.*[5]] A good
  pomander; a little decayed in the scent, but six grains of musk,
  ground with rose-water and tempered with a little civet, shall
  fetch her again presently.

PASS. Oh, ay, as a bawd with aqua-vitae.[6]

BIL. And, what, dost thou rail upon the ladies as thou wert
  wont?   20

PASS. I were better roast a live cat, and might do it with more
  safety. I am as secret to [the] thieves as their painting. There's
  Maquerelle, oldest bawd and a perpetual beggar. Did you
  never hear of her trick to be known in the city?

BIL. Never.

PASS. Why, she gets all the picture-makers to draw her picture;

[1] Expose.   [2] Join forces.   [3] This scene added in Q₃.
[4] Apparently a nonce word. Coiled up (?), inconvenienced (?)—*O.E.D.*
A printer's error for 'cloistered' (= confined, restricted)?
[5] A ball of perfume.   [6] Spirits.

when they have done, she most courtly finds fault with them
one after another, and never fetcheth them; they, in revenge
of this, execute her in pictures as they do in Germany, and
hang her in their shops. By this means is she better known to
the stinkards [1] than if she had been five times carted.[2]

BIL. 'Fore God, an excellent policy!

PASS. Are there any revels tonight, my Lord?

BIL. Yes.

PASS. Good my Lord, give me leave to break a fellow's pate that
hath abused me.

BIL. Whose pate?

PASS. Young Ferrard, my Lord.

BIL. Take heed, he's very valiant; I have known him fight eight
quarrels in five days, believe it.

PASS. Oh, is he so great a quarreller? Why, then, he's an arrant
coward.

BIL. How prove you that?

PASS. Why, thus: he that quarrels seeks to fight; and he that
seeks to fight seeks to die; and he that seeks to die seeks never
to fight more; and he that will quarrel, and seeks means never
to answer a man more, I think he's a coward.

BIL. Thou canst prove anything.

PASS. Anything but a rich knave, for I can flatter no man.

BIL. Well, be not drunk, good fool; I shall see you anon in the
presence.   *Exeunt.*

[ACT V. SCENE 2]

[*An anteroom in the citadel*]

Enter MALVOLE *and* MAQUERELLE, *at several doors opposite,*
singing

MAL. 'The Dutchman for a drunkard,'—

MAQ. 'The Dane for golden locks,'—

MAL. 'The Irishman for usquebaugh,' [3]

MAQ. 'The Frenchman for the (   ).'

MAL. Oh, thou art a blessed creature! Had I a modest woman
to conceal, I would put her to thy custody; for no reasonable

---

[1] The mob.   [2] Carried publicly · n a cart, a punishment for bawds, etc.
[3] Whisky.

creature would ever suspect her to be in thy company. Ha,
thou art a melodious Maquerelle, thou picture of a woman,
and substance of a beast.

Enter PASSARELLO [1]

MAQ. Oh, fool, will ye be ready anon to go with me to the revels? 10
The hall will be so pestered [2] anon.
PASS. Ay, as the country is with attorneys.
MAL. What hast thou there, fool?
PASS. Wine. I have learned to drink since I went with my lord
ambassador; I'll drink to the health of Madam Maquerelle.
MAL. Why, thou wast wont to rail upon her.
PASS. Ay, but since I borrowed money of her, I'll drink to her
health now, as gentlemen visit brokers, or as knights send
venison to the city, either to take up more money or to procure
longer forbearance. 20
MAL. Give me the bowl. I drink a health to Altofront, our
deposed duke.
PASS. I'll take it;—so. Now I'll begin a health to Madam
Maquerelle.
MAL. Phew! I will not pledge her.
PASS. Why? I pledged your lord.
MAL. I care not.
PASS. Not pledge Madam Maquerelle? Why, then, will I spew
up your lord again with this fool's finger.
MAL. Hold; I'll take it. 30
MAQ. Now thou hast drunk my health, fool, I am friends with
thee.
PASS. Art? Art?
'When Griffon [3] saw the reconciled quean
Offering about his neck her arms to cast,
He threw off sword and heart's malignant spleen,
And lovely her below the loins embrac'd.' [4]—
Adieu, Madam Maquerelle. *Exit* PASSARELLO.
MAL. And how dost thou think o' this transformation of state
now? 40
MAQ. Verily, very well; for we women always note, the falling
of the one is the rising of the other; some must be fat, some
must be lean; some must be fools, and some must be lords;

---

[1] Lines 10–38 added in Q_3. [2] Crowded.
[3] A hero in Ariosto, *Orlando Furioso* (1516). [4] Not identified.

some must be knaves, and some must be officers; some must be beggars, and some must be knights; some must be cuckolds, and some must be citizens. As, for example, I have two court-dogs, the most fawning curs, the one called Watch, th' other Catch; now I, like Lady Fortune, sometimes love this dog, sometimes raise that dog, sometimes favour Watch, most commonly fancy Catch. Now that dog which I favour I feed, and he's so ravenous that what I give he never chaws it, gulps it down whole, without any relish of what he has, but with a greedy expectation of what he shall have. The other dog now—

MAL. No more dog, sweet Maquerelle, no more dog. And what hope hast thou of the Duchess Maria? Will she stoop to the duke's lure? Will she come, thinkest?

MAQ. Let me see; where's the sign [1] now? Ha' ye e'er a calendar? Where's the sign, trow you?

MAL. Sign! Why, is there any moment in that?

MAQ. Oh, believe me, a most secret power! Look ye, a Chaldean or an Assyrian (I am sure 'twas a most sweet Jew) told me, court any woman in the right sign, you shall not miss; but you must take her in the right vein then; as when the sign is in Pisces, a fishmonger's wife is very sociable; in Cancer, a precisian's [2] wife is very flexible; in Capricorn, a merchant's wife hardly holds out; in Libra, a lawyer's wife is very tractable, especially if her husband be at the term; [3] only in Scorpio 'tis very dangerous meddling. Has the duke sent any jewel, any rich stones?

MAL. Ay, I think those are the best signs to take a lady in.

Enter captain

By your favour, signior, I must discourse with the Lady Maria, Altofront's duchess; I must enter for the duke.

CAPT. She here shall give you interview. I received the guardship of this citadel from the good Altofront, and for his use I'll keep't till I am of no use.

MAL. Wilt thou? O Heavens, that a Christian should be found in a buff jerkin! Captain Conscience, I love thee, Captain. We attend. (*Exit captain.*) And what hope hast thou of this duchess' easiness?

---

[1] Astrological sign.   [2] Puritan's.   [3] Court session.

MAQ. 'Twill go hard. She was a cold creature ever; she hated
monkeys, fools, jesters, and gentlemen ushers extremely; she
had the vile trick on't, not only to be truly modestly honourable in her own conscience, but she would avoid the least
wanton carriage that might incur suspect; as, God bless me,
she had almost brought bed-pressing out of fashion; I could
scarce get a fine [1] for the lease of a lady's favour once in a
fortnight.

MAL. Now, in the name of immodesty, how many maidenheads   90
hast thou brought to the block?

MAQ. Let me see; Heaven forgive us our misdeeds,—here's the
duchess.

Enter MARIA *and captain* [2]

MAL. God bless thee, lady!

MARIA. Out of thy company!

MAL. We have brought thee tender [3] of a husband.

MARIA. I hope I have one already.

MAQ. Nay, by mine honour, madam, as good ha' ne'er a
husband as a banished husband; he's in another world now.
I'll tell thee, lady, I have heard of a sect that maintained,   100
when the husband was asleep, the wife might lawfully entertain another man, for then her husband was as dead; much
more when he is banished.

MARIA. Unhonest creature!

MAQ. Pish! Honesty is but an art to seem so.
Pray ye, what's honesty, what's constancy,
But fables feign'd, odd old fools' chat,
Devis'd by jealous fools, to wrong our liberty?

MAL. Molly, he that loves thee is a duke, Mendoza; he will
maintain thee royally, love thee ardently, defend thee power-   110
fully, marry thee sumptuously, and keep thee in despite of
Rosicleer or Donzel del Phoebo. [4] There's jewels; if thou wilt,
so; if not, so.

MARIA. Captain, for God's sake, save poor wretchedness
From tyranny of lustful insolence!
Enforce me in the deepest dungeon dwell,
Rather than here; here round about is hell.
O my dear'st Altofront, where'er thou breathe,

---

[1] Fee.   [2] V. 2—quartos.   [3] A formal offer.
[4] Heroes in *The Mirror of Knighthood* (1583–1601).

Let my soul sink into the shades beneath,
Before I stain thine honour; this thou hast,
And long as I can die, I will live chaste!

MAL. 'Gainst him that can enforce, how vain is strife?

MARIA. She that can be enforc'd has here a knife!
She that through force her limbs with lust enrolls
Wants Cleopatra's asps or Portia's coals.
God amend you!   *Exit with captain.*

MAL. Now the fear of the devil for ever go with thee!
Maquerelle, I tell thee, I have found an honest woman!
Faith, I perceive, when all is done, there is of women, as of all
other things, some good, most bad; some saints, some sinners.
For as nowadays no courtier but has his mistress, no captain
but has his cockatrice,[1] no cuckold but has his horns, and no
fool but has his feather; even so, no woman but has her weak-
ness and feather too, no sex but has his—I can hunt the letter
no farther. [*Aside.*] O God, how loathsome this toying is to
me! That a duke should be forced to fool it! Well, *stultorum
plena sunt omnia*;[2] better play the fool lord than be the fool
lord.—Now where's your sleights, Madam Maquerelle?

MAQ. Why, are ye ignorant that 'tis said a squeamish, affected
niceness is natural to women, and that the excuse of their
yielding is only, forsooth, the difficult obtaining? You must
put her to't; women are flax, and will fire in a moment.

MAL. Why, was the flax put into thy mouth, and yet thou—
Thou set fire, thou inflame her?

MAQ. Marry, but I'll tell ye now, you were too hot.

MAL. The fitter to have enflamed the flax-woman.

MAQ. You were too boisterous, spleeny, for, indeed,—

MAL. Go, go; thou art a weak pandress; now I see,
Sooner earth's fire Heaven itself shall waste,
Than all with heat can melt a mind that's chaste.
Go, thou the duke's lime-twig![3] I'll make the duke turn thee
out of thine office. What, not get one touch of hope, and had
her at such advantage!

MAQ. Now, o' my conscience, now I think in my discretion, we
did not take her in the right sign; the blood was not in the true
vein, sure.   *Exeunt.*

[1] Whore.
[2] 'All places are full of fools' (Cicero, *Epistolae ad Familiares*, ix. 22).
[3] Trap.

[ACT V. SCENE 3]

[*A room in the palace*]

Enter BILIOSO [1]

BIL. Make way there! The duke returns from the enthrone-
ment. Malvole—

MAL. Out, rogue!

BIL. Malvole—

MAL. 'Hence, ye gross-jawed, peasantly—out, go!' [2]

BIL. Nay, sweet Malvole, since my return I hear you are become
the thing I always prophesied would be, an advanced virtue, a
worthily employed faithfulness, a man o' grace, dear friend.
Come, what? *Si quoties peccant homines . . .;* [3] if as often as
courtiers play the knaves, honest men should be angry . . .   10
—Why, look ye, we must collogue [4] sometimes, forswear
sometimes.

MAL. Be damned sometimes.

BIL. Right; *nemo omnibus horis sapit*: 'no man can be honest at
all hours.' Necessity often depraves virtue.

MAL. I will commend thee to the duke.

BIL. Do; let's be friends, man.

MAL. And knaves, man.

BIL. Right; let us prosper and purchase; [5] our lordships shall
live, and our knavery be forgotten.   20

MAL. He that by any ways gets riches, his means never shame
him.

BIL. True.

MAL. For impudency and faithlessness are the mainstays to
greatness.

BIL. By the Lord, thou art a profound lad.

MAL. By the Lord, thou art a perfect knave. Out, ye ancient
damnation!

BIL. Peace, peace; and thou wilt not be a friend to me as I am a
knave, be not a knave to me as I am thy friend, and disclose   30
me. Peace; cornets!

---

[1] Lines 1—31 added in Q₃.
[2] Bilioso's words at II. 2. 62.
[3] 'If as often men sin . . .' (Ovid, *Tristia*, II. 33).
[4] Feign.   [5] Become rich.

Enter PREPASSO *and* FERRARDO, *two pages with lights,*
CELSO *and* EQUATO, MENDOZA *in duke's robes, and*
GUERRINO [1]

MEND. On, on; leave us, leave us.

      Exeunt all saving MALVOLE *and* MENDOZA.

  Stay, where is the hermit?

MAL. With Duke Pietro, with Duke Pietro.

MEND. Is he dead? Is he poisoned?

MAL. Dead as the duke is.

MEND. Good, excellent. He will not blab; secureness lives in
secrecy. Come hither, come hither.

MAL. Thou hast a certain strong villainous scent about thee my
nature cannot endure.

MEND. Scent, man? What returns Maria? What answer to our
suit?

MAL. Cold, frosty; she is obstinate.

MEND. Then she's but dead; 'tis resolute, she dies.
Black deed only through black deed safely flies.

MAL. Phew! *Per scelera semper sceleribus tutum est iter.* [2]

MEND. What, art a scholar? Art a politician? Sure, thou art an
an arrant knave.

MAL. Who, I? I have been twice an under-sheriff, man.

MEND. Hast been with Maria? [3]

MAL. As your scrivener to your usurer, I have dealt about
taking this commodity, but she's cold-frosty. Well, I will go
rail upon some great man, that I may purchase the bastinado, [4]
or else go marry some rich Genoan lady, and instantly go
travel.

MEND. Travel when thou art married?

MAL. Ay, 'tis your young lord's fashion to do so, though he
were so lazy, being a bachelor, that he would never travel so
far as the university; yet when he married her, tales of—and,
Catso, for England.

MEND. And why for England?

MAL. Because there is no brothel-houses there.

MEND. Nor courtesans?

<hr>

 [1] V. 3—quartos.
 [2] 'The safe way through crimes is always by crimes' (Seneca, *Agamemnon*,
I. 115).
 [3] Lines 50–65 added in Q₃. 'Hast been . . . cold-frosty' (lines 50–2) were
perhaps intended to cancel part of the dialogue beginning at line 41.
 [4] Bring a beating upon myself.

MAL. Neither; your whore went down with the stews,[1] and
    your punk [2] came up with your Puritan.

MEND. Canst thou empoison? Canst thou empoison?

MAL. Excellently; no Jew, 'pothecary, or politician better.
    Look ye, here's a box; whom wouldst thou empoison?
    Here's a box [*Passes it to* MENDOZA.] which, opened and the
    fume taken up in conduits through which the brain purges   70
    itself, doth instantly for twelve hours' space bind up all show
    of life in a deep senseless sleep; here's another [*Passes it to*
    MENDOZA.] which, being opened under the sleeper's nose,
    chokes all the pores of life, kills him suddenly.

MEND. I'll try experiments; 'tis good not to be deceived. So, so;
    Catso!   *Seems to poison* MALVOLE.
    Who would fear that may destroy?
    Death hath no teeth or tongue;
    And he that's great, to him are slaves
    Shame, murder, fame and wrong.   80

Enter CELSO

Celso?

CEL. My honoured Lord.

MEND. The good Malvole, that plain-tongu'd man,
    Alas, is dead on sudden, wondrous strangely.
    He held in our esteem good place. Celso,
    See him buried, see him buried.

CEL. I shall observe ye.

MEND. And, Celso, prithee let it be thy care tonight
    To have some pretty show, to solemnize
    Our high instalment, some music, masquery.   90
    We'll give fair entertain unto Maria,
    The duchess to the banish'd Altofront.
    Thou shalt conduct her from the citadel
    Unto the palace. Think on some masquery.

CEL. Of what shape, sweet Lord?

MEND. Why, shape? Why, any quick-done fiction;
    As some brave spirits of the Genoan dukes
    To come out of Elysium, forsooth,

---

[1] Areas occupied by brothels; notorious stews in Southwark were abolished
in 1546.
[2] Prostitute. The sentence seems to imply that an earlier situation revived
under another name.

Led in by Mercury, to gratulate [1]
Our happy fortune; some such anything,
Some far-fet trick, good for ladies, some stale toy
Or other; no matter, so it be of our devising.
Do thou prepar't; 'tis but for a fashion sake.
Fear not, it shall be grac'd, man, it shall take.

CEL. All service.

MEND. All thanks; our hand shall not be close [2] to thee.
Farewell.
[*Aside.*] Now is my treachery secure, nor can we fall;
Mischief that prospers, men do virtue call.
I'll trust no man; he that by tricks gets wreaths
Keeps them with steel; no man securely breathes
Out of deserved ranks; the crowd will mutter, 'Fool!'
Who cannot bear with spite, he cannot rule.
The chiefest secret for a man of state
Is to live senseless [3] of a strengthless hate.   [*Exit.*]

MAL. (*Starts up and speaks.*) Death of the damned thief! I'll
make one i' the masque; thou shalt ha' some brave spirits of
the antique dukes!

CEL. My Lord, what strange delusion?

MAL. Most happy, dear Celso; poisoned with an empty box!
I'll give thee all anon. My lady comes to court; there is a
whirl of fate comes tumbling on; the castle's captain stands for
me, the people pray for me, and the great leader of the just
stands for me! Then courage, Celso;
For no disastrous chance can ever move him
That leaveth [4] nothing but a God above him.   [*Exeunt.*]

[ACT V. SCENE 4]

[*The presence-chamber*]

Enter PREPASSO *and* BILIOSO, *two pages before them,*
MAQUERELLE, BIANCA, *and* EMILIA

BIL. Make room there, room for the ladies! Why, gentlemen,
will ye not suffer the ladies to be entered in the great chamber?

---

[1] Salute.   [2] Niggardly.   [3] Unconscious.
[4] Feareth(?)—so emended in several modern editions.

Why, gallants! And you, sir, to drop your torch where the
beauties must sit too!

PREP. And there's a great fellow plays the knave; why dost not
strike him?

BIL. Let him play the knave, a' God's name. Think'st thou I
have no more wit than to strike a great fellow? The music,
more lights, revelling-scaffolds! Do you hear? Let there be
oaths enow ready at the door; swear out the devil himself.   10
Let's leave the ladies, and go see if the lords be ready for
them.   *All save the ladies depart.*

MAQ. And, by my troth, beauties, why do you not put you into
the fashion? This is a stale cut; you must come into fashion.
Look ye, you must be all felt, felt and feather, a felt [1] upon
your bare hair; look ye, these tiring things [2] are justly out of
request now; and—do ye hear?—you must wear falling-
bands; [3] you must come into the falling fashion. There is such
a deal o' pinning these ruffs, when the fine clean fall is worth
all; and again, if you should chance to take a nap in the after-   20
noon, your falling-band requires no poting-stick [4] to recover
his form. Believe me, no fashion to the falling, I say.

BIAN. And is not Signior Saint Andrew [5] a gallant fellow now?

MAQ. By my maidenhead, la, honour and he agrees as well
together as a satin suit and woollen stockings.

EMIL. But is not Marshal Make-room, my servant in reversion,[6] a proper gentleman?

MAQ. Yes, in reversion, as he had his office; as, in truth, he
hath all things in reversion. He has his mistress in reversion,
his clothes in reversion, his wit in reversion; and, indeed, is a   30
suitor to me for my dog in reversion; but, in good verity, la,
he is as proper a gentleman in reversion as—and, indeed, as
fine a man as may be, having a red beard and a pair of warped
legs.[7]

BIAN. But, i' faith, I am most monstrously in love with Count
Quidlibet-in-quodlibet; [8] is he not a pretty, dapper, unidle
gallant?

[1] i.e. hat.   [2] Head-dresses.

[3] Flat collars, a style which succeeded ruffs. Falling bands seem not to have
been in style for women until the reign of James I.

[4] A device for crimping ruffs, etc.

[5] A few copies of Q₁ have 'Jaques' or 'James' added here, a hit at King
James.

[6] By right of succession, i.e. at second hand.

[7] A description of Marston himself.

[8] Freely translated: 'Whatever you want wherever you want it.'

MAQ. He is even one of the most busy-fingered lords; he will
    put the beauties to the squeak most hideously.

Enter BILIOSO

BIL. Room! Make a lane there! The duke is entering. Stand
    handsomely for beauty's sake. Take up [1] the ladies there. So,
    cornets, cornets!

> *Enter* PREPASSO, *joins to* BILIOSO; *two pages and lights,*
> FERRARDO, MENDOZA; *at the other door, two pages with
> lights, and the captain leading in* MARIA; *the duke meets
> MARIA and closeth with her; the rest fall back* [2]

MEND. Madam, with gentle ear receive my suit:
    A kingdom's safety should o'erpeise [3] slight rites;
    Marriage is merely nature's policy.
    Then, since unless our royal beds be join'd,
    Danger and civil tumult frights the state,
    Be wise as you are fair, give way to fate.
MARIA. What wouldst thou, thou affliction to our house?
    Thou ever-devil, 'twas thou that banish'st
    My truly noble lord.
MEND. I?
MARIA. Ay, by thy plots, by thy black stratagems.
    Twelve moons have suff'red change since I beheld
    The loved presence of my dearest lord.
    O thou far worse than death! He parts but soul
    From a weak body; but thou soul from soul
    Disseverest, that which God's hand did knit.
    Thou scant [4] of honour, full of devilish wit!
MEND. We'll check your too intemperate lavishness;
    I can and will.
MARIA. What canst?
MEND. Go to; in banishment thy husband dies.
MARIA. He ever is at home that's ever wise.
MEND. You'st [5] ne'er meet more; reason should love control.
MARIA. Not meet?
    She that dear loves, her love's still in her soul.
MEND. You are but a woman, lady; you must yield.

---

[1] Conduct.   [2] V. 4—quartos.
[3] Outweigh.   [4] Dearth.   [5] 'You must'

MARIA. Oh, save me, thou innated bashfulness,
   Thou only ornament of woman's modesty!   70
MEND. Modesty? Death, I'll torment thee!
MARIA. Do; urge all torments, all afflictions try;
   I'll die my lord's, as long as I can die.
MEND. Thou obstinate, thou shalt die. Captain, that lady's life
   Is forfeited to justice: We have examin'd her,
   And we do find she hath empoisoned
   The reverend hermit; therefore we command
   Severest custody. Nay, if you'll do's no good,
   You'll do's no harm; a tyrant's peace is blood.
MARIA. Oh, thou art merciful! O gracious devil,   80
   Rather by much let me condemned be
   For seeming murder than be damn'd for thee!
   I'll mourn no more; come, gird my brows with flowers;
   Revel and dance, soul, now thy wish thou hast;
   Die like a bride, poor heart; thou shalt die chaste.

Enter AURELIA in mourning habit

AUR. 'Life is a frost of cold felicity,
   And death the thaw of all our vanity.' [1]
   Was't not an honest priest that wrote so?
MEND. Who let her in?
BIL. Forbear!   90
PREP. Forbear!
AUR. Alas, calamity is everywhere;
   Sad misery, despite your double doors,
   Will enter even in court.
BIL. Peace!
AUR. I ha' done.
BIL. One word—take heed!
AUR. I ha' done.

Enter MERCURY with loud music

MERC. Cyllenian Mercury, the god of ghosts,
   From gloomy shades that spread the lower coasts,   100
   Calls four high-famed Genoan dukes to come,
   And make this presence their Elysium,

---

[1] Thomas Bastard, *Chrestoleros*, iv. 32 (1598).

    To pass away this high triumphal night
    With song and dances, court's more soft delight.
AUR. Are you god of ghosts? I have a suit depending [1] in hell
    betwixt me and my conscience; I would fain have thee help
    me to an advocate.
BIL. Mercury shall be your lawyer, lady.
AUR. Nay, faith, Mercury has too good a face to be a right [2]
    lawyer.
PREP. Peace, forbear! Mercury presents the masque.
    *Cornets; the song to the cornets, which playing, the masque
      enters.* MALVOLE, PIETRO, FERNEZE, *and* CELSO *in
      white robes, with dukes' crowns upon laurel wreaths, pisto-
      lets and short swords under their robes*
MEND. Celso, Celso, court Maria for our love.—Lady, be
    gracious, yet grace—
                    MALVOLE *takes his wife* MARIA *to dance.*
MARIA. With me, sir?
MAL.   Yes, more loved than my breath,
    With you I'll dance.
MARIA.   Why, then you dance with death.
    But, come, sir, I was ne'er more apt to mirth.
    Death gives eternity a glorious breath;
    Oh, to die honour'd, who would fear to die!
MAL. They die in fear who live in villainy.
MEND. Yes, believe him, lady, and be rul'd by him.
                  PIETRO *takes his wife* AURELIA *to dance.*
PIET. Madam, with me?
AUR. Wouldst then be miserable?
PIET. I need not wish.
AUR. Oh, yet forbear my hand. Away! Fly, fly!
    Oh, seek not her that only seeks to die!
PIET. Poor loved soul!
AUR. What, wouldst court misery?
PIET. Yes.
AUR. She'll come too soon. O my grieved heart!
PIET. Lady, ha' done, ha' done.
    Come, let's dance; be once from sorrow free.
AUR. Art a sad man?
PIET. Yes, sweet.
AUR. Then we'll agree.

               [1] Pending.   [2] True.

FERNEZE *takes* MAQUERELLE, *and* CELSO, BIANCA; *then
the cornets sound the measure, one change and rest*

FERN. (*To* BIANCA.) Believe it, lady; shall I swear? Let me
enjoy you in private, and I 'll marry you,[1] by my soul.

BIAN. I had rather you would swear by your body; I think that
would prove the more regarded oath with you.

FERN. I 'll swear by them both, to please you.

BIAN. Oh, damn them not both to please me, for God's sake.   140

FERN. Faith, sweet creature, let me enjoy you tonight, and I 'll
marry you tomorrow fortnight, by my troth, la.

MAQ. On his troth, la! Believe him not; that kind of cony-
catching [2] is as stale as Sir Oliver Anchovy's perfumed jerkin.
Promise of matrimony by a young gallant to bring a virgin
lady into a fool's paradise, make her a great woman, and then
cast her off! 'Tis as common, as natural to a courtier, as
jealousy to a citizen, gluttony to a Puritan, wisdom to an
alderman, pride to a tailor, or an empty hand-basket to one of
these sixpenny damnations.[3] Of his troth, la! Believe him not;   150
traps to catch polecats! [3]

MAL. (*To* MARIA.) Keep your face constant. Let no sudden
passion
   Speak in your eyes.   [*Reveals himself to her.*]

MARIA. O my Altofront!

PIET. [*To* AURELIA.]   A tyrant's jealousies
   Are very nimble; you receive it all.[4]   [*Reveals himself to her.*]

AUR. My heart, though not my knees, doth humbly fall
   Low as the earth to thee.

PIET. Peace! Next change; no words.   160

MARIA. Speech to such? [5] Ay, oh, what will affords!
   *Cornets sound the measure over again; which danced, they
   unmask. They environ* MENDOZA, *bending their pistols on
   him*

MEND. Malvole!

MAL. No.

MEND. Altofront! Duke Pietro! Ferneze! Ha?

ALL. Duke Altofront! Duke Altofront!   *Cornets, a flourish.*

MEND. Are we surpris'd? What strange delusions mock
   Our senses? Do I dream, or have I dreamt
   This two days' space? Where am I?

---

[1] She is already married to Bilioso.   [2] Trickery.
[3] Prostitutes.   [4] Bear the brunt.
[5] i.e. Pietro, with whom she now dances.

They seize upon MENDOZA.

MAL. Where an arch-villain is—

MEND. Oh, lend me breath till I am fit to die!
For peace with Heaven, for your own souls' sake,
Vouchsafe me life!

PIET. Ignoble villain, whom neither Heaven nor hell,
Goodness of God or man, could once make good!—

MAL. Base, treacherous wretch, what grace canst thou expect,
That hast grown impudent in gracelessness?

MEND. Oh, life!

MAL. Slave, take thy life.
Wert thou defenced [1] through blood and wounds,
The sternest horror of a civil fight,
Would I achieve [2] thee; but prostrate at my feet,
I scorn to hurt thee; 'tis the heart of slaves
That deigns to triumph over peasants' graves;
For such thou art, since birth doth ne'er enroll
A man 'mong monarchs, but a glorious soul.
Oh, I have seen strange accidents of state: [3]
The flatterer, like the ivy, clip the oak,
And waste it to the heart; lust so confirm'd
That the black act of sin itself not sham'd
To be term'd courtship.
Oh, they that are as great as be their sins,
Let them remember that th'inconstant people
Love many princes merely for their faces
And outward shows; and they do covet more
To have a sight of these than of their virtues.
Yet thus much let the great ones still conceive,
When they observe not Heaven's impos'd conditions,
They are no kings, but forfeit their commissions.

MAQ. Oh, good my Lord, I have lived in the court this twenty
year; they that have been old courtiers and come to live in the
city, they are spited at and thrust to the walls like apricots,
good my Lord.

BIL. My Lord, I did know your lordship in this disguise; you
heard me ever say if Altofront did return I would stand for
him; besides, 'twas your lordship's pleasure to call me wittol
and cuckold; you must not think, but that I knew you, I
would have put it up [4] so patiently.

---

[1] Protected.   [2] Bring thee to an end.
[3] Lines 186–207 added in Q₃.   [4] Tolerated it.

MAL. (*To* PIETRO *and* AURELIA.) You o'er-joy'd spirits, wipe
    your long-wet eyes.—

Hence with this man. (*Kicks out* MENDOZA.) An eagle takes not   210
flies.

(*To* PIETRO *and* AURELIA.) You to your vows.—(*To*
    MAQUERELLE.) And thou unto the suburbs.[1]

(*To* BILIOSO.) You to my worst friend I would hardly give;
Thou art a perfect old knave.—(*To* CELSO *and the captain.*)
    All pleas'd, live
You two unto my breast;—(*To* MARIA.) thou to my heart;
The rest of idle actors idly part.
And as for me, I here assume my right,
To which I hope all's pleas'd; to all, good night.   220
      Cornets, a flourish. Exeunt omnes.

FINIS

An imperfect ode, being but one staff, spoken
by the Prologue

To wrest each hurtless thought to private sense
  Is the foul use of ill-bred impudence;
    Immodest censure now grows wild,
      All over-running.
  Let innocence be ne'er so chaste,
      Yet at the last
      She is defil'd
With too nice-brained cunning.
    O you of fairer soul,
      Control   230
    With an Herculean arm
      This harm;
And once teach all old freedom of a pen,
Which still must write of fools whiles 't writes of men.

[1] The location of the brothels.

Epilogue

Your modest silence, full of heedy stillness,
Makes me thus speak: a voluntary illness [1]
Is merely [2] senseless; but unwilling error,
Such as proceeds from too rash youthful fervour,
May well be call'd a fault, but not a sin;
Rivers take names from founts where they begin.
Then let not too severe an eye peruse
The slighter bracks [3] of our reformed Muse,
Who could herself herself of faults detect,
But that she knows 'tis easy to correct.
Though some men's labour, troth, to err is fit,
As long as wisdom's not profess'd, but wit.
Then, till another's [4] happier Muse appears,
Till his Thalia [5] feast your learned ears,
To whose desertful lamps [6] pleas'd Fates impart
Art above nature, judgment above art,
Receive this piece which hope nor fear yet daunteth;
He that knows most knows most how much he wanteth.

FINIS

[1] Defect   [2] Wholly.   [3] Flaws.   [4] Ben Jonson's.
[5] Muse of comic poetry.   [6] Studies at night.

THOMAS MIDDLETON
(1580–1627)

Born London; studied at Queen's College, Oxford.
Wrote pageants, masques, and pamphlets; was City
Chronologer (1620–7). A varied dramatic achievement:
comedies, among them *A Trick to Catch the Old One*,
A Chaste Maid in Cheapside; tragedies, *Women Beware
Women*, *The Changeling* (with Rowley); and a political
satire, *A Game at Chess*.

WILLIAM ROWLEY
(*c.* 1585–1626)

A character actor with various companies for many
years. Collaborated with several other dramatists; with
Middleton he wrote *A Fair Quarrel*, *The Spanish Gipsy*,
etc. Wrote independently several undistinguished plays,
including *All's Lost by Lust* and *A Shoemaker a
Gentleman*.

THE CHANGELING (1622)

The Changeling is distinguished by its having in juxtaposition two remarkably diverse plots: a powerful tragedy (largely conceived and written by Middleton) and a coarse, farcical comedy (by Rowley). To a superficial view, in their impact or effect the two plots are less than a unified whole, linked as they are in fact only in the denouement, but in intention the union is clear and implies the close collaboration of the authors.

The major plot centres on the changing loyalties of Beatrice, whose career ends tragically because of her faulty judgment. The secondary plot, set in a madhouse, reveals how Isabella is tempted by two pretended idiots (i.e. changelings) to be disloyal to her husband, as Beatrice is tempted to be disloyal to her original fiancé; by contrast, however, Isabella sensibly resists the temptation and is thus able to repulse her blackmailer.

The contrasts between the two women create the principal interest in the Rowley subplot, which is to modern taste distinctly uncouth. Rowley's liking for coarse jokes and puns, in uninspired prose, and his rough-hewn versification contribute to this plot little that is positive, but the madhouse scenes are not likely to have given much offence to the original audience; public visits to London's Bedlam were a popular pastime in the seventeenth century, and the studies of Robert Reed junior (*Bedlam on the Jacobean Stage*, 1952) suggest that the underplot owes something to the nefarious activities of a contemporary administrator of Bethlehem Hospital, Dr Hildish Crooke.[1]

The collaboration of the authors was close; therefore it is impossible to label exactly the contributions of each writer. Middleton's is the main hand in the principal plot, although Rowley wrote most of Act I, Scene 1 and Act V, Scene 3, and contributed to a few other scenes in it. The subplot is Rowley's, apart from some small touches of Middleton.

---

[1] The text of the subplot fails to reveal until late in the action the fact that Antonio and Franciscus are not really insane. If the viewer of the play were unaware of their true condition he would miss much of the humour and irony of the madhouse scenes; thus it is likely that both disguised men reveal themselves in mime to the audience when they first appear. (It is hardly necessary to point out that the dialogue of pretended fools and madmen need not be entirely coherent.)

Middleton's writing in *The Changeling* is marked by a delicacy of touch in both style and characterization, a skill in language and metre, and an unusual emphasis on verbal and dramatic irony. Middleton was, however, responsible for the episodes of the virginity tests, which strike the modern reader or viewer as implausible.

Those parts of the play most dramatically and emotionally effective concern Beatrice's ingenuous involvement with the Iago-like De Flores, her revulsion, in a brilliantly conceived scene (III. 4), when she ultimately realizes her situation, and finally, in distinctive contrast, her gradual habituation to an intimate relationship with him. It is her naïve, self-confident belief that she may both possess her cake and eat it which destroys her. The remainder of the *dramatis personae* are not without distinctive personalities; yet none is developed with the penetration that Beatrice is.

The major plot was primarily indebted to stories in Reynolds's *God's Revenge against Murder* (1621) and Cespedes's *Gerardo, The Unfortunate Spaniard* (1622); the subplot had no literary source. *The Changeling* was first produced in 1622, was popular on the stage for many years, but was not published until 1653. Two subsequent issues of the play (later in 1653 and in 1668) are the same printing as the first, with revised title-pages.

THE CHANGELING
by
Thomas Middleton
and
William Rowley
[1622]

Dramatis Personae

VERMANDERO, father to Beatrice
TOMAZO de PIRACQUO, a noble lord
ALONZO de PIRACQUO, his brother, suitor to Beatrice
ALSEMERO, a nobleman, afterwards married to Beatrice
JASPERINO, his friend
ALIBIUS, a jealous doctor
LOLLIO, his man
PEDRO, friend to Antonio
ANTONIO, the changeling
FRANCISCUS, the counterfeit madman
DE FLORES, servant to Vermandero
MADMEN, SERVANTS
BEATRICE [-JOANNA], daughter to Vermandero
DIAPHANTA, her waiting-woman
ISABELLA, wife to Alibius
SCENE: Alicante, [Spain].

Act I. [Scene 1]

[*A street near the harbour of Alicante*]

Enter ALSEMERO

ALS. 'Twas in the temple where I first beheld her,
    And now again the same; what omen yet
    Follows of that? None but imaginary.
    Why should my hopes or fate be timorous?
    The place is holy, so is my intent;
    I love her beauties to the holy purpose,[1]
    And that, methinks, admits comparison
    With man's first creation, the place bless'd,[2]
    And is his right home back, if he achieve it.
    The church hath first begun our interview,   10
    And that's the place must join us into one;
    So there's beginning and perfection too.

Enter JASPERINO

JAS. Oh, sir, are you here? Come, the wind's fair with you;
    Y'are like to have a swift and pleasant passage.
ALS. Sure, y'are deceived, friend; 'tis contrary
    In my best judgment.
JAS.   What, for Malta?
    If you could buy a gale amongst the witches,[3]
    They could not serve you such a lucky pennyworth [4]
    As comes a' God's name.[5]
ALS.   Even now I observ'd
    The temple's vane to turn full in my face;   20
    I know 'tis against me.
JAS.   Against you?
    Then you know not where you are.
ALS.   Not well, indeed.
JAS. Are you not well, sir?
ALS.   Yes, Jasperino;

---

[1] Matrimony.   [2] Paradise.   [3] Witches were reputed to sell winds.
[4] Bargain.   [5] i.e. free.

    Unless there be some hidden malady
    Within me, that I understand not.
JAS.   And that
    I begin to doubt, sir. I never knew
    Your inclinations to travel at a pause
    With any cause to hinder it, till now.
    Ashore you were wont to call your servants up,
    And help to trap your horses for the speed; [1]
    At sea I have seen you weigh the anchor with 'em,
    Hoist sails for fear to lose the foremost breath,
    Be in continual prayers for fair winds,
    And have you chang'd your orisons?
ALS.   No, friend,
    I keep the same church, same devotion.
JAS. Lover I'm sure y'are none; the stoic was
    Found in you long ago. Your mother nor
    Best friends, who have set snares of beauty—ay,
    And choice ones too—could never trap you that way.
    What might be the cause?
ALS.   Lord, how violent
    Thou art! I was but meditating of
    Somewhat I heard within the temple.
JAS.   Is this
    Violence? 'Tis but idleness compar'd
    With your haste yesterday.
ALS.   I'm all this while
    A-going, man.

Enter servants

JAS.   Backwards, I think, sir. Look, your servants.
1 SERV. The seamen call; shall we board your trunks?
ALS. No, not today.
JAS.   'Tis the critical day,
    It seems, and the sign in Aquarius.[2]
2 SERV. [*Aside.*] We must not to sea today; this smoke will bring
    forth fire!
ALS. Keep all on shore; I do not know the end,
    Which need I must do, of an affair in hand
    Ere I can go to sea.

       [1] To assist in harnessing the horses to expedite departure.
       [2] Foreboding storms.

1 SERV.   Well, your pleasure.
2 SERV. [*Aside.*] Let him e'en take his leisure too; we are safer
  on land.   *Exeunt servants.*

Enter BEATRICE, DIAPHANTA, *and servants.* [ALSEMERO
  greets BEATRICE *and kisses her*]

JAS. [*Aside.*] How now! The laws of the Medes are changed
  sure! [1] Salute a woman? He kisses too. Wonderful! Where
  learnt he this? And does it perfectly too; in my conscience, he
  ne'er rehearsed it before. Nay, go on; this will be stranger and   60
  better news at Valencia than if he had ransomed half Greece
  from the Turk.
BEA. You are a scholar, sir?
ALS.   A weak one, lady.
BEA. Which of the sciences [2] is this love you speak of?
ALS. From your tongue I take it to be music.
BEA. You are skilful in't, can sing at first sight.
ALS. And I have show'd you all my skill at once.
  I want more words to express me further,
  And must be forc'd to repetition:
  I love you dearly.
BEA.   Be better advis'd, sir;   70
  Our eyes are sentinels unto our judgments,
  And should give certain judgment what they see;
  But they are rash sometimes and tell us wonders
  Of common things, which, when our judgments find,
  They then can check the eyes and call them blind.
ALS. But I am further, lady; yesterday
  Was mine eyes' employment, and hither now
  They brought my judgment, where are both agreed.
  Both houses [3] then consenting, 'tis agreed;
  Only there wants the confirmation   80
  By the hand royal—that's your part, lady.
BEA. Oh, there's one above me, sir.— [*Aside.*] For five days past—
  To be recall'd! Sure, mine eyes were mistaken;
  This was the man was meant me. That he should come
  So near his time, and miss it!
JAS. [*Aside.*] We might have come by the carriers [4] from

---

[1] 'The unalterable has been altered.'
[2] Descriptive of any scholarly activity.
[3] Fig., houses of parliament.   [4] Overland porters.

Valencia, I see, and saved all our sea provision; we are at
farthest sure. Methinks I should do something too;
I meant to be a venturer [1] in this voyage.
Yonder's another vessel; I'll board her.
If she be lawful prize, down goes her top-sail!

                           [Approaches DIAPHANTA.]

Enter DE FLORES

DE F. Lady, your father—
BEA.   Is in health, I hope.
DE F. Your eye shall instantly instruct you, lady;
  He's coming hitherward.
BEA.   What needed then
  Your duteous preface? I had rather
  He had come unexpected; you must stall [2]
  A good presence with unnecessary blabbing;
  And how welcome for your part you are,
  I'm sure you know.
DE F. [*Aside.*]   Will't never mend, this scorn,
  One side nor other? Must I be enjoin'd
  To follow still whilst she flies from me? Well,
  Fates do your worst, I'll please myself with sight
  Of her, at all opportunities,
  If but to spite her anger; I know she had
  Rather see me dead than living, and yet
  She knows no cause for't but a peevish will.   [*Exit.*]
ALS. You seem'd displeased, lady, on the sudden.
BEA. Your pardon, sir, 'tis my infirmity;
  Nor can I other reason render you
  Than his or hers,[3] of some particular thing
  They must abandon as a deadly poison,
  Which to a thousand other tastes were wholesome;
  Such to mine eyes is that same fellow there,
  The same that report [4] speaks of the basilisk.[5]
ALS. This is a frequent frailty in our nature;
  There's scarce a man among a thousand sound,
  But hath his imperfection: one distastes

----

[1] Sharer, investor.   [2] Diminish interest in.
[3] This or that.   [4] Rumour, legend.
[5] A mythical serpent reputed to kill with its glance.

The scent of roses, which to infinites [1]
Most pleasing is and odoriferous;
One oil,[2] the enemy of poison,   120
Another wine, the cheerer of the heart,
And lively refresher of the countenance.
Indeed, this fault, if so it be, is general;
There's scarce a thing but is both lov'd and loath'd;
Myself, I must confess, have the same frailty.

BEA. And what may be your poison, sir? I am bold with you.

ALS. And what might be your desire? Perhaps a cherry.[3]

BEA. I am no enemy to any creature
My memory has, but yon gentleman.

ALS. He does ill to tempt your sight, if he knew it.   130

BEA. He cannot be ignorant of that, sir;
I have not spar'd to tell him so; and I want [4]
To help myself, since he's a gentleman
In good respect with my father, and follows him.

ALS. He's out of his place then now.   [They talk apart.]

JAS. I am a mad wag, wench.

DIA. So methinks; but for your comfort I can tell you, we have
a doctor in the city that undertakes the cure of such.

JAS. Tush, I know what physic is best for the state of mine own
body.   140

DIA. 'Tis scarce a well-governed state, I believe.

JAS. I could show thee such a thing with an ingredient that we
two would compound together, and if it did not tame the
maddest blood i' th' town for two hours after, I'll ne'er
profess physic again.

DIA. A little poppy, sir, were good to cause you sleep.

JAS. Poppy? I'll give thee a pop i' th' lips for that first, and
begin there! Poppy is one simple [5] indeed, and cuckoo [6]
(what you call't) another. I'll discover [7] no more now;
another time I'll show thee all.   [Exit.]   150

Enter VERMANDERO, [DE FLORES,] *and servants*

BEA. My father, sir.

VER.   Oh, Joanna, I came to meet thee;
Your devotion's ended?

---

[1] Many people.   [2] Some volatile oils were used in medicine.
[3] i.e. anything trivial.   [4] Lack means.
[5] A remedy with one ingredient.   [6] The cuckoo-flower.   [7] Reveal.

BEA.   For this time, sir.—
  [*Aside.*] I shall change my saint, I fear me; I find
  A giddy turning in me.—Sir, this while
  I am beholding to this gentleman,
  Who left his own way to keep me company,
  And in discourse I find him much desirous
  To see your castle. He hath much deserv'd it, sir,
  If ye please to grant it.
VER.   With all my heart, sir.
  Yet there's an article [1] between; I must know
  Your country. We use not to give survey
  Of our chief strengths to strangers; our citadels
  Are plac'd conspicuous to outward view,
  On promonts' tops; but within are secrets.
ALS. A Valencian, sir.
VER.   A Valencian?
  That's native, sir; of what name, I beseech you?
ALS. Alsemero, sir.
VER.   Alsemero; not the son
  Of John de Alsemero?
ALS.   The same, sir.
VER. My best love bids you welcome.
BEA. [*Aside.*]   He was wont
  To call me so,[2] and then he speaks a most
  Unfeigned truth.
VER.   Oh, sir, I knew your father;
  We two were in acquaintance long ago,
  Before our chins were worth Julan down,[3]
  And so continued till the stamp of time
  Had coin'd us into silver. Well, he's gone;
  A good soldier went with him.
ALS. You went together [4] in that, sir.
VER. No, by Saint Jaques,[5] I came behind him;
  Yet I have done somewhat too. An unhappy day
  Swallowed him at last at Gibraltar [6]
  In fight with those rebellious Hollanders,
  Was it not so?
ALS.   Whose death I had reveng'd,

---

[1] Proviso.   [2] i.e. his best love.
[3] The first growth of beard (an Elizabethan coinage).
[4] Were equal in valour.   [5] The patron saint of Spain.
[6] The scene of a Dutch victory over the Spanish in 1607.

Or follow'd him in fate, had not the late league [1]
Prevented me.
VER.   Ay, ay, 'twas time to breathe.
Oh, Joanna, I should ha' told thee news:
I saw Piracquo lately.
BEA. [*Aside.*]   That's ill news.
VER. He's hot preparing for this day of triumph:
Thou must be a bride within this sevennight.
ALS. [*Aside.*]   Ha!
BEA. Nay, good sir, be not so violent; with speed
I cannot render satisfaction   190
Unto the dear companion of my soul,
Virginity, whom I thus long have liv'd with,
And part with it so rude and suddenly.
Can such friends divide, never to meet again,
Without a solemn farewell?
VER.   Tush, tush! There's a toy.[2]
ALS. [*Aside.*] I must now part, and never meet again
With any joy on earth.—Sir, your pardon,
My affairs call on me.
VER.   How, sir? By no means;
Not chang'd so soon, I hope. You must see my castle,
And her best entertainment ere we part;   200
I shall think myself unkindly used else.
Come, come, let's on. I had good hope your stay
Had been awhile with us in Alicant;
I might have bid you to my daughter's wedding.
ALS. [*Aside.*] He means to feast me, and poisons me before-
    hand.—
I should be dearly glad to be there, sir,
Did my occasions suit as I could wish.
BEA. I shall be sorry if you be not there
When it is done, sir,— [*Aside.*] but not so suddenly.   210
VER. I tell you, sir, the gentleman's complete,
A courtier and a gallant, enrich'd
With many fair and noble ornaments; [3]
I would not change him for a son-in-law
For any he in Spain, the proudest he,
And we have great ones, that you know.
ALS.   He's much
Bound to you, sir.

----

[1] A truce, 1607–21.   [2] A trifle, whim.   [3] Attributes.

VER.   He shall be bound to me,
  As fast as this tie can hold him; I'll want
  My will else.
BEA. [*Aside.*] I shall want mine if you do it.
VER. But come; by the way I'll tell you more of him.
ALS. [*Aside.*] How shall I dare to venture in his castle,
  When he discharges murderers [1] at the gate?
  But I must on, for back I cannot go.
BEA. [*Aside*] Not this serpent gone yet?   [*Drops a glove.*[2]]
VER.   Look, girl, thy glove's fall'n.
  Stay, stay; De Flores, help a little.
              [*Exeunt* VERMANDERO, ALSEMERO, *and servants.*]
DE F.   Here, lady.
BEA. Mischief on your officious forwardness!
  Who bade you stoop? They touch my hand no more.
  There! For t'other's sake I part with this;
                    [*Throws the other glove at him.*]
  Take 'um and draw thine own skin off with 'um.
                         Exeunt BEATRICE *and* DIAPHANTA.
DE F. Here's a favour come with a mischief! Now I know
  She had rather wear my pelt tann'd in a pair
  Of dancing pumps than I should thrust my fingers
  Into her sockets here. I know she hates me,
  Yet cannot choose but love her;
  No matter; if but to vex her, I'll haunt her still;
  Though I get nothing else, I'll have my will.   *Exit.*

[ACT I. SCENE 2]

[ALIBIUS'S *house*]

Enter ALIBIUS *and* LOLLIO

ALIB. Lollio, I must trust thee with a secret,
  But thou must keep it.
LOL. I was ever close to a secret, sir.
ALIB. The diligence that I have found in thee,
  The care and industry already past,

---

                    [1] Small cannon.   [2] For Alsemero to retrieve.

Assures me of thy good continuance.
Lollio, I have a wife.

LOL. Fie, sir, 'tis too late to keep her secret; she's known to be
married all the town and country over.

ALIB. Thou goest too fast, my Lollio; that knowledge   10
I allow no man can be barr'd it;
But there is a knowledge which is nearer,
Deeper, and sweeter, Lollio.

LOL. Well, sir, let us handle that between you and I.

ALIB. 'Tis that I go about, man. Lollio,
My wife is young.

LOL. So much the worse to be kept secret, sir.

ALIB. Why, now thou meet'st the substance of the point;
I am old, Lollio.

LOL. No, sir, 'tis I am old Lollio.   20

ALIB. Yet why may not this [1] concord and sympathize?
Old trees and young plants often grow together,
Well enough agreeing.

LOL. Ay, sir, but the old trees raise themselves higher and
broader than the young plants.

ALIB. Shrewd application! There's the fear, man:
I would wear my ring on my own finger;
Whilst it is borrowed it is none of mine,
But his that useth it.

LOL. You must keep it on still then; if it but lie by,   30
One or other will be thrusting into't.

ALIB. Thou conceiv'st me, Lollio; here thy watchful eye
Must have employment; I cannot always be
At home.

LOL.   I dare swear you cannot.

ALIB.   I must look out. [2]

LOL. I know't; you must look out. 'Tis every man's case.

ALIB. Here, I do say, must thy employment be:
To watch her treadings, and in my absence
Supply my place.

LOL. I'll do my best, sir; yet surely I cannot see who you
should have cause to be jealous of.   40

ALIB. Thy reason for that, Lollio? 'Tis a comfortable
question. [3]

LOL. We have but two sorts of people in the house, and both

---

[1] The marital situation.   [2] Attend to business affairs.
[3] A question which may have a reassuring answer.

under the whip; that's fools and madmen. The one has not
wit enough to be knaves, and the other not knavery enough to
be fools.

ALIB. Ay, those are all my patients, Lollio.
I do profess the cure of either sort;
My trade, my living 'tis; I thrive by it.
But here's the care that mixes with my thrift:
The daily visitants, that come to see
My brainsick patients, I would not have
To see my wife. Gallants I do observe,
Of quick enticing eyes, rich in habits,
Of stature and proportion very comely;
These are most shrewd temptations, Lollio.

LOL. They may be easily answered, sir: if they come to see the
fools and madmen, you and I may serve the turn, and let my
mistress alone; she's of neither sort.

ALIB. 'Tis a good ward; [1] indeed, come they to see
Our madmen or our fools, let 'um see no more
Than what they come for; by that consequent
They must not see her; I'm sure she's no fool.

LOL. And I'm sure she's no madman.

ALIB. Hold that buckler [2] fast, Lollio; my trust
Is on thee, and I account it firm and strong.
What hour is't, Lollio?

LOL. Towards belly-hour, sir.

ALIB. Dinner time? Thou mean'st twelve o'clock?

LOL. Yes, sir, for every part has his hour: we wake at six and
look about us, that's eye-hour; at seven we should pray, that's
knee-hour; at eight walk, that's leg-hour; at nine gather
flowers and pluck a rose, [3] that's nose-hour; at ten we drink,
that's mouth-hour; at eleven lay about us for victuals, that's
hand-hour; at twelve go to dinner, that's belly-hour.

ALIB. Profoundly, Lollio! It will be long
Ere all thy scholars learn this lesson, and
I did look to have a new one ent'red.—Stay;
I think my expectation is come home.

Enter PEDRO *and* ANTONIO (*disguised as an idiot*)

PED. Save you, sir; my business speaks itself;
This sight takes off the labour of my tongue.

---

[1] Defence.   [2] Shield.   [3] Relieve oneself.

ALIB. Ay, ay, sir; 'tis plain enough: you mean him for my patient.

PED. And if your pains prove but commodious,[1] to give but some little strength to the sick and weak part of nature in him, these are but patterns [2] [*Gives* ALIBIUS *money.*] to show you of the whole pieces that will follow to you, beside the charge of diet, washing and other necessaries fully defrayed.

ALIB. Believe it, sir, there shall no care be wanting.

LOL. Sir, an officer in this place may deserve something; the   90
trouble will pass through my hands.

PED. 'Tis fit something should come to your hands then, sir.
                                    [*Gives* LOLLIO *money.*]

LOL. Yes, sir, 'tis I must keep him sweet,[3] and read to him; what is his name?

PED. His name is Antonio; marry, we use but half to him, only Tony.[4]

LOL. Tony, Tony; 'tis enough, and a very good name for a fool. What's your name, Tony?

ANT. He, he, he! Well, I thank you, cousin. He, he, he!

LOL. Good boy; hold up your head. He can laugh; I perceive   100
by that he is no beast.

PED. Well, sir,
If you can raise him but to any height,
Any degree of wit,—might he attain,
As I might say, to creep but on all four
Towards the chair of wit, or walk on crutches,
'Twould add an honour to your worthy pains,
And a great family might pray for you,
To which he should be heir, had he discretion
To claim and guide his own; assure you, sir,   110
He is a gentleman.

LOL. Nay, there's nobody doubted that; at first sight I knew him for a gentleman—he looks no other yet.

PED. Let him have good attendance and sweet lodging.

LOL. As good as my mistress lies in, sir; and as you allow us time and means, we can raise him to the higher degree of discretion.

PED. Nay, there shall no cost want, sir.

LOL. He will hardly be stretched up to the wit of a magnifico.

---

[1] Beneficial.   [2] Samples.
[3] Clean.   [4] A conventional name for a simpleton.

PED. Oh no, that's not to be expected; far shorter will be enough.

LOL. I'll warrant you [I'll] make him fit to bear office in five weeks; I'll undertake to wind him up to the wit of constable.

PED. If it be lower than that it might serve turn.

LOL. No, fie; to level him with a headborough,[1] beadle,[2] or watchman were but little better than he is. Constable I'll able[3] him; if he do come to be a justice afterwards, let him thank the keeper. Or I'll go further with you: say I do bring him up to my own pitch, say I make him as wise as myself.

PED. Why, there I would have it.

LOL. Well, go to; either I'll be as arrant a fool as he, or he shall be as wise as I, and then I think 'twill serve his turn.

PED. Nay, I do like thy wit passing well.

LOL. Yes, you may; yet if I had not been a fool, I had had more wit than I have too; remember what state you find me in.

PED. I will, and so leave you. Your best cares, I beseech you.

Exit PEDRO.

ALIB. Take you none with you; leave 'um all with us.

ANT. Oh, my cousin's gone. Cousin, cousin, oh!

LOL. Peace, peace, Tony! You must not cry, child; you must be whipped if you do. Your cousin is here still; I am your cousin, Tony.

ANT. He, he! Then I'll not cry, if thou be'st my cousin. He, he, he!

LOL. I were best try his wit a little, that I may know what form to place him in.

ALIB. Ay, do, Lollio, do.

LOL. I must ask him easy questions at first. Tony, how many true[4] fingers has a tailor on his right hand?

ANT. As many as on his left, cousin.

LOL. Good; and how many on both?

ANT. Two less than a deuce, cousin.

LOL. Very well answered; I come to you again, cousin Tony: How many fools goes to[5] a wise man?

ANT. Forty in a day sometimes, cousin.

LOL. Forty in a day? How prove you that?

ANT. All that fall out amongst themselves, and go to a lawyer to be made friends.

---

[1] A kind of constable, sharing in his proverbial stupidity.
[2] A minor parish official.   [3] Qualify.
[4] Honest.   [5] Lollio's meaning is 'make'.

LOL. A parlous[1] fool! He must sit in the fourth form at least,
I perceive that; I come again, Tony: How many knaves make
an honest man?   160

ANT. I know not that, cousin.

LOL. No, the question is too hard for you. I'll tell you, cousin;
there's three knaves may make an honest man; a sergeant, a
jailer, and a beadle; the sergeant catches him, the jailer holds
him, the beadle lashes him; and if he be not honest then, the
hangman must cure him.

ANT. Ha, ha, ha! That's fine sport, cousin.

ALIB. This was too deep a question for the fool, Lollio.

LOL. Yes, this might have served yourself, though I say't;
once more, and you shall go play, Tony.   170

ANT. Ay, play at push-pin,[2] cousin; ha, he!

LOL. So thou shalt; say how many fools are here.

ANT. Two, cousin, thou and I.

LOL. Nay, y'are too forward there, Tony; mark my question:
How many fools are here? A fool before a knave, a fool behind
a knave, between every two fools a knave; how many fools,
how many knaves?

ANT. I never learnt so far, cousin.

ALIB. Thou putt'st too hard questions to him, Lollio.

LOL. I'll make him understand it easily. Cousin, stand there.   180

ANT. Ay, cousin.

LOL. Master, stand you next the fool.

ALIB. Well, Lollio?

LOL. Here's my place. Mark now, Tony; there's a fool before
a knave.

ANT. That's I, cousin.

LOL. Here's a fool behind a knave—that's I; and between us
two fools there is a knave—that's my master; 'tis but we
three,[3] that's all.

ANT. We three, we three, cousin.   *Madmen shout within.*   190

1 MADMAN. (*Within.*) Put's head i' th' pillory, the bread's too
little.

2 MADMAN. (*Within.*) Fly, fly, and he catches the swallow.

3 MADMAN. (*Within.*) Give her more onion, or the devil put
the rope about her crag.[4]

---

[1] Shrewd.   [2] A child's game.
[3] An allusion to an old joke involving a picture of two idiots with the
inscription, 'We three, loggerheads be'. (The spectator is the third.)
[4] Neck.

LOL. You may hear what time of day it is, the chimes of Bedlam goes.

ALIB. Peace, peace, or the wire [1] comes!

3 MADMAN. (*Within.*) Cat whore, cat whore! Her parmasant,[2] her parmasant!

ALIB. Peace, I say!—Their hour's come; they must be fed, Lollio.

LOL. There's no hope of recovery of that Welsh madman—was undone by a mouse that spoiled him a parmasant; lost his wits for't.[3]

ALIB. Go to your charge, Lollio, I'll to mine.

LOL. Go you to your madmen's ward; let me alone with your fools.

ALIB. And remember my last charge, Lollio.   *Exit.*

LOL. Of which your patients do you think I am? Come, Tony, you must amongst your school-fellows now; there's pretty scholars amongst 'um, I can tell you; there's some of 'em at *stultus, stulta, stultum.*[4]

ANT. I would see the madmen, cousin, if they would not bite me.

LOL. No, they shall not bite thee, Tony.

ANT. They bite when they are at dinner, do they not, coz?

LOL. They bite at dinner, indeed, Tony. Well, I hope to get credit by thee; I like thee the best of all the scholars that ever I brought up, and thou shalt prove a wise man, or I'll prove a fool myself.   *Exeunt.*

ACT II. [SCENE 1]

[VERMANDERO'S *castle*]

Enter BEATRICE *and* JASPERINO *severally*

BEA. Oh, sir, I'm ready now for that fair service
Which makes the name of friend sit glorious on you.
Good angels and this conduct [5] be your guide;
Fitness of time and place is there set down, sir.
                    [*Gives him a letter.*]

---

[1] Whip.   [2] Parmesan cheese.
[3] Several contemporary jokes centred on the Welsh fondness for cheese.
[4] Capable of declining the Latin for 'stupid'.   [5] Message.

JAS. The joy I shall return rewards my service.   *Exit.*
BEA. How wise is Alsemero in his friend!
    It is a sign he makes his choice with judgment.
    Then I appear in nothing more approv'd
    Than making choice of him;
    For 'tis a principle, he that can choose   10
    That bosom well, who of his thought partakes,
    Proves most discreet in every choice he makes.
    Methinks I love now with the eyes of judgment,
    And see the way to merit, clearly see it.
    A true deserver like a diamond sparkles;
    In darkness you may see him; that's in absence,
    Which is the greatest darkness falls on love;
    Yet he is best discern'd then
    With intellectual eyesight. What's Piracquo
    My father spends his breath for? And his blessing   20
    Is only mine as I regard [1] his name;
    Else it goes from me, and turns head against me,
    Transform'd into a curse. Some speedy way
    Must be remember'd; he's so forward too,
    So urgent that way, scarce allows me breath
    To speak to [2] my new comforts.

Enter DE FLORES

DE F. [*Aside.*]   Yonder's she;
    Whatever ails me, now alate especially,
    I can as well be hang'd as refrain seeing her;
    Some twenty times a day, nay, not so little,
    Do I force errands, frame ways and excuses   30
    To come into her sight, and I have small reason for't,
    And less encouragement; for she baits me still
    Every time worse than other, does profess herself
    The cruellest enemy to my face in town,
    At no hand can abide the sight of me,
    As if danger or ill luck hung in my looks.
    I must confess my face is bad enough,
    But I know far worse has better fortune,
    And not endur'd alone, but doted on;
    And yet such pick-hair'd [3] faces, chins like witches',   40

[1] Respect.   [2] Consider.   [3] Thin-bearded.

Here and there five hairs, whispering in a corner,
As if they grew in fear one of another,
Wrinkles like troughs, where swine-deformity swills
The tears of perjury that lie there like wash
Fallen from the slimy and dishonest eye;
Yet such a one plucks sweets without restraint,
And has the grace of beauty to his sweet.
Though my hard fate has thrust me out to servitude,
I tumbled into th' world a gentleman.
She turns her blessed eye upon me now,
And I'll endure all storms before I part with't.
BEA. [*Aside.*] Again!
  This ominous ill-fac'd fellow more disturbs me
  Than all my other passions.[1]
DE F. [*Aside.*]   Now't begins again;
  I'll stand this storm of hail though the stones pelt me.
BEA. Thy business? What's thy business?
DE F. [*Aside.*]   Soft and fair,
  I cannot part so soon now.
BEA. [*Aside.*]   The villain's fix'd—
  Thou standing [2] toad-pool!
DE F. [*Aside.*]   The shower falls amain now.
BEA. Who sent thee? What's thy errand? Leave my sight.
DE F. My lord your father charg'd me to deliver
  A message to you.
BEA.   What, another since?
  Do't and be hang'd then; let me be rid of thee.
DE F. True service merits mercy.
BEA.   What's thy message?
DE F. Let beauty settle but in patience,
  You shall hear all.
BEA.   A dallying, trifling torment!
DE F. Signior Alonzo de Piracquo, lady,
  Sole brother to Tomazo de Piracquo;—
BEA. Slave, when wilt make an end?
DE F.   Too soon I shall.
BEA. What all this while of him?
DE F.   The said Alonzo,
  With the foresaid Tomazo,—
BEA.   Yet again?

Afflictions.   [2] Stagnant.

DE F. Is new alighted.

BEA.   Vengeance strike the news!
  Thou thing most loath'd, what cause was there in this
  To bring thee to my sight?

DE F.   My lord your father
  Charg'd me to seek you out.

BEA.   Is there no other
  To send his errand by?

DE F.   It seems 'tis my luck
  To be i' th' way still.

BEA.   Get thee from me!

DE F. [*Aside.*]   So!
  Why, am not I an ass to devise ways
  Thus to be rail'd at? I must see her still;
  I shall have a mad qualm within this hour again,
  I know't, and, like a common Garden bull,   80
  I do but take breath to be lugg'd again.[1]
  What this may bode I know not; I'll despair the less,
  Because there's daily precedents of bad faces
  Belov'd beyond all reason; these foul chops
  May come into favour one day 'mongst his fellows.
  Wrangling has prov'd the mistress of good pastime;
  As children cry themselves asleep, I ha' seen
  Women have chid themselves abed to men.   *Exit.*

BEA. I never see this fellow, but I think
  Of some harm towards me; danger's in my mind still;   90
  I scarce leave trembling of an hour after.
  The next good mood I find my father in,
  I'll get him quite discarded. Oh, I was
  Lost in this small disturbance and forgot
  Affliction's fiercer torrent that now comes
  To bear down all my comforts.

Enter VERMANDERO, ALONZO, *and* TOMAZO

VER.   Y'are both welcome,
  But an especial one belongs to you, sir,
  To whose most noble name our love presents
  The addition [2] of a son, our son Alonzo.

---

[1] An allusion to bull-baiting at Paris Garden, Southwark.
[2] Title.

ALON. The treasury of honour cannot bring forth
  A title I should more rejoice in, sir.
VER. You have improv'd [1] it well. Daughter, prepare;
  The day will steal upon thee suddenly.
BEA. [*Aside.*] Howe'er, I will be sure to keep the night,[2]
  If it should come so near me.

                    [BEATRICE *and* VERMANDERO *talk apart.*]

TOM.   Alonzo.
ALON.   Brother?
TOM. In troth I see small welcome in her eye.
ALON. Fie, you are too severe a censurer
  Of love in all points; there's no bringing on [3] you.
  If lovers should mark everything a fault,
  Affection would be like an ill-set book,
  Whose faults might prove as big as half the volume.
BEA. That's all I do entreat.
VER.   It is but reasonable;
  I'll see what my son says to't. Son Alonzo,
  Here's a motion made but to reprieve
  A maidenhead three days longer; the request
  Is not far out of reason, for indeed
  The former time is pinching.
ALON.   Though my joys
  Be set back so much time as I could wish
  They had been forward, yet since she desires it,
  The time is set as pleasing as before;
  I find no gladness wanting.
VER.   May I ever
  Meet it in that point still! Y'are nobly welcome, sirs.

                    Exeunt VERMANDERO *and* BEATRICE.

TOM. So; did you mark the dullness of her parting now?
ALON. What dullness? Thou art so exceptious [4] still.
TOM. Why, let it go then; I am but a fool
  To mark your harms so heedfully.
ALON.   Where's the oversight?
TOM. Come, your faith's cozen'd [5] in her, strongly cozen'd;
  Unsettle your affection with all speed
  Wisdom can bring it to; your peace is ruin'd else.
  Think what a torment 'tis to marry one
  Whose heart is leap'd into another's bosom;

----

[1] Proved.   [2] Stand guard.   [3] Persuading.
[4] Captious.   [5] Deceived.

If ever pleasure she receive from thee,
It comes not in thy name, or of thy gift;
She lies but with another in thine arms,
He the half-father unto all thy children
In the conception; if he get 'em not,
She helps to get 'em for him,[1] and how dangerous
And shameful her restraint [2] may go in time to,
It is not to be thought on without sufferings.

ALON. You speak as if she lov'd some other then.   140

TOM. Do you apprehend so slowly?

ALON.   Nay, and that
Be your fear only, I am safe enough.
Preserve your friendship and your counsel, brother,
For time of more distress; I should depart
An enemy, a dangerous, deadly one,
To any but thyself, that should but think
She knew the meaning of inconstancy,
Much less the use and practice; yet w'are friends;
Pray, let no more be urg'd; I can endure
Much, till I meet an injury to her,   150
Then I am not myself. Farewell, sweet brother;
How much w'are bound to Heaven to depart lovingly.

                                                    Exit.

TOM. Why, here is love's tame madness; thus a man
Quickly steals into his vexation.   *Exit.*

[ACT II. Scene 2]

[*Another room in the castle*]

Enter DIAPHANTA *and* ALSEMERO

DIA. The place is my charge; you have kept your hour,
And the reward of a just meeting bless you.
I hear my lady coming. Complete gentleman,
I dare not be too busy with my praises,
Th'are dangerous things to deal with.   *Exit.*

ALS.   This goes well;

---

[1] Quartos add, 'in his passions', probably intended to be cancelled.
[2] i.e. restraining her.

These women are the ladies' cabinets:
Things of most precious trust are lock'd into 'em.

Enter BEATRICE

BEA. I have within my eye all my desires.
  Requests that holy prayers ascend Heaven for,
  And bring 'em down to furnish our defects,[1]
  Come not more sweet to our necessities
  Than thou unto my wishes.
ALS.   W'are so like
  In our expressions, lady, that unless I borrow
  The same words, I shall never find their equals.
BEA. How happy were this meeting, this embrace,
  If it were free from envy! This poor kiss,
  It has an enemy, a hateful one,
  That wishes poison to't; how well were I now
  If there were none such name known as Piracquo,
  Nor no such tie as the command of parents!
  I should be but too much blessed.
ALS.   One good service
  Would strike off both your fears; and I'll go near it too,
  Since you are so distress'd; remove the cause,
  The command ceases; so there's two fears blown out
  With one and the same blast.
BEA.   Pray, let me find you, sir.
  What might that service be so strangely happy?
ALS. The honourablest piece 'bout man: valour.
  I'll send a challenge to Piracquo instantly.
BEA. How! Call you that extinguishing of fear,
  When 'tis the only way to keep it flaming?
  Are not you ventured in the action,
  That's all my joys and comforts? Pray, no more, sir.
  Say you prevail'd, your danger 'tis and not mine; then
  The law would claim you from me, or obscurity
  Be made the grave to bury you alive.
  I'm glad these thoughts come forth; oh, keep not one
  Of this condition, sir! Here was a course
  Found to bring sorrow on her way to death;
  The tears would ne'er ha' dried till dust had chok'd 'em.
  Blood-guiltiness becomes a fouler visage,—
                    [1] Supply our deficiencies.

   [*Aside.*] And now I think on one. I was to blame,
   I ha' marr'd so good a market with my scorn;
   'T had been done questionless; the ugliest creature
   Creation fram'd for some use, yet to see
   I could not mark so much where it should be.
ALS. Lady,—
BEA. [*Aside.*] Why, men of art make much of poison,
   Keep one to expel another. Where was my art?
ALS. Lady, you hear not me.
BEA.   I do especially, sir;
   The present times are not so sure of our side   50
   As those hereafter may be; we must use 'em then
   As thrifty folk their wealth, sparingly now,
   Till the time opens.
ALS.   You teach wisdom, lady.
BEA. Within there, Diaphanta!

Enter DIAPHANTA

DIA.   Did you call, madam?
BEA. Perfect your service, and conduct this gentleman
   The private way you brought him.
DIA.   I shall, madam.
ALS. My love's as firm as love e'er built upon.
          Exeunt ALSEMERO *and* DIAPHANTA.

Enter DE FLORES

DE F. [*Aside.*] I have watch'd this meeting, and do wonder
   much
   What shall become of t'other; I'm sure both   60
   Cannot be serv'd unless she transgress; haply
   Then I'll put in for one; for if a woman
   Fly from one point, from him she makes a husband,
   She spreads and mounts then like arithmetic,
   One, ten, a hundred, a thousand, ten thousand,
   Proves in time sutler [1] to an army royal.
   Now do I look to be most richly rail'd at,
   Yet I must see her.
BEA. [*Aside.*]   Why, put case I loath'd him
   As much as youth and beauty hates a sepulchre,
                  [1] Provisioner.

Must I needs show it? Cannot I keep that secret,
And serve my turn upon him? See, he's here.—
De Flores!

DE F. [*Aside.*] Ha, I shall run mad with joy!
 She call'd me fairly by my name, De Flores,
 And neither rogue nor rascal!

BEA.   What ha' you done
 To your face alate? Y'ave met with some good physician;
 Y'ave prun'd [1] yourself, methinks; you were not wont
 To look so amorously.[2]

DE F. [*Aside.*]   Not I;
 'Tis the same physnomy, to a hair and pimple,
 Which she call'd scurvy scarce an hour ago;
 How is this?

BEA.   Come hither; nearer, man.

DE F. [*Aside.*] I'm up to the chin in Heaven!

BEA.   Turn, let me see;
 Vah, 'tis but the heat of the liver,[3] I perceiv't;
 I thought it had been worse.

DE F. [*Aside.*]   Her fingers touch'd me!
 She smells all amber.[4]

BEA. I'll make a water [5] for you shall cleanse this
 Within a fortnight.

DE F.   With your own hands, lady?

BEA. Yes, mine own, sir; in a work of cure
 I'll trust no other.

DE F. [*Aside.*]   'Tis half an act of pleasure
 To hear her talk thus to me.

BEA.   When w'are us'd
 To a hard face, 'tis not so unpleasing;
 It mends still in opinion, hourly mends,
 I see it by experience.

DE F. [*Aside.*]   I was bless'd
 To light upon this minute; I'll make use on't.

BEA. Hardness becomes the visage of a man well:
 It argues service, resolution, manhood,
 If cause were of employment.

DE F.   'Twould be soon seen,
 If e'er your ladyship had cause to use it.

---

[1] Trimmed.   [2] Like a lover.
[3] Considered to be the seat of love and of violent passions.
[4] Ambergris, an ingredient of perfume.   [5] A lotion.

I would but wish the honour of a service
So happy as that mounts to.
BEA.   We shall try you—   100
  O my De Flores!
DE F. [*Aside.*]   How's that? She calls me hers
  Already: 'My De Flores!'—You were about
  To sigh out somewhat, madam.
BEA.   No, was I?
  I forgot—Oh!
DE F.   There 'tis again, the very fellow on't.
BEA. You are too quick, sir.
DE F.   There's no excuse for't now;
  I heard it twice, madam. That sigh would fain
  Have utterance; take pity on't,
  And lend it a free word; 'las, how it labours
  For liberty; I hear the murmur yet
  Beat at your bosom.
BEA.   Would Creation—   110
DE F. Ay, well said, that's it.
BEA.   Had form'd me man!
DE F. Nay, that's not it.
BEA.   Oh, 'tis the soul of freedom!
  I should not then be forc'd to marry one
  I hate beyond all depths; I should have power
  Then to oppose my loathings, nay, remove 'em
  For ever from my sight.
DE F. [*Aside.*]   O bless'd occasion!—
  Without change to your sex, you have your wishes.
  Claim so much man in me.
BEA.   In thee, De Flores?
  There's small cause for that.
DE F.   Put it not from me;
  It's a service that I kneel for to you.   120
BEA. You are too violent to mean faithfully.
  There's horror in my service, blood and danger;
  Can those be things to sue for?
DE F.   If you knew
  How sweet it were to me to be employ'd
  In any act of yours, you would say then
  I fail'd, and us'd not reverence enough
  When I receiv'd the charge on't.
BEA. [*Aside.*]   This is much,

Methinks; belike his wants are greedy, and
To such gold tastes like angel's food.—Rise.
DE F. I'll have the work first.
BEA. [*Aside.*]   Possible his need   1
Is strong upon him.—There's to encourage thee;
                                  Gives him money.
As thou art forward and thy service dangerous,
Thy reward shall be precious.
DE F.   That I have thought on;
I have assur'd myself of that beforehand,
And know it will be precious—the thought ravishes.
BEA. Then take him to thy fury!
DE F.   I thirst for him.
BEA. Alonzo de Piracquo!
DE F.   His end's upon him;
He shall be seen no more.
BEA.   How lovely now
Dost thou appear to me! Never was man
Dearlier rewarded.
DE F.   I do think of that.
BEA. Be wondrous careful in the execution.
DE F. Why, are not both our lives upon the cast?[1]
BEA. Then I throw all my fears upon thy service.
DE F. They ne'er shall rise to hurt you.
BEA.   When the deed's done,
I'll furnish thee with all things for thy flight;
Thou may'st live bravely in another country.
DE F. Ay, ay, we'll talk of that hereafter.
BEA. [*Aside.*]   I shall rid myself
Of two inveterate loathings at one time,
Piracquo, and his dog-face.   *Exit.*
DE F.   Oh, my blood!
Methinks I feel her in my arms already,
Her wanton fingers combing out this beard,
And, being pleased, praising this bad face.
Hunger and pleasure, they'll commend sometimes
Slovenly dishes, and feed heartily on 'em,
Nay, which is stranger, refuse daintier for 'em.
Some women are odd feeders—I'm too loud.
Here comes the man goes supperless to bed,
Yet shall not rise tomorrow to his dinner.

               [1] Throw, as in games of chance.

Enter ALONZO

ALON. De Flores.
DE F.   My kind, honourable Lord.
ALON. I am glad I ha' met with thee.
DE F.   Sir?
ALON.   Thou canst show me   160
  The full strength of the castle?
DE F.   That I can, sir.
ALON. I much desire it.
DE F.   And if the ways and straits [1]
  Of some of the passages be not too tedious for you,
  I will assure you, worth your time and sight, my Lord.
ALON. Pooh, that shall be no hindrance.
DE F.   I'm your servant then.
  'Tis now near dinner time; 'gainst your lordship's rising,
  I'll have the keys about me.
ALON.   Thanks, kind De Flores.
DE F. [*Aside.*] He's safely thrust upon me beyond hopes.
                                        Exeunt.

ACT III. [SCENE 1]

[*A passageway in the castle*]

In the act-time DE FLORES *hides a naked rapier*

Enter ALONZO *and* DE FLORES

DE F. Yes, here are all the keys; I was afraid, my Lord,
  I'd wanted for the postern [2]—this is it.
  I've all, I've all, my Lord; this for the sconce. [3]
ALON. 'Tis a most spacious and impregnable fort.
DE F. You'll tell me more, my Lord; this descent
  Is somewhat narrow; we shall never pass
  Well with our weapons, they'll but trouble us.
                [DE FLORES *removes his sword.*]
ALON. Thou say'st true.
DE F.   Pray, let me help your lordship.

---

[1] Narrow places.   [2] Side door.
[3] A small, isolated fortification.

ALON. 'Tis done. Thanks, kind De Flores.
DE F.   Here are hooks, my Lord,
  To hang such things on purpose.
ALON.   Lead, I'll follow thee.
                Exeunt at one door and enter at the other.

[ACT III. SCENE 2]
[*An isolated part of the castle*]

[*Enter* ALONZO *and* DE FLORES]

DE F. All this is nothing; you shall see anon
  A place you little dream on.
ALON.   I am glad
  I have this leisure. All your master's house
  Imagine I ha' taken a gondola.
DE F. All but myself, sir; [*Aside.*] which makes up my safety.—
  My Lord, I'll place you at a casement here
  Will show you the full strength of all the castle.
  Look; spend your eye awhile upon that object.
ALON. Here's rich variety, De Flores.
DE F.   Yes, sir.
ALON. Goodly munition.
DE F.   Ay, there's ordnance, sir,
  No bastard [1] metal, will ring you a peal like bells
  At great men's funerals. Keep your eye straight, my Lord;
  Take special notice of that sconce before you;
  There you may dwell awhile.
ALON.   I am upon't.
DE F. And so am I.
  [DE FLORES *retrieves the hidden rapier and stabs* ALONZO.]
ALON.   De Flores! Oh, De Flores!
  Whose malice hast thou put on?
DE F.   Do you question
  A work of secrecy? I must silence you.
ALON. Oh, oh, oh!
DE F.   I must silence you.
  So, here's an undertaking well accomplish'd.

---

[1] Debased.

This vault serves to good use now. Ha, what's that   20
Threw sparkles in my eye? Oh, 'tis a diamond
He wears upon his finger; it was well found;
This will approve [1] the work. What, so fast on?
Not part in death? I'll take a speedy course then:
Finger and all shall off. So; now I'll clear
The passages from all suspect or fear.   *Exit with the body.*

[ACT III. SCENE 3]

[ALIBIUS's *house*]

Enter ISABELLA *and* LOLLIO

ISA. Why, sirrah? Whence have you commission
  To fetter the doors against me? If you
  Keep me in a cage, pray whistle to me;
  Let me be doing something.

LOL. You shall be doing, if it please you;
  I'll whistle to you if you'll pipe after.

ISA. Is it your master's pleasure or your own,
  To keep me in this pinfold? [2]

LOL. 'Tis for my master's pleasure, lest being taken in another
  man's corn, you might be pounded in another place.   10

ISA. 'Tis very well, and he'll prove very wise.

LOL. He says you have company enough in the house, if you
  please to be sociable, of all sorts of people.

ISA. Of all sorts? Why, here's none but fools and madmen.

LOL. Very well; and where will you find any other, if you should
  go abroad? There's my master and I to boot too.

ISA. Of either sort one,[3] a madman and a fool.

LOL. I would even participate of both then, if I were as you; I
  know y'are half mad already, be half foolish too.

ISA. Y'are a brave,[4] saucy rascal. Come on, sir,   20
  Afford me then the pleasure of your bedlam;
  You were commending once today to me
  Your last-come lunatic; what a proper [5]
  Body there was without brains to guide it,

---

    [1] Confirm.   [2] A pound.   [3] One of each kind.
    [4] Bold.   [5] Handsome.

And what a pitiful delight appear'd
In that defect, as if your wisdom had found
A mirth in madness; pray, sir, let me partake,
If there be such a pleasure.

Lol. If I do not show you the handsomest, discreetest madman, one that I may call the understanding madman, then
say I am a fool.

Isa. Well, a match; I will say so.

Lol. When you have [had] a taste of the madman, you shall, if
you please, see Fools' College, o' th' side. I seldom lock there;
'tis but shooting a bolt or two, and you are amongst 'em.

Exit Lollio; *re-enters presently with* Franciscus

Come on, sir, let me see how handsomely you'll behave
yourself now.

Fran. How sweetly she looks! Oh, but there's a wrinkle in her
brow as deep as philosophy. Anacreon,[1] drink to my mistress'
health; I'll pledge it. Stay, stay, there's a spider in the cup;
no, 'tis but a grape-stone. Swallow it; fear nothing, poet; so,
so, lift higher.

Isa. Alack, alack, 'tis too full of pity
To be laugh'd at. How fell he mad? Canst thou tell?

Lol. For love, mistress; he was a pretty poet too, and that set
him forwards first; the Muses then forsook him; he ran mad
for a chambermaid, yet she was but a dwarf neither.

Fran. Hail, bright Titania![2]
Why stand'st thou idle on these flow'ry banks?
Oberon is dancing with his Dryades;
I'll gather daisies, primroses, violets,
And bind them in a verse of poesy.

Lol. Not too near; you see your danger.

                              [*Threatens* Franciscus *with his whip*.]

Fran. Oh, hold thy hand, great Diomede;[3]
Thou feed'st thy horses well, they shall obey thee.
Get up,[4] Bucephalus[5] kneels.   [*Kneels*.]

---

[1] A Greek lyric poet, said to have choked to death on a grape-stone whilst
drinking wine.
[2] The queen of the fairies and wife of Oberon.
[3] A mythological Greek king who fed his horses human flesh.
[4] Mount.
[5] The charger of Alexander the Great; it knelt to allow him to mount.

LOL. You see how I awe my flock; a shepherd has not his dog
    at more obedience.

ISA. His conscience is unquiet; sure that was
    The cause of this. A proper gentleman.   60

FRAN. Come hither, Aesculapius; [1] hide the poison. [2]

LOL. Well, 'tis hid.   [FRANCISCUS rises.]

FRAN. Didst thou never hear of one Tiresias, [3]
    A famous poet?

LOL. Yes, that kept tame wild geese.

FRAN. That's he; I am the man.

LOL. No.

FRAN. Yes, but make no words on't; I was a man
    Seven years ago.

LOL. A stripling, I think, you might.   70

FRAN. Now I'm a woman, all feminine.

LOL. I would I might see that.

FRAN. Juno struck me blind.

LOL. I'll ne'er believe that; for a woman, they say, has an eye
    more than a man.

FRAN. I say she struck me blind.

LOL. And Luna [4] made you mad; you have two trades to beg
    with.

FRAN. Luna is now big-bellied, and there's room
    For both of us to ride with Hecate; [5]   80
    I'll drag thee up into her silver sphere,
    And there we'll kick the dog [6]—and beat the bush, [6]—
    That barks against the witches of the night,
    The swift lycanthropi [7] that walks the round;
    We'll tear their wolvish skins and save the sheep.
                       [Attempts to seize LOLLIO.]

LOL. Is't come to this? Nay, then my poison comes forth
    again. Mad slave indeed! Abuse your keeper!

ISA. I prithee, hence with him, now he grows dangerous.

FRAN. (Sings.) Sweet love, pity me.
    Give me leave to lie with thee.   90

[1] The Greek god of healing.   [2] i.e. the whip.
[3] The Theban prophet; one of many legends about him describes his
blindness and how he was led by birds; another legend tells of his sexual
metamorphoses.
[4] The Roman goddess of the moon.
[5] The Greek goddess of magic and witchcraft; by confusion and mistaken
evolution identified with Selene, the Greek goddess of the moon.
[6] Legendary possessions of the man in the moon.
[7] Victims of wolf madness.

LOL. No, I'll see you wiser first; to your kennel.

FRAN. No noise, she sleeps; draw all the curtains round,
Let no soft sound molest the pretty soul,
But love, and love creeps in at a mousehole.

LOL. I would you would get into your hole! *Exit* FRANCISCUS.
Now, mistress, I will bring you another sort; you shall be
fooled another while. Tony! Come hither, Tony; look who's
yonder, Tony.

Enter ANTONIO

ANT. Cousin, is it not my aunt? [1]

LOL. Yes, 'tis one of 'um, Tony.

ANT. He, he, how do you, uncle?   1

LOL. Fear him not, mistress, 'tis a gentle nigget; [2] you may
play with him, as safely with him as with his bawble. [3]

ISA. How long hast thou been a fool?

ANT. Ever since I came hither, cousin.

ISA. Cousin? I'm none of thy cousins, fool.

LOL. Oh, mistress, fools have always so much wit as to claim
their kindred.

MADMAN. (*Within.*) Bounce, bounce! He falls, he falls!

ISA. Hark you, your scholars in the upper room are out of order.   1

LOL. Must I come amongst you there? Keep you the fool,
mistress; I'll go up and play left-handed [4] Orlando [5] amongst
the madmen.   *Exit.*

ISA. Well, sir.

ANT. 'Tis opportuneful now, sweet lady. Nay,
Cast no amazing eye upon this change.   [*Reveals himself.*]

ISA. Ha!

ANT. This shape of folly shrouds your dearest love,
The truest servant to your powerful beauties,
Whose magic had this force thus to transform me.   12

ISA. You are a fine fool indeed.

ANT.   Oh, 'tis not strange;
Love has an intellect that runs through all
The scrutinous sciences, and, like a cunning poet,
Catches a quantity of every knowledge,

---

[1] Bawd or prostitute.
[2] Fool.
[3] The sceptre of a licensed fool; it was often obscenely suggestive.
[4] Perhaps a pun on 'sinister'.
[5] Orlando Furioso, the hero of several medieval romances.

Yet brings all home into one mystery,
Into one secret that he proceeds in.
ISA. Y'are a parlous [1] fool.
ANT. No danger in me; I bring naught but love
And his soft-wounding shafts to strike you with.
Try but one arrow; if it hurt you,   130
I'll stand you twenty back in recompense.   [*Kisses her.*]
ISA. A forward fool too!
ANT.   This was love's teaching;
A thousand ways he fashion'd out my way,
And this I found the safest and the nearest
To tread the Galaxia [2] to my star.
ISA. Profound withal! Certain, you dream'd of this;
Love never taught it waking.
ANT.   Take no acquaintance
Of these outward follies; there's within
A gentleman that loves you.
ISA.   When I see him,
I'll speak with him; so, in the meantime, keep   140
Your habit, it becomes you well enough.
As you are a gentleman, I'll not discover you;
That's all the favour that you must expect;
When you are weary, you may leave the school,
For all this while you have but play'd the fool.

Enter LOLLIO

ANT. And must again.—He, he, I thank you, cousin,
I'll be your valentine tomorrow morning.
LOL. How do you like the fool, mistress?
ISA. Passing well, sir.
LOL. Is he not witty, pretty well, for a fool?   150
ISA. If he hold on as he begins, he is like
To come to something.
LOL. Ay, thank a good tutor. You may put him to't; he begins
to answer pretty hard questions. Tony, how many is five times
six?
ANT. Five times six is six times five.
LOL. What arithmetician could have answered better? How
many is one hundred and seven?
ANT. One hundred and seven is seven hundred and one, cousin.

----

[1] Shrewd.   [2] The Milky Way.

LOL. This is no wit to speak on! Will you be rid of the fool now? 1

ISA. By no means, let him stay a little.

MADMAN. (*Within.*) Catch there, catch the last couple in hell![1]

LOL. Again must I come amongst you? Would my master were
come home! I am not able to govern both these wards
together.   *Exit.*

ANT. Why should a minute of love's hour be lost?

ISA. Fie, out again! I had rather you kept
Your other posture; you become not your tongue
When you speak from your clothes.[2]

ANT.   How can he freeze,
Lives near so sweet a warmth? Shall I alone   1
Walk through the orchard of the Hesperides,[3]
And cowardly not dare to pull an apple?

                                    Enter LOLLIO *above.*

This with the red cheeks I must venture for.

                                    [*Attempts to kiss her.*]

ISA. Take heed, there's giants keep 'em.

LOL. [*Aside.*] How now, fool, are you good at that? Have you
read Lipsius?[4] He's past *Ars Amandi*;[5] I believe I must put
harder questions to him, I perceive that.

ISA. You are bold without fear too.

ANT.   What should I fear,
Having all joys about me? Do you smile,
And love shall play the wanton on your lip,   1
Meet and retire, retire and meet again.
Look you but cheerfully, and in your eyes
I shall behold mine own deformity,
And dress myself up fairer; I know this shape
Becomes me not, but in those bright mirrors
I shall array me handsomely.

LOL. [*Aside.*]   Cuckoo, cuckoo![6]   *Exit.*

        Enter madmen above, some as birds, other as beasts

ANT. What are these?

ISA.   Of fear enough to part us;
Yet they are but our school of lunatics,

---

[1] In the game of barley-break (V. 3. 161-2) couples were tagged in a
marked area called hell.

[2] i.e. his fool's garments.

[3] The nymphs who guarded the golden apples in the Isles of the Blest.

[4] A Flemish scholar whose name is used for the sake of the pun.

[5] An alternative title of Ovid's *Ars Amatoria*.

[6] Lollio's anticipation of Alibius's cuckoldry.

That act their fantasies in any shapes
Suiting their present thoughts; if sad, they cry;   190
If mirth by their conceit, they laugh again.
Sometimes they imitate the beasts and birds,
Singing, or howling, braying, barking; all
As their wild fancies prompt 'um.   [*Exeunt madmen.*]
ANT.   These are no fears.
ISA. But here's a large one, my man.

Enter LOLLIO

ANT. Ha, he, that's fine sport indeed, cousin.
LOL. I would my master were come home; 'tis too much for one
  shepherd to govern two of these flocks, nor can I believe that
  one churchman can instruct two benefices at once; there will
  be some incurable mad on the one side, and very fools on the   200
  other. Come, Tony.
ANT. Prithee, cousin, let me stay here still.
LOL. No, you must to your book now; you have played
  sufficiently.
ISA. Your fool is grown wondrous witty.
LOL. Well, I'll say nothing; but I do not think but he will put
  you down one of these days. *Exeunt* LOLLIO *and* ANTONIO.
ISA. Here the restrained current might make breach,
  Spite of the watchful bankers; [1] would a woman stray,
  She need not gad abroad to seek her sin,   210
  It would be brought home one way or other:
  The needle's point will to the fixed north,
  Such drawing arctics women's beauties are.

Enter LOLLIO

LOL. How dost thou, sweet rogue?
ISA. How now?
LOL. Come, there are degrees; one fool may be better than
  another.
ISA. What's the matter?
LOL. Nay, if thou giv'st thy mind to fool's-flesh, have at thee!
                                    [*Attempts to kiss her.*]
ISA. You bold slave, you!   220
LOL. I could follow now as t'other fool did:

---

[1] Dike-tenders.

'What should I fear,
Having all joys about me? Do you but smile,
And love shall play the wanton on your lip,
Meet and retire, retire and meet again.
Look you but cheerfully, and in your eyes
I shall behold my own deformity,
And dress myself up fairer; I know this shape
Becomes me not,—'
and so as it follows, but is not this the more foolish way?   2
Come, sweet rogue; kiss me, my little Lacedemonian![1] Let
me feel how thy pulses beat; thou hast a thing about thee would
do a man pleasure, I'll lay my hand on't.

ISA. Sirrah, no more! I see you have discovered
This love's knight-errant, who hath made adventure
For purchase of my love. Be silent, mute,
Mute as a statue, or his injunction,
For me enjoying, shall be to cut thy throat;
I'll do it, though for no other purpose, and
Be sure he'll not refuse it.

LOL.   My share, that's all;   2
I'll have my fool's part with you.

ISA.   No more! Your master.

Enter ALIBIUS

ALIB. Sweet, how dost thou?

ISA.   Your bounden servant, sir.

ALIB. Fie, fie, sweetheart, no more of that.

ISA. You were best lock me up.

ALIB. In my arms and bosom, my sweet Isabella,
I'll lock thee up most nearly. Lollio,
We have employment, we have task in hand;
At noble Vermandero's, our castle's captain,
There is a nuptial to be solemniz'd,—
Beatrice-Joanna, his fair daughter, bride,—   2
For which the gentleman hath bespoke our pains;
A mixture of our madmen and our fools,
To finish, as it were, and make the fag
Of all the revels, the third night from the first;
Only an unexpected passage over,[2]
To make a frightful pleasure, that is all,
But not the all I aim at; could we so act it,
To teach it in a wild, distracted measure,

[1] Strumpet.   [2] A surprise incursion of the madmen and fools.

Though out of form and figure, breaking time's head,—
It were no matter, 'twould be heal'd again   260
In one age or other, if not in this.
This, this,[1] Lollio; there's good reward begun,
And will beget a bounty be it known.[2]

LOL. This is easy, sir, I'll warrant you; you have about you
fools and madmen that can dance very well, and 'tis no
wonder: your best dancers are not the wisest men; the reason
is, with often jumping they jolt their brains down into their
feet, that their wits lie more in their heels than in their
heads.

ALIB. Honest Lollio, thou giv'st me a good reason
And a comfort in it.

ISA.   Y'ave a fine trade on't;   270
Madmen and fools are a staple commodity.

ALIB. Oh, wife, we must eat, wear clothes, and live;
Just at the lawyer's haven we arrive,[3]
By madmen and by fools we both do thrive.   *Exeunt.*

[ACT III. SCENE 4]

[*The castle*]

Enter VERMANDERO, ALSEMERO, JASPERINO, *and*
BEATRICE

VER. Valencia speaks so nobly of you, sir,
I wish I had a daughter now for you.

ALS. The fellow of this creature were a partner
For a king's love.

VER.   I had her fellow once, sir,
But Heaven has married her to joys eternal;
'Twere sin to wish her in this vale again.
Come, sir, your friend and you shall see the pleasures
Which my health chiefly joys in.

ALS. I hear the beauty of this seat largely.[4]

VER. It falls much short of that.
                    Exeunt [*men*]. *Manet* BEATRICE.

---

[1] Plan, scheme.
[2] 'We can expect a generous payment (for the show) and perhaps future commissions.'
[3] i.e. to become wealthy(?).   [4] Far and wide.

BEA.   So, here's one step
　Into my father's favour; time will fix him.
　I have got him now the liberty of the house;
　So wisdom by degrees works out her freedom;
　And if that eye be dark'ned that offends me—
　I wait but that eclipse [1]—this gentleman
　Shall soon shine glorious in my father's liking,
　Through the refulgent virtue of my love.

Enter DE FLORES

DE F. [*Aside.*] My thoughts are at a banquet! For the deed,
　I feel no weight in't; 'tis but light and cheap
　For the sweet recompense that I set down for't.
BEA. De Flores.
DE F.   Lady?
BEA.   Thy looks promise cheerfully.
DE F. All things are answerable: time, circumstance,
　Your wishes, and my service.
BEA.   Is it done then?
DE F. Piracquo is no more.
BEA. My joys start at mine eyes; our sweet'st delights
　Are evermore born weeping.
DE F.   I've a token for you.
BEA. For me?
DE F. But it was sent somewhat unwillingly;
　I could not get the ring without the finger.
BEA. Bless me! What hast thou done?
DE F.   Why, is that more
　Than killing the whole man? I cut his heart-strings.
　A greedy hand thrust in a dish of court
　In a mistake hath had as much as this.
BEA. 'Tis the first token my father made me send him.
DE F. And I [have] made him send it back again
　For his last token. I was loath to leave it,
　And I'm sure dead men have no use of jewels.
　He was as loath to part with't, for it stuck
　As if the flesh and it were both one substance.
BEA. At the stag's fall the keeper has his fees;
　'Tis soon appli'd,—all dead men's fees are yours, sir.

---

[1] The death of Alonzo.

I pray, bury the finger, but the stone
You may make use on shortly; the true value,
Take 't of my truth, is near three hundred ducats.[1]

DE F. 'Twill hardly buy a capcase [2] for one's conscience though,
To keep it from the worm,[3] as fine as 'tis.
Well, being my fees, I'll take it;
Great men have taught me that, or else my merit
Would scorn the way on 't.

BEA.   It might justly, sir.   50
Why, thou mistak'st, De Flores, 'tis not given
In state of recompense.

DE F.   No, I hope so, lady;
You should soon witness my contempt to 't then.

BEA. Prithee, thou look'st as if thou wert offended.

DE F. That were strange, lady; 'tis not possible
My service should draw such a cause from you.
Offended? Could you think so? That were much
For one of my performance, and so warm
Yet in my service.

BEA. 'Twere misery in me to give you cause, sir.

DE F. I know so much, it were so; misery   60
In her most sharp condition.

BEA.   'Tis resolv'd then,
Look you, sir, here's three thousand golden florins; [4]
I have not meanly thought upon thy merit.

DE F. What, salary? Now you move me.

BEA.   How, De Flores?

DE F. Do you place me in the rank of verminous fellows,
To destroy things for wages? Offer gold
[For] the life blood of man? Is anything
Valued too precious for my recompense?

BEA. I understand thee not.

DE F.   I could ha' hir'd
A journeyman in murder at this rate,   70
And mine own conscience might have [slept at ease],
And have had the work brought home.

BEA. [Aside.]   I'm in a labyrinth.

---

[1] Perhaps £100, but there is no need to assume that Middleton had any precise interest in or knowledge of foreign currency values.
[2] Receptacle.
[3] The remorse of conscience.
[4] Perhaps about £450, probably presented in the form of a draft or note of hand.

What will content him? I would fain be rid of him.—
 I'll double the sum, sir.
DE F.   You take a course
 To double my vexation, that's the good you do.
BEA. [*Aside.*] Bless me! I am now in worse plight than I was;
 I know not what will please him.—For my fear's sake,
 I prithee make away with all speed possible;
 And if thou be'st so modest not to name
 The sum that will content thee, paper blushes not;
 Send thy demand in writing, it shall follow thee;
 But prithee take thy flight.
DE F.   You must fly too then.
BEA. I?
DE F. I'll not stir a foot else.
BEA.   What's your meaning?
DE F. Why, are not you as guilty, in, I'm sure,
 As deep as I? And we should stick together.
 Come, your fears counsel you but ill; my absence
 Would draw suspect upon you instantly;
 There were no rescue for you.
BEA. [*Aside.*]   He speaks home.
DE F. Nor is it fit we two engag'd so jointly
 Should part and live asunder.
BEA.   How now, sir?
 This shows not well.
DE F.   What makes your lip so strange?[1]
 This must not be betwixt us.
BEA. [*Aside.*]   The man talks wildly.
DE F. Come, kiss me with a zeal now.
BEA. [*Aside.*]   Heaven, I doubt[2] him!
DE F. I will not stand so long to beg 'em shortly.
BEA. Take heed, De Flores, of forgetfulness;
 'Twill soon betray us.
DE F.   Take you heed first;
 Faith, y'are grown much forgetful; y'are to blame in't.
BEA. [*Aside.*] He's bold, and I am blam'd for 't!
DE F.   I have eas'd
 You of your trouble; think on 't. I'm in pain,
 And must be eas'd of you; 'tis a charity.
 Justice invites your blood to understand me.

[1]Unfriendly.   [2]Fear.

BEA. I dare not.

DE F.   Quickly!

BEA.   Oh, I never shall!
  Speak it yet further off that I may lose
  What has been spoken, and no sound remain on't.
  I would not hear so much offence again
  For such another deed!

DE F.   Soft, lady, soft;
  The last is not yet paid for. Oh, this act
  Has put me into spirit! I was as greedy on't
  As the parch'd earth of moisture, when the clouds weep.   110
  Did you not mark, I wrought myself into't,
  Nay, sued and kneel'd for't? Why was all that pains took?
  You see I have thrown contempt upon your gold;
  Not that I want it [not], for I do piteously;
  In order I will come unto't, and make use on't,
  But 'twas not held so precious to begin with,
  For I place wealth after the heels of pleasure;
  And were I not resolv'd in my belief
  That thy virginity were perfect in thee,
  I should but take my recompense with grudging,   120
  As if I had but half my hopes I agreed for.

BEA. Why, 'tis impossible thou canst be so wicked,
  Or shelter such a cunning cruelty,
  To make his death the murderer of my honour!
  Thy language is so bold and vicious,
  I cannot see which way I can forgive it
  With any modesty.

DE F.   Push! You forget yourself!
  A woman dipp'd in blood, and talk of modesty!

BEA. Oh, misery of sin! Would I had been bound
  Perpetually unto my living hate   130
  In that Piracquo than to hear these words!
  Think but upon the distance that creation
  Set 'twixt thy blood and mine, and keep thee there.

DE F. Look but in your conscience, read me there;
  'Tis a true book; you'll find me there your equal.
  Push! Fly not to your birth, but settle you
  In what the act has made you; y'are no more now.
  You must forget your parentage to me: [1]

[1] 'Your aristocratic ancestry in your relationship with me.'

Y'are the deed's creature; by that name
You lost your first condition, and I challenge you,
As peace and innocency has turn'd you out,
And made you one with me.

BEA.   With thee, foul villain?

DE F. Yes, my fair murd'ress; do you urge [1] me,
Though thou writ'st maid, thou whore in thy affection?
'Twas chang'd from thy first love, and that's a kind
Of whoredom in thy heart; and he's chang'd now,
To bring thy second on, thy Alsemero,
Whom (by all sweets that ever darkness tasted),
If I enjoy thee not, thou ne'er enjoy'st!
I'll blast the hopes and joys of marriage,
I'll confess all; my life I rate at nothing.

BEA. De Flores,—

DE F.   I shall rest from all lovers' plagues then;
I live in pain now; that shooting eye
Will burn my heart to cinders.

BEA.   Oh, sir, hear me!

DE F. She that in life and love refuses me,
In death and shame my partner she shall be.

BEA. [Kneels.] Stay, hear me once for all: I make thee master
Of all the wealth I have in gold and jewels;
Let me go poor unto my bed with honour,
And I am rich in all things.

DE F.   Let this silence thee:
The wealth of all Valencia shall not buy
My pleasure from me;
Can you weep Fate from its determin'd purpose?
So soon may [you] weep me.

BEA.   Vengeance begins;
Murder, I see, is followed by more sins.
Was my creation in the womb so curs'd,
It must engender with a viper first?

DE F. Come, rise, and shroud your blushes in my bosom;
Silence is one of pleasure's best receipts.
My peace is wrought for ever in this yielding.
'Las, how the turtle [2] pants! Thou'lt love anon
What thou so fear'st and faint'st to venture on.   Exeunt.

---

[1] Provoke.   [2] Turtle dove.

ACT IV

[Dumb show]

*Enter gentlemen, VERMANDERO meeting them with action of
wonderment at the flight of ALONZO PIRACQUO. Enter
ALSEMERO, with JASPERINO and gallants; VERMANDERO
points to him, the gentlemen seeming to applaud the choice.
[Exeunt] ALSEMERO, JASPERINO, and gentlemen;
BEATRICE, the bride, following in great state, accompanied
with DIAPHANTA, ISABELLA, and other gentlewomen;
DE FLORES after all, smiling at the accident.[1] ALONZO'S
ghost appears to DE FLORES in the midst of his smile,
startles him, showing him the hand whose finger he had cut
off. They pass over in great solemnity*

[ACT IV. SCENE 1]

[ALSEMERO'S *apartment in the castle*]

Enter BEATRICE

BEA. This fellow has undone me endlessly;
    Never was bride more fearfully distress'd;
    The more I think upon th' ensuing night,
    And whom I am to cope with in embraces,
    One who's ennobled both in blood and mind,
    So clear in understanding,—that's my plague now—
    Before whose judgment will my fault appear
    Like malefactors' crimes before tribunals.
    There's no hiding on't, the more I dive
    Into my own distress; how a wise man   10
    Stands for [2] a great calamity! There's no venturing
    Into his bed, what course soe'er I light upon
    Without my shame,[3] which may grow up to danger;
    He cannot but in justice strangle me
    As I lie by him, as a cheater use me;
    'Tis a precious craft to play with a false die

---

[1]Event.   [2]Endures.   [3]Shaming myself.

Before a cunning gamester. Here's his closet,
The key left in't, and he abroad i' th' park;
Sure 'twas forgot—I'll be so bold as look in't.
Bless me! A right physician's closet 'tis,
Set round with vials, every one her mark too.
Sure he does practise physic for his own use,
Which may be safely call'd your great man's wisdom.[1]
What manuscript lies here? 'The Book of Experiment,
Call'd Secrets in Nature'; so 'tis, 'tis so;
'How to know whether a woman be with child or no';
I hope I am not yet! If he should try it though!
Let me see; folio forty-five. Here 'tis,
The leaf tuck'd down upon't, the place suspicious.
'If you would know whether a woman be with child or not,
give her two spoonfuls of the white water in glass C'; where's
that glass C? Oh, yonder I see't now. 'And if she be with
child, she sleeps full twelve hours after; if not, not.'
None of that water comes into my belly!
I'll know you from a hundred; I could break you now,
Or turn you into milk, and so beguile
The master of the mystery, but I'll look to you.
Ha! That which is next is ten times worse:
'How to know whether a woman be a maid or no.'
If that should be appli'd, what would become of me?
Belike he has a strong faith of my purity,
That never yet made proof;[2] but this he calls
'A merry sleight, but true experiment, the author Antonius
Mizaldus.'[3] 'Give the party you suspect the quantity of a
spoonful of the water in glass M, which, upon her that is a
maid, makes three several effects: 'twill make her incon-
tinently gape, then fall into a sudden sneezing, last into a
violent laughing; else dull, heavy, and lumpish.'
Where had I been?
I fear it, yet 'tis seven hours to bed time.

Enter DIAPHANTA

DIA. Cuds,[4] madam, are you here?

[1] Since his knowledge of medicine protects him against illness or death.
[2] Has never been put to the test.
[3] A French astrologer and scholar, 1520–78; similar tests appear in his writings, but not in his *De Arcanis Naturae* (*Secrets in Nature*).
[4] A mild oath, derived from 'God's'.

BEA. [*Aside.*]   Seeing that wench now,
  A trick comes in my mind; 'tis a nice piece [1]
  Gold cannot purchase.—I come hither, wench,
  To look [2] my lord.
DIA.   Would I had such a cause
  To look him too! Why, he's i' th' park, madam.
BEA. There let him be.
DIA.   Ay, madam, let him compass
  Whole parks and forests, as great rangers [3] do;
  At roosting time a little lodge can hold 'em.
  Earth-conquering Alexander, that thought the world
  Too narrow for him, in the end had but his pit-hole.[4]   60
BEA. I fear thou art not modest, Diaphanta.
DIA. Your thoughts are so unwilling to be known, madam;
  'Tis ever the bride's fashion towards bed time
  To set light by her joys, as if she ow'd [5] 'em not.
BEA. Her joys? Her fears, thou would'st say.
DIA.   Fear of what?
BEA. Art thou a maid,[6] and talk'st so to a maid?
  You leave a blushing business behind,
  Beshrew your heart for 't.
DIA.   Do you mean good sooth,[7] madam?
BEA. Well, if I'd thought upon the fear at first,
  Man should have been unknown.
DIA.   Is't possible?   70
BEA. I will give a thousand ducats to that woman
  Would try what my fears were, and tell me true
  Tomorrow, when she gets from 't; as she likes,
  I might perhaps be drawn to 't.
DIA.   Are you in earnest?
BEA. Do you get the woman, then challenge me,
  And see if I'll fly from 't; but I must tell you
  This by the way, she must be a true maid,
  Else there's no trial; my fears are not hers else.
DIA. Nay, she that I would put into your hands, madam,
  Shall be a maid.
BEA.   You know I should be sham'd else,   80
  Because she lies for me.
DIA.   'Tis a strange humour;

---

[1] A scrupulous girl.   [2] Seek.   [3] Gamekeepers.
[4] Cf. *Hamlet*, v. 1. 225–6.   [5] Owned.   [6] Virgin.
[7] In truth.

But are you serious still? Would you resign
Your first night's pleasure, and give money too?

BEA. As willingly as live.—[*Aside.*] Alas, the gold
Is but a by-bet [1] to wedge in the honour.

DIA. I do not know how the world goes abroad
For faith or honesty; there's both requir'd in this.
Madam, what say you to me, and stray no further?
I've a good mind, in troth, to earn your money.

BEA. Y'are too quick, I fear, to be a maid.

DIA. How? Not a maid? Nay, then you urge me, madam;
Your honourable self is not a truer
With all your fears upon you—

BEA. [*Aside.*] Than I with all my lightsome joys about me.

DIA. Bad enough then.

BEA. I'm glad to hear't; then you dare put your honesty [2]
Upon an easy trial.

DIA.   Easy? Anything.

BEA. I'll come to you straight.   [*Goes to the closet.*]

DIA.   She will not search me, will she,
Like the forewoman of a female jury?

BEA. Glass M; ay, this is it. Look, Diaphanta,
You take no worse than I do.

DIA.   And in so doing,
I will not question what 'tis, but take it.

BEA. [*Aside.*] Now if the experiment be true, 'twill praise itself,
And give me noble ease. Begins already;

                         [DIAPHANTA *gapes.*]

There's the first symptom; and what haste it makes
To fall into the second—there by this time!

                         [DIAPHANTA *sneezes*].

Most admirable secret! On the contrary,
It stirs me not a whit, which most concerns it.

DIA. Ha, ha, ha!

BEA. [*Aside.*] Just in all things and in order,
As if 'twere circumscrib'd; one accident [3]
Gives way unto another.

DIA.   Ha, ha, ha!

BEA. How now, wench?

DIA.   Ha, ha, ha! I am so, so light
At heart—Ha, ha, ha!—so pleasurable.
But one swig more, sweet madam.

[1] A supplementary incentive.   [2] Chastity.   [3] Symptom.

BEA.   Ay, tomorrow;
   We shall have time to sit by't.
DIA.   Now I'm sad again.
BEA. [*Aside.*] It lays itself so gently too.—Come, wench,
   Most honest Diaphanta I dare call thee now.
DIA. Pray tell me, madam, what trick call you this?
BEA. I'll tell thee all hereafter; we must study
   The carriage of this business.
DIA.   I shall carry't well,   120
   Because I love the burden.
BEA.   About midnight
   You must not fail to steal forth gently,
   That I may use the place.
DIA.   Oh, fear not, madam,
   I shall be cool by that time. The bride's place,
   And with a thousand ducats! I'm for a justice now,
   I bring a portion with me; I scorn small fools.   *Exeunt.*

[ACT IV. SCENE 2]
[*Another room in the castle*]

Enter VERMANDERO *and servant*

VER. I tell thee, knave, mine honour is in question,
   A thing till now free from suspicion,
   Nor ever was there cause. Who of my gentlemen
   Are absent? Tell me and truly how many and who.
SERV. Antonio, sir, and Franciscus.
VER. When did they leave the castle?
SERV. Some ten days since, sir, the one intending for Briamata,
   th' other for Valencia.
VER. The time accuses 'um; a charge of murder
   Is brought within my castle gate, Piracquo's murder.   10
   I dare not answer faithfully [1] their absence;
   A strict command of apprehension
   Shall pursue 'um suddenly, and either wipe
   The stain off clear, or openly discover it.

---

[1] Explain in good faith.

Provide me winged warrants for the purpose.

[Exit servant.]

See, I am set on again.

Enter TOMAZO

TOM. I claim a brother of you.
VER.   Y'are too hot;
Seek him not here.
TOM.   Yes, 'mongst your dearest bloods,
If my peace find no fairer satisfaction;
This is the place must yield account for him,
For here I left him, and the hasty tie
Of this snatch'd marriage gives strong testimony
Of his most certain ruin.
VER.   Certain falsehood!
This is the place indeed; his breach of faith
Has too much marr'd both my abused love,
The honourable love I reserv'd for him,
And mock'd my daughter's joy. The prepar'd morning
Blush'd at his infidelity; he left
Contempt and scorn to throw upon those friends
Whose belief hurt 'em; oh, 'twas most ignoble
To take his flight so unexpectedly,
And throw such public wrongs on those that lov'd him.
TOM. Then this is all your answer.
VER.   'Tis too fair
For one of his alliance; and I warn you
That this place no more see you.   *Exit.*

Enter DE FLORES

TOM.   The best is,
There is more ground to meet a man's revenge on.
Honest De Flores?
DE F.   That's my name indeed.
Saw you the bride? Good sweet sir, which way took she?
TOM. I have bless'd mine eyes from seeing such a false one.
DE F. *[Aside.]* I'd fain get off; this man's not for my company,
I smell his brother's blood when I come near him.
TOM. Come hither, kind and true one; I remember
My brother lov'd thee well.

DE F.   Oh, purely, dear sir.
  [*Aside.*] Methinks I am now again a-killing on him,
  He brings it so fresh to me.
TOM.   Thou canst guess, sirrah,—
  One honest friend has an instinct of jealousy—
  At some foul guilty person.
DE F.   'Las, sir,
  I am so charitable I think none
  Worse than myself. You did not see the bride then?
TOM. I prithee name her not. Is she not wicked?   50
DE F. No, no, a pretty, easy, round-pack'd [1] sinner,
  As your most ladies are, else you might think
  I flatter'd her; but, sir, at no hand wicked,
  Till th' are so old their chins and noses meet,
  And they salute witches. I am call'd, I think, sir.
  [*Aside.*] His company ev'n o'erlays [2] my conscience.   *Exit.*
TOM. That De Flores has a wondrous honest heart;
  He'll bring it out in time, I'm assur'd on't.

Enter ALSEMERO

  Oh, here's the glorious master of the day's joy;
  'Twill not be long till he and I do reckon.—Sir.   60
ALS. You are most welcome.
TOM.   You may call that word back;
  I do not think I am, nor wish to be.
ALS. 'Tis strange you found your way to this house then.
TOM. Would I'd ne'er known the cause! I'm none of those, sir,
  That come to give you joy and swill your wine;
  'Tis a more precious liquor that must lay
  The fiery thirst I bring.
ALS.   Your words and you
  Appear to me great strangers.
TOM.   Time and our swords
  May make us more acquainted; this the business:
  I should have [had] a brother in your place;   70
  How treachery and malice have dispos'd of him,
  I'm bound to inquire of him which holds his right,
  Which never could come fairly.
ALS.   You must look
  To answer for that word, sir.

         [1] Plump(?).   [2] Presses hard upon.

Tom.   Fear you not,
  I'll have it [1] ready drawn at our next meeting.
  Keep your day solemn. Farewell, I disturb it not;
  I'll bear the smart with patience for a time.   *Exit.*
Als. 'Tis somewhat ominous this, a quarrel enter'd
  Upon this day; my innocence relieves me.

              Enter Jasperino

  I should be wondrous sad else. Jasperino,
  I have news to tell thee, strange news.
Jas.   I ha' some too,
  I think as strange as yours. Would I might keep
  Mine, so my faith and friendship might be kept in't!
  Faith, sir, dispense a little with my zeal,
  And let it cool in this. [2]
Als.   This puts me on,
  And blames thee for thy slowness.
Jas.   All may prove nothing,
  Only a friendly fear that leap'd from me, sir.
Als. No question it may prove nothing; let's partake it though.
Jas. 'Twas Diaphanta's chance (for to that wench
  I pretend [3] honest love, and she deserves it)
  To leave me in a back part of the house,
  A place we chose for private conference;
  She was no sooner gone, but instantly
  I heard your bride's voice in the next room to me,
  And, lending more attention, found De Flores
  Louder than she.
Als.   De Flores? Thou art out now.
Jas. You'll tell me more anon.
Als.   Still I'll prevent [4] thee:
  The very sight of him is poison to her.
Jas. That made me stagger too, but Diaphanta
  At her return confirm'd it. [5]
Als.   Diaphanta!
Jas. Then fell we both to listen, and words pass'd
  Like those that challenge interest in a woman.
Als. Peace! Quench thy zeal; 'tis dangerous to thy bosom.

---

[1] i.e. 'my sword'.   [2] In this matter.   [3] Proffer.
[4] Anticipate.   [5] Beatrice and De Flores's present relationship.

JAS. Then truth is full of peril.
ALS.   Such truths are.
  Oh, were she the sole glory of the earth,
  Had eyes that could shoot fire into kings' breasts,
  And touch'd,[1] she sleeps not here! Yet I have time,
  Though night be near, to be resolv'd hereof,
  And prithee do not weigh me by my passions.
JAS. I never weigh'd friend so.
ALS.   Done charitably.   110
  That key will lead thee to a pretty secret,
  By a Chaldean taught me, and I have
  My study upon some.[2] Bring from my closet
  A glass incrib'd there with the letter M,
  And question not my purpose.
JAS.   It shall be done, sir.   *Exit*.
ALS. How can this hang together? Not an hour since
  Her woman came pleading her lady's fears,
  Deliver'd her for the most timorous virgin
  That ever shrunk at man's name, and so modest,
  She charg'd her weep out her request to me   120
  That she might come obscurely to my bosom.

Enter BEATRICE

BEA. [*Aside*.] All things go well; my woman's preparing yonder
  For her sweet voyage, which grieves me to lose;
  Necessity compels it; I lose all else.
ALS. [*Aside*.] Push! Modesty's shrine is set in yonder forehead;
  I cannot be too sure though.—My Joanna.
BEA. Sir, I was bold to weep a message to you;
  Pardon my modest fears.
ALS. [*Aside*.]   The dove's not meeker;
  She's abus'd,[3] questionless.—

Enter JASPERINO

                              Oh, are you come, sir?
BEA. [*Aside*.] The glass, upon my life! I see the letter.   130
JAS. Sir, this is M.
ALS.   'Tis it.
BEA. [*Aside*.]   I am suspected.

        [1] Soiled.   [2] i.e. some secrets.   [3] Maligned.

ALS. How fitly our bride comes to partake with us!

BEA. What is't, my Lord?

ALS.   No hurt.

BEA.   Sir, pardon me,
I seldom taste of any composition.[1]

ALS. But this, upon my warrant, you shall venture on.

BEA. I fear 'twill make me ill.

ALS.   Heaven forbid that!

BEA. [*Aside.*] I'm put now to my cunning; th' effects I know,
If I can now but feign 'em handsomely.   [*Drinks.*]

ALS. [*To* JASPERINO.] It has that secret virtue it ne'er miss'd,
    sir,
Upon a virgin.

JAS. [*To* ALSEMERO.] Treble qualitied?
                              [BEATRICE *gapes and sneezes.*]

ALS. [*To* JASPERINO]. By all that's virtuous, it takes there,
    proceeds!

JAS. [*To* ALSEMERO.] This is the strangest trick to know a
    maid by.

BEA. Ha, ha, ha!
You have given me joy of heart to drink, my Lord.

ALS. No, thou hast given me such joy of heart
That never can be blasted.

BEA.   What's the matter, sir?

ALS. [*To* JASPERINO.] See, now 'tis settled in a melancholy,
Keeps both the time and method.—My Joanna,
Chaste as the breath of Heaven, or morning's womb,
That brings the day forth, thus my love encloses thee.
                                             Exeunt.

[ACT IV. SCENE 3]

[ALIBIUS'S *house*]

Enter ISABELLA *and* LOLLIO

ISA. O Heaven! Is this the waning moon?
Does love turn fool, run mad, and all at once?

---

[1] Mixed drink.

Sirrah, here's a madman, akin to the fool too,
A lunatic lover.

LOL. No, no, not he I brought the letter from?

ISA. Compare his inside with his out, and tell me.

[Gives him the letter.]

LOL. The out's mad, I'm sure of that; I had a taste on't.
[Reads.] 'To the bright Andromeda, chief chambermaid to
the Knight of the Sun,[1] at the sign of Scorpio, in the middle
region, sent by the bellows-mender of Aeolus. Pay the post.'   10
This is stark madness.

ISA. Now mark the inside. [Takes the letter again.] 'Sweet lady,
having now cast off this counterfeit cover of a madman, I
appear to your best judgment a true and faithful lover of your
beauty.'

LOL. He is mad still.

ISA. 'If any fault you find, chide those perfections in you which
made me imperfect. 'Tis the same sun that causeth to grow
and enforceth to wither,—'

LOL. Oh, rogue!   20

ISA. '—Shapes and transhapes, destroys and builds again; I
come in winter to you dismantled of my proper ornaments;
by the sweet splendour of your cheerful smiles, I spring and
live a lover.'

LOL. Mad rascal still!

ISA. 'Tread him not under foot, that shall appear an honour to
your bounties. I remain—mad till I speak with you, from
whom I expect my cure—Yours all, or one beside himself,
Franciscus.'

LOL. You are like to have a fine time on't; my master and I   30
may give over our professions: I do not think but you can cure
fools and madmen faster than we, with little pains too.

ISA. Very likely.

LOL. One thing I must tell you, mistress: you perceive that I
am privy to your skill; if I find you minister once and set up
the trade, I put in for my thirds [2]—I shall be mad or fool else.

ISA. The first place is thine, believe it, Lollio,
If I do fall.

LOL. I fall upon you.

ISA. So.   40

LOL. Well, I stand to my venture.

---

[1] A hero in *The Mirror of Knighthood* (1583–1601).
[2] The third part of booty, etc., traditionally retained by the captor.

Isa. But thy counsel now; how shall I deal with 'um?

Lol. Why, do you mean to deal with 'um?

Isa. Nay, the fair understanding,[1] how to use 'um.

Lol. Abuse [2] 'um! That's the way to mad the fool and make a fool of the madman, and then you use 'um kindly.

Isa. 'Tis easy; I'll practise, do thou observe it.
   The key of thy wardrobe.

Lol. There fit yourself for 'um, and I'll fit 'um both for you.
                                    [*Gives her the key.*]

Isa. Take thou no further notice than the outside.   *Exit.*

Lol. Not an inch; I'll put you to the inside.

Enter ALIBIUS

Alib. Lollio, art there? Will all be perfect, think'st thou?
   Tomorrow night, as if to close up the
   Solemnity, Vermandero expects us.

Lol. I mistrust the madmen most; the fools will do well enough, I have taken pains with them.

Alib. Tush, they cannot miss; the more absurdity,
   The more commends it, so no rough behaviours
   Affright the ladies; they are nice [3] things, thou know'st.

Lol. You need not fear, sir; so long as we are there with our commanding pizzles,[4] they'll be as tame as the ladies themselves.

Alib. I will see them once more rehearse before they go.

Lol. I was about it, sir. Look you to the madmen's morris, and let me alone with the other; there is one or two that I mistrust their fooling; I'll instruct them, and then they shall rehearse the whole measure.

Alib. Do, do; I'll see the music prepar'd; but, Lollio,
   By the way, how does my wife brook her restraint?
   Does she not grudge at it?

Lol. So, so; she takes some pleasure in the house, she would abroad else; you must allow her a little more length; she's kept too short.

Alib. She shall along to Vermandero's with us;
   That will serve her for a month's liberty.

Lol. What's that on your face, sir?

Alib. Where, Lollio? I see nothing.

---

[1] 'Understand me fairly or modestly.'   [2] Deceive.
[3] Fastidious.   [4] Whips.

Lol. Cry you mercy,[1] sir, 'tis your nose; it showed like the
    trunk of a young elephant.[2]

Alib. Away, rascal! I 'll prepare the music, Lollio.   80

                                              [*Exit* Alibius.]

Lol. Do, sir, and I 'll dance the whilst. Tony, where art thou,
    Tony?

Enter Antonio

Ant. Here, cousin; where art thou?

Lol. Come, Tony, the footmanship I taught you.

Ant. I had rather ride, cousin.

Lol. Ay, a whip take you; but I 'll keep you out. Vault in; look
    you, Tony: fa, la, la, la, la.   [*Dances.*]

Ant. Fa, la, la, la, la.   [*Dances.*]

Lol. There, an honour.[3]

Ant. Is this an honour, coz?   90

Lol. Yes, and it please your worship.

Ant. Does honour bend in the hams, coz?

Lol. Marry, does it; as low as worship, squireship, nay, yeo-
    manry itself sometimes, from whence it first stiffened. There,
    rise; a caper.

Ant. Caper after an honour, coz?

Lol. Very proper; for honour is but a caper, rises as fast and
    high, has a knee or two, and falls to the ground again. You can
    remember your figure, Tony?

Ant. Yes, cousin; when I see thy figure, I can remember mine.   100

Enter Isabella, [*dressed like a madwoman*]

Isa. Hey, how he treads the air! Shough,[4] shough, t'other way!
    He burns his wings else; here 's wax enough below, Icarus,
    more than will be cancelled[5] these eighteen moons; he 's
    down, he 's down! What a terrible fall he had!
    Stand up, thou son of Cretan Dedalus,
    And let us tread the lower labyrinth;
    I 'll bring thee to the clue.[6]

Ant. Prithee, coz, let me alone.

Isa.   Art thou not drown'd?

---

[1] 'I beg your pardon.'   [2] An allusion to cuckoldry.
[3] A bow.   [4] i.e. 'Shoo!'   [5] Used up.
[6] The thread used by Theseus to find his way out of the labyrinth.

About thy head I saw a heap of clouds,
Wrapp'd like a Turkish turban; on thy back
A crook'd chameleon-colour'd rainbow hung
Like a tiara down unto thy hams.
Let me suck out those billows in thy belly;
Hark how they roar and rumble in the straits!
Bless thee from the pirates.

ANT. Pox upon you! Let me alone.

ISA. Why shouldst thou mount so high as Mercury,
Unless thou hadst reversion of his place?
Stay in the moon with me, Endymion,
And we will rule these wild, rebellious waves
That would have drown'd my love.

ANT.   I'll kick thee if
Again thou touch me, thou wild, unshapen antic;
I am no fool, you bedlam!

ISA. But you are, as sure as I am, mad.
Have I put on this habit of a frantic,
With love as full of fury, to beguile
The nimble eye of watchful jealousy,
And am I thus rewarded?   [*Reveals herself.*]

ANT.   Ha, dearest beauty!

ISA. No, I have no beauty now,
Nor ever had, but what was in my garments.
You, a quick-sighted lover! Come not near me;
Keep your caparisons,[1] y'are aptly clad;
I came a feigner to return stark mad.   *Exit.*

ANT. Stay, or I shall change condition,
And become as you are.

Enter LOLLIO

LOL. Why, Tony, whither now? Why, fool?

ANT. Whose fool, usher of idiots? You coxcomb!
I have fool'd too much.

LOL. You were best be mad another while then.

ANT. So I am, stark mad. I have cause enough,
And I could throw the full effects on thee,
And beat thee like a fury.

LOL. Do not, do not; I shall not forbear the gentleman under
the fool, if you do. Alas, I saw through your fox-skin[2] before

---

[1] Trappings.   [2] Disguise.

now; come, I can give you comfort; my mistress loves you,
and there is as arrant a madman i' th' house as you are a fool—
your rival—whom she loves not; if after the masque we can
rid her of him, you earn her love, she says, and the fool shall
ride her.

ANT. May I believe thee?   150

LOL. Yes, or you may choose whether you will or not.

ANT. She's eas'd of him; I have a good quarrel on't.

LOL. Well, keep your old station yet, and be quiet.

ANT. Tell her I will deserve her love.   [*Exit.*]

LOL. And you are like to have your desire.

Enter FRANCISCUS

FRAN. [*Sings.*] Down, down, down a-down a-down, and then
          with a horse-trick,[1]
     To kick Latona's [2] forehead, and break her bowstring.

LOL. [*Aside.*] This is t'other counterfeit; I'll put him out of
     his humour. [*Takes out a letter and reads.*] 'Sweet lady, having   160
     now cast [off] this counterfeit cover of a madman, I appear to
     your best judgment a true and faithful lover of your beauty.'
     This is pretty well for a madman.

FRAN. Ha! What's that?

LOL. 'Chide those perfections in you which [have] made me
     imperfect.'

FRAN. [*Aside.*] I am discovered to the fool.

LOL. I hope to discover the fool in you ere I have done with
     you. 'Yours all, or one beside himself, Franciscus.' This
     madman will mend sure.   170

FRAN. What do you read, sirrah?

LOL. Your destiny, sir; you'll be hanged for this trick, and
     another that I know.

FRAN. Art thou of counsel with thy mistress?

LOL. Next her apron strings.

FRAN. Give me thy hand.

LOL. Stay; let me put yours in my pocket first. Your hand is
     true, is it not? It will not pick? [3] I partly fear it, because I think
     it does lie.

FRAN. Not in a syllable.   180

---

[1] Prank.
[2] Latona (Leto) was sometimes identified with Diana, her daughter.
[3] Steal.

LOL. So; if you love my mistress so well as you have handled
the matter here, you are like to be cured of your madness.

FRAN. And none but she can cure it.

LOL. Well, I'll give you over then, and she shall cast your
water [1] next.

FRAN. Take for thy pains past.   [*Gives* LOLLIO *money.*]

LOL. I shall deserve more, I hope; my mistress loves you, but
must have some proof of your love to her.

FRAN. There I meet my wishes.

LOL. That will not serve; you must meet her enemy and yours.   19

FRAN. He's dead already.

LOL. Will you tell me that, and I parted but now with him?

FRAN. Show me the man.

LOL. Ay, that's the right course now; see him before you kill
him in any case, and yet it needs not go so far neither; 'tis but
a fool that haunts the house and my mistress in the shape of
an idiot; bang but his fool's coat well-favouredly, and 'tis well.

FRAN. Soundly, soundly!

LOL. Only reserve him till the masque be past; and if you find
him not now in the dance yourself, I'll show you. In, in! My   20
master!

FRAN. He handles him like a feather. Hey!   [*Exit.*]

Enter ALIBIUS

ALIB. Well said; [2] in a readiness, Lollio?

LOL. Yes, sir.

ALIB. Away then, and guide them in, Lollio;
Entreat your mistress to see this sight.
Hark, is there not one incurable fool
That might be begg'd? [3] I have friends.

LOL.   I have him for you,
One that shall deserve it too.   [*Exit.*]

[*Enter* ISABELLA, *and re-enter* LOLLIO, *with*] *the madmen
and fools* [*who*] *dance*

ALIB. Good boy, Lollio,   21
'Tis perfect; well, fit but once these strains,
We shall have coin and credit for our pains.   *Exeunt.*

---

[1] 'Diagnose your disease.'   [2] 'Well done.'
[3] To apply to the king for the guardianship of an idiot (in order to profit
from his estate). Alibius evidently seeks a fool to pass over to a friend.

ACT V. [SCENE 1]
[*A hallway in the castle*]

Enter BEATRICE. *A clock strikes one*

BEA. One struck, and yet she lies by't! Oh, my fears!
    This strumpet serves her own ends, 'tis apparent now,
    Devours the pleasure with a greedy appetite,
    And never minds my honour or my peace,
    Makes havoc of my right; but she pays dearly for't.
    No trusting of her life with such a secret,
    That cannot rule her blood to keep her promise.
    Beside, I have some suspicion of her faith to me
    Because I was suspected of my lord,
    And it must come from her. (*Clock strikes two.*) Hark!   10
      By my horrors,
    Another clock strikes two!

Enter DE FLORES

DE F.   Pist, where are you?
BEA. De Flores?
DE F.   Ay; is she not come from him yet?
BEA. As I am a living soul, not.
DE F.   Sure the devil
    Hath sow'd his itch within her; who would trust
    A waiting-woman?
BEA.   I must trust somebody.
DE F. Push! They are termagants; [1]
    Especially when they fall upon their masters,
    And have their ladies' first-fruits; th' are mad whelps,
    You cannot stave 'em off from game royal; then   20
    You are so harsh and hardy, ask no counsel,
    And I could have help'd you to an apothecary's daughter,
    Would have fall'n off before eleven, and thank'd you too.
BEA. O me, not yet? This whore forgets herself.
DE F. The rascal fares so well. Look, y'are undone:
    The day-star, by this hand! See Phosphorus plain yonder.

---

[1] Shrews.

BEA. Advise me now to fall upon some ruin,
There is no counsel safe else.
DE F.   Peace; I ha't now;
For we must force a rising; there's no remedy.
BEA. How? Take heed of that.   3*
DE F. Tush; be you quiet, or else give over all.
BEA. Prithee, I ha' done then.
DE F.   This is my reach: [1] I'll set
Some part afire of Diaphanta's chamber.
BEA. How, fire, sir? That may endanger the whole house.
DE F. You talk of danger when your fame's on fire!
BEA. That's true; do what thou wilt now.
DE F.   Push; I aim
At a most rich success, strikes all dead sure;
The chimney being afire, and some light parcels [2]
Of the least danger in her chamber only,
If Diaphanta should be met by chance then,   4*
Far from her lodging—which is now suspicious—
It would be thought her fears and affrights then
Drove her to seek for succour; if not seen
Or met at all, as that's the likeliest,
For her own shame she'll hasten towards her lodging;
I will be ready with a piece [3] high-charg'd,
As 'twere to cleanse the chimney; there 'tis proper now,
But she shall be the mark.
BEA.   I'm forc'd to love thee now,
'Cause thou provid'st so carefully for my honour.
DE F. 'Slid,[4] it concerns the safety of us both,   5*
Our pleasure and continuance.
BEA.   One word now,
Prithee: how for the servants?
DE F.   I'll dispatch them
Some one way, some another in the hurry,
For buckets, hooks, ladders; fear not you,
The deed shall find its time, and I've thought since
Upon a safe conveyance for the body too.
How this fire purifies wit! Watch you your minute.
BEA. Fear keeps my soul upon't; I cannot stray from't.

Enter ALONZO'S *ghost*

[1] Plan.   [2] Portions.   [3] Firearm.
[4] 'By God's lid.'

DE F. Ha! What art thou that tak'st away the light
    'Twixt that star and me? I dread thee not;   60
    'Twas but a mist of conscience. All's clear again.   *Exit.*
BEA. Who's that, De Flores? Bless me! It slides by;
                                    [Exit ghost.]
    Some ill thing haunts the house; 't has left behind it
    A shivering sweat upon me; I'm afraid now.
    This night has been so tedious. O this strumpet!
    Had she a thousand lives, he should not leave her
    Till he had destroy'd the last. List! O my terrors!
    Three struck by Saint Sebastian's!   *Clock strikes three.*
WITHIN. Fire, fire, fire!
BEA. Already! How rare is that man's speed!   70
    How heartily he serves me! His face loathes [1] one;
    But look upon his care, who would not love him?
    The east is not more beauteous than his service.
WITHIN. Fire fire, fire!

Enter DE FLORES; *servants pass over, ring a bell*

DE F. Away, dispatch! Hooks, buckets, ladders! That's well
    said.
    The fire-bell rings, the chimney works; my charge; [2]
    The piece is ready.   *Exit.*
BEA.   Here's a man worth loving.—

Enter DIAPHANTA

    Oh, y'are a jewel!
DIA.   Pardon frailty, madam;
    In troth, I was so well I ev'n forgot myself.   80
BEA. Y'have made trim work.
DIA.   What?
BEA.   Hie quickly to your chamber;
    Your reward follows you.
DIA.   I never made
    So sweet a bargain.   *Exit.*

Enter ALSEMERO

---

[1] Disgusts.   [2] Load of powder.

ALS.   O my dear Joanna;
  Alas, art thou risen too? I was coming,
  My absolute treasure.
BEA.   When I miss'd you,
  I could not choose but follow.
ALS.   Th'art all sweetness;
  The fire is not so dangerous.
BEA.   Think you so, sir?
ALS. I prithee tremble not; believe me, 'tis not.

Enter VERMANDERO *and* JASPERINO

VER. Oh, bless my house and me!
ALS.   My lord your father.

Enter DE FLORES *with a piece*

VER. Knave, whither goes that piece?
DE F.   To scour the chimney.   90
                                Exit.

VER. Oh, well said, well said;
  That fellow's good on all occasions.
BEA. A wondrous necessary man, my Lord.
VER. He hath a ready wit; he's worth 'em all, sir;
  Dog [1] at a house on fire; I ha' seen him sing'd ere now.
                    The piece goes off.

  Ha, there he goes.
BEA.   'Tis done.
ALS.   Come, sweet, to bed now.
  Alas, thou wilt get cold.
BEA.   Alas, the fear keeps that out;
  My heart will find no quiet till I hear
  How Diaphanta, my poor woman, fares;
  It is her chamber, sir, her lodging chamber.   100
VER. How should the fire come there?
BEA. As good a soul as ever lady countenanc'd,
  But in her chamber negligent and heavy;
  She 'scap'd a mine [2] twice.
VER.   Twice?
BEA.   Strangely twice, sir.

---

[1] Adept.   [2] i.e. a dangerous situation.

VER. Those sleepy sluts are dangerous in a house,
   And they be ne'er so good.

Enter DE FLORES

DE F.   O poor virginity,
   Thou hast paid dearly for't.
VER.   Bless us! What's that?
DE F. A thing you all knew once—Diaphanta's burnt.
BEA. My woman, oh, my woman!
DE F.   Now the flames
   Are greedy of her; burnt, burnt, burnt to death, sir.   110
BEA. Oh, my presaging soul!
ALS.   Not a tear more;
   I charge you by the last embrace I gave you
   In bed before this rais'd us.
BEA.   Now you tie me;
   Were it my sister, now she gets no more.

Enter servant

VER. How now?
SERV.   All danger's past; you may now take
   Your rest, my lords, the fire is throughly quench'd.
   Ah, poor gentlewoman, how soon was she stifled!
BEA. De Flores, what is left of her inter,
   And we as mourners all will follow her;
   I will entreat that honour to my servant,   120
   Ev'n of my lord himself.
ALS.   Command it, sweetness.
BEA. Which of you spied the fire first?
DE F.   'Twas I, madam.
BEA. And took such pains in't too? A double goodness!
   'Twere well he were rewarded.
VER.   He shall be.
   De Flores, call upon me.
ALS.   And upon me, sir.
          Exeunt [all except DE FLORES].
DE F. Rewarded? Precious! Here's a trick beyond me;
   I see in all bouts both of sport and wit,
   Always a woman strives for the last hit.   *Exit.*

[ACT V. SCENE 2]

[*A room in the castle*]

Enter TOMAZO

TOM. I cannot taste the benefits of life
With the same relish I was wont to do.
Man I grow weary of, and hold his fellowship
A treacherous, bloody friendship; and because
I am ignorant in whom my wrath should settle,
I must think all men villains, and the next
I meet, whoe'er he be, the murderer
Of my most worthy brother. Ha! What's he?

Enter DE FLORES *and passes over the stage*

Oh, the fellow that some call honest De Flores;
But methinks honesty was hard bested
To come there for a lodging, as if a queen
Should make her palace of a post-house.
I find a contrariety in nature
Betwixt that face and me; the least occasion
Would give me game upon him; [1] yet he's so foul
One would scarce touch him with a sword he loved
And made account of; so most deadly venemous,
He would go near to poison any weapon
That should draw blood on him; one must resolve
Never to use that sword again in fight,
In way of honest manhood, that strikes him;
Some river must devour't; 'twere not fit
That any man should find it. What, again?

Enter DE FLORES

He walks a' purpose by, sure, to choke me up,
To infect my blood.
DE F.   My worthy noble Lord!

[1] 'Provoke me to fight with him.'

TOM. Dost offer to come near and breathe upon me?

                                        [*Strikes him.*]

DE F. A blow!   [*Draws his sword.*]

TOM.   Yea, are you so prepar'd?   [*Draws.*]
  I'll rather, like a soldier, die by th' sword
  Than like a politician by thy poison.

DE F. Hold, my Lord, as you are honourable.   30

TOM. All slaves that kill by poison are still cowards.

DE F. [*Aside.*] I cannot strike; I see his brother's wounds
  Fresh bleeding in his eye, as in a crystal.—
  I will not question this; I know y'are noble;

                                        [*Sheathes his sword.*]

  I take my injury with thanks given, sir,
  Like a wise lawyer; and as a favour
  Will wear it for the worthy hand that gave it.—
  [*Aside.*] Why this from him that yesterday appear'd
  So strangely loving to me?
  Oh, but instinct is of a subtler strain;   40
  Guilt must not walk so near his lodge again;
  He came near me now.   *Exit.*

TOM. All league with mankind I renounce for ever,
  Till I find this murderer; not so much
  As common courtesy but I'll lock up;
  For in the state of ignorance I live in,
  A brother may salute his brother's murderer,
  And wish good speed to th' villain in a greeting.

              Enter VERMANDERO, ALIBIUS, *and* ISABELLA

VER. Noble Piracquo.

TOM.   Pray keep on your way, sir;
  I've nothing to say to you.

VER.   Comforts bless you, sir.   50

TOM. I have forsworn compliment, in troth I have, sir;
  As you are merely man, I have not left
  A good wish for you, nor any here.

VER. Unless you be so far in love with grief
  You will not part from't upon any terms,
  We bring that news will make a welcome for us.

TOM. What news can that be?

VER.   Throw no scornful smile
  Upon the zeal I bring you; 'tis worth more, sir.

Two of the chiefest men I kept about me [1]
 I hide not from the law or your just vengeance.
TOM. Ha!
VER. To give your peace more ample satisfaction
 Thank these discoverers.
TOM.   If you bring that calm,
 Name but the manner I shall ask forgiveness in
 For that contemptuous smile upon you;
 I'll perfect it with reverence that belongs
 Unto a sacred altar.   [Kneels.]
VER.   Good sir, rise;
 Why, now you overdo so much a' this hand
 As you fell short a' t'other. Speak, Alibius.
ALIB. 'Twas my wife's fortune, as she is most lucky
 At a discovery, to find out lately
 Within our hospital of fools and madmen
 Two counterfeits slipp'd into these disguises;
 Their names, Franciscus and Antonio.
VER. Both mine, sir, and I ask no favour for 'em.
ALIB. Now that which draws suspicion to their habits,
 The time of their disguisings agrees justly
 With the day of the murder.
TOM.   O bless'd revelation!
VER. Nay, more, nay, more, sir; I'll not spare mine own
 In way of justice. They both feign'd a journey
 To Briamata, and so wrought out their leaves;
 My love was so abus'd [2] in't.
TOM.   Time's too precious
 To run in waste now; you have brought a peace
 The riches of five kingdoms could not purchase.
 Be my most happy conduct; I thirst for 'em;
 Like subtle lightning will I wind about 'em,
 And melt their marrow in 'em.   Exeunt.

---

[1] In this apparent exaggeration of the status of Antonio and Franciscus, Vermandero is emphasizing his magnanimous gesture.
[2] Thus deceived.

[ACT V. SCENE 3]

[ALSEMERO'S *apartment in the castle*]

Enter ALSEMERO *and* JASPERINO

JAS. Your confidence, I'm sure, is now of proof; [1]
  The prospect from the garden has show'd
  Enough for deep suspicion.
ALS.   The black mask
  That so continually was worn upon't
  Condemns the face for ugly ere't be seen;
  Her despite to him, and so seeming bottomless.
JAS. Touch it home then; 'tis not a shallow probe
  Can search this ulcer soundly; I fear you'll find it
  Full of corruption. 'Tis fit I leave you;
  She meets you opportunely from that walk;   10
  She took the back door at his parting with her.   *Exit.*
ALS. Did my fate wait for this unhappy stroke
  At my first sight of woman?

Enter BEATRICE

                    She's here.
BEA. Alsemero!
ALS.   How do you?
BEA.   How do I?
  Alas, how do you? You look not well.
ALS. You read me well enough, I am not well.
BEA. Not well, sir? Is't in my power to better you?
ALS. Yes.
BEA.   Nay, then y'are cur'd again.
ALS. Pray resolve me one question, lady.
BEA.   If I can.
ALS. None can so sure. Are you honest?   20
BEA. Ha, ha, ha! That's a broad question, my Lord.
ALS. But that's not a modest answer, my lady.
  Do you laugh? My doubts are strong upon me.
BEA. 'Tis innocence that smiles, and no rough brow

---

[1] 'Your confidence in my veracity has been confirmed'

    Can take away the dimple in her cheek.
    Say I should strain a tear to fill the vault,[1]
    Which would you give the better faith to?
ALS. 'Twere but hypocrisy of a sadder colour,
    But the same stuff; neither your smiles nor tears
    Shall move or flatter me from my belief:
    You are a whore.
BEA.   What a horrid sound it hath!
    It blasts a beauty to deformity;
    Upon what face soever that breath falls,
    It strikes it ugly; oh, you have ruin'd
    What you can ne'er repair again.
ALS.   I'll all
    Demolish, and seek out truth within you,
    If there be any left. Let your sweet tongue
    Prevent [2] your heart's rifling, there I'll ransack
    And tear out my suspicion.
BEA.   You may, sir;
    'Tis an easy passage; yet, if you please,
    Show me the ground whereon you lost your love;
    My spotless virtue may but tread on that
    Before I perish.
ALS.   Unanswerable!
    A ground you cannot stand on; you fall down
    Beneath all grace and goodness when you set
    Your ticklish heel on't; there was a visor
    O'er that cunning face, and that became you;
    Now Impudence in triumph rides upon't;
    How comes this reconcilement else
    'Twixt you and your despite, your rancorous loathing,
    De Flores? He that your eye was sore at sight of,
    He's now become your arm's supporter, your
    Lip's saint.
BEA.   Is there the cause?
ALS.   Worse; your lust's devil,
    Your adultery!
BEA.   Would any but yourself say that,
    'Twould turn him to a villain.
ALS.   'Twas witness'd
    By the counsel of your bosom, Diaphanta.
BEA. Is your witness dead then?

                [1] The sky.   [2] Forestall.

ALS.   'Tis to be fear'd
　　It was the wages of her knowledge; poor soul,
　　She liv'd not long after the discovery.
BEA.　Then hear a story of not much less horror   60
　　Than this your false suspicion is beguil'd with;
　　To your bed's scandal I stand up [1] innocence,
　　Which even the guilt of one black other deed
　　Will stand for proof of: your love has made me
　　A cruel murd'ress.
ALS.   Ha!
BEA.   A bloody one.
　　I have kiss'd poison for't, strok'd a serpent;
　　That thing of hate, worthy in my esteem
　　Of no better employment, and him most worthy
　　To be so employ'd, I caus'd to murder
　　That innocent Piracquo, having no   70
　　Better means than that worst to assure
　　Yourself to me.
ALS.   Oh, the place itself e'er since
　　Has crying been for vengeance, the temple
　　Where blood [2] and beauty first unlawfully
　　Fir'd their devotion and quench'd the right one; [3]
　　'Twas in my fears at first; 'twill have it now. [4]
　　Oh, thou art all deform'd!
BEA.   Forget not, sir,
　　It for your sake was done; shall greater dangers
　　Make the less welcome?
ALS.   Oh, thou shouldst have gone
　　A thousand leagues about to have avoided   80
　　This dangerous bridge of blood! Here we are lost.
BEA.　Remember I am true unto your bed.
ALS.　The bed itself's a charnel, the sheets shrouds
　　For murder'd carcasses. It must ask pause
　　What I must do in this; meantime you shall
　　Be my prisoner only. Enter my closet;   *Exit* BEATRICE.
　　I'll be your keeper yet. Oh, in what part
　　Of this sad story shall I first begin? Ha!
　　This same fellow has put me in. [5]

　　　　　　　[1] Put forward.   [2] Passion.
　　　　　　[3] i.e. religious devotion (I. 1. 5–12).
　　　　　　[4] 'The temple will have vengeance now.'
　　　　　　[5] Suggested an approach.

Enter DE FLORES

                                    De Flores!
DE F. Noble Alsemero!
ALS.   I can tell you
  News, sir; my wife has her commended to you.
DE F. That's news indeed, my Lord; I think she would
  Commend me to the gallows if she could,
  She has ever lov'd me so well; I thank her.
ALS. What's this blood upon your band,[1] De Flores?
DE F. Blood? No, sure 'twas wash'd since.
ALS.   Since when, man?
DE F. Since t'other day I got a knock
  In a sword-and-dagger school; I think 'tis out.
ALS. Yes, 'tis almost out; but 'tis perceiv'd though.
  I had forgot my message; this it is: 10
  What price goes murder?
DE F.   How, sir?
ALS.   I ask you, sir.
  My wife's behindhand with [2] you, she tells me,
  For a brave bloody blow you gave for her sake
  Upon Piracquo.
DE F.   Upon? 'Twas quite through him, sure;
  Has she confess'd it?
ALS.   As sure as death to both of you,
  And much more than that.
DE F.   It could not be much more;
  'Twas but one thing, and that—she is a whore.
ALS. It could not choose but follow. O cunning devils,
  How should blind men know you from fair-fac'd saints?
BEA. (*Within.*) He lies, the villain does belie me!   1
DE F. Let me go to her, sir.
ALS.   Nay,[3] you shall to her.
  Peace, crying crocodile, your sounds are heard!
  Take your prey to you; get you in to her, sir.
                                    Exit DE FLORES.
  I'll be your pander now; rehearse again
  Your scene of lust, that you may be perfect
  When you shall come to act it to the black audience
  Where howls and gnashings shall be music to you.

                    [1] Collar.   [2] Indebted to.   [3] Indeed.

Clip your adult'ress freely; 'tis the pilot
Will guide you to the Mare Mortuum,[1]
Where you shall sink to fathoms bottomless.   120

Enter VERMANDERO, ALIBIUS, ISABELLA, TOMAZO,
    FRANCISCUS, *and* ANTONIO

VER. Oh, Alsemero, I have a wonder for you.
ALS. No, sir, 'tis I, I have a wonder for you.
VER. I have suspicion near as proof itself
    For Piracquo's murder.
ALS.   Sir, I have proof
    Beyond suspicion for Piracquo's murder.
VER. Beseech you, hear me: these two have been disguis'd
    E'er since the deed was done.
ALS.   I have two other
    That were more close disguis'd than your two could be
    E'er since the deed was done.
VER. You'll hear me: these mine own servants—   130
ALS. Hear me: those nearer than your servants,
    That shall acquit them and prove them guiltless.
FRAN. That may be done with easy truth, sir.
TOM. How is my cause bandied through your delays!
    'Tis urgent in my blood and calls for haste;
    Give me a brother alive or dead—
    Alive, a wife with him; if dead, for both
    A recompense for murder and adultery.[2]
BEA. (*Within.*) Oh, oh, oh!
ALS.   Hark! 'Tis coming to you.
DE F. (*Within.*) Nay, I'll along for company.
BEA. (*Within.*)   Oh, oh!   140
VER. What horrid sounds are these?
ALS.   Come forth, you twins
    Of mischief.

Enter DE FLORES, *bringing in* BEATRICE [*wounded*]

DE F.   Here we are; if you have any more
    To say to us, speak quickly; I shall not

_____
[1] The Dead Sea.
[2] Adultery in the sense that Alonzo has been supplanted from his rightful
place by Alsemero (Tomazo knows nothing about Beatrice's relationship
with De Flores).

Give you the hearing else; I am so stout yet,
And so, I think, that broken rib of mankind.[1]

VER. A host of enemies ent'red my citadel
Could not amaze like this! Joanna, Beatrice-Joanna!

BEA. Oh, come not near me, sir, I shall defile you;
I am that of your blood was taken from you
For your better health;[2] look no more upon't,
But cast it to the ground regardlessly;
Let the common sewer take it from distinction.[3]
Beneath the stars, upon yon meteor[4]
Ever hung my fate, 'mongst things corruptible;
I ne'er could pluck it from him; my loathing
Was prophet to the rest, but ne'er believ'd;
Mine honour fell with him, and now my life.
Alsemero, I am a stranger to your bed;
Your bed was cozen'd on the nuptial night,
For which your false bride died.

ALS.   Diaphanta!

DE F. Yes, and the while I coupled with your mate
At barley-break; now we are left in hell.[5]

VER. We are all there, it circumscribes [us] here.

DE F. I lov'd this woman in spite of her heart;
Her love I earn'd out of Piracquo's murder.

TOM. Ha, my brother's murderer?

DE F.   Yes, and her honour's prize
Was my reward. I thank life for nothing
But that pleasure; it was so sweet to me
That I have drunk it up all, left none behind
For any man to pledge me.

VER.   Horrid villain!
Keep life in him for further tortures.

DE F.   No!
I can prevent you; here's my penknife still;
It is but one thread more,—and now 'tis cut.

                                    [Stabs himself.]

Make haste, Joanna, by that token to thee;
Canst not forget, so lately put in mind,
I would not go to leave thee far behind.   Dies.

---

[1] The fallen Eve.   [2] Impurities removed by bloodletting.
[3] Perception.   [4] i.e. De Flores.
[5] An allusion to being the triumphant partners in the game of barley-break
(III. 3. 162, and note).

BEA. Forgive me, Alsemero, all forgive;
    'Tis time to die when 'tis a shame to live.   *Dies.*
VER. Oh, my name is ent'red now in that record,[1]
    Where till this fatal hour 'twas never read.   180
ALS. Let it be blotted out; let your heart lose it,
    And it can never look you in the face,
    Nor tell a tale behind the back of life
    To your dishonour; justice hath so right
    The guilty hit that innocence is quit
    By proclamation, and may joy again.
    Sir, you are sensible of what truth hath done;
    'Tis the best comfort that your grief can find.
TOM. Sir, I am satisfied; my injuries
    Lie dead before me; I can exact no more   190
    Unless my soul were loose, and could o'ertake
    Those black fugitives that are fled from thence,
    To take a second vengeance; but there are wraths
    Deeper than mine, 'tis to be fear'd, about 'em.
ALS. What an opacous body had that moon
    That last chang'd on us! Here's beauty chang'd
    To ugly whoredom; here, servant obedience
    To a master-sin, imperious murder;
    I, a suppos'd husband, chang'd embraces
    With wantonness, but that was paid before;[2]   200
    Your[3] change is come too, from an ignorant wrath
    To knowing friendship. Are there any more on's?
ANT. Yes, sir, I was changed too, from a little ass as I was to a
    great fool as I am, and had like to ha' been changed[4] to the
    gallows, but that you know my innocence[5] always excuses me.
FRAN. I was chang'd from a little wit to be stark mad,
    Almost for the same purpose.
ISA. [*To* ALIBIUS.]   Your change is still
    Behind,[6] but deserve best your transformation:
    You are a jealous coxcomb, keep schools of folly,
    And teach your scholars how to break your own head.[7]   210
ALIB. I see all apparent, wife, and will change now
    Into a better husband, and never keep
    Scholars that shall be wiser than myself.

---

[1] The heavenly book of misdeeds.
[2] Paid for earlier by Diaphanta's death.
[3] Tomazo's.   [4] A pun on chained.   [5] A pun on idiocy.
[6] To come.   [7] Make you a cuckold.

ALS. [*To* VERMANDERO.] Sir, you have yet a son's duty living,
    Please you accept it; let that your sorrow,
    As it goes from your eye, go from your heart;
    Man and his sorrow at the grave must part.

Epilogue

ALS. All we can do to comfort one another,
    To stay a brother's sorrow for a brother,
    To dry a child from the kind father's eyes,
    Is to no purpose, it rather multiplies;
    Your only smiles have power to cause relive
    The dead again, or in their rooms to give
    Brother a new brother, father a child;
    If these appear, all griefs are reconcil'd.   *Exeunt omnes.*

FINIS

PHILIP MASSINGER
(1583–1640)

Born Salisbury; studied at Oxford. In London from 1606, and wrote for the King's Men during most of his career. Collaborated widely and wrote some fifteen plays independently, mostly comedies and tragicomedies (*The Great Duke of Florence*, *The Maid of Honour*, etc.), and a few tragedies (*The Duke of Milan*).

A New Way to Pay Old Debts (1625)

This romantic yet unromantic comedy has many remarkably modern characteristics, dealing as it does with the dual themes of the power of money and social climbing. Massinger's strictures on the misuse of economic and political power in the microcosm of rural Nottinghamshire had their relevance to a broader framework in seventeenth-century England and anticipate features of social and economic life in the twentieth century. Further, those aspects of the play concerning marriages that cut across established social plateaus have their modern pertinence.

Massinger was no social rebel, and he allowed his characters to marry only within their appropriate classes; he showed an obviously critical attitude towards the proposed marriage between Lord Lovell, the distinguished soldier-nobleman, and Margaret Overreach, the attractive daughter of the parvenu. This loveless match promoted by Margaret's father is by no means comparable to the romance between the young nobleman Rowland Lacy and Rose Otley, the daughter of a prosperous merchant, in *The Shoemakers' Holiday*. Dekker clearly approved of this union. (There are, as well, obvious contrasts between the rise of Eyre and that of Overreach.)

In spite of certain modern traits in *A New Way to Pay Old Debts*, many aspects of the play are rather old-fashioned; Massinger tended to fill it with type figures deriving from the Morality tradition, and he wrote in facile yet flat blank verse. There is not a line of prose in the play; the underlings speak verse as fluent as that of their betters. The involved periodic structure of several of the longer speeches causes the reader to lose his grip on the syntax. The author handled least effectively the sentimental passages of the play and failed to exploit fully many potentialities for humour.

Only one character stands out; the dynamic role of Sir Giles Overreach has been the principal motivation for a series of revivals of the play, several of them in modern times. Although Sir Giles represented a type, he comes alive still as a rapacious moneylender, a rural empire-builder (a kind of miniature

Tamburlaine), and an exponent of the familiar ambition of pushing his family upward on the social ladder.

The contemporary careers of Sir Giles Mompesson and his hangers-on provided Massinger with his original inspiration; the facts of Mompesson's misuse of a monopoly in gold and silver thread manufacturing and the licensing of inns and taverns were much modified, but the plot had a considerable indebtedness to Middleton's *A Trick to Catch the Old One* (1608). This satiric comedy is more ironic in tone than *A New Way* and lacks Massinger's moral seriousness, but Massinger created a smooth-flowing plot with enough lively action to cover the flat spots.

An interesting, though suspect, plot device is that of the crucial secret (whispered to Lady Allworth by Wellborn) which remains hidden from the audience until its gradual revelation much later in the play. Here the author missed an opportunity for dramatic irony. Less persuasive is the 'detective-story' incident involving disappearing ink, etc.; Marrall's motives remain ambiguous, for at the time the deed was originally performed the schemer could have had little assurance that its beneficiary, Wellborn, would later be in a position to reward him.

The first, and only early, edition of the play (1633) is the basis of this edition.

A New Way to Pay Old Debts
by Philip Massinger
[1625]

To the Right Honourable Robert, Earl of Carnarvon,
Master Falconer of England:

My good Lord, pardon, I beseech you, my boldness, in presuming to shelter this comedy under the wings of your lordship's favour and protection. I am not ignorant, having never yet deserved [1] you in my service, that it cannot but meet with a severe construction, if in the clemency of your noble disposition, you fashion not a better defence for me than I can fancy for myself. All I can allege is that divers Italian princes and lords of eminent rank in England have not disdained to receive and read poems of this nature, nor am I wholly lost in my hopes but that your honour, who have ever expressed yourself a favourer and friend to the Muses, may vouchsafe, in your gracious acceptance of this trifle, to give me encouragement to present you with some laboured work, and of a higher strain hereafter. I was born a devoted servant to the thrice-noble family of your incomparable lady,[2] and am most ambitious, but with a becoming distance, to be known to your lordship, which, if you please to admit, I shall embrace it as a bounty, that while I live shall oblige me to acknowledge you for my noble patron, and profess myself to be

Your honour's true servant,

PHILIP MASSINGER.

[1] Benefited.

[2] Massinger's father was the principal business agent of William Herbert, the third Earl of Pembroke; the daughter of his younger brother married Robert Dormer, Earl of Carnarvon, in 1625.

To the Ingenious Author, Master Philip Massinger
on his Comedy called
A New Way to Pay Old Debts:

'Tis a rare charity, and thou couldst not
So proper to the time have found a plot;
Yet whilst you teach to pay, you lend the age
We wretches live in, that to come, the stage,
The thronged audience that was thither brought,
Invited by your fame, and to be taught
This lesson. All are grown indebted more,
And when they look for freedom ran in score.
It was a cruel courtesy to call
In hope of liberty, and then enthrall.
The nobles are your bondmen gentry, and
All besides those that did not understand;
They were no men of credit, bankrupts born,
Fit to be trusted with no stock but scorn.
You have more wisely credited to such
That, though they cannot pay, can value much.
I am your debtor too, but to my shame
Repay you nothing back but your own fame.

HENRY MOODY, miles.[1]

To his friend the author:

You may remember how you chid me when
I rank'd you equal with those glorious men,
Beaumont and Fletcher; if you love not praise
You must forbear the publishing of plays:
The crafty mazes of the cunning plot,
The polish'd phrase, the sweet expressions; got
Neither by theft nor violence, the conceit
Fresh and unsullied. All is of weight,[2]
Able to make the captive reader know
I did but justice when I plac'd you so.
A shamefast blushing would become the brow
Of some weak virgin writer; we allow
To you a kind of pride, and there, where most
Should blush at commendations, you should boast.
If any think I flatter, let him look
Off from my idle trifles on thy book.

THOMAS JAY, miles.

[1] Knight.   [2] Importance.

Dramatis Personae

LOVELL, an English lord
SIR GILES OVERREACH, a cruel extortioner, [uncle to Wellborn]
[FRANK] WELLBORN, a prodigal
[TOM] ALLWORTH, a young gentleman, page to Lord Lovell, [stepson to the Lady Allworth]
GREEDY, a hungry justice of the peace
MARRALL, a term-driver,[1] a creature of Sir Giles Overreach
ORDER, [a steward] ⎫
AMBLE, [an usher]   ⎪
FURNACE, [a cook]   ⎬ servants to the Lady Allworth
WATCHALL, [a porter] ⎭
WILLDO, a parson
TAPWELL, an alehouse keeper
THREE CREDITORS, [SERVANTS, ETC.]
THE LADY ALLWORTH, a rich widow
MARGARET, daughter to Overreach
WAITING-WOMAN
CHAMBERMAID
FROTH, Tapwell's wife
[SCENE: Rural Nottinghamshire.]

[1] A hanger-on at the law courts.

ACT I. SCENE 1

[*Before* TAPWELL'S *alehouse*]

Enter WELLBORN, TAPWELL, *and* FROTH

WELL. No bouse?[1] Nor no tobacco?

TAP.   Not a suck, sir;
  Nor the remainder of a single can
  Left by a drunken porter, all night-pall'd[2] too.

FROTH. Not the dropping of the tap for your morning's
     draught, sir;
  'Tis verity, I assure you.

WELL.   Verity, you brach![3]
  The devil turn'd precisian?[4] Rogue, what am I?

TAP. Troth, durst I trust you with a looking-glass,
  To let you see your trim shape, you would quit[5] me,
  And take the name yourself.

WELL.   How, dog?

TAP.   Even so, sir;   10
  And I must tell you, if you but advance
  Your Plymouth cloak,[6] you shall be soon instructed
  There dwells, and within call, if it please your worship,
  A potent monarch call'd the constable,
  That does command a citadel call'd the stocks;
  Whose guards are certain files of rusty billmen,[7]
  Such as with great dexterity will hale
  Your tatter'd, lousy—

WELL.   Rascal! Slave!

FROTH.   No rage, sir.

TAP. At his own peril. Do not put yourself
  In too much heat, there being no water near   20
  To quench your thirst; and sure, for other liquor,
  As mighty ale, or beer, they are things, I take it,
  You must no more remember; not in a dream, sir.

---

[1] Drink.   [2] Flat.   [3] Bitch.
[4] Puritan.   [5] Absolve.
[6] A cudgel; so called from the ruse of destitute seamen who carried a stick
or cudgel to give the impression that they were travellers.
[7] Churlish watchmen armed with halberds.

WELL. Why, thou unthankful villain, dar'st thou talk thus?
  Is not thy house and all thou hast my gift?
TAP. I find it not in chalk;[1] and Timothy Tapwell
  Does keep no other register.
WELL.   Am not I he
  Whose riots fed and cloth'd thee? Wert thou not
  Born on my father's land, and proud to be
  A drudge in his house?
TAP.   What I was, sir, it skills [2] not;
  What you are, is apparent. Now for a farewell;
  Since you talk of father, in my hope it will torment you,
  I'll briefly tell your story. Your dead father,
  My quondam master, was a man of worship,
  Old Sir John Wellborn, justice of the peace and quorum,[3]
  And stood fair to be *custos rotulorum*; [4]
  Bare the whole sway of the shire, kept great house,
  Reliev'd the poor, and so forth; but he dying,
  And the twelve hundred a year coming to you,
  Late Master Francis, but now forlorn Wellborn—
WELL. Slave, stop, or I shall lose myself!
FROTH.   Very hardly;
  You cannot out of your way.[5]
TAP.   But to my story—
  You were then a lord of acres, the prime gallant,
  And I your under-butler. Note the change now:
  You had a merry time of 't—hawks and hounds,
  With choice of running horses, mistresses
  Of all sorts and all sizes; yet so hot
  As their embraces made your lordships [6] melt;
  Which your uncle, Sir Giles Overreach, observing
  (Resolving not to lose a drop of 'em),
  On foolish mortgages, statutes,[7] and bonds,
  For a while suppli'd your looseness, and then left you.
WELL. Some curate hath penn'd this invective, mongrel,
  And you have studied it.
TAP.   I have not done yet.
  Your land gone, and your credit not worth a token,[8]

---

[1] On the tavern reckoning-board.   [2] Matters.
[3] An important justice whose presence was necessary to constitute a bench.
[4] The justice responsible for the keeping of county records.
[5] 'You are already lost.'   [6] Estates.
[7] Recognizances involving the penalty of forfeiture of land.
[8] A tradesman's counter, used as small change.

You grew the common borrower; no man scap'd
Your paper-pellets,[1] from the gentleman
To the beggars on highways, that sold you switches
In your gallantry.

WELL.   I shall switch your brains out.

TAP. Where [2] poor Tim Tapwell, with a little stock,   60
Some forty pounds or so, bought a small cottage,
Humbled myself to marriage with my Froth here,
Gave entertainment—

WELL.   Yes, to whores and canters,[3]
Clubbers by night.

TAP.   True, but they brought in profit,
And had a gift to pay for what they call'd for,
And stuck not [4] like your mastership. The poor income
I glean'd from them hath made me in my parish
Thought worthy to be scavenger,[5] and in time
May rise to be overseer of the poor; [6]
Which if I do, on your petition, Wellborn,   70
I may allow you thirteen pence a quarter,
And you shall thank my worship.

WELL.   Thus, you dogbolt,[7]
And thus!—   *Beats and kicks him.*

TAP. [*To* FROTH.] Cry out for help!

WELL.   Stir, and thou diest.
Your potent prince, the constable, shall not save you.
Hear me, ungrateful hell-hound: did not I
Make purses [8] for you? Then you lick'd my boots,
And thought your holiday cloak too coarse to clean 'em.
'Twas I that, when I heard thee swear, if ever
Thou couldst arrive at forty pounds, thou wouldst
Live like an emperor,—'twas I that gave it   80
In ready gold. Deny this, wretch.

TAP.   I must, sir;
For, from the tavern to the taphouse, all,
On forfeiture of their licences, stand bound
Never to remember who their best guests were,
If they grew poor like you.

---

[1] i.e. I O U s.   [2] Whereas.   [3] Users of cant; thieves, etc.
[4] Were not grudging.   [5] Road or street cleaner.
[6] An unpaid position, but it probably had greater prestige than that of scavenger.
[7] Wretch.   [8] Accumulate money.

WELL.   They are well rewarded
That beggar themselves to make such cuckolds rich.
Thou viper, thankless viper! Impudent bawd!
But since you are grown forgetful, I will help
Your memory, and tread thee into mortar,
Not leave one bone unbroken.   [*Beats him again.*]
TAP.   Oh!
FROTH.   Ask mercy.

Enter ALLWORTH

WELL. 'Twill not be granted.
ALL.   Hold, for my sake, hold!
Deny me, Frank? They are not worth your anger.
WELL. For once thou hast redeem'd them from this sceptre;
[*Holds up his cudgel.*]
But let 'em vanish, creeping on their knees,
And if they grumble, I revoke my pardon.
FROTH. This comes of your prating, husband; you presum'd
On your ambling wit, and must use your glib tongue,
Though you are beaten lame for't.
TAP.   Patience, Froth;
There's law to cure our bruises.
                    They go off on their hands and knees.
WELL.   Sent to your mother?
ALL. My lady, Frank, my patroness, my all!
She's such a mourner for my father's death,
And in her love to him so favours me
That I cannot pay too much observance to her.
There are few such stepdames.
WELL.   'Tis a noble widow,
And keeps her reputation pure and clear
From the least taint of infamy; her life,
With splendour of her actions, leaves no tongue
To envy or detraction. Prithee, tell me,
Has she no suitors?
ALL.   Even the best of the shire, Frank,
My lord [1] excepted; such as sue and send,
And send and sue again, but to no purpose.
Their frequent visits have not gain'd her presence;
Yet she's so far from sullenness and pride

                    [1] Lovell.

That I dare undertake you shall meet from her
A liberal entertainment. I can give you
A catalogue of her suitors' names.
WELL.   Forbear it,
  While I give you good counsel. I am bound to it;
  Thy father was my friend, and that affection
  I bore to him, in right descends to thee;
  Thou art a handsome and a hopeful youth,   120
  Nor will I have the least affront stick on thee,
  If I with any danger can prevent it.
ALL. I thank your noble care; but, pray you, in what
  Do I run the hazard?
WELL.   Art thou not in love?
  Put it not off with wonder.[1]
ALL.   In love, at my years?
WELL. You think you walk in clouds, but are transparent.
  I have heard all, and the choice that you have made,
  And with my finger can point out the north star
  By which the loadstone of your folly's guided;
  And to confirm this true, what think you of   130
  Fair Margaret, the only child and heir
  Of Cormorant Overreach? Does it blush and start
  To hear her only nam'd? Blush at your want
  Of wit and reason.
ALL.   You are too bitter, sir.
WELL. Wounds of this nature are not to be cur'd
  With balms, but corrosives. I must be plain;
  Art thou scarce manumis'd [2] from the porter's lodge,[3]
  And yet sworn servant to the pantofle,[4]
  And dar'st thou dream of marriage? I fear
  'Twill be concluded for impossible   140
  That there is now, nor e'er shall be hereafter,
  A handsome page or player's boy of fourteen
  But either loves a wench, or drabs love him,
  Court-waiters [5] not exempted.
ALL.   This is madness.
  Howe'er you have discover'd my intents,
  You know my aims are lawful, and if ever
  The queen of flowers, the glory of the spring,

---

[1] Surprise.   [2] Freed.   [3] Where underlings were punished.
[4] Slippers; i.e. 'You are still in service, fetching your master's slippers, etc.'
[5] Pages at court.

The sweetest comfort to our smell, the rose,
Sprang from an envious briar, I may infer
There's such disparity in their conditions,
Between the goodness of my soul, the daughter,
And the base churl, her father.

WELL.   Grant this true,
As I believe it, canst thou ever hope
To enjoy a quiet bed with her whose father
Ruin'd thy state?

ALL.   And yours too.

WELL.   I confess it;
True. I must tell you as a friend, and freely,
That where impossibilities are apparent,
'Tis indiscretion to nourish hopes.
Canst thou imagine—let not self-love blind thee—
That Sir Giles Overreach, that, to make her great
In swelling titles, without touch of conscience
Will cut his neighbour's throat, and I hope his own too,
Will e'er consent to make her thine? Give o'er,
And think of some course suitable to thy rank,
And prosper in it.

ALL.   You have well advis'd me.
But, in the meantime, you that are so studious
Of my affairs wholly neglect your own.
Remember yourself, and in what plight you are.

WELL. No matter, no matter.

ALL.   Yes, 'tis much material.
You know my fortune and my means; yet something
I can spare from myself to help your wants.

WELL.   How's this?

ALL. Nay, be not angry. There's eight pieces [1]
To put you in better fashion.

WELL.   Money from thee?
From a boy, a stipendiary? [2] One that lives
At the devotion of a stepmother
And the uncertain favour of a lord?
I'll eat my arms first! Howsoe'er blind Fortune
Hath spent the utmost of her malice on me,
Though I am vomited out of an alehouse,
And thus accoutred; know not where to eat,

---

[1] Gold coins, probably unites, worth twenty-two shillings each.
[2] Dependant.

Or drink, or sleep, but underneath this canopy [1]—
Although I thank thee, I despise thy offer;
And as I in my madness broke my state [2]
Without th'assistance of another's brain,
In my right wits I'll piece it; at the worst,
Die thus and be forgotten!

ALL.   A strange humour!   *Exeunt.*

ACT I. SCENE 2

[*The hall in* LADY ALLWORTH's *house*]

Enter ORDER, AMBLE, FURNACE, *and* WATCHALL

ORDER. Set all things right, or, as my name is Order,
  And by this staff of office that commands you,
  This chain and double ruff, symbols of power,
  Whoever misses in his function, [3]
  For one whole week he makes forfeiture of his breakfast
  And privilege in the wine-cellar.
AMBLE.   You are merry,
  Good master steward.
FURN.   Let him; I'll be angry.
AMBLE. Why, fellow Furnace, 'tis not twelve o'clock yet,
  Nor dinner taking up; then 'tis allow'd
  Cooks, by their places, may be choleric.   10
FURN. You think you have spoke wisely, goodman Amble,
  My lady's go-before.
ORDER.   Nay, nay, no wrangling.
FURN. Twit me with the authority of the kitchen?
  At all hours and all places I'll be angry;
  And, thus provok'd, when I am at my prayers
  I will be angry!
AMBLE.   There was no hurt meant.
FURN. I am friends with thee, and yet I will be angry.
ORDER. With whom?
FURN.   No matter whom; yet now I think on't,
  I am angry with my lady.
WATCH.   Heaven forbid, man!

---

[1] The sky.   [2] Bankrupted my estate.   [3] Duty.

ORDER. What cause has she given thee?

FURN.   Cause enough, master steward;
  I was entertain'd [1] by her to please her palate,
  And, till she forswore eating, I perform'd it.
  Now, since our master, noble Allworth, died,
  Though I crack my brains to find out tempting sauces,
  And raise fortifications in the pastry
  Such as might serve for models in the Low Countries,
  Which, if they had been practised at Breda,[2]
  Spinola might have thrown his cap at it,[3] and ne'er took it.

AMBLE. But you had wanted matter [4] there to work on.

FURN. Matter? With six eggs and a strike [5] of rye meal,
  I had kept the town till doomsday, perhaps longer.

ORDER. But what's this to your pet against my lady?

FURN. What's this? Marry, this: when I am three parts roasted,
  And the fourth part parboil'd to prepare her viands.
  She keeps her chamber, dines with a panada [6]
  Or water-gruel, my sweat never thought on.

ORDER. But your art is seen in the dining-room.

FURN.   By whom?
  By such as pretend love to her, but come
  To feed upon her. Yet of all the harpies
  That do devour her, I am out of charity
  With none so much as the thin-gutted squire
  That's stol'n into commission.[7]

ORDER.   Justice Greedy?

FURN. The same, the same. Meat's cast away upon him,
  It never thrives. He holds this paradox:
  Who eats not well, can ne'er do justice well;
  His stomach's as insatiable as the grave,
  Or strumpets' ravenous appetites.   ALLWORTH knocks.

WATCH.   One knocks.

ORDER. Our late young master.   [ALLWORTH enters.]

AMBLE.   Welcome, sir.

FURN.   Your hand;
  If you have a stomach, a cold bake-meat's ready.

ORDER. His father's picture in little.

FURN.   We are all your servants.

---

[1] Employed.
[2] A Dutch city, captured by the Spanish under Spinola in 1625.
[3] Given up.   [4] Provisions.   [5] A bushel.
[6] A bread pudding.   [7] Office.

AMBLE. In you he lives.

ALL.   At once, my thanks to all.
This is some comfort. Is my lady stirring?

Enter LADY ALLWORTH, *waiting-woman, and chambermaid*

ORDER. Her presence answer for us.

LADY.   Sort those silks well.
I'll take the air alone.
                              Exeunt waiting-woman and chambermaid.

FURN.   You air and air;
But will you never taste but spoon-meat [1] more?
To what use serve I?

LADY.   Prithee, be not angry;
I shall ere long. I' the meantime, there is gold
To buy thee aprons and a summer suit.

FURN. I am appeas'd, and Furnace now grows cool.

LADY. And as I gave directions, if this morning   60
I am visited by any, entertain 'em
As heretofore; but say, in my excuse,
I am indispos'd.

ORDER.   I shall, madam.

LADY.   Do, and leave me.
Nay, stay you, Allworth.   *Exeunt servants.*

ALL.   I shall gladly grow here,
To wait on your commands.

LADY.   So soon turn'd courtier?

ALL. Style not that courtship, madam, which is duty,
Purchas'd on your part.

LADY.   Well, you shall o'ercome;
I'll not contend in words. How is it with
Your noble master?

ALL.   Ever like himself,
No scruple lessen'd in the full weight of honour.   70
He did command me,—pardon my presumption—
As his unworthy deputy, to kiss
Your ladyship's fair hands.

LADY.   I am honour'd in
His favour to me. Does he hold his purpose
For the Low Countries?

                              [1] A liquid diet.

ALL.   Constantly, good madam;
But he will in person first present his service.

LADY. And how approve you of his course? You are yet
Like virgin parchment, capable of any
Inscription, vicious or honourable.
I will not force your will, but leave you free
To your own election.

ALL.   Any form you please
I will put on; but, might I make my choice,
With humble emulation I would follow
The path my lord marks to me.

LADY.   'Tis well answer'd,
And I commend your spirit. You had a father,
Bless'd be his memory, that some few hours
Before the will of Heaven took him from me,
Who did commend you, by the dearest ties
Of perfect love between us, to my charge;
And, therefore, what I speak you are bound
To hear with such respect as if he liv'd in me.
He was my husband, and howe'er you are not
Son of my womb, you may be of my love,
Provided you deserve it.

ALL.   I have found you,
Most honour'd madam, the best mother to me,
And, with my utmost strengths of care and service,
Will labour you never may repent
Your bounties shower'd upon me.

LADY.   I much hope it.
These were your father's words: 'If e'er my son
Follow the war, tell him it is a school
Where all the principles tending to honour
Are taught, if truly followed; but for such
As repair thither as a place in which
They do presume they may with licence practise
Their lusts and riots, they shall never merit
The noble name of soldiers. To dare boldly
In a fair cause, and for the country's safety
To run upon the cannon's mouth undaunted,
To obey their leaders and shun mutinies,
To bear with patience the winter's cold
And summer's scorching heat, and not to faint,
When plenty of provision fails, with hunger—

Are the essential parts make up a soldier,
Not swearing, dice, or drinking.'
ALL.   There's no syllable
You speak, but is to me an oracle,
Which but to doubt were impious.
LADY.   To conclude:
Beware ill company, for often men
Are like to those with whom they do converse;
And from one man I warn you, and that's Wellborn;
Not 'cause he's poor—that rather claims your pity;   120
But that he's in his manners so debauch'd,
And hath to vicious courses sold himself,
'Tis true, your father lov'd him, while he was
Worth the loving; but if he had liv'd
To have seen him as he is, he had cast him off
As you must do.
ALL.   I shall obey in all things.
LADY. You follow me to my chamber, you shall have gold
To furnish you like my son, and still [1] suppli'd,
As I hear from you.
ALL.   I am still your creature.   *Exeunt.*

ACT I. SCENE 3

[*The hall in* LADY ALLWORTH'S *house*]

Enter OVERREACH, GREEDY, ORDER, AMBLE, FURNACE,
WATCHALL, *and* MARRALL

GREEDY. Not to be seen?
OVER.   Still cloister'd up? Her reason,
I hope, assures her, though she make herself
Close prisoner ever for her husband's loss,
'Twill not recover him.
ORDER.   Sir, it is her will,
Which we that are her servants ought to serve it,
And not dispute. Howe'er, you are nobly welcome,
And if you please to stay, that you may think so,
There came not six days since, from Hull, a pipe [2]

---

[1] Ever more.   [2] Cask.

Of rich Canary, which shall spend itself
For my lady's honour.

GREEDY.   Is it of the right race? [1]

ORDER. Yes, Master Greedy.

AMBLE. [*Aside.*]   How his mouth runs o'er.

FURN. [*Aside.*] I'll make it run and run.—Save your good
    worship.

GREEDY. Honest master cook, thy hand again. How I love thee!
    Are the good dishes still in being? Speak, boy.

FURN. If you have a mind to feed, there is a chine
    Of beef, well season'd.

GREEDY.   Good!

FURN.   A pheasant, larded. [2]

GREEDY. That I might now give thanks for't!

FURN.   Other kickshaws. [3]
    Besides, there came last night from the forest of Sherwood,
    The fattest stag I ever cook'd.

GREEDY.   A stag, man?

FURN. A stag, sir; part of it prepar'd for dinner,
    And bak'd in puff-paste. [4]

GREEDY.   Puff-paste too, Sir Giles!
    A ponderous chine of beef! A pheasant larded!
    And red deer too, Sir Giles, and bak'd in puff-paste!
    All business set aside; let us give thanks here.

FURN. [*Aside.*] How the lean skeleton's rapt!

OVER.   You know we cannot.

MAR. Your worships are to sit on a commission, [5]
    And if you fail to come, you lose the cause.

GREEDY. Cause me no causes. I'll prove it, for such a dinner
    We may put off a commission: you shall find it
    Henrici decimo quarto. [6]

OVER.   Fie, Master Greedy;
    Will you lose me a thousand pounds for a dinner?
    No more, for shame. We must forget the belly
    When we think of profit.

GREEDY.   Well, you shall o'errule me.
    I could ev'n cry now. Do you hear, master cook—
    Send but a corner of that immortal pasty,

---

[1] Vintage.   [2] Greased, or stuffed with bacon.
[3] Delicacies.   [4] Fine pastry.
[5] A trial for bankruptcy (II. 1. 1–8).
[6] In a law of the fourteenth year of Henry's reign.

And I, in thankfulness, will by your boy
Send you a brace of threepences.
FURN.   Will you be so prodigal?

Enter WELLBORN [*unkempt*]

OVER. Remember me to your lady. Who have we here?
WELL. You know me.
OVER.   I did once, but now I will not;   40
Thou art no blood of mine. Avaunt, thou beggar!
If ever thou presume to own me more,
I'll have thee cag'd and whipp'd.
GREEDY.   I'll grant the warrant.
Think of Pie Corner,[1] Furnace.
                Exeunt OVERREACH, GREEDY, *and* MARRALL.
WATCH.   Will you out, sir?
I wonder how you durst creep in.
ORDER.   This is rudeness
And saucy impudence.
AMBLE.   Cannot you stay
To be serv'd among your fellows, from the basket,[2]
But you must press into the hall?
FURN.   Prithee, vanish
Into some outhouse, though it be the pigsty;
My scullion shall come to thee.

Enter ALLWORTH

WELL.   This is rare.   50
Oh, here's Tom Allworth. Tom!
ALL.   We must be strangers;
Nor would I have you seen here for a million.
                                         Exit ALLWORTH.
WELL. Better and better. He contemns me too?

Enter waiting-woman and chambermaid

WOMAN. Foh, what a smell's here! What thing's this?
CHAMB.   A creature

---

[1] An allusion to the pasty (line 36), and to an area of London noted for pastry shops.
[2] A container of scraps for the poor, placed at the gate.

Made out of the privy. Let us hence for love's sake,
Or I shall swoon.
WOMAN.   I begin to faint already.
     Exeunt waiting-woman and chambermaid.
WATCH. Will know your way?
AMBLE.   Or shall we teach it you,
By the head and shoulders?
WELL.   No, I will not stir;
Do you mark, I will not. Let me see the wretch
That dares attempt to force me. Why, you slaves,
Created only to make legs [1] and cringe,
To carry in a dish, and shift a trencher,
That have not souls only to hope a blessing
Beyond black jacks [2] or flagons; you that were born
Only to consume meat, and drink, and batten
Upon reversions; [3] who advances? Who
Shows me the way?

   Enter LADY ALLWORTH, *waiting-woman, and chambermaid*

ORDER.   My lady!
CHAMB.   Here's the monster!
WOMAN. Sweet madam, keep your glove to your nose.
CHAMB.   Or let me
Fetch some perfumes may be predominant;
You wrong yourself else.
WELL.   Madam, my designs
Bear me to you.
LADY.   To me?
WELL.   And though I have met with
But ragged entertainment from your grooms here,
I hope from you to receive that noble usage
As may become the true friend of your husband,
And then I shall forget thee.
LADY.   I am amaz'd
To see and hear this rudeness. Dar'st thou think,
Though sworn, that it can ever find belief,
That I, who to the best men of this country
Deni'd my presence since my husband's death,
Can fall so low as to change words with thee?

    [1] Bow.   [2] Leather jugs for beer.
    [3] Feed upon leftovers.

Thou son of infamy, forbear my house,
And know and keep the distance that's between us;
Or, though it be against my gentle temper,
I shall take order you no more shall be
An eyesore to me.

WELL.   Scorn me not, good lady;
But, as in form you are angelical,
Imitate the heavenly natures, and vouchsafe
At the least awhile to hear me. You will grant
The blood that runs in this arm is as noble
As that which fills your veins; those costly jewels   90
And those rich clothes you wear, your men's observance
And women's flattery are in you no virtues,
Nor these rags, with my poverty, in me vices.
You have a fair fame, and, I know, deserve it—
Yet, lady, I must say—in nothing more
Than in the pious sorrow you have shown
For your late noble husband.

ORDER. [*Aside.*]   How she starts!

FURN. [*Aside.*] And hardly can keep finger from the eye,
To hear him nam'd.

LADY.   Have you aught else to say?

WELL. That husband, madam, was once in his fortune   100
Almost as low as I. Want, debts, and quarrels
Lay heavy on him; let it not be thought
A boast in me, though I say, I reliev'd him.
'Twas I that gave him fashion;[1] mine the sword
That did on all occasions second his;
I brought him on and off with honour, Lady,
And when in all men's judgments he was sunk,
And in his own hopes not to be buoy'd up,
I stepp'd unto him, took him by the hand,
And set him upright.

FURN. [*Aside.*]   Are not we base rogues   110
That could forget this?

WELL.   I confess, you made him
Master of your estate; nor could your friends,
Though he brought no wealth with him, blame you for't;
For he had a shape, and to that shape a mind
Made up of all parts either great or noble,

---

[1] Suitable apparel

So winning a behaviour, not to be
Resisted, madam.
LADY.   'Tis most true, he had.
WELL. For his sake then, in that I was his friend,
Do not contemn me.
LADY.   For what's past, excuse me;
I will redeem it. Order, give the gentleman
A hundred pounds.
WELL.   No, madam, on no terms;
I will not beg or borrow sixpence of you,
But be suppli'd elsewhere, or want thus ever.
Only one suit I make, which you deny not
To strangers; and 'tis this.   *Whispers to her.*
LADY.   Fie! Nothing else?
WELL. Nothing; unless you please to charge your servants
To throw away a little respect upon me.
LADY. What you demand is yours.
WELL.   I thank you, Lady.
Now what can be wrought out of such a suit
Is yet supposition. I have said all;
When you please, you may retire. [*Exit* LADY ALLWORTH.]
                    Nay, all's forgotten,
And for a lucky omen to my project,
Shake hands, and end all quarrels in the cellar.
ORDER. Agreed, agreed.
FURN.   Still merry Master Wellborn. *Exeunt.*

ACT II. SCENE 1

[*A room in* OVERREACH'S *house*]

Enter OVERREACH *and* MARRALL

OVER. He's gone, I warrant thee; this commission crush'd him.[1]
MAR. Your worship have the way on't, and ne'er miss
To squeeze these unthrifts into air; and yet
The chapfall'n [2] justice did his part, returning
For your advantage the certificate,
Against his conscience and his knowledge too,

---

[1] The situation was alluded to in I. 3. 27-8.   [2] Thin-jawed.

With your good favour, to the utter ruin
Of the poor farmer.
OVER.   'Twas for these good ends
I made him a justice. He that bribes his belly
Is certain to command his soul.
MAR.   I wonder,   10
Still with your licence, why, your worship having
The power to put this thin-gut in commission,
You are not in 't yourself.
OVER.   Thou art a fool.
In being out of office, I am out of danger;
Where, if I were a justice, besides the trouble,
I might, or out of wilfulness or error,
Run myself finely into a *praemunire*,[1]
And so become a prey to the informer.
No, I 'll have none of 't; 'tis enough I keep
Greedy at my devotion; so he serve   20
My purposes, let him hang or damn, I care not;
Friendship is but a word.
MAR.   You are all wisdom.
OVER. I would be worldly wise; for the other wisdom,
That does prescribe us a well-govern'd life,
And to do right to others as ourselves,
I value not an atom.
MAR.   What course take you,
With your good patience, to hedge in the manor
Of your neighbour, Master Frugal? As 'tis said
He will not sell, nor borrow, nor exchange,
And his land, lying in the midst of your many lordships,[2]   30
Is a foul blemish.
OVER.   I have thought on 't, Marrall,
And it shall take. I must have all men sellers,
And I the only purchaser.
MAR.   'Tis most fit, sir.
OVER. I 'll therefore buy some cottage near his manor,
Which done, I 'll make my men break ope his fences,
Ride o'er his standing corn, and in the night
Set fire on his barns, or break his cattle's legs.
These trespasses draw on suits, and suits, expenses,
Which I can spare, but will soon beggar him.

---

[1] A penalty involving forfeiture of one's goods.   [2] Estates.

When I have harried him thus two or three year,
Though he sue *in forma pauperis*,[1] in spite
Of all his thrift and care, he'll grow behindhand.
MAR. The best I ever heard! I could adore you.
OVER. Then, with the favour of my man of law,
I will pretend some title. Want will force him
To put it to arbitrament; then, if he sell
For half the value, he shall have ready money,
And I possess his land.
MAR.   'Tis above wonder!
Wellborn was apt[2] to sell, and needed not
These fine arts, sir, to hook him in.
OVER.   Well thought on.
[*Aside.*] This varlet, Marrall, lives too long, to upbraid me
With my close cheat put upon him.[3]—Will nor cold
Nor hunger kill him?
MAR.   I know not what to think on't.
I have us'd all means; and the last night I caus'd
His host, the tapster, to turn him out of doors;
And have been since with all your friends and tenants,
And, on the forfeit of your favour, charg'd 'em,
Though a crust of mouldy bread would keep him from
   starving,
Yet they should not relieve him. This is done, sir.
OVER. That was something, Marrall, but thou must go further,
And suddenly, Marrall.
MAR.   Where and when you please, sir.
OVER. I would have thee seek him out, and, if thou canst,
Persuade him that 'tis better steal than beg;
Then, if I prove he has but robb'd a henroost,
Not all the world shall save him from the gallows.
Do anything to work him to despair,
And 'tis thy masterpiece.
MAR.   I will do my best, sir.
OVER. I am now on my main work with the Lord Lovell,
The gallant-minded, popular Lord Lovell,
The minion of the people's love. I hear
He's come into the country, and my aims are
To insinuate myself into his knowledge,
And then invite him to my house.

---

[1] As a pauper (in order to escape court fees).
[2] Willing.   [3] Wellborn.

MAR.   I have you;
  This points at my young mistress.
OVER.   She must part with
  That humble title, and write 'honourable',
  'Right honourable', Marrall, my right honourable daughter,
  If all I have, or e'er can get, will do it.
  I will have her well attended; there are ladies
  Of arrant [1] knights decay'd and brought so low,   80
  That for cast [2] clothes and meat will gladly serve her.
  And 'tis my glory, though I come from the city,
  To have their issue whom I have undone,
  To kneel to mine as bondslaves.
MAR.   'Tis fit state, sir.
OVER. And therefore I'll not have a chambermaid
  That ties her shoes, or any meaner office,
  But such whose fathers were right worshipful.
  'Tis a rich man's pride, there having ever been
  More than a feud, a strange antipathy,
  Between us and true gentry.

Enter WELLBORN

MAR.   See who's here, sir.   90
OVER. Hence, monster! Prodigy!
WELL.   Sir, your wife's nephew;
  She and my father tumbled in one belly.
OVER. Avoid my sight; thy breath's infectious, rogue!
  I shun thee as a leprosy, or the plague.
  Come hither, Marrall; [*Aside.*] This is the time to work him.
MAR. [*Aside.*] I warrant you, sir.   *Exit* OVERREACH.
WELL.   By this light, I think he's mad.
MAR. Mad? Had you took compassion on yourself,
  You long since had been mad.
WELL.   You have took a course,
  Between you and my venerable uncle,
  To make me so.
MAR.   The more pale-spirited you,   100
  That would not be instructed. I swear deeply—
WELL. By what?
MAR.   By my religion.

----

[1] Notorious.   [2] Discarded.

WELL.   Thy religion!
  The devil's creed! But what would you have done?
MAR. Had there been but one tree in all the shire,
  Nor any hope to compass a penny halter,
  Before, like you, I had outliv'd my fortunes,
  A withe [1] had serv'd my turn to hang myself.
  I am zealous for your cause; pray you, hang yourself,
  And presently, as you love your credit.
WELL.   I thank you.
MAR. Will you stay till you die in a ditch, or lice devour you?
  Or if you dare not do the feat yourself,
  But that you'll put the state to charge and trouble,
  Is there no purse to be cut, house to be broken,
  Or market-woman with eggs that you may murder,
  And so dispatch the business?
WELL.   Here's variety,
  I must confess; but I'll accept of none
  Of all your gentle offers, I assure you.
MAR. Why, have you hope ever to eat again,
  Or drink, or be the master of three farthings?
  If you like not hanging, drown yourself; take some course
  For your reputation.
WELL.   'Twill not do, dear tempter,
  With all the rhetoric the fiend hath taught you.
  I am as far as thou art from despair;
  Nay, I have confidence, which is more than hope,
  To live, and suddenly, better than ever.
MAR. Ha, ha! These castles you build in the air
  Will not persuade me or to give or lend
  A token to you.
WELL.   I'll be more kind to thee;
  Come, thou shalt dine with me.
MAR.   With you?
WELL.   Nay, more: dine gratis.
MAR. Under what hedge, I pray you? Or at whose cost?
  Are they padders [2] or Abram-men [3] that are your consorts?
WELL. Thou art incredulous; but thou shalt dine,
  Not alone at her house, but with a gallant lady;
  With me, and with a lady.
MAR.   Lady? What lady?

----

[1] A pliant branch, as of willow.   [2] Footpads.
[3] Fraudulent vagabonds.

With the Lady of the Lake, or Queen of Fairies?
For I know it must be an enchanted dinner.
WELL. With the Lady Allworth, knave.
MAR.   Nay, now there's hope
Thy brain is crack'd.
WELL.   Mark there, with what respect
I am entertain'd.
MAR.   With choice, no doubt, of dog-whips.
Why, dost thou ever hope to pass her porter?   140
WELL. 'Tis not far off; go with me; trust thine own eyes.
MAR. Troth, in my hope, or my assurance rather,
To see thee curvet,[1] and mount like a dog in a blanket,[2]
If ever thou presume to pass her threshold,
I will endure thy company.
WELL.   Come along then.   *Exeunt.*

ACT II. SCENE 2

[LADY ALLWORTH'S *house*]

Enter ALLWORTH, *waiting-woman, chambermaid,* ORDER,
AMBLE, FURNACE, *and* WATCHALL

WOMAN. Could you not command your leisure one hour
   longer?
CHAMB. Or half an hour?
ALL.   I have told you what my haste is;
Besides, being now another's, not my own,
Howe'er I much desire to enjoy you longer,
My duty suffers, if to please myself,
I should neglect my lord.
WOMAN.   Pray you, do me the favour
To put these few quince-cakes into your pocket;
They are of mine own preserving.
CHAMB.   And this marmalade;
'Tis comfortable for your stomach.
WOMAN.   And at parting,   10
Excuse me if I beg a farewell from you.

---

[1] Leap.   [2] As tossed by children.

CHAMB. You are still before me. I move the same suit, sir.
                    ALLWORTH *kisses them severally.*

FURN. [*Aside.*] How greedy these chamberers are of a beardless
    chin!
    I think the tits [1] will ravish him.
ALL.   My service
    To both.
WOMAN.   Ours waits on you.
CHAMB.   And shall do ever.
ORDER. You are my lady's charge; be therefore careful
    That you sustain your parts.
WOMAN.   We can bear, I warrant you.
                    Exeunt waiting-woman and chambermaid.
FURN. Here, drink it off; the ingredients are cordial,[2]
    And this the true elixir; [3] it hath boil'd
    Since midnight for you. 'Tis the quintessence
    Of five cocks of the game, ten dozen of sparrows,
    Knuckles of veal, potato roots and marrow,
    Coral and ambergris.[4] Were you two years elder,
    And had a wife or gamesome mistress,
    I durst trust you with neither. You need not bait [5]
    After this, I warrant you; though your journey's long,
    You may ride on the strength of this till tomorrow morning.
ALL. Your courtesies overwhelm me; I much grieve
    To part from such true friends; and yet find comfort;
    My attendance on my honourable lord,
    Whose resolution holds to visit my lady,
    Will speedily bring me back.

Knocking at the gate; MARRALL *and* WELLBORN *within.*

MAR.   Dar'st thou venture further?
WELL. Yes, yes, and knock again.
ORDER.   'Tis he; disperse.
AMBLE. Perform it bravely.
FURN.   I know my cue, ne'er doubt me.
                    The servants go off several ways.

---

    [1] Minxes.   [2] Restorative.
    [3] A miraculous protractor of life.
    [4] All of these ingredients were then used for aphrodisiac or medicinal
purposes.
    [5] Take nourishment.

WATCH. [*Re-entering with* MARRALL *and* WELLBORN.] Beast
    that I was to make you stay! [1] Most welcome;
  You were long since expected.
WELL.   Say so much
  To my friend, I pray you.
WATCH.   For your sake, I will, sir.
MAR. For his sake!
WELL.   Mum; this is nothing.
MAR.   More than ever   40
  I would have believ'd, though I had found it in my primer.[2]
ALL. When I have giv'n you reasons for my late harshness
  You'll pardon and excuse me; for, believe me,
  Though now I part abruptly, in my service
  I will deserve it.
MAR. [*Aside.*]   Service! With a vengeance!
WELL. I am satisfied; farewell, Tom.
ALL.   All joy stay with you.
                               Exit ALLWORTH.

Enter AMBLE

AMBLE. You are happily encount'red; I yet never
  Presented one so welcome as I know
  You will be to my lady.
MAR.   This is some vision,
  Or sure these men are mad, to worship a dunghill;   50
  It cannot be a truth.
WELL.   Be still a pagan,
  An unbelieving infidel; be so, miscreant,
  And meditate on blankets, and on dog whips.

Enter FURNACE

FURN. I am glad you are come; until I know your pleasure
  I know not how to serve up my lady's dinner.
MAR. [*Aside.*] His pleasure! Is it possible?
WELL.   What's thy will?
FURN. Marry, sir, I have some grouse and turkey chicken,[3]
  Some rails and quails; and my lady will'd me to ask you

---

[1] Wait.   [2] A prayer-book for children.
[3] Young turkey.

What kind of sauces best affect your palate,
That I may use my utmost skill to please it.

MAR. [*Aside.*] The devil's ent'red this cook. Sauce for his palate,
That, on my knowledge, for almost this twelve-month,
Durst wish but cheese-parings and brown bread on Sundays!
                    [WELLBORN *talks apart with* FURNACE.]

WELL. That way I like 'em best.

FURN.   It shall be done, sir.
                              Exit FURNACE.

WELL. What think you of the hedge we shall dine under?
Shall we feed gratis?

MAR.   I know not what to think;
Pray you, make me not mad.

Enter ORDER

ORDER.   This place becomes you not;
Pray you, walk, sir, to the dining-room.

WELL.   I am well here,
Till her ladyship quits her chamber.

MAR.   Well here, say you?
'Tis a rare change! But yesterday you thought
Yourself well in a barn, wrapp'd up in pease-straw.

Enter waiting-woman and chambermaid

WOMAN. Oh, sir, you are wish'd for.

CHAMB.   My lady dreamt, sir, of you.

WOMAN. And the first command she gave after she rose
Was, her devotions done, to give her notice
When you approach'd here.

CHAMB.   Which is done, on my virtue.

MAR. I shall be converted; I begin to grow
Into a new belief, which saints nor angels
Could have won me to have faith in.

Enter LADY ALLWORTH

WOMAN.   Sir, my lady.

LADY. I come to meet you, and languish'd till I saw you.
This first kiss is for form; I allow a second
To such a friend.

MAR. [*Aside.*]   To such a friend! Heav'n bless me!
WELL. I am wholly yours; yet, madam, if you please
  To grace this gentleman with a salute—
MAR. [*Aside.*] Salute me at his bidding!
WELL.   —I shall receive it
  As a most high favour.
LADY.   Sir, you may command me.
WELL. Run backward from a lady? And such a lady?
MAR. To kiss her foot is, to poor me, a favour
  I am unworthy of.   *Offers to kiss her foot.*
LADY.   Nay, pray you, rise;
  And since you are so humble, I'll exalt you;
  You shall dine with me today, at mine own table.   90
MAR. Your ladyship's table? I am not good enough
  To sit at your steward's board.
LADY.   You are too modest;
  I will not be deni'd.

                Enter FURNACE

FURN.   Will you still be babbling,
  Till your meat freeze on the table? The old trick still;
  My art ne'er thought on.
LADY.   Your arm, Master Wellborn.
  [*To* MARRALL.] Nay, keep us company.
MAR.   I was never so grac'd.
    Exeunt WELLBORN, LADY ALLWORTH, MARRALL,
    AMBLE, *waiting-woman, and chambermaid*
ORDER. So; we have play'd our parts, and are come off well;
  But if I know the mystery, why my lady
  Consented to it, or why Master Wellborn
  Desir'd it, may I perish!
FURN.   Would I had   100
  The roasting of his heart that cheated him,
  And forces the poor gentleman to these shifts!
  By fire, for cooks are Persians,[1] and swear by it,
  Of all the griping and extorting tyrants
  I ever heard or read of, I ne'er met
  A match to Sir Giles Overreach.
WATCH.   What will you take
  To tell him so, fellow Furnace?

----

[1] i.e. fire-worshippers.

FURN.   Just as much
  As my throat is worth, for that would be the price on't.
  To have a usurer that starves himself,
  And wears a cloak of one-and-twenty years   10
  On a suit of fourteen groats,[1] bought of the hangman,[2]
  To grow rich, and then purchase,[3] is too common;
  But this Sir Giles feeds high, keeps many servants,
  Who must at his command do any outrage;
  Rich in his habit, vast in his expenses;
  Yet he to admiration [4] still increases
  In wealth and lordships.
ORDER.   He frights men out of their estates,
  And breaks through all law-nets, made to curb ill men,
  As they were cobwebs. No man dares reprove him.
  Such a spirit to dare and power to do were never   12
  Lodg'd so unluckily.

Enter AMBLE

AMBLE.   Ha, ha! I shall burst.
ORDER. Contain thyself, man.
FURN.   Or make us partakers
  Of your sudden mirth.
AMBLE.   Ha, ha! My lady has got
  Such a guest at her table, this term-driver, Marrall,
  This snipe of an attorney!
FURN.   What of him, man?
AMBLE. The knave thinks still he's at the cook's shop in Ram
      Alley,[5]
  Where the clerks divide, and the elder is to choose; [6]
  And feeds so slovenly!
FURN.   Is this all?
AMBLE.   My lady
  Drank to him for fashion sake, or to please Master Wellborn;   13
  As I live, he rises, and takes up a dish,
  In which there were some remnants of a boil'd capon,
  And pledges her in white broth! [7]

---

[1] i.e. almost worthless (a groat was valued at fourpence or less).
[2] The hangman received the clothing of his victims.
[3] Acquire property.   [4] Wonder.
[5] A London street noted for restaurants.
[6] Where the law students divide a purchase, and the senior chooses the
best portion (perhaps with some acrimony).   [7] Gravy.

FURN.   Nay, 'tis like
  The rest of his tribe.
AMBLE.   And when I brought him wine,
  He leaves his stool, and, after a leg [1] or two
  Most humbly thanks my worship.
ORDER.   Rose already!
AMBLE. I shall be chid.

Enter LADY ALLWORTH, WELLBORN, *and* MARRALL

FURN. [*Aside.*]   My lady frowns.
LADY [*To* AMBLE.]   You wait well!
  Let me have no more of this; I observ'd your jeering.
  Sirrah, I'll have you know, whom I think worthy
  To sit at my table, be he ne'er so mean,   140
  When I am present, is not your companion. [2]
ORDER. [*Aside.*] Nay, she'll preserve what's due to her.
FURN. [*Aside.*]   This refreshing
  Follows your flux of laughter.
LADY. [*To* WELLBORN.]   You are master
  Of your own will. I know so much of manners,
  As not to inquire your purposes.—In a word,
  To me you are ever welcome, as to a house
  That is your own.
WELL. [*Aside to* MARRALL.] Mark that.
MAR. [*Aside to* WELLBORN.]   With reverence, sir,
  And it like your worship.
WELL.   Trouble yourself no farther,
  Dear madam; my heart's full of zeal and service,
  However in my language I am sparing.   150
  Come, Master Marrall.
MAR.   I attend your worship.
                      Exeunt WELLBORN *and* MARRALL.
LADY. I see in your looks you are sorry, and you know me
  An easy mistress. Be merry; I have forgot all.
  Order and Furnace, come with me; I must give you
  Further directions.
ORDER.   What you please.
FURN.   We are ready.   *Exeunt.*

---

[1] A bow.   [2] Equal.

ACT II. SCENE 3

[*The road near* OVERREACH'S *house*]

Enter WELLBORN *and* MARRALL

WELL. I think I am in a good way.

MAR.   Good sir, the best way,
The certain best way.

WELL.   There are casualties
That men are subject to.

MAR.   You are above 'em;
And as you are already worshipful,
I hope ere long you will increase in worship,
And be right worshipful.

WELL.   Prithee, do not flout me;
What I shall be, I shall be. Is't for your ease
You keep your hat off?

MAR.   Ease? And it like your worship,
I hope Jack Marrall shall not live so long,
To prove himself such an unmannerly beast,
Though it hail hazel-nuts, as to be cover'd
When your worship's present.

WELL. [*Aside.*]   Is not this a true rogue,
That out of mere hope of a future coz'nage [1]
Can turn thus suddenly? 'Tis rank already.

MAR. I know your worship's wise, and needs no counsel;
Yet if, in my desire to do you service,
I humbly offer my advice, but still
Under correction, I hope I shall not
Incur your high displeasure.

WELL.   No, speak freely.

MAR. Then, in my judgment, sir, my simple judgment,
Still with your worship's favour, I could wish you
A better habit; [2] for this cannot be
But much distasteful to the noble lady
—I say no more—that loves you; for, this morning,
To me, and I am but a swine to her,
Before th' assurance of her wealth perfum'd you,
You savour'd not of amber. [3]

---

[1] Trickery.   [2] Attire.
[3] Ambergris, an ingredient of perfume.

WELL.   I do now then?
MAR. This your batoon [1] hath got a touch of it.
                    Kisses the end of WELLBORN'*s cudgel.*
  Yet, if you please, for change,[2] I have twenty pounds here,
  Which, out of my true love, I presently   30
  Lay down at your worship's feet; 'twill serve to buy you
  A riding-suit.
WELL.   But where's the horse?
MAR.   My gelding
  Is at your service; nay, you shall ride me,
  Before your worship shall be put to the trouble
  To walk afoot. Alas, when you are lord
  Of this lady's manor, as I know you will be,
  You may, with the lease of glebe land [3] call'd Knave's Acre,
  A place I would manure,[4] requite your vassal.
WELL. I thank thy love, but must make no use of it;
  What's twenty pounds?
MAR.   'Tis all that I can make, sir.   40
WELL. Dost thou think, though I want clothes, I could not
      have 'em,
  For one word to my lady?
MAR.   As I know not that!
WELL. Come, I'll tell thee a secret, and so leave thee.
  I'll not give her the advantage, though she be
  A gallant-minded lady, after we are married
  (There being no woman but is sometimes froward),
  To hit me in the teeth, and say she was forc'd
  To buy my wedding-clothes, and took me on
  With a plain riding-suit and an ambling nag.   50
  No, I'll be furnish'd something like myself;
  And so farewell. For thy suit touching Knave's Acre,
  When it is mine, 'tis thine.
MAR.   I thank your worship.
                                Exit WELLBORN.

  How was [I] cozen'd in the calculation
  Of this man's fortune! My master cozen'd too,
  Whose pupil I am in the art of undoing men,
  For that is our profession. Well, well, Master Wellborn,
  You are of a sweet nature, and fit again to be cheated;
  Which, if the Fates please, when you are possess'd

---

[1] Baton, stick.   [2] A change of garments.
[3] Land which was a part of a clergyman's benefice.   [4] Cultivate.

Of the land and lady, you sans question shall be,
I'll presently think of the means.   *Walks by, musing.*

Enter OVERREACH, [*addressing a servant within*]

OVER.   Sirrah, take my horse;
I'll walk to get me an appetite. 'Tis but a mile,
And exercise will keep me from being pursy.—[1]
Ha! Marrall! Is he conjuring? Perhaps
The knave has wrought the prodigal to do
Some outrage on himself, and now he feels
Compunction in his conscience for't; no matter,
So it be done.—Marrall!

MAR.   Sir.

OVER.   How succeed we
In our plot on Wellborn?

MAR.   Never better, sir.

OVER. Has he hang'd or drown'd himself?

MAR.   No, sir, he lives;
Lives once more to be made a prey to you,
A greater prey than ever.

OVER.   Art thou in thy wits?
If thou art, reveal this miracle, and briefly.

MAR. A lady, sir, is fall'n in love with him.

OVER. With him? What lady?

MAR.   The rich Lady Allworth.

OVER. Thou dolt! How dar'st thou speak this?

MAR.   I speak truth;
And I do so but once a year, unless
It be to you, sir. We din'd with her ladyship,
I thank his worship.

OVER.   His worship!

MAR.   As I live, sir;
I din'd with him, at the great lady's table,
Simple [2] as I stand here, and saw when she kiss'd him,
And would, at his request, have kiss'd me too;
But I was not so audacious as some youths are,
And dare do anything, be it ne'er so absurd,
And sad after performance.

OVER.   Why, thou rascal,
To tell me these impossibilities!

---

[1] Short-winded.   [2] Humble.

Dine at her table? And kiss him? Or thee?
Impudent varlet! Have not I myself,
To whom great countesses' doors have oft flew open,
Ten times attempted, since her husband's death,   90
In vain to see her, though I came a suitor?
And yet your good solicitorship and rogue Wellborn
Were brought into her presence, feasted with her?
But that I know thee a dog that cannot blush,
This most incredible lie would call up one
On thy buttermilk cheeks.

MAR.   Shall I not trust my eyes, sir,
Or taste? I feel her good cheer in my belly.

OVER. You shall feel me, if you give not over, sirrah!
Recover your brains again, and be no more gull'd
With a beggar's plot, assisted by the aids   100
Of serving-men and chambermaids; for beyond these
Thou never saw'st a woman, or I'll quit you
From my employments.

MAR.   Will you credit this yet?
On my confidence of their marriage, I offer'd Wellborn—
(*Aside.*) I would give a crown now I durst say 'his worship'—
My nag and twenty pounds.

OVER.   Did you so, idiot?
                                Strikes him down.
Was this the way to work him to despair,
Or rather to cross me?

MAR.   Will your worship kill me?

OVER. No, no; but drive the lying spirit out of you.

MAR. He's [1] gone.

OVER.   I have done then. Now, forgetting   110
Your late imaginary feast and lady,
Know my Lord Lovell dines with me tomorrow;
Be careful naught be wanting to receive him,
And bid my daughter's women trim her up.
Though they paint her, so [2] she catch the lord, I'll thank 'em.
There's a piece for thy late blows.

MAR. (*Aside.*)   I must yet suffer;
But there may be a time.

OVER.   Do you grumble?

MAR.   No, sir.
                                                Exeunt.

---

[1] It's.   [2] If.

ACT III. SCENE 1

[*The road to* OVERREACH'S *house*]

Enter LORD LOVELL, ALLWORTH, *and servants*

LOV. Walk the horses down the hill; something in private
    I must impart to Allworth.   *Exeunt servants.*
ALL.   Oh, my Lord,
    What sacrifice of reverence, duty, watching,
    Although I could put off the use of sleep
    And ever wait on your commands to serve 'em;
    What dangers, though in ne'er so horrid shapes,
    Nay, death itself, though I should run to meet it,
    Can I, and with a thankful willingness, suffer!
    But still the retribution will fall short
    Of your bounties shower'd upon me.
LOV.   Loving youth,
    Till what I purpose be put into act,
    Do not o'er-prize it. Since you have trusted me
    With your soul's nearest, nay, her dearest, secret,
    Rest confident 'tis in a cabinet lock'd
    Treachery shall never open. I have found you—
    For so much to your face I must profess,
    Howe'er you guard [1] your modesty with a blush for't—
    More zealous in your love and service to me
    Than I have been in my rewards.
ALL.   Still great ones,
    Above my merit.
LOV.   Such your gratitude calls 'em;
    Nor am I of that harsh and rugged temper
    As some great men are tax'd with, who imagine
    They part from the respect due to their honours
    If they use not all such as follow 'em,
    Without distinction of their births, like slaves.
    I am not so condition'd; I can make
    A fitting difference between my footboy
    And a gentleman by want compell'd to serve me.

[1] Adorn.

ALL. 'Tis thankfully acknowledg'd; you have been
    More like a father to me than a master.   30
    Pray you, pardon the comparison.
Lov.   I allow it;
    And to give you assurance I am pleas'd in it,
    My carriage and demeanour to your mistress,
    Fair Margaret, shall truly witness for me
    I can command my passions.
ALL.   'Tis a conquest
    Few lords can boast of when they are tempted. Oh!
Lov. Why do you sigh? Can you be doubtful of me?
    By that fair name I in the wars have purchas'd,
    And all my actions hitherto untainted,
    I will not be more true to mine own honour   40
    Than to my Allworth.
ALL.   As you are the brave Lord Lovell,
    Your bare word only given is an assurance
    Of more validity and weight to me
    Than all the oaths bound up with imprecations,
    Which, when they would deceive, most courtiers practise;
    Yet, being a man (for, sure, to style you more
    Would relish of gross flattery), I am forc'd,
    Against my confidence of your worth and virtues,
    To doubt, nay, more, to fear.
Lov.   So young, and jealous?
ALL. Were you to encounter with a single foe,   50
    The victory were certain; but to stand
    The charge of two such potent enemies,
    At once assaulting you, as wealth and beauty,
    And those too seconded by power, is odds
    Too great for Hercules.
Lov.   Speak your doubts and fears,
    Since you will nourish 'em, in plainer language,
    That I may understand 'em.
ALL.   What's your will,
    Though I lend arms against myself (provided
    They may advantage you), must be obeyed.
    My much-lov'd Lord, were Margaret only fair,   60
    The cannon of her more than earthly form,
    Though mounted high, commanding all beneath it,
    And ramm'd with bullets of her sparkling eyes,
    Of all the bulwarks that defend your senses

Could batter none but that which guards your sight.
But when the well-tim'd accents of her tongue
Make music to you, and with numerous [1] sounds
Assault your hearing (such as if Ulysses
Now liv'd again, howe'er he stood the Sirens,
Could not resist), the combat must grow doubtful
Between your reason and rebellious passions.
Add this too: when you feel her touch and breath,
Like a soft western wind when it glides o'er
Arabia, creating gums and spices;
And, in the van, the nectar of her lips,
Which you must taste, bring the battalia [2] on,
Well arm'd, and strongly lin'd [3] with her discourse
And knowing manners, to give entertainment;
Hippolitus himself would leave Diana,[4]
To follow such a Venus.

LOV.   Love hath made you
Poetical, Allworth.

ALL.   Grant all these beat off,
Which, if it be in man to do, you'll do it,
Mammon, in Sir Giles Overreach, steps in
With heaps of ill-got gold and so much land,
To make her more remarkable, as would tire
A falcon's wings in one day to fly over.
Oh, my good Lord, these powerful aids, which would
Make a mis-shapen Negro beautiful
(Yet are but ornaments to give her lustre,
That in herself is all perfection), must
Prevail for her. I here release your trust;
'Tis happiness enough for me to serve you,
And sometimes with chaste eyes to look upon her.

LOV. Why, shall I swear?

ALL.   Oh, by no means, my Lord;
And wrong not so your judgment to the world
As from your fond indulgence to a boy,
Your page, your servant, to refuse a blessing
Divers great men are rivals for.

LOV.   Suspend

---

[1] Harmonious.   [2] Battle array.   [3] Reinforced.
[4] Hippolitus was said to have been revived and adopted as a favourite by
Diana after his death, which had resulted from the intrigue of his stepmother,
Phaedra.

Your judgment till the trial. How far is it
T' Overreach' house?

ALL.   At the most, some half-hour's riding;   100
You'll soon be there.

LOV.   And you the sooner freed
From your jealous cares.

ALL.   O that I durst hope it!   *Exeunt.*

ACT III. SCENE 2

[OVERREACH'S *house*]

Enter OVERREACH, GREEDY, *and* MARRALL

OVER. Spare for no cost; let my dressers crack with the weight
Of curious viands.

GREEDY.   'Store indeed's no sore,' [1] sir.

OVER. That proverb fits your stomach, Master Greedy.
And let no plate be seen but what's pure gold,
Or such whose workmanship exceeds the matter
That it is made of; let my choicest linen
Perfume the room, and, when we wash, the water,
With precious powders mix'd, so please my lord
That he may with envy wish to bathe so ever.

MAR. 'Twill be very chargeable.[2]

OVER.   Avaunt, you drudge!   10
Now all my labour'd ends are at the stake,
Is't a time to think of thrift? Call in my daughter.

                                   [*Exit* MARRALL.]
And, Master Justice, since you love choice dishes,
And plenty of 'em—

GREEDY.   As I do indeed, sir,
Almost as much as to give thanks for 'em.

OVER. I do confer that providence,[3] with my power
Of absolute command to have abundance,
To your best care.

GREEDY.   I'll punctually discharge it,

---

[1] 'No harm done in having adequate supplies.'
[2] Expensive.   [3] Provision.

And give the best directions. Now am I,
In my own conceit, a monarch; at the least
Arch-president of the boil'd, the roast, the bak'd;
For which I will eat often, and give thanks
When my belly's brac'd up like a drum, and that's pure
    justice.   *Exit* GREEDY.

OVER. It must be so. Should the foolish girl prove modest,
She may spoil all. She had it not from me,
But from her mother; I was ever forward,
As she must be, and therefore I'll prepare her.

Enter MARGARET

Alone—and let your women wait without.
MARG. Your pleasure, sir?
OVER.   Ha, this is a neat dressing!
These orient pearls and diamonds well plac'd too!
The gown affects [1] me not; it should have been
Embroider'd o'er and o'er with flowers of gold;
But these rich jewels and quaint fashion help it.
And how below? Since oft the wanton eye,
The face observ'd, descends unto the foot,
Which being well proportion'd as yours is,
Invites as much as perfect white and red,
Though without art. How like you your new woman,
The Lady Downfall'n?
MARG.   Well, for a companion;
Not as a servant.
OVER.   Is she humble, Meg,
And careful too, her ladyship forgotten?
MARG. I pity her fortune.
OVER.   Pity her? Trample on her!
I took her up in an old tamin [2] gown,
Even starv'd for want of twopenny chops, to serve thee;
And if I understand she but repines [3]
To do thee any duty, though ne'er so servile,
I'll pack her to her knight, where I have lodg'd him,
Into the Counter,[4] and there let 'em howl together.
MARG. You know your own ways; but, for me, I blush
When I command her, that was once attended

---

[1] Pleases.   [2] A thin woollen cloth.
[3] Grudges.   [4] A London prison.

With persons not inferior to myself
In birth.

OVER.   In birth? Why, art thou not my daughter,
The bless'd child of my industry and wealth?
Why, foolish girl, was't not to make thee great
That I have ran, and still pursue, those ways
That hale down curses on me, which I mind not?
Part with these humble thoughts, and apt [1] thyself
To the noble state I labour to advance thee,
Or, by my hopes to see thee honourable,   60
I will adopt a stranger to my heir,
And throw thee from my care. Do not provoke me.

MARG. I will not, sir; mould me which way you please.

Enter GREEDY

OVER. How, interrupted?

GREEDY.   'Tis a matter of importance.
The cook, sir, is self-will'd, and will not learn
From my experience; there's a fawn brought in, sir,
And, for my life, I cannot make him roast it
With a Norfolk dumpling in the belly of it;
And, sir, we wise men know, without the dumpling
'Tis not worth threepence.

OVER.   Would it were whole in thy belly,   70
To stuff it out! Cook it any way! Prithee, leave me.

GREEDY. Without order for the dumpling?

OVER.   Let it be dumpl'd
Which way thou wilt, or tell him I will scald him
In his own cauldron.

GREEDY.   I had lost my stomach
Had I lost my mistress' dumpling; I'll give thanks for't.

                          Exit GREEDY.

OVER. But to our business, Meg. You have heard who dines
here?

MARG. I have, sir.

OVER.   'Tis an honourable man;
A lord, Meg, and commands a regiment
Of soldiers, and, what's rare, is one himself,   80
A bold and understanding one; and to be
A lord and a good leader, on one volume,

                        [1] Fit.

Is granted unto few but such as rise up
The kingdom's glory.

Enter GREEDY

GREEDY.   I'll resign my office,
If I be not better obey'd.
OVER.   'Slight, art thou frantic?
GREEDY. Frantic? 'Twould make me a frantic and stark mad,
Were I not a justice of peace and coram [1] too,
Which this rebellious cook cares not a straw for.
There are a dozen of woodcocks—
OVER.   Make thyself
Thirteen,[2] the baker's dozen.
GREEDY.   I am contented,
So they may be dress'd to my mind; he has found out
A new device for sauce, and will not dish 'em
With toasts and butter. My father was a tailor,
And my name, though a justice, Greedy Woodcock;
And ere I 'll see my lineage so abus'd,
I 'll give up my commission.
OVER. [*Calls within.*]   Cook! Rogue, obey him!—
I have given the word; pray you, now remove yourself
To a collar of brawn,[3] and trouble me no farther.
GREEDY. I will, and meditate what to eat at dinner.

Exit GREEDY.

OVER. And as I said, Meg, when this gull disturb'd us,
This honourable lord, this colonel,
I would have thy husband.
MARG.   There 's too much disparity
Between his quality [4] and mine, to hope it.
OVER. I more than hope 't, and doubt not to effect it.
Be thou no enemy to thyself; my wealth
Shall weigh his titles down and make you equals.
Now for the means to assure him thine, observe me; [5]
Remember he 's a courtier and a soldier,
And not to be trifl'd with; and, therefore, when
He comes to woo you, see you do not coy it.

---

[1] i.e. quorum (I. 1. 35).
[2] The thirteenth woodcock; i.e. fool.
[3] Boar's flesh, often the shoulder or neck.
[4] Rank, birth.   [5] 'Pay attention to me.

This mincing modesty hath spoil'd many a match
By a first refusal, in vain after [1] hop'd for.

MARG. You'll have me, sir, preserve the distance that
Confines a virgin?

OVER.   Virgin me no virgins;
I must have you lose that name, or you lose me.
I will have you private; [2]—start not—I say, private;
If thou art my true daughter, not a bastard,
Thou wilt venture alone with one man, though he came
Like Jupiter to Semele, [3] and come off [4] too;
And, therefore, when he kisses you, kiss close.   120

MARG. I have heard this is the strumpet's fashion, sir,
Which I must never learn.

OVER.   Learn anything,
And from any creature that may make thee great;
From the devil himself.

MARG.   This is but devilish doctrine.

OVER. Or, if his blood grow hot, suppose he offer
Beyond this, do not you stay [5] till it be cool,
But meet his ardour; if a couch be near,
Sit down on't and invite him.

MARG.   In your house,
Your own house, sir? For Heaven's sake, what are you then?
Or what shall I be, sir?

OVER.   Stand not on form;   130
Words are no substances.

MARG.   Though you could dispense
With your own honour, cast aside religion,
The hope of Heaven or the fear of hell, excuse me.
In worldly policy this is not the way
To make me his wife; his whore, I grant it may do;
My maiden honour so soon yielded up,
Nay, prostituted, cannot but assure him
I that am light to him will not hold weight
When he is tempted by others; so, in judgment,
When to his lust I have given up my honour,   140
He must and will forsake me.

OVER.   How? Forsake thee?

---

[1] Later.   [2] Intimate.
[3] She had asked to see him in all his splendour, but was overwhelmed by
his radiance.
[4] 'Acquit yourself well.'   [5] Delay.

Do I wear a sword for fashion? Or is this arm
Shrunk up or wither'd? Does there live a man
Of that large list I have encount'red with
Can truly say I e'er gave inch of ground
Not purchas'd with his blood that did oppose me?
Forsake thee when the thing is done? He dares not!
Give me but proof he has enjoy'd thy person,
Though all his captains, echoes to his will,
Stood arm'd by his side to justify the wrong,
And he himself in the head of his bold troop,
Spite of his lordship and his colonelship,
Or the judge's favour, I will make him render
A bloody and a strict accompt, and force him,
By marrying thee, to cure thy wounded honour.
I have said it.

Enter MARRALL

MAR.   Sir, the man of honour's come,
    Newly alighted.
OVER. [*To* MARGARET.] In, without reply,
    And do as I command, or thou art lost.— *Exit* MARGARET.
    Is the loud music I gave order for
    Ready to receive him?
MAR.   'Tis, sir.
OVER.   Let 'em sound
    A princely welcome. [*Exit* MARRALL.] Roughness, awhile
        leave me;
    For fawning now, a stranger to my nature,
    Must make way for me.

Loud music. Enter LOVELL, ALLWORTH, GREEDY, MARRALL

LOV.   Sir, you meet your trouble.
OVER. What you are pleas'd to style so is an honour
    Above my worth and fortunes.
ALL. [*Aside.*]   Strange, so humble.
OVER. A justice of peace, my Lord.
LOV.   Your hand, good sir.
GREEDY. [*Aside.*] This is a lord, and some think this a favour;
    But I had rather have my hand in my dumpling.

OVER. Room for my lord!

LOV.   I miss, sir, your fair daughter,   170
 To crown my welcome.

OVER.   May it please my lord
 To taste a glass of Greek wine first, and suddenly
 She shall attend my lord.

LOV.   You'll be obey'd, sir.
                        Exeunt all except OVERREACH.

OVER. 'Tis to my wish; as soon as come, ask for her!

Enter MARGARET

Why, Meg! Meg Overreach! How, tears in your eyes?
Ha! Dry 'em quickly, or I'll dig 'em out.
Is this a time to whimper? Meet that greatness
That flies into thy bosom; think what 'tis
For me to say, 'My honourable daughter';
And thou, when I stand bare, to say, 'Put on',   180
Or, 'Father, you forget yourself'; no more!
But be instructed, or expect—He comes.

    Enter LOVELL, ALLWORTH, GREEDY, MARRELL; *they
    salute*

A black-brow'd girl, my Lord.

LOV.   As I live, a rare one.

ALL. [*Aside*.] He's took already; I am lost.

OVER. [*Aside*.]   That kiss
 Came twanging off; I like it.—Quit the room.
                    Exeunt ALLWORTH, GREEDY, *and* MARRALL.
 A little bashful, my good Lord, but you,
 I hope, will teach her boldness.

LOV.   I am happy
 In such a scholar; but—

OVER.   I am past learning,
 And therefore leave you to yourselves.—
 [*Aside to* MARGARET.]   Remember.
                        Exit OVERREACH.

LOV. You see, fair lady, your father is solicitous;   190
 You have to change the barren name of virgin
 Into a hopeful wife.

MARG.   His haste, my Lord,
  Holds no power o'er my will.
LOV.   But o'er your duty.
MARG. Which, forc'd too much, may break.
LOV.   Bend rather, sweetest;
  Think of your years.
MARG.   Too few to match with yours,
  And choicest fruits too soon pluck'd, rot and wither.
LOV. Do you think I am old?
MARG.   I am sure I am too young.
LOV. I can advance you.
MARG.   To a hill of sorrow,
  Where every hour I may expect to fall,
  But never hope firm footing. You are noble,
  I of low descent, however rich;
  And tissues match'd with scarlet suit but ill.[1]
  Oh, my good Lord, I could say more, but that
  I dare not trust these walls.
LOV.   Pray you, trust my ear then.

Enter OVERREACH *apart, listening*

OVER. [*Aside.*] Close at it! Whispering! This is excellent!
  And, by their postures, a consent on both parts.

Enter GREEDY

GREEDY. Sir Giles, Sir Giles!
OVER.   The great fiend stop that clapper!
GREEDY. It must ring out, sir, when my belly rings noon;
  The bak'd meats [2] are run out, the roast turn'd powder.
OVER. I shall powder you!
GREEDY.   Beat me to dust; I care not.
  In such a cause as this, I'll die a martyr.
OVER. Marry, and shall, you barathrum of the shambles! [3]
                                        Strikes him.
GREEDY. How! Strike a justice of peace? 'Tis petty treason,

---

[1] The rich and expensive garments worn by the nobility are in sharp
contrast to the garments of any other station in life, even the gowns of high
civic officials or the fine cloth called scarlet.
[2] Meat pies.
[3] 'You bottomless pit of the butcher shops.'

Edwardi quinto! But that you are my friend,
I would commit you without bail or mainprize.[1]

OVER. Leave your bawling, sir, or I shall commit you
Where you shall not dine today! Disturb my lord
When he is in discourse?

GREEDY.   Is't a time to talk
When we should be munching?

LOV.   Ha! I heard some noise.

OVER. Mum, villain, vanish. Shall we break a bargain   220
Almost made up?

            [*Exit* OVERREACH,] *thrusting* GREEDY *off*.

LOV.   Lady, I understand you,
And rest most happy in your choice, believe it;
I'll be a careful pilot to direct
Your yet uncertain bark to a port of safety.

MARG. So shall your honour save two lives, and bind us
Your slaves for ever.

LOV.   I am in the act rewarded,
Since it is good; howe'er, you must put on
An amorous carriage towards me to delude
Your subtle father.

MARG.   I am prone to that.

LOV. Now break we off our conference. Sir Giles!   230
Where is Sir Giles?

Enter OVERREACH *and the rest*

OVER.   My noble Lord. And how
Does your lordship find her?

LOV.   Apt, Sir Giles, and coming,
And I like her the better.

OVER.   So do I too.

LOV. Yet should we take forts at the first assault,
'Twere poor in the defendant; I must confirm her
With a love-letter or two, which I must have
Deliver'd by my page, and you give way to't.

OVER. With all my soul. [*To* ALLWORTH.] A towardly
    gentleman;
Your hand, good Master Allworth. Know my house   240
Is ever open to you.

ALL. [*Aside*.]   'Twas shut till now.

                    [1] Surety.

OVER. Well done, well done, my honourable daughter;
  Th'art so already. Know this gentle youth,
  And cherish him, my honourable daughter.
MARG. I shall, with my best care.

Noise within, as of a coach.

OVER.   A coach!
GREEDY.   More stops
  Before we go to dinner! Oh, my guts!

Enter LADY ALLWORTH and WELLBORN

LADY. [To WELLBORN.]   If I find welcome,
  You share in it; if not, I'll back again,
  Now I know your ends; for I come arm'd for all
  Can be objected.
LOV.   How! The Lady Allworth!
OVER. And thus attended!

  LOVELL salutes LADY ALLWORTH, who salutes MARGARET.

MAR. [To OVERREACH.]   No, I am a dolt;
  The spirit of lies had ent'red me.[1]
OVER. [To MARRALL.]   Peace, patch.[2]
  'Tis more than wonder! An astonishment
  That does possess me wholly!
LOV.   Noble lady,
  This is a favour, to prevent my visit,[3]
  The service of my life can never equal.
LADY. My Lord, I laid wait for you, and much hop'd
  You would have made my poor house your first inn;
  And, therefore, doubting that you might forget me,
  Or too long dwell here, having such ample cause
  In this unequall'd beauty for your stay,
  And fearing to trust any but myself
  With the relation of my service to you,
  I borrow'd so much from my long restraint,
  And took the air in person to invite you.
LOV. Your bounties are so great they rob me, madam,
  Of words to give you thanks.
LADY.   Good Sir Giles Overreach.

Salutes him.

---

[1] See II. 3, 106, 109.   [2] Fool.
[3] 'To anticipate my visit to you.'

How dost thou, Marrall? Lik'd you my meat so ill,
You'll dine no more with me?
GREEDY.   I will, when you please,
And it like your ladyship.
LADY.   When you please, Master Greedy;
If meat can do it, you shall be satisfied.   270
And now, my Lord, pray take into your knowledge
This gentleman; howe'er his outside's coarse,
His inward linings are as fine and fair
As any man's. (*Presents* WELLBORN.) —Wonder not I speak
at large.— [1]
And howsoe'er his humour carries him
To be thus accoutred, or what taint soever,
For his wild life, hath stuck upon his fame,
He may ere long, with boldness, rank himself
With some that have contemn'd him. Sir Giles Overreach,   280
If I am welcome, bid him so.
OVER.   My nephew.
He has been too long a stranger. Faith, you have;
Pray, let it be mended.   LOVELL *confers with* WELLBORN.
MAR. [*To* OVERREACH.] Why, sir, what do you mean?
This is 'rogue Wellborn, monster, prodigy,
That should hang or drown himself'; no man of worship,
Much less your nephew.
OVER. [*To* MARRALL.]   Well, sirrah, we shall reckon
For this hereafter.
MAR. [*Aside.*]   I'll not lose my jeer,
Though I be beaten dead for't.
WELL.   Let my silence plead
In my excuse, my Lord, till better leisure
Offer itself to hear a full relation   290
Of my poor fortunes.
LOV.   I would hear, and help 'em.
OVER. Your dinner waits you.
LOV.   Pray you, lead; we follow.
                         [WELLBORN *stands aside.*]
LADY. Nay, you are my guest; come, dear Master Wellborn.
                         Exeunt all except GREEDY.
GREEDY. 'Dear Master Wellborn!' So she said! Heav'n!
    Heav'n!

---

[1] Freely.

If my belly would give me leave, I could ruminate
All day on this. I have granted twenty warrants
To have him committed, from all prisons in the shire,
To Nottingham jail; and now 'Dear Master Wellborn!'
And 'My good nephew!' But I play the fool
To stand here prating, and forget my dinner.

Enter MARRALL

  Are they set, Marrall?
MAR.   Long since. Pray you, a word, sir.
GREEDY. No wording now.
MAR.   In troth, I must; my master,
  Knowing you are his good friend, makes bold with you
  And does entreat you, more guests being come in
  Than he expected, especially his nephew,
  The table being full too, you would excuse him,
  And sup with him on the cold meat.[1]
GREEDY.   How! No dinner,
  After all my care?
MAR.   'Tis but a penance for
  A meal; besides, you broke your fast.
GREEDY.   That was
  But a bit to stay my stomach. A man in commission
  Give place to a tatterdemalion?
MAR.   No bug [2] words, sir;
  Should his worship hear you—
GREEDY.   Lose my dumpling too,
  And butter'd toasts, and woodcocks?
MAR.   Come, have patience;
  If you will dispense a little with your worship,[3]
  And sit with the waiting-women, you'll have dumpling,
  Woodcock, and butter'd toasts too.
GREEDY.   This revives me;
  I will gorge there sufficiently.
MAR.   This is the way, sir.   *Exeunt.*

---

[1] This episode may have been an inconsistent afterthought by Massinger,
or intended as a trick upon Greedy devised by either Sir Giles or Marrall;
III. 1, 1–13 indicate that Overreach joined his guests at dinner.
[2] Threatening.
[3] Importance.

ACT III. SCENE 3
[OVERREACH'S *house*]

Enter OVERREACH, *as from dinner*

OVER. She's caught! O women! She neglects my lord,
  And all her compliments appli'd to Wellborn!
  The garments of her widowhood laid by,
  She now appears as glorious as the spring.
  Her eyes fix'd on him; in the wine she drinks,
  He being her pledge, she sends him burning kisses,
  And sits on thorns till she be private with him.
  She leaves my meat to feed upon his looks;
  And if in our discourse he be but nam'd,
  From her a deep sigh follows; but why grieve I   10
  At this? It makes for me; if she prove his,
  All that is hers is mine, as I will work him.

Enter MARRALL

MAR. Sir, the whole board is troubled at your rising.
OVER. No matter, I'll excuse it. Prithee, Marrall,
  Watch for an occasion to invite my nephew
  To speak with me in private.
MAR.   Who? The rogue
  The lady scorn'd to look on?
OVER.   You are a wag.

Enter LADY ALLWORTH *and* WELLBORN

MAR. See, sir, she's come, and cannot be without him.
LADY. With your favour, sir, after a plenteous dinner,
  I shall make bold to walk a turn or two   20
  In your rare garden.
OVER.   There's an arbour too,
  If your ladyship please to use it.
LADY.   Come, Master Wellborn.
    Exeunt LADY ALLWORTH *and* WELLBORN.
OVER. Grosser and grosser! Now I believe the poet [1]

---

[1] Ovid (*Metamorphoses*, xv. 500 ff.).

Feign'd not, but was historical, when he wrote
Pasiphaë was enamour'd of a bull; [1]
This lady's lust's more monstrous.

Enter LOVELL, MARGARET, *and the rest*

                                        My good Lord,
Excuse my manners.
LOV.   There needs none, Sir Giles;
I may ere long say 'Father', when it pleases
My dearest mistress to give warrant to it.
OVER. She shall seal to it, my Lord, and make me happy.

Enter LADY ALLWORTH *and* WELLBORN

MARG. My lady is return'd.
LADY.   Provide my coach;
I'll instantly away. My thanks, Sir Giles,
For our entertainment.
OVER.   'Tis your nobleness
To think it such.
LADY.   I must do you a further wrong,
In taking away your honourable guest.
LOV. I wait on you, madam; farewell, good Sir Giles.
LADY. Good Mistress Margaret. Nay, come, Master Wellborn,
I must not leave you behind; in sooth, I must not.
OVER. Rob me not, madam, of all joys at once;
Let my nephew stay behind; he shall have my coach,
And, after some small conference between us,
Soon overtake your ladyship.
LADY.   Stay not long, sir.
LOV. [*To* MARGARET.] This parting kiss; you shall every day
    hear from me
By my faithful page.
ALL.   'Tis a service I am proud of.
    Exeunt LADY ALLWORTH, LOVELL, ALLWORTH, *and*
        MARRALL.
OVER. Daughter, to your chamber. (*Exit* MARGARET.) You
    may wonder, nephew,

---

[1] Pasiphaë, the wife of Minos, was enamoured of Tauros; the Minotaur
was born of their union.

After so long an enmity between us,
I should desire your friendship.

WELL.   So I do, sir;
'Tis strange to me.

OVER.   But I'll make it no wonder;   50
And, what is more, unfold my nature to you.
We worldly men, when we see friends and kinsmen
Past hope sunk in their fortunes, lend no hand
To lift 'em up, but rather set our feet
Upon their heads, to press 'em to the bottom;
As, I must yield, with you I practis'd it.
But now I see you in a way to rise,
I can and will assist you. This rich lady—
And I am glad of't—is enamour'd of you;
'Tis too apparent, nephew.

WELL.   No such thing;   60
Compassion rather, sir.

OVER.   Well, in a word,
Because your stay is short, I'll have you seen
No more in this base shape; nor shall she say
She married you like a beggar, or in debt.

WELL. (*Aside.*) He'll run into the noose, and save my labour!

OVER. You have a trunk of rich clothes not far hence
In pawn; I will redeem 'em; and, that no clamour
May taint your credit for your petty debts,
You shall have a thousand pounds to cut 'em off,
And go a free man to the wealthy lady.   70

WELL. This done, sir, out of love, and no ends else—

OVER. As it is, nephew.

WELL.   —Binds me still your servant.

OVER. No compliments! You are stay'd for; ere y'ave supp'd
You shall hear from me. My coach, knaves, for my nephew!
Tomorrow I will visit you.

WELL.   Here's an uncle
In a man's extremes! [1] How much they do belie you,
That say you are hard-hearted!

OVER.   My deeds, nephew,
Shall speak my love; what men report I weigh not.   *Exeunt.*

---

[1] Extremities.

ACT IV. SCENE 1

[LADY ALLWORTH's *house*]

Enter LOVELL *and* ALLWORTH

LOV. 'Tis well.—Give me my cloak.—I now discharge you
  From further service. Mind your own affairs;
  I hope they will prove successful.
ALL.   What is bless'd
  With your good wish, my Lord, cannot but prosper.
  Let after times report, and to your honour,
  How much I stand engag'd,[1] for I want language
  To speak my debt; yet, if a tear or two
  Of joy for your much goodness can supply
  My tongue's defects, I could—
LOV.   Nay, do not melt;
  This ceremonial thanks to me's superfluous.
OVER. (*Within.*) Is my lord stirring?
LOV. 'Tis he. Oh, here's your letter. Let him in.

Enter OVERREACH, GREEDY, *and* MARRALL

OVER. A good day to my lord.
LOV.   You are an early riser, Sir Giles.
OVER. And reason, to attend your lordship.
LOV. And you too, Master Greedy, up so soon?
GREEDY. In troth, my Lord, after the sun is up
  I cannot sleep, for I have a foolish stomach
  That croaks for breakfast. With your lordship's favour,
  I have a serious question to demand
  Of my worthy friend Sir Giles.
LOV.   Pray you, use your pleasure.
GREEDY. How far, Sir Giles, and pray you answer me
  Upon your credit, hold you it to be
  From your manor-house to this of my Lady Allworth's?
OVER. Why, some four mile.
GREEDY.   How! Four mile? Good Sir Giles,
  Upon your reputation, think better;
  For if you do abate but one half-quarter

[1] Indebted.

Of five, you do yourself the greatest wrong
That can be in the world; for four miles' riding
Could not have rais'd so huge an appetite
As I feel gnawing in me.

MAR.   Whether you ride   30
Or go on foot, you are that way still [1] provided,
And it please your worship.

OVER. [*To* MARRALL.]   How now, sirrah? Prating
Before my lord? No deference? Go to my nephew;
See all his debts discharg'd, and help his worship
To fit on his rich suit.

MAR. [*Aside.*]   I may fit [2] you too.
Toss'd like a dog still!   *Exit.*

LOV.   I have writ this morning
A few lines to my mistress, your fair daughter.

OVER. 'Twill fire her, for she 's wholly yours already.
Sweet Master Allworth, take my ring; 'twill carry you
To her presence, I dare warrant you; and there plead   40
For my good lord, if you shall find occasion.
That done, pray ride to Nottingham; get a licence,
Still by this token. I 'll have it dispatch'd,
And suddenly, my Lord, that I may say,
My honourable, nay, right honourable daughter.

GREEDY. Take my advice, young gentleman: get your breakfast;
'Tis unwholesome to ride fasting. I 'll eat with you,
And eat to purpose.

OVER.   Some Fury 's in that gut;
Hungry again! Did you not devour this morning
A shield of brawn,[3] and a barrel of Colchester oysters?   50

GREEDY. Why, that was, sir, only to scour my stomach,
A kind of preparative. Come, gentleman,
I will not have you feed like the hangman of Flushing,
Alone,[4] while I am here.

LOV. [*To* ALLWORTH.]   Haste your return.

ALL. I will not fail, my Lord.

GREEDY.   Nor I, to line
My Christmas coffer.[5]   *Exeunt* GREEDY *and* ALLWORTH.

OVER.   To my wish, we are private.

[1] Always.   [2] Punish.
[3] The rolled skin of a boar's flank, stuffed with meat and cooked.
[4] Perhaps the hangman of Flushing (a port in the Netherlands, for several
years in English hands) suffered an unusual degree of social ostracism.
[5] A box for the collection of gratuities; here, Greedy's stomach.

I come not to make offer with my daughter
A certain portion; that were poor and trivial.
In one word, I pronounce all that is mine,
In lands or leases, ready coin or goods,
With her, my Lord, comes to you; nor shall you have
One motive to induce you to believe
I live too long, since every year I'll add
Something unto the heap, which shall be yours too.

Lov. You are a right kind father.

Over.   You shall have reason
To think me such. How do you like this seat?
It is well wooded and well water'd, the acres
Fertile and rich; would it not serve for change
To entertain your friends in a summer progress? [1]
What thinks my noble lord?

Lov.   'Tis a wholesome air,
And well-built pile; and she that's mistress of it
Worthy the large revenue.

Over.   She the mistress?
It may be so for a time; but let my lord
Say only that he likes it, and would have it,
I say, ere long 'tis his.

Lov.   Impossible.

Over. You do conclude too fast, not knowing me,
Nor the engines [2] that I work by. 'Tis not alone
The Lady Allworth's lands, for those once Wellborn's,
As by her dotage on him I know they will be,
Shall soon be mine; but point out any man's
In all the shire, and say they lie convenient
And useful to your lordship, and once more
I say aloud, they are yours.

Lov.   I dare not own
What's by unjust and cruel means extorted;
My fame and credit are more dear to me
Than so to expose 'em to be censur'd by
The public voice.

Over.   You run, my Lord, no hazard.
Your reputation shall stand as fair
In all good men's opinions as now;
Nor can my actions, though condemn'd for ill,

---

[1] Tour or visit.   [2] Devices.

Cast any foul aspersion upon yours;
For though I do contemn report [1] myself
As mere sound, I still will be so tender
Of what concerns you, in all points of honour,
That the immaculate whiteness of your fame
Nor your unquestion'd integrity
Shall e'er be sullied by one taint or spot
That may take from your innocence or candour.[2]
All my ambition is to have my daughter
Right honourable, which my lord can make her;   100
And might I live to dance upon my knee
A young Lord Lovell, born by her unto you,
I write *nil ultra* to my proudest hopes.
As for possessions and annual rents,
Equivalent to maintain you in the port [3]
Your noble birth and present state requires,
I do remove that burden from your shoulders,
And take it on my own; for, though I ruin
The country to supply your riotous waste,
The scourge of prodigals, want, shall never find you.   110

Lov. Are you not frighted with the imprecations
And curses of whole families, made wretched
By your sinister practices?

OVER.   Yes, as rocks are,
When foamy billows split themselves against
Their flinty ribs; or as the moon is mov'd
When wolves, with hunger pin'd, howl at her brightness.
I am of a solid temper, and, like these,
Steer on a constant course; with mine own sword,
If call'd into the field, I can make that right,
Which fearful enemies murmur'd at as wrong.   120
Now, for these other piddling complaints
Breath'd out in bitterness, as when they call me
Extortioner, tyrant, cormorant, or intruder
On my poor neighbour's right, or grand encloser
Of what was common,[4] to my private use;
Nay, when my ears are pierc'd with widows' cries,
And undone orphans wash with tears my threshold,
I only think what 'tis to have my daughter
Right honourable; and 'tis a powerful charm

---

[1] Rumour, gossip.   [2] Purity.
[3] Style.   [4] i.e. common land.

Makes me insensible of remorse or pity,
Or the least sting of conscience.

Lov.   I admire [1]
The toughness of your nature.

Over.   'Tis for you,
My Lord, and for my daughter, I am marble;
Nay, more; if you will have my character
In little, I enjoy more true delight
In my arrival to my wealth these dark
And crooked ways than you shall e'er take pleasure
In spending what my industry hath compass'd.
My haste commands me hence. In one word, therefore,
Is it a match?

Lov.   I hope that is past doubt now.

Over. Then rest secure; not the hate of all mankind here,
Nor fear of what can fall on me hereafter
Shall make me study aught but your advancement
One story higher. An earl, if gold can do it!
Dispute not my religion nor my faith;
Though I am borne thus headlong by my will,
You may make choice of what belief you please;
To me they are equal. So, my Lord, good morrow.   *Exit.*

Lov. He's gone! I wonder how the earth can bear
Such a portent! [2] I that have liv'd a soldier
And stood the enemy's violent charge undaunted,
To hear this blasphemous beast, am bath'd all over
In a cold sweat. Yet, like a mountain, he,
Confirm'd in atheistical assertions,
Is no more shaken than Olympus [3] is
When angry Boreas loads his double head
With sudden drifts of snow.

Enter Lady Allworth, Amble, *and waiting-woman*

Lady.   Save you, my Lord.
Disturb I not your privacy?

Lov.   No, good madam;
For your own sake I am glad you came no sooner,
Since this bold bad man, Sir Giles Overreach,
Made such a plain discovery of himself,

---

[1] Wonder at.   [2] A prodigy.
[3] More accurately, Parnassus.

And read this morning such a devilish matins
That I should think it a sin next to his
But to repeat it.

LADY.   I ne'er press'd, my Lord,
On others' privacies; yet against my will,
Walking, for health' sake, in the gallery
Adjoining to your lodgings, I was made
(So vehement and loud he was) partaker
Of his tempting offers.

LOV.   Please you to command
Your servant hence, and I shall gladly hear   170
Your wiser counsel.

LADY.   'Tis, my Lord, but a woman's,
But true and hearty.—Wait in the next room,
But be within call; yet not so near to force me
To whisper my intents.

AMBLE.   We are taught better
By you, good madam.

WOMAN.   And well know our distance.

LADY. Do so, and talk not; 'twill become your breeding.
                Exeunt AMBLE *and waiting-woman.*
Now, my good Lord, if I may use my freedom,
As to an honour'd friend—

LOV.   You lessen else
Your favour to me.

LADY.   I dare then say thus:
As you are noble—howe'er common men   180
Make sordid wealth the object and sole end
Of their industrious aims—'twill not agree
With those of eminent blood, who are engag'd
More to prefer [1] their honours than to increase
The state left 'em by their ancestors,
To study large additions to their fortunes,
And quite forget their births; though I must grant
Riches well got to be a useful servant,
But a bad master.

LOV.   Madam, 'tis confess'd;
But what infer you from it?

LADY.   This, my Lord;   190
That as all wrongs, though thrust into one scale,
Slide of themselves off when right fills the other

                [1] Promote.

And cannot bide the trial, so all wealth,
I mean if ill-acquir'd, cemented to honour
By virtuous ways achiev'd and bravely purchas'd,
Is but as rubbage pour'd into a river,
Howe'er intended to make good the bank,
Rendering the water that was pure before
Polluted and unwholesome. I allow
The heir of Sir Giles Overreach, Margaret,
A maid well qualified, and the richest match
Our north part can make boast of, yet she cannot,
With all that she brings with her, fill their mouths [1]
That never forget who was her father;
Or that my husband Allworth's lands, and Wellborn's,—
How wrung from both needs now no repetition—
Were real motives that more work'd your lordship
To join your families than her form and virtues;
You may conceive the rest.

Lov.   I do, sweet madam,
  And long since have consider'd it; I know
  The sum of all that makes a just man happy
  Consists in the well choosing of his wife;
  And there, well to discharge it, does require
  Equality of years, of birth, of fortune;
  For beauty, being poor and not cried up
  By birth or wealth, can truly mix with neither.
  And wealth, where there's such difference in years
  And fair descent, must make the yoke uneasy;
  But I come nearer.

Lady.   Pray you, do, my Lord.

Lov. Were Overreach' states thrice centupl'd, his daughter
  Millions of degrees much fairer than she is,
  Howe'er I might urge precedents to excuse me,
  I would not adulterate my blood
  By marrying Margaret, and so leave my issue
  Made up of several pieces, one part scarlet
  And the other London blue.[2] In my own tomb
  I will inter my name first.

Lady. (Aside.)   I am glad to hear this.—
  Why then, my Lord, pretend you marriage to her?

---

[1] Stop the gossip.
[2] 'One part of a brilliant colour, or high-ranking, in contrast to another in the colour worn by servants, etc.'

Dissimulation but ties false knots
On that straight line by which you hitherto   230
Have measur'd all your actions.
LOV.   I make answer,
And aptly, with a question. Wherefore have you,
That since your husband's death have liv'd a strict
And chaste nun's life, on the sudden giv'n yourself
To visits and entertainments? Think you, madam,
'Tis not grown public conference; or the favours
Which you too prodigally have thrown on Wellborn,
Being too reserv'd before, incur not censure?
LADY. I am innocent here, and, on my life, I swear
My ends are good.
LOV.   On my soul, so are mine   240
To Margaret; but leave both to the event;
And since this friendly privacy does serve
But as an offer'd means unto ourselves
To search each other farther, you having shown
Your care of me, I my respect to you,
Deny me not, but still in chaste words, madam,
An afternoon's discourse.
LADY.   So I shall hear you.   [*Exeunt.*]

ACT IV. SCENE 2

[*Before* TAPWELL'S *alehouse*]

Enter TAPWELL *and* FROTH

TAP. Undone! Undone! This was your counsel, Froth!
FROTH. Mine! I defy thee. Did not Master Marrall—
He has marr'd all, I am sure—strictly command us,
On pain of Sir Giles Overreach' displeasure,
To turn the gentleman out of doors?
TAP.   'Tis true;
But now he's his uncle's darling, and has got
Master Justice Greedy, since he fill'd his belly,
At his commandment, to do anything.
Woe, woe to us!
FROTH.   He may prove merciful.

TAP. Troth, we do not deserve it at his hands.
  Though he knew all the passages [1] of our house,
  As the receiving of stolen goods and bawdry,
  When he was rogue Wellborn no man would believe him,
  And then his information could not hurt us;
  But now he is right worshipful again,
  Who dares but doubt [2] his testimony? Methinks
  I see thee, Froth, already in a cart,[3]
  For a close bawd, thine eyes ev'n pelted out
  With dirt and rotten eggs, and my hand hissing,
  If I scape the halter, with the letter R [4]
  Printed upon it.
FROTH.   Would that were the worst!
  That were but nine days' wonder. As for credit,[5]
  We have none to lose; but we shall lose the money
  He owes us and his custom; there's the hell on't.
TAP. He has summon'd all his creditors by the drum,[6]
  And they swarm about him like so many soldiers
  On the pay day, and has found out such a new way
  To pay old debts, as 'tis very likely
  He shall be chronicl'd for it.
FROTH.   He deserves it
  More than ten pageants. But are you sure his worship
  Comes this way to my lady's?
A CRY WITHIN. Brave Master Wellborn!
TAP.   Yes, I hear him.
FROTH. Be ready with your petition, and present it
  To his good grace.

> *Enter* WELLBORN *in a rich habit*, MARRALL, GREEDY,
>   ORDER, FURNACE, *and three creditors*. TAPWELL,
>   *kneeling, delivers his bill of debt*

WELL.   How's this? Petition'd too?
  But note what miracles the payment of
  A little trash and a rich suit of clothes
  Can work upon these rascals! I shall be,
  I think, Prince Wellborn.

---

[1] Occurrences.   [2] Fear.
[3] Being publicly carted was the usual punishment for bawdry.
[4] For 'Rogue'.   [5] Reputation.
[6] By public announcement.

MAR.   When your worship's married,
You may be; I know what I hope to see you.

WELL. Then look thou for advancement.

MAR.   To be known   60
Your worship's bailiff is the mark I shoot at.

WELL. And thou shalt hit it.

MAR.   Pray you, sir, dispatch
These needy followers, and for my admittance,[1]
Provided you'll defend me from Sir Giles,
Whose service I am weary of, I'll say something
You shall give thanks for.

WELL.   Fear me not [2] Sir Giles.

In this interim, TAPWELL *and* FROTH *flatter and bribe*
JUSTICE GREEDY

GREEDY. Who, Tapwell? I remember thy wife brought me,
Last New Year's tide, a couple of fat turkeys.

TAP. And shall do every Christmas, let your worship
But stand my friend now.

GREEDY.   How? With Master Wellborn?   50
I can do anything with him on such terms.—
See you this honest couple? They are good souls
As ever drew out faucet; have they not
A pair of honest faces?

WELL.   I o'erheard you,
And the bribe he promis'd; you are cozen'd in 'em;
For, of all the scum that grew rich by my riots,
This, for a most unthankful knave, and this,
For a base bawd and whore, have worst deserv'd me,
And therefore speak not for 'em. By your place
You are rather to do me justice; lend me your ear: 60
Forget his turkeys, and call in his licence,
And, at the next fair, I'll give you a yoke of oxen
Worth all his poultry.

GREEDY.   I am chang'd on the sudden
In my opinion. Come near; nearer, rascal.
And, now I view him better, did you e'er see
One look so like an archknave? His very countenance,
Should an understanding judge but look upon him,
Would hang him, though he were innocent.

TAP., FROTH.   Worshipful sir!—

---

[1] 'My appointment as your bailiff.'
[2] 'Do not fear' (ethical dative).

GREEDY. No. Though the great Turk came, instead of turkeys,
   To beg any favour, I am inexorable.   7
   Thou hast an ill name; besides thy musty ale,
   That hath destroy'd many of the king's liege people,
   Thou never hadst in thy house, to stay men's stomachs,
   A piece of Suffolk cheese, or gammon of bacon,
   Or any esculent,[1] as the learned call it
   For their emolument, but sheer drink only;
   For which gross fault, I here do damn thy licence,
   Forbidding thee ever to tap or draw;
   For instantly, I will, in mine own person,
   Command the constable to pull down thy sign,   8
   And do it before I eat.
FROTH.   No mercy?
GREEDY.   Vanish!
   If I show any, may my promis'd oxen gore me!
                              Exit GREEDY.
TAP. Ungrateful knaves are ever so rewarded.
                    Exeunt TAPWELL *and* FROTH.
WELL. Speak; what are you?
1 CREDITOR.   A decay'd vintner, sir,
   That might have thriv'd, but that your worship broke me
   With trusting you with muscadine and eggs,
   And five-pound suppers, with your after drinkings,[2]
   When you lodg'd upon the Bankside.
WELL.   I remember.
1 CRED. I have not been hasty, nor e'er laid to arrest you;
   And therefore, sir,—
WELL.   Thou art an honest fellow: 9
   I'll set thee up again. [*To* MARRALL.] See his bill paid.—
   What are you?
2 CRED.   A tailor once, but now mere botcher.[3]
   I gave you credit for a suit of clothes,
   Which was all my stock, but you failing in payment,
   I was remov'd from the shop-board, and confin'd
   Under a stall.[4]
WELL.   See him paid;—and botch no more.
2 CRED. I ask no interest, sir.

---

[1] Food.   [2] Drinks consumed between and after meals.
[3] Patcher.
[4] i.e. 'I was compelled to give up my shop and to do business from behind
a market stall or booth.'

WELL.   Such tailors need not;
If their bills are paid in one-and-twenty years,
They are seldom losers. [*To* 3 CRED.] Oh, I know thy face;
Thou wert my surgeon. You must tell no tales;   100
Those days are done. I will pay you in private.

ORDER. A royal gentleman!

FURN.   Royal as an emperor!
He'll prove a brave master; my good lady knew
To choose a man.

WELL.   See all men else discharg'd;
And since old debts are clear'd by a new way,
A little bounty will not misbecome me.
There's something, honest cook, for thy good breakfasts;
[*To* ORDER.] And this for your respect; take't; 'tis good gold,
And I able to spare it.

ORDER.   You are too munificent.

FURN. He was ever so.

WELL.   Pray you, on before.

3 CRED.   Heaven bless you!   110

            Exeunt ORDER, FURNACE, *and third creditor.*

MAR. At four o'clock the rest know where to meet me.

WELL. Now, Master Marrall, what's the weighty secret
You promis'd to impart?

MAR.   Sir, time nor place
Allow me to relate each circumstance;
This only, in a word: I know Sir Giles
Will come upon you for security
For his thousand pounds, which you must not consent to.
As he grows in heat, as I am sure he will,
Be you but rough, and say he's in your debt
Ten times the sum, upon sale of your land;   120
I had a hand in't—I speak it to my shame—
When you were defeated of it.

WELL.   That's forgiven.

MAR. I shall deserv't. Then urge him to produce
The deed in which you pass'd it over to him,
Which I know he'll have about him to deliver
To the Lord Lovell, with many other writings
And present moneys. I'll instruct you further,
As I wait upon your worship. If I play not my prize [1]

---

[1] 'If I do not take my part.'

To your full content and your uncle's much vexation,
Hang up Jack Marrall.

WELL.   I rely upon thee.   *Exeunt.*

ACT IV. SCENE 3

[OVERREACH's *house*]

Enter ALLWORTH *and* MARGARET

ALL. Whether to yield the first praise to my lord's
   Unequall'd temperance or your constant sweetness
   That I yet live, my weak hands fasten'd on
   Hope's anchor, spite of all storms of despair,
   I yet rest doubtful.

MARG.   Give it to Lord Lovell;
   For what in him was bounty, in me's duty.
   I make but payment of a debt to which
   My vows in that high office [1] regist'red
   Are faithful witnesses.

ALL.   'Tis true, my dearest;
   Yet when I call to mind how many fair ones
   Make wilful shipwreck of their faiths and oaths
   To God and man, to fill the arms of greatness,
   And you rise up no less than a glorious star,
   To the amazement of the world, that hold out
   Against the stern authority of a father,
   And spurn at honour when it comes to court you;
   I am so tender of your good that faintly,
   With your wrong, I can wish myself that right
   You yet are pleas'd to do me.

MARG.   Yet and ever.
   To me what's title, when content is wanting?
   Or wealth rak'd up together with much care,
   And to be kept with more, when the heart pines
   In being dispossess'd of what it longs for
   Beyond the Indian mines? [2] Or the smooth brow
   Of a pleas'd sire that slaves me to his will,

---

[1] Heaven.   [2] i.e. more than the wealth of the Indies.

And, so his ravenous humour may be feasted
By my obedience and he see me great,
Leaves to my soul nor faculties nor power
To make her own election?

ALL.   But the dangers
That follow the repulse!

MARG.   To me they are nothing;   30
Let Allworth love, I cannot be unhappy.
Suppose the worst, that in his rage he kill me,
A tear or two, by you dropp'd on my hearse
In sorrow for my fate, will call back life
So far as but to say that I die yours;
I then shall rest in peace; or should he prove
So cruel as one death would not suffice
His thirst of vengeance, but with ling'ring torments
In mind and body I must waste to air,
In poverty join'd with banishment; so you share   40
In my afflictions, which I dare not wish you,
So high I prize you, I could undergo 'em
With such a patience as should look down
With scorn on his worst malice.

ALL.   Heaven avert
Such trials of your true affection to me!
Nor will it unto you that are all mercy
Show so much rigour; but since we must run
Such desperate hazards, let us do our best
To steer between 'em.

MARG.   Your lord's ours, and sure;
And, though but [1] a young actor, second me   50
In doing to the life what he has plotted;
The end may yet prove happy. Now, my Allworth—

Enter OVERREACH [*behind*]

ALL. [*Aside to* MARGARET.] To your letter, and put on a
    seeming anger.

MARG. I'll pay my lord all debts due to his title,
And when, with terms not taking from his honour,
He does solicit me, I shall gladly hear him.
But in this peremptory, nay, commanding, way,
T'appoint a meeting and, without my knowledge,

_____
[1] 'Though you (Allworth) are but . . .'

A priest to tie the knot can ne'er be undone
Till death unloose it, is a confidence [1]
In his lordship will deceive him.

ALL.   I hope better,
My good lady.

MARG.   Hope, sir, what you please; for me,
I must take a safe and secure course; I have
A father, and without his full consent,
Though all lords of the land kneel'd for my favour
I can grant nothing.

OVER. [*Coming forward.*] I like this obedience;
But whatsoever my lord writes must and shall be
Accepted and embrac'd. Sweet Master Allworth,
You show yourself a true and faithful servant
To your good lord; he has a jewel of you.
How? Frowning, Meg? Are these looks to receive
A messenger from my lord? What's this? Give me it.

MARG. A piece of arrogant paper, like th' inscriptions.

OVER. (*Reads the letter.*) 'Fair mistress, from your servant
        learn all joys
That we can hope for, if deferr'd, prove toys;
Therefore this instant, and in private, meet
A husband that will gladly at your feet
Lay down his honours, tend'ring them to you
With all content, the church being paid her due.'
Is this the arrogant piece of paper? Fool!
Will you still be one? In the name of madness, what
Could his good honour write more to content you?
Is there aught else to be wish'd after these two
That are already offer'd? Marriage first,
And lawful pleasure after. What would you more?

MARG. Why, sir, I would be married like your daughter,
Not hurried away i' th' night I know not whither,
Without all ceremony, no friends invited
To honour the solemnity.

ALL.   An't please your honour,
For so before tomorrow I must style you,
My lord desires this privacy, in respect
His honourable kinsmen are far off,
And his desires to have it done brook not
So long delay as to expect [2] their coming;

---

[1] Presumption.   [2] Await.

And yet he stands resolv'd, with all due pomp,
As running at the ring,[1] plays, masques, and tilting,
To have his marriage at court celebrated,
When he has brought your honour up to London.   100
OVER. He tells you true. 'Tis the fashion, on my knowledge;
Yet the good lord, to please your peevishness,
Must lose a night forsooth, and lose a night
In which perhaps he might get two boys on thee.
Tempt me no farther; this goad   *[Touches his sword.]*
Shall prick you to him.
MARG.   I could be contented,
Were you but by, to do a father's part,
And give me in the church.
OVER.   So my lord have you,
What do I care who gives you? Since my lord
Does purpose to be private, I'll not cross him.   110
I know not, Master Allworth, how my lord
May be provided, and therefore there's a purse
Of gold; 'twill serve this night's expense. Tomorrow
I'll furnish him with any sums; in the meantime,
Use my ring to my chaplain; he is benefic'd
At my manor of Gotham, and call'd Parson Willdo.
'Tis no matter for a licence; I'll bear him out in't.
MARG. With your favour, sir, what warrant is your ring?
He may suppose I got that twenty ways,
Without your knowledge; and then to be refus'd   120
Were such a stain upon me. If you pleas'd, sir,
Your presence would do better.
OVER.   Still perverse?
I say again, I will not cross my lord;
Yet I'll prevent [2] you too. Paper and ink, there!
ALL. I can furnish you.
OVER.   I thank you; I can write then.
                                OVERREACH writes.
ALL. You may, if you please, put out the name of my lord,
In respect he comes disguis'd, and only write,
'Marry her to this gentleman.'
OVER.   Well advis'd;
'Tis done. Away! (MARGARET *kneels.*) My blessing, girl?
Thou hast it.   130

----

[1] Riding at a ring suspended on a post.
[2] Anticipate.

Nay, no reply; begone! Good Master Allworth,
This shall be the best night's work you ever made.
ALL. I hope so, sir.   *Exeunt* ALLWORTH *and* MARGARET.
OVER.   Farewell. Now all's cock-sure; [1]
Methinks I hear already knights and ladies
Say, 'Sir Giles Overreach, how is it with
Your honourable daughter? Has her honour
Slept well tonight?' Or 'Will her honour please
To accept this monkey, dog, or parakeet'
(This is state in [2] ladies), 'or my eldest son
To be her page and wait upon her trencher?'   14
My ends, my ends are compass'd! Then for
Wellborn and the lands. Were he once married to the widow,
I have him here! I can scarce contain myself,
I am so full of joy, nay, joy all over.   *Exit.*

ACT V

[LADY ALLWORTH'S *house*]

Enter LADY ALLWORTH, LORD LOVELL, *and* AMBLE

LADY. By this you know how strong the motives were
That did, my Lord, induce me to dispense
A little with my gravity to advance,
In personating [3] some few favours to him,
The plots and projects of the downtrod Wellborn;
Nor shall I e'er repent, although I suffer
In some few men's opinions for't, the action.
For he that ventur'd all for my dear husband
Might justly claim an obligation from me
To pay him such a courtesy; which had I
Coyly or over-curiously [4] denied,
It might have argu'd me of little love
To the deceas'd.
LOV.   What you intended, madam,
For the poor gentleman hath found good success,
For, as I understand, his debts are paid,

---

[1] Secure.   [2] The manner, behaviour of.
[3] Putting forward in a feigned character.   [4] Fastidiously.

And he once more furnish'd for fair employment;
But all the arts that I have us'd to raise
The fortunes of your joy and mine, young Allworth,
Stand yet in supposition,[1] though I hope well,
For the young lovers are in wit more pregnant   20
Than their years can promise; and for their desires,
On my knowledge, they are equal.

LADY.   As my wishes
Are with yours, my Lord; yet give me leave to fear
The building, though well grounded; to deceive
Sir Giles, that's both a lion and a fox
In his proceedings, were a work beyond
The strongest undertakers, not the trial
Of two weak innocents.

LOV.   Despair not, madam;
Hard things are compass'd oft by easy means,
And judgment, being a gift deriv'd from Heaven,   30
Though sometimes lodg'd i' th' hearts of worldly men,
That ne'er consider from whom they receive it,
Forsakes such as abuse the giver of it.
Which is the reason that the politic
And cunning statesman that believes he fathoms
The counsels of all kingdoms on the earth
Is by simplicity oft overreach'd.

LADY. May he be so! Yet, in his name to express it
Is a good omen.

LOV.   May it to myself
Prove so, good lady, in my suit to you.   40
What think you of the motion?

LADY.   Troth, my Lord,
My own unworthiness may answer for me;
For had you, when that I was in my prime
(My virgin-flower uncropp'd), presented me
With this great favour, looking on my lowness,
Not in a glass of self-love, but of truth,
I could not but have thought it as a blessing
Far, far beyond my merit.

LOV.   You are too modest,
And undervalue that which is above
My title or whatever I call mine.   50
I grant, were I a Spaniard, to marry

                    [1] Unsettled.

A widow might disparage me, but being
A true-born Englishman, I cannot find
How it can taint my honour; nay, what's more,
That which you think a blemish is to me
The fairest lustre. You already, madam,
Have given sure proofs how dearly you can cherish
A husband that deserves you; which confirms me
That, if I am not wanting in my care
To do you service, you'll be still the same   60
That you were to your Allworth. In a word,
Our years, our states, our births are not unequal,
You being descended nobly and alli'd so;
If then you may be won to make me happy,
But join your lips to mine, and that shall be
A solemn contract.

LADY.   I were blind to my own good
Should I refuse it; yet, my Lord, receive me
As such a one, the study of whose whole life
Shall know no other object but to please you.

LOV. If I return not, with all tenderness,   70
Equal respect to you, may I die wretched!

LADY. There needs no protestation, my Lord,
To her that cannot doubt—

Enter WELLBORN

                    You are welcome, sir;
Now you look like yourself.

WELL.   And will continue
Such in my free acknowledgment that I am
Your creature, madam, and will never hold
My life mine own, when you please to command it.

LOV. It is a thankfulness that well becomes you;
You could not make choice of a better shape
To dress your mind in.

LADY.   For me, I am happy   80
That my endeavours prosper'd. Saw you of late
Sir Giles, your uncle?

WELL.   I heard of him, madam,
By his minister, Marrall; he's grown into strange passions
About his daughter. This last night he look'd for [1]

---

[1] Expected.

Your lordship at his house, but missing you,
And she not yet appearing, his wisehead [1]
Is much perplex'd and troubl'd.

Lov.   It may be,
Sweetheart, my project took.

Lady.   I strongly hope.

Over. [*Within.*] Ha! Find her, booby, thou huge lump of
   nothing;   90
I'll bore thine eyes out else!

Well.   May it please your lordship,
For some ends of mine own, but to withdraw
A little out of sight, though not of hearing,
You may perhaps have sport.

Lov.   You shall direct me.
                                    He steps aside.

Enter Overreach, *with distracted looks, driving in*
   Marrall *before him*

Over. I shall *sol-fa* you,[2] rogue!

Mar.   Sir, for what cause
Do you use me thus?

Over.   Cause, slave? Why, I am angry,
And thou a subject only fit for beating,
And so to cool my choler. Look to the writing;
Let but the seal be broke upon the box
That has slept in my cabinet these three years,   100
I'll rack thy soul for't.

Mar. (*Aside.*)   I may yet cry quittance,[3]
Though now I suffer, and dare not resist.

Over. Lady, by your leave, did you see my daughter-lady,
And the lord her husband? Are they in your house?
If they are, discover, that I may bid 'em joy;
And, as an entrance to her place of honour,
See your ladyship on her left hand, and make curtsies
When she nods on you; which you must receive
As a special favour.

Lady.   When I know, Sir Giles,
Her state requires such ceremony, I shall pay it;   110
But, in the meantime, as I am myself,

---

[1] One who considers himself wise, always used ironically.
[2] Make you sing, i.e. 'beat you'.   [3] Retaliation.

I give you to understand I neither know
Nor care where her honour is.

OVER.   When you once see her
Supported, and led by the hand of her lord her husband,
You'll be taught better. Nephew!

WELL.   Sir.

OVER.   No more?

WELL. 'Tis all I owe you.

OVER.   Have your redeem'd rags
Made you thus insolent?

WELL. (*In scorn.*)   Insolent to you?
Why, what are you, sir, unless in your years,
At the best more than myself?

OVER. [*Aside.*]   His fortune swells him;
'Tis rank [1] he's married.

LADY. [*Aside.*]   This is excellent.   12

OVER. Sir, in calm language, though I seldom use it,
I am familiar with the cause that makes you
Bear up thus bravely; there's a certain buzz
Of a stol'n marriage,—do you hear?—of a stol'n marriage,
In which 'tis said there's somebody hath been cozen'd;
I name no parties.

WELL.   Well, sir, and what follows?

OVER. Marry, this, since you are peremptory: remember
Upon mere hope of your great match, I lent you
A thousand pounds; put me in good security,
And suddenly, by mortgage or by statute,[2]   1
Of some of your new possessions, or I'll have you
Dragg'd in your lavender [3] robes to the jail. You know me,
And therefore do not trifle.

WELL.   Can you be
So cruel to your nephew now he's in
The way to rise? Was this the courtesy
You did me 'in pure love and no ends else'?

OVER. End me no ends. Engage the whole estate,
And force your spouse to sign it, you shall have
Three or four thousand more, to roar and swagger
And revel in bawdy taverns.

WELL.   And beg after!   14
Mean you not so?

---

[1] Obvious.   [2] Recognizance.
[3] From a slang phrase which implied 'lately in pawn'.

OVER.   My thoughts are mine, and free.
   Shall I have security?
WELL.   No, indeed you shall not,
   Nor bond nor bill nor bare acknowledgment;
   Your great looks fright not me.
OVER.   But my deeds shall!
   Outbrav'd?   *They both draw.*
LADY.   Help! Murder, murder!
               Servants enter [and separate them].
WELL.   Let him come on,
   With all his wrongs and injuries about him,
   Arm'd with his cutthroat practices to guard him;
   The right that I bring with me will defend me,
   And punish his extortion.
OVER.   That I had thee
   But single in the field!
LADY.   You may, but make not   150
   My house your quarrelling scene.
OVER.   Were't in a church,
   By Heaven and hell, I'll do't!
MAR. [*Aside to* WELLBORN.]   Now put him to
   The showing of the deed.
WELL.   This rage is vain, sir;
   For fighting, fear not, you shall have your hands full,
   Upon the least incitement; and whereas
   You charge me with a debt of a thousand pounds,
   If there be law, howe'er you have no conscience,
   Either restore my land, or I'll recover
   A debt that's truly due to me from you,
   In value ten times more than what you challenge.   160
OVER. I in thy debt? Oh, impudence! Did I not purchase
   The land left by thy father, that rich land
   That had continued in Wellborn's name
   Twenty descents, which, like a riotous fool,
   Thou didst make sale of? Is not here enclos'd
   The deed that does confirm it mine?
MAR. [*Aside.*]   Now, now!
WELL. I do acknowledge none; I ne'er pass'd o'er
   Any such land. I grant for a year or two
   You had it in trust, which if you do discharge,
   Surrend'ring the possession, you shall ease   170
   Yourself and me of chargeable suits in law,

Which, if you prove not honest, as I doubt it,
Must of necessity follow.

LADY.   In my judgment
He does advise you well.

OVER.   Good! Good! Conspire
With your new husband, lady; second him
In his dishonest practices, but when
This manor is extended [1] to my use,
You'll speak in a humbler key, and sue for favour.

LADY. Never! Do not hope it.

WELL.   Let despair first seize me.

OVER. Yet to shut up thy mouth, and make thee give   1
Thyself the lie, the loud lie, I draw out
The precious evidence; if thou can forswear
Thy hand and seal, and make a forfeit of
Thy ears to the pillory,[2] see— (*Opens the box.*) here's that will make
My interest clear. Ha!

LADY.   A fair [3] skin of parchment.

WELL. Indented.[4] I confess, and labels [5] too,
But neither wax nor words. How! Thunderstruck?
Not a syllable to insult with? My wise uncle,
Is this your precious evidence? Is this that makes   1
Your interest clear?

OVER.   I am o'erwhelm'd with wonder!
What prodigy is this? What subtle devil
Hath raz'd out the inscription? The wax
Turn'd to dust! The rest of my deeds whole,
As when they were deliver'd, and this only
Made nothing! Do you deal with witches, rascal?
There is a statute [6] for you, which will bring
Your neck in a hempen circle; yes, there is;
And now 'tis better thought, for, cheater, know
This juggling will not save you.

WELL.   To save thee   2
Would beggar the stock of money.

OVER.   Marrall!

---

[1] Seized.
[2] To be put in the pillory and to have one's ears cut off were likely penalties for perjury.   [3] Unmarked.
[4] Divided irregularly, to match the duplicate copy made from the same parchment.   [5] With tabs for seals.
[6] The law which prescribed hanging as the penalty for witchcraft.

MAR.   Sir.

OVER. (*Flattering him.*) Though the witnesses are dead, your
 testimony;
 Help with an oath or two. And for thy master,
 Thy liberal master, my good honest servant,
 I know you will swear anything, to dash
 This cunning sleight; besides, I know thou art
 A public notary, and such stand in law
 For a dozen witnesses; the deed, being drawn too
 By thee, my careful Marrall, and deliver'd   210
 When thou wert present, will make good my title.
 Wilt thou not swear this?

MAR.   I? No, I assure you.
 I have a conscience not sear'd up like yours;
 I know no deeds.

OVER.   Wilt thou betray me?

MAR.   Keep him
 From using of his hands; I'll use my tongue
 To his no little torment.

OVER.   Mine own varlet
 Rebel against me?

MAR.   Yes, and uncase [1] you too.
 The idiot, the patch, the slave, the booby,
 The property fit only to be beaten
 For your morning exercise, your football, or   220
 Th'unprofitable lump of flesh, your drudge,
 Can now anatomize [2] you, and lay open
 All your black plots, and level with the earth
 Your hill of pride, and, with these gabions [3] guarded,
 Unload my great artillery, and shake,
 Nay, pulverize the walls you think defend you.

LADY. How he foams at the mouth with rage!

WELL.   To him again!

OVER. Oh, that I had thee in my gripe, I would tear thee
 Joint after joint!

MAR.   I know that you are a tearer,
 But I'll have first your fangs par'd off, and then   230
 Come nearer to you; when I have discover'd, [4]
 And made it good before the judge, what ways

[1] Strip.   [2] Dissect.
[3] Wicker baskets filled with earth, used to defend a military position.
[4] Revealed.

And devilish practices you us'd to cozen
With an army of whole families, who yet live,
And, but [1] enroll'd for soldiers, were able
To take in [2] Dunkirk.

WELL.   All will come out.

LADY.   The better.

OVER. But that I will live, rogue, to torture thee,
And make thee wish, and kneel in vain, to die,
These swords that keep thee from me should fix here,
Although they made my body but one wound,   2
But I would reach thee.

LOV. (*Aside.*)   Heaven's hand in this;
One bandog [3] worry the other!

OVER.   I play the fool,
And make my anger but ridiculous.
There will be a time and place, there will be, cowards,
When you shall feel what I dare do.

WELL.   I think so;
You dare do any ill, yet want true valour
To be honest and repent.

OVER.   They are words I know not,
Nor e'er will learn. Patience, the beggar's virtue,
Shall find no harbour here; after these storms
At length a calm appears.

Enter GREEDY *and* PARSON WILLDO

                     Welcome, most welcome.   2
There's a comfort in thy looks; is the deed done?
Is my daughter married? Say but so, my chaplain,
And I am tame.

WILLDO.   Married? Yes, I assure you.

OVER. Then vanish, all sad thoughts. There's more gold for
    thee.
My doubts and fears are in the titles drown'd
Of my right honourable, my right honourable daughter.

GREEDY. Here will I be feasting; at least for a month
I am provided. Empty guts, croak no more;
You shall be stuff'd like bagpipes, not with wind,   2
But bearing [4] dishes.

---

[1] If they were.   [2] Capture.
[3] Chained dog.   [4] Substantial.

OVER. (*Whispering to* WILLDO.) Instantly be here?—
  To my wish, to my wish! Now you that plot against me,
  And hop'd to trip my heels up, that contemn'd me,
  Think on't and tremble. (*Loud music.*) They come!
    I hear the music.
  A lane there for my lord!
WELL.   This sudden heat
  May yet be cool'd, sir.
OVER.   Make way there for my lord!

Enter MARGARET *and* ALLWORTH

MARG. Sir, first your pardon, then your blessing, with
  Your full allowance of the choice I have made.   *Kneels.*
  As ever you could make use of your reason,   270
  Grow not in passion; since you may as well
  Call back the day that's past, as untie the knot
  Which is too strongly fasten'd. Not to dwell
  Too long on words: this is my husband.
OVER.   How!
ALL. So I assure you; all the rites of marriage,
  With every circumstance,[1] are past. Alas, sir,
  Although I am no lord, but a lord's page,
  Your daughter, and my lov'd wife, mourns not for it;
  And for [2] right honourable son-in-law, you may say
  Your dutiful daughter.
OVER. [*To* WILLDO.]   Devil, are they married?   280
WILLDO. Do a father's part, and say, 'Heaven give 'em joy!'
OVER. Confusion and ruin! Speak, and speak quickly,
  Or thou art dead.
WILLDO.   They are married.
OVER.   Thou hadst better
  Have made contract with the king of fiends
  Than these. My brain turns!
WILLDO.   Why this rage to me?
  Is not this your letter, sir, and these the words:
  'Marry her to this gentleman'?
OVER.   I [3] cannot,
  Nor will I e'er believe it!—'Sdeath, I will not!—
  That I, that in all passages I touch'd
  At worldly profit have not left a print   290

_____
    [1] Detail.   [2] Instead of.   [3] It—quarto.

Where I have trod for the most curious search
To trace my footsteps, should be gull'd by children,
Baffl'd and fool'd, and all my hopes and labours
Defeated and made void!

WELL.   As it appears,
You are so, my grave uncle.

OVER.   Village nurses
Revenge their wrongs with curses; I 'll not waste
A syllable, but thus I take the life
Which, wretched, I gave to thee.   *Offers to kill* MARGARET.

LOV. [*Advances.*]   Hold, for your own sake!
Though charity to your daughter hath quite left you,
Will you do an act, though in your hopes lost here,
Can leave no hope of peace or rest hereafter?
Consider; at the best you are but a man,
And cannot so create your aims but that
They may be cross'd.

OVER.   Lord, thus I spit at thee
And at thy counsel, and again desire thee,
And as thou art a soldier, if thy valour
Dares show itself where multitude and example
Lead not the way, let's quit the house, and change
Six words in private.

LOV.   I am ready.

LADY.   Stay, sir;
Contest with one distracted?

WELL.   You'll grow like him,
Should you answer his vain challenge.

OVER. [*To* LOVELL.]   Are you pale?
Borrow his [1] help; though Hercules call it odds,
I 'll stand against both as I am, hemm'd in thus.
Since, like a Libyan lion in the toil,[2]
My fury cannot reach the coward hunters,
And only spends itself, I 'll quit the place.
Alone I can do nothing; but I have servants
And friends to second me, and if I make not
This house a heap of ashes—By my wrongs,
What I have spoke I will make good!—or leave
One throat uncut—If it be possible,
Hell, add to my afflictions!   *Exit* OVERREACH.

MAR.   Is 't not brave sport?

---

[1] Wellborn's.   [2] Trap.

GREEDY. Brave sport? I am sure it has ta'en away my stomach;
  I do not like the sauce.
ALL.   Nay, weep not, dearest,
  Though it express your pity; what's decreed
  Above we cannot alter.
LADY.   His threats move me
  No scruple, madam.
MAR.   Was it not a rare trick,
  And it please your worship, to make the deed nothing?
  I can do twenty neater, if you please
  To purchase and grow rich; for I will be   330
  Such a solicitor and steward for you
  As never worshipful had.
WELL.   I do believe thee;
  But first discover the quaint means you us'd
  To raze out the conveyance.[1]
MAR.   They are mysteries
  Not to be spoke in public: certain minerals
  Incorporated in the ink and wax.
  Besides, he gave me nothing, but still fed me
  With hopes and blows, and that was the inducement
  To this conundrum. If it please your worship
  To call to memory, this mad beast once caus'd me   340
  To urge you or to drown or hang yourself;
  I'll do the like to him if you command me.
WELL. You are a rascal. He that dares be false
  To a master, though unjust, will ne'er be true
  To any other. Look not for reward
  Or favour from me; I will shun thy sight
  As I would a basilisk's.[2] Thank my pity
  If thou keep thy ears; howe'er, I will take order
  Your practice shall be silenc'd.
GREEDY.   I'll commit him,
  If you'll have me, sir.
WELL.   That were to little purpose;   350
  His conscience be his prison. Not a word,
  But instantly begone.
ORDER.   Take this kick with you.
AMBLE. And this.
FURN.   If that I had my cleaver here,
  I would divide your knave's head.

    [1] Deed.   [2] A serpent whose glance was reputed to kill.

MAR.   This is the haven
  False servants still [1] arrive at.   *Exit* MARRALL.

                    Enter OVERREACH

LADY.   Come again?
LOV. Fear not, I am your guard.
WELL.   His looks are ghastly.
WILLDO. Some little time I have spent, under your favours,
  In physical studies,[2] and, if my judgment err not,
  He's mad beyond recovery; but [3] observe him,
  And look to yourselves.
OVER.   Why, is not the whole world   3(
  Included in myself? To what use then
  Are friends and servants? Say there were a squadron
  Of pikes, lin'd through with shot,[4] when I am mounted
  Upon my injuries, shall I fear to charge 'em?
  No; I'll through the battalia,[5] and, that routed,
                    Flourishing his sword, sheathed.
  I'll fall to execution. Ha! I am feeble;
  Some undone widow sits upon mine arm,
  And takes away the use of 't; and my sword,
  Glu'd to my scabbard with wrong'd orphans' tears,
  Will not be drawn. Ha! What are these? Sure, hangmen   3;
  That come to bind my hands, and then to drag me
  Before the judgment seat. Now they are new shapes,
  And do appear like Furies, with steel whips
  To scourge my ulcerous soul. Shall I then fall
  Ingloriously, and yield? No; spite of fate,
  I will be forc'd to hell like to myself.
  Though you were legions of accursed spirits,
  Thus would I fly among you.   [*Rushes forward and falls.*]
WELL.   There's no help;
  Disarm him first, then bind him.
GREEDY.   Take a *mittimus*,[6]
  And carry him to Bedlam.
LOV.   How he foams!   3{
WELL. And bites the earth!

----

          [1] A!ways.   [2] The study of physic, or medicine.
          [3] Only.   [4] Interspersed with musketeers.
          [5] Battle array.   [6] A writ of confinement.

WILLDO.   Carry him to some dark room;
  There try what art can do for his recovery.
                            Servants force OVERREACH *off.*
MARG. Oh, my dear father!
ALL.   You must be patient, mistress.
LOV. Here is a precedent to teach wicked men
  That when they leave religion and turn atheists,
  Their own abilities leave 'em. Pray you, take comfort;
  I will endeavour you shall be his guardians
  In his distractions; and for your land, Master Wellborn,
  Be it good or ill in law, I'll be an umpire
  Between you and this, th'undoubted heir   390
  Of Sir Giles Overreach. For me, here's the anchor
  That I must fix on.
ALL.   What you will determine,
  My Lord, I will allow of.
WELL.   'Tis the language
  That I speak too; but there is something else
  Besides the repossession of my land
  And payment of my debts that I must practise:
  I had a reputation, but 'twas lost
  In my loose course, and, till I redeem it
  Some noble way, I am but half made up.
  It is a time of action; if your lordship   400
  Will please to confer a company upon me
  In your command, I doubt not in my service
  To my king and country but I shall do something
  That may make me right again.
LOV.   Your suit is granted,
  And you lov'd for the motion.
WELL. [*Comes downstage.*]   Nothing wants then
  But your allowance [1]—

The Epilogue

But your allowance, and in that our all
Is comprehended; it being known, nor we
Nor he that wrote the comedy can be free

[1] Approval.

Without your manumission;[1] which if you
Grant willingly, as a fair favour due   410
To the poet's and our labours—as you may,
For we despair not, gentlemen, of the play—
We jointly shall profess your grace hath might
To teach us action, and him how to write.

FINIS

[1] Release (by your applause).

GLOSSARY

MOST of the puzzling words in the plays are explained in a note on the page in which they appear; a few occur frequently and are thus included here to avoid overloading the text. Several of the words below have alternative meanings which their contexts will make clear.

'a, he, she, it.
a', in, on.
and, if.
angels, coins worth about 6s. 8d. each.
appeal, a charge, an accusation.
Catso, an exclamation or oath.
challenge, to claim.
charges, expenses.
clip, to embrace.
close, secret.
cornuto, a cuckold.
cousin, coz, in colloquial usage, a casual or distant relationship.
credit, reputation.
cross, a piece of money.
discover, reveal.
doubt, to fear.
firk, to frisk, cheat, beat.
fond, foolish.
forsooth, truly, indeed.
go to, an expression of impatience.
Godamercy, may God reward you; i.e. thank you.
marry, indeed.
mean, inferior.
minion, favourite.
pair, pack (of cards).
portagues, gold coins worth almost £5 each.
possets, hot mixed drinks.
presently, at once, soon.
purchase, to acquire wealth or property.
quean, a jade.
receipt, recipe.
sleight, a trick.
still, always, ever more.
straight, immediately.
touse, to disorder.

389

trencher, a plate, square or round, often made of wood.
true, honest.
unthrift, a prodigal, spendthrift.
use, to be accustomed to.
want, to lack.
wittol, a complacent cuckold.